IF I

GO

MISSING

OTHER BOOKS BY LESLIE WOLFE

DETECTIVE KAY SHARP SERIES

The Girl from Silent Lake

Beneath Blackwater River

The Angel Creek Girls

The Girl on Wildfire Ridge

Missing Girl at Frozen Falls

TESS WINNETT SERIES

Dawn Girl

The Watson Girl

Glimpse of Death

Taker of Lives

Not Really Dead

Girl With A Rose

Mile High Death

The Girl They Took

The Girl Hunter

BAXTER & HOLT SERIES

Las Vegas Girl

Casino Girl

Las Vegas Crime

ALEX HOFFMANN SERIES

Executive

Devil's Move

The Backup Asset

The Ghost Pattern

Operation Sunset

STANDALONE TITLES

The Surgeon

The Girl You Killed

Stories Untold

Love, Lies and Murder

IF I
GO
MISSING

LESLIE WOLFE

**GRAND
CENTRAL**

New York Boston

Copyright © 2023 by Leslie Wolfe
Excerpt from *The Surgeon* copyright © 2023 by Leslie Wolfe

Cover design by Lisa Brewster. Cover photo by Shutterstock.
Cover copyright © 2024 by Hachette Book Group, Inc.

Grand Central Publishing
Hachette Book Group
1290 Avenue of the Americas, New York, NY 10104
grandcentralpublishing.com
@grandcentralpub

First published in 2023 by Bookouture, an imprint of Storyfire, Ltd.
First Grand Central Publishing Edition: December 2024

Grand Central Publishing is a division of Hachette Book Group, Inc.
The Grand Central Publishing name and logo is a registered trademark of Hachette Book Group, Inc.

The publisher is not responsible for websites (or their content) that are not owned by the publisher.

The Hachette Speakers Bureau provides a wide range of authors for speaking events. To find out more, go to hachettespeakersbureau.com or email HachetteSpeakers@hbgusa.com.

Grand Central Publishing books may be purchased in bulk for business, educational, or promotional use. For information, please contact your local bookseller or the Hachette Book Group Special Markets Department at special.markets@hbgusa.com.

Library of Congress Cataloging-in-Publication Data has been applied for.

ISBN: 978-1-5387-6953-9 (trade paperback)

Printed in the United States of America

LSC-C

Printing 1, 2024

A special thank you to my New York City legal eagle and friend, Mark Freyberg, who expertly guided me through the intricacies of the judicial system.

IF I
GO
MISSING

ONE

If you're reading this, I've gone missing.

And I have just these pages to get you to know me, to understand what I'm about, to care about me enough to leave the rut of your daily routine behind and invest a little bit of your most precious asset—your time—in finding me. In bringing me home.

My plan is to make it as easy as possible. Enclosed in this binder you will find the tidbits that form a person's existence. Mine. A jigsaw puzzle made of photos, bank accounts, social media usernames and passwords, fingerprints, and DNA. Twenty-nine years of personal history told in a few pictures; some faded with time, others crisp and fresh and new, all equally meaningful. If I put it in here, whatever it may be, it's important for you to look at it with an open mind and decide if it had anything to do with my disappearance.

If I could, now that I'm writing this, I wouldn't be shy; I'd tell you straight up what's going on. But I can't. I don't have a crystal ball to know what the future will hold. As I'm sitting at my desk, in my peaceful den, typing this letter, it's no easy task to look ahead at such a horrifying possibility.

Going missing. The thought brings shivers to my spine.

How does one begin to know what will be the critical information needed to solve my disappearance? How do I choose from the vast number of memories contained within my life's journey, those that would help you find me?

Nevertheless, I have to try, blindly, like someone feeling their way through the deepest darkness, frail yet unstoppable, seeking the power of light to shine over them and set them free.

Although it's deathly serious, building this binder reminds me of a game I used to play with my best friend, as a child. Or—I should be precise—as a teenager, just starting to look at life differently, yet still believing in the magic that had lit our childhoods with enchantment. I remember going on two- or three-day outings here and there, ready to explore the world, to conquer it, to make it ours. I remember the pervasive smell of mothballs that ruined our appetite and gave us headaches, yet didn't stop us from writing secret missives that could only be read in a mirror's reflection, using one of da Vinci's favorite ways to encode messages. I'm a lefty, so mirror writing comes easier to me than it would to most people. But that's not the point: I digress.

Life feels this way to me right now, like a mirror-written letter I cannot comprehend. But if you can find the right mirror, my life will bare its secrets in front of your eyes. And you'll understand everything I'm trying to say here but cannot find the words for.

You see, I'm afraid for my life. And I'm not sure whether the secret I discovered is the reason why I've gone missing and you're reading this. All I know is that I'm caught in a quagmire of shadows and deceit, an inescapable trap that might have swallowed me already.

My only hope is you. Most people like crime in fiction, on television, or in books. Those people shy away from looking at crime's realities, repelled, shrouding themselves in disbelief, thinking that denial will be the protective shield that will keep their lives pristine and safe. Others are the exact opposite, eager to stare at blood puddles and flare their nostrils at the first whiff of death, unrelentingly looking for scapegoats and making up lies to support their fictitious scenarios as they go along. To them, the lure of someone else's misery is heady and unescapable.

Neither can be trusted to find the truth. Especially when that truth is wrapped in a lie, shielded from the light of day in such ways that no one can see it. Serving the lie in perpetuity, just as a host organism serves and feeds the parasite coiled around its heart.

This is the kind of person you'll need to be to find me: different; someone who chose to fight crime, not just be entertained by it in fiction and the news media. Someone with an unrelenting passion for making people's lives a little better at the worst moments of their existence. I'm hoping that's who you are, hell-bent on a mission to find out what's real, and that you won't stop until you get answers.

You were meant for this.

Only you can find me.

Please do.

Before I end this message, I have to apologize to my dear husband. I'm so sorry for hiding this binder. Just know I didn't hide it from you, and I hope you found it easily. You know everything about me anyway; probably nothing within its pages is a surprise to you. I hid it because it gives whoever finds it complete access to my life, to everything I am, I own, and I love. You're already privy to all that, but such power in the hands of the wrong people could have terrifying consequences. So, I kept it hidden, away from nosy housekeepers and the occasional overnight visitors, and you obviously found it and gave it to the detective investigating my disappearance. Thank you for doing all that. Maybe it will help bring me back a little bit sooner.

To all the people who care about me, I want to say something, knowing it won't bring much relief to the anguish you must be feeling right now. Here it is, nevertheless. I'm strong, resilient, and I can endure. My parents raised me well. I won't go down without a fight. Just know that, and know I'm counting the seconds until we're reunited.

So please flip through the pages and find answers to your questions, some of which you haven't yet asked. It's in your power to save me. No one else can.

Please find me.

TWO

"Alana, we talked about this."

The disappointment in my husband's voice is unmistakable. I glance at him quickly before resuming the delicate task of layering a wilted salad. His eyes shift away from mine. He's avoiding me without a word, without moving. Seeing him turn away from me like that makes me sad.

He's right. We did talk about it. And I made him a promise.

Opening the fridge, I make room for the salad bowl, then slip it in there and set a timer for ten minutes. "You're right," I say, walking over to the kitchen island and pulling a bar stool to the side, so I can face him. "And we're going, just like we discussed. Tomorrow."

He lights up, showing his gratitude with a warm smile. "That's my girl." He walks over to the pantry and opens the door with the mindless gesture of someone who does that hundreds of times a day. He chooses a Burgundy from the bottom shelf and quickly uncorks it. The cork pops out with a joyful sound. The gurgling of red filling two tall glasses is next, for a moment the only sound in the serene kitchen.

I hold my hand up to stop him from filling my glass; I'll only take a sip.

He hands a glass to me, then plants a quick kiss on my lips. I raise the glass, noticing how the sun's late afternoon rays light up the liquid with ruby sparkles. Then I look into his eyes, relishing the warmth I find in them, the love, the enduring patience.

"I love you, Daniel," I say simply.

His smile wanes. Lines furrow his brow under strands of unruly light-brown hair. He abandons his glass on the granite counter without touching it. "What's wrong, baby?"

A sigh swells my chest. It's my turn to look away, wishing I was better at hiding my emotions. "I'm a bit scared of this fertility treatment, that's all."

His eyebrows pop up a little, and I smile. I've always loved this about my husband: his thoughts are written on his face clearly, in an endearing kind of way; almost naïve, but not really. With strangers he's as composed as the best of them, but not with me. "What are you afraid of?" he asks, his voice kind, understanding, yet touched by anxiety.

I bite my lip, weighing my words before I answer. Then I decide to go with humor. I'm a coward: I don't want to ruin a perfectly good Sunday afternoon by starting to spew things as unpalatable and disturbing as the truth. I'd rather we enjoyed our wine while we wait for the salad to chill, then have a peaceful dinner. We rarely have that privilege, with him working long hours at his restaurant.

"Twins." The reply comes out in a blurt.

His jaw loosens. "What?"

I tilt my head slightly and stare at him. "Yeah, well, it's a risk with fertility shots. They stimulate ovulation, sometimes way too much. We might get twins." My breath shatters unexpectedly, and I place the untouched glass on the counter. My hand finds my abdomen and rubs it gently as if I were already pregnant. He can't see what I'm doing from where he's sitting, on the other side of the kitchen island. I struggle to find the source of my earlier humor. It's as if it has dried out, leaving behind an arid, doom-laden expanse. But I somehow manage. "I can handle two, I guess. Can you?"

His smile lights up the room, golden glimmers of joy in his eyes. Seeing him like that unsettles me. "Are you kidding me right now?" he asks, springing to his feet and rushing around the counter so he can wrap his arms around me. "You have nothing to worry about." He buries his head in my hair and whispers in my ear. "I can handle five if you'll give them to me."

I push him away gently. Everything is a joke to my husband. Sometimes I wonder if he wants children so badly because he's still one at heart. "This is serious, Daniel. We could—"

"We'll be fine, I promise. The restaurant is making enough money to feed us."

"And put us through college too? All five of us?" I quip, head slightly tilted like before, but for a different reason. I'm not doubting him anymore. I'm shamelessly flirting with him, while wondering, in the back of my mind, how long an abandoned salad can survive in the fridge before it goes mushy.

There's something inherently hot about Daniel when he looks at me like this. His tousled, sun-kissed hair still smelling of shower gel, his full lips sketching a lopsided smile, the afternoon stubble that grazes against my lips when he draws near. There's a hunger in his touch that lights a fire in me.

This time, the fire quickly dies when I remember what we were talking about. Fertility treatments. Tomorrow's appointment is for the first round of shots, in the afternoon. Remembering that has the effect of ice water poured over my head—bucketloads of it—while I silently scream inside.

I pull away gently and take a step or two back, then check the time. "Dinner's ready."

He stands in place, seeming a little stunned, his hands finding his pockets after hovering hesitantly in midair for a split second, frowning as he watches me. I'm grateful I have something to do, and I do it quickly, albeit not as effectively as a *restaurateur*.

He laughs when I call him that. He says having a place called Dan's Diner, which he runs with his little brother, Jason, is not really worthy of French-inspired words any more than it is worthy of a Michelin Star. I always remind him of where that place is, in one of the most desirable locations on the California coast, overlooking Pacific sunsets from its large patio, at the heart of a serene little town called Half Moon Bay. People drive across the Santa Cruz Mountains for his clam chowder, coming from San Francisco and all the way from San Jose.

Dishes clatter in my hands for a few moments, then we're finally seated, hearty servings of wilted salad on our dinner plates, warm rolls fresh out of the oven. Daniel tops up our wine and sets the bottle down by his side. There's still about a third of it left. Then he smiles at me, serenely and a bit pensively. He reminds me of a young Paul Newman when he does that.

"Well, bon appétit," I say, uttering two of the very few words of French I speak.

He looks at the food critically yet humorously. The lump of lettuce has shifted from underneath the layer of ham and mushrooms smothered in lemon juice, looking wilted, of course. It's supposed to. Still, the result of my labor is visually unappealing. I couldn't make a living working in a restaurant if my life depended on it.

"Nice try," he says, then unloads a forkful in his mouth and chews heartily. "Mm, it's really good."

My cheeks catch fire. I don't need his mercy. "Thanks, but—"

"No, really, this is fantastic," he adds, cleaning his plate at full speed. "I think I want to add this to our menu."

"Really?" I taste the salad and it *is* good. It's slightly wilted, yet the iceberg is still crisp and crunchy. The ham has left salty goodness throughout, mixed to perfection with lemon juice. Herbs and pepper added nice accents to it. I smile, filled with the pride of the beginner in the presence of her first masterpiece.

"What's it called?" Daniel reaches for a second serving.

"Wilted salad. I found the recipe online." I take another mouthful and savor the blend of tastes in my mouth. "You mean it? You'd put my salad on your menu?"

He raises the glass. "Absolutely. Timing's a beast, though. We can't have customers wait ten minutes for refrigeration after prep. We can't make it ahead of time, either, because it would lose texture quickly, even if cold stored." He stares absent-mindedly at the empty plate where the salad has left traces of its juices. "We'd have to make it fresh and front staff would have to work with us, buy us the time, even if we use the blast chiller for half a minute or so." Another moment of thinking. "I'd add shallots and a touch of Dijon for a high-powered mouthfeel."

I shrug. I'm not qualified to foresee what Dijon and shallots would do to my recipe. Unlike Daniel, I can't imagine the taste of foods in my mind. "Add it to the appetizer menu," I suggest. "People who order appetizers have more time to spend at their table."

He looks at me intently. A slow-burning heat ignites inside me under his gaze, fertility treatments be damned.

"A salad on the appetizer menu? You're not just a pretty face," he whispers, tracing his finger along my hand. "Why don't we—"

A loud noise disrupts the loaded hush of our kitchen. It comes from outside our house and sounds like the tailgate of a large truck being slammed. A couple of men's voices shout something unintelligible, then silence. We both rise from the table and go into the living room to take a look.

Movers are unloading furniture in the driveway of the house next door, the only other house in our small cul-de-sac. They move quickly, loading boxes on dollies and rushing them inside. The truck bears a logo I recognize, a local high-end mover. Not someone like Allied or Mayflower, which means our new neighbor didn't come from out of state.

"Did you know Mrs. Moore was selling?" I ask, and Daniel shakes his head. "Maybe she's renting it out. I didn't see a for sale sign."

For a moment, I wonder why Mrs. Moore didn't tell me about this. Not that she had to, but I like to think of her as my friend. She's almost seventy, and I knew this was going to happen at some point. I just wish I could've said goodbye properly over a nice dinner and a glass of wine in our backyard.

"She might've gone to live with her son," I say, although Daniel didn't ask. He's just looking out the window, seemingly fascinated with how the movers are doing their job. "I hope he likes Marcello."

"Who?"

"Her cat." I chuckle lightly. We visited with the neighbor and her cat countless times. Each time she regaled us with the story of how her cat got his name: his eyes reminded her of an old flame of hers when she was a young nurse, and she spent a few days in the arms of a young Italian doctor named Marcello.

Such a lighthearted, romantic little story, and Daniel manages to forget it every time.

We watch the movers for another minute or so, then I head back into the kitchen and reach into the freezer for an apple pie. I warm it in the oven just enough to thaw it. While I wait, I touch up my lipstick and run a brush through my hair. A critical, uncompromising look in the mirror returns an image I'm not particularly proud of, but not ashamed of either. My light-brown hair, mid-back length and slightly wavy, looks dull, strands clumping together despite my brushing. It needs a trim and some conditioner. I look a bit tired and pale, which is understandable considering I spent all day helping Daniel with bookkeeping for the diner.

"Ah, going over to meet the neighbors?" Daniel asks, looking at the pie I extract from the oven.

I pull off the oven mitts and abandon them on the stove. "Might as well." This is one American tradition I absolutely love. When we moved in, Mrs. Moore showed up and welcomed us to the neighborhood, then invited us to dinner at her place. It was a blessing I still remember fondly. Otherwise, it would've been the diner, and both Daniel and I have eaten enough of everything on that menu to last us a lifetime. Actually, that's why Daniel doesn't cook for us at home too often. Only I do. He takes a break from cooking, and I take a break from his menu choices. Good deal overall, except I'm a rather mediocre cook.

I smooth my clothes and run my hand through my hair one more time before grabbing the pie and leaving the house. Daniel clearly has no intention to come with; he'd actually be happy to go back to his accounting chores.

As I reach the sidewalk, the truck is pulling away, bouncing lightly on its large wheels as it takes the turn onto the main road.

The door to the neighbors' house is closed. I clear my throat and prepare to flash a welcoming smile, then ring the bell.

The door swings open. A man, dressed in a white shirt and gray slacks, greets me with an inquisitive glance that immediately shifts to recognition. As our eyes meet, I feel faint, like I can't breathe. Memories rush through my brain, unwanted, overwhelming.

The sound of the pie smashing to the ground is distant and vague, as if it were happening to someone else. As if I were hearing it on TV from another room.

The clacking of approaching stiletto heels gets my attention. I turn my bewildered eyes away from the splattered pie, just as she comes into view. The slender young woman is approaching quickly from the living room in a flutter of red ruffles and waves of long blonde hair. She gasps, then greets me warmly as I gawk in disbelief.

"Oh, my gosh, Alana, what a surprise!"

She wraps her arms around me and squeezes me tightly while managing to avoid stepping into the splashes of apple pie. As if in a dream, I lift my arms and put them around her slender body, even as my head is spinning.

Somehow, I manage to close my gaping mouth and whisper her name.

"Chloe."

THREE

For about a year after we met, I couldn't understand why Chloe Avery wasn't enrolled in one of those posh private schools that lined Silicon Valley. Her family had money. More than that, her parents *came* from money, a distinction of some importance when considering one's choices in education.

Unlike Chloe, I didn't have a choice. For me, public school was the only option. But as a sixteen-year-old starting her junior year of high school, my mind wasn't on schooling options.

I'm thinking of it now because I didn't think of it when I met her for the first time.

That was almost twelve years ago.

We were different, like night and day. She was spirited and passionate and bubbly, always smiling and tossing her long blonde hair over her shoulder to get it out of the way, in a signature move she repeated without the tiniest shred of self-consciousness. She had an innate restlessness that drove her to explore the world hungrily, as if running out of time. Every day she'd come up with a new idea, an activity we'd never tried before, a food she wanted us to taste, or rumors of some place we could visit.

And she was beautiful. Breathtakingly so.

She could've been a supermodel if only she'd sent a head-shot to some agencies. Fascinated with her looks, I tried to talk her into it. But she didn't care about any of that. It was her time to live, "to experience freedom," as she used to say, batting her long eyelashes and looking at me pleadingly with big, round eyes that reminded me of a deer. Same soft, hazel irises, same vulnerability that has made generations of kids want to adopt Bambi. But she wasn't weak. She was one of the strongest people I ever met. Underneath that façade of delicate beauty and carefree enjoyment of life, I discovered a steely inner core, a side to her that would surprise many people.

We couldn't've been more different, Chloe and me.

Unlike her, I was a bit of a tomboy, athletic and focused on finishing school with good grades so I could get into a good college; maybe earn myself a scholarship while I was at it. Long, light-brown hair, which I wore loose or sometimes tied in a ponytail, and blue-gray eyes were my best features. For the rest, I thought of myself as painfully plain.

I worked evenings, some weekends, and all summer long, because my mother's two jobs just didn't make ends meet. My dad had left us about a year after I was born, disappearing without a word or a forwarding address. Some of the very few pictures I found in an old shoebox show the toddler I used to be, seated on my mother's lap, smiling carelessly and wiggling my fingers in the air, her eyes with dark circles under them, although she pushed herself to smile. Those pictures show the very modest furnished room we used to live in until I was eight or nine.

By the time I met Chloe, my life had not evolved much from that tiny, furnished rental. We'd moved a couple of times, my mother still clinging to live life in Half Moon Bay, California, her hometown and mine, when she could've maybe lived a better life in Kansas or somewhere like that. But, like me, she loved this town deeply: the salty air, the dense fog rolling in at night; the small, rural community that comes together after the hordes of seasonal tourists have gone home.

We lived in a one-bedroom apartment when I was in high school, and I also had a work permit that allowed me to take a job after school. During summertime, I worked on one of the local farms, a family-oriented tourist attraction that offered a petting zoo, pony rides, and pick-your-own berries. I fed the animals, cleaned their stalls, picked fruit, welcomed tourists. I was kind of a jack of all trades, master of some. I didn't have a passion for it, not even close, but it was money that my mother and I both needed. A few evenings a week, I took a shift at the local hardware store, where I put on an apron that smelled of dust and WD-40 and helped late-afternoon customers find the air filter, the power tools, or the screws they were looking for. There wasn't any time in my life for friendships or fun.

Yet Chloe and I became close friends. In a matter of days, faster than I'd thought possible. We simply gelled. I can't speak of what she liked about me, but I liked her honesty, her direct-ness, the joy that exuded from her as if every day was a gift that she couldn't wait to unwrap. Some of that joy rubbed off on me, and I cherished it, like sunshine in an otherwise dreary climate of long days spent working under the pervasive cloud of poverty.

I didn't expect our friendship to last. I was dreading the moment she'd come to realize that other girls in our class were way more fun than I was. Soon, she'd find something better to do than wait for me to finish my shift so we could catch a movie I cringed about paying for. While she had new outfits to try on, I had five ponies to groom before I could finish for the day. She smelled of Jo Malone or Acqua di Parma, while I sometimes dipped into the freezing Pacific waters to rinse off the stench of manure from my hair before I met with her. That was only if I didn't have the time to swing by my apartment for a shower, but still. I would have been mortified if she ever found that out about me, even today.

Our friendship endured and grew stronger. We were a good fit, Chloe and I, and her unusual upbringing kept the issue of money from causing damage. She was graceful about it, not flaunting it like other kids would do without giving it a second thought. She respected that I had to work, and had offered a couple of times to pay for ice cream and movie tickets, but she didn't insist when I said I wanted to pay my own way. When I met her parents, I learned where all that was coming from.

She invited me to her house a few months into my junior year. It was almost Thanksgiving, and the ocean breeze was biting, a miserable, damp wind that had killed our plans to walk by the cliffs. Instead, she drove into town and picked me up for Sunday lunch with her family.

I was shy and so painfully uncomfortable it hurts to remember. I was completely intimidated in her presence, not just then but most of the time. Their house, custom-built on a cliff rising about fifty feet above sea level, ten miles south of the town, was the most beautiful I'd ever seen. Single story, with large windows that let the views fill every room with the movement and sound and taste of the Pacific, it took my breath away.

Chloe's bedroom was not what I'd expected. It was simple, yet I could sense the wealth behind it. But that was it for luxury. What I thought was a massive window turned out to be a sliding door, and she had a small terrace built above the drop, waves crashing under our feet, where she and I curled up on lounge chairs, wrapped up in warm blankets, and looked at the ocean, chatting about small stuff. Just typical girl talk, Chloe keen as always on gossiping about all the boys in school and I happy to listen, fascinated with what other people's lives could be like.

Lunch that day must've been average for them, but to me it was like nothing I'd ever tasted. A hearty potato soup with sour cream and thinly minced shallots. A slice of pot roast that melted in my mouth. Eating at a casual pace took all the willpower I had.

Her parents were charming, just like Chloe. I could see the family resemblance. She got her high forehead from her father, Harold Avery. Her fascinating eyes and her blonde locks came from her mother, Denise. All three of them were beautiful people and I was in awe of them, their life, the way the world moved for them. Not like it happened for my mom and me, in moments of crisis alternating with a plain, white-knuckled fight for survival, the good and the bad mixed together in a shapeless clump.

Denise was a dentist with a bustling practice in Santa Clara. Harold was a commercial real estate attorney. Years later, I realized that meant he was the man who large technology firms hired when they planned to build another headquarters or needed a zoning change. His perceptive eyes drilled into me, asking me about my life with real or perfectly feigned curiosity. An occasional approving smile stretched his lips while he listened. I remember rebelling that day, deciding not to hold anything back. To not lie, nor be ashamed of my reality. So, there I was, a bit flustered but bravely forging ahead, sharing my work experience at the farm, talking about pony rides and tourists picking strawberries.

I don't remember seeing even the smallest hint of arrogance or contempt in Harold's attitude or Denise's. If anything, I felt appreciated. Before dessert was served, I felt I belonged, as paradoxical as it would seem now or did back then.

And I understood why Chloe wasn't attending some fancy private school in San Jose. They were down-to-earth, unpretentious people, and probably wanted their daughter to be raised the same way.

The rest of the school year went by smoothly, with me working a few nights per week and a full day on Saturdays, and

Chloe taking us exploring every bit of time off I could get to hang out with her. Ice cream from the carton served on a blanket by the sea, digging in heartily with plastic spoons bent to the breaking point. A pottery workshop that proved to us both that spinning clay wasn't our thing. Weekend trips to cabins in the mountains, keys borrowed from family friends and acquaintances who owned vacation properties. Then, when the weather warmed up a bit, camping trips at the state beach with a bunch of other juniors and some seniors too. Our first beer, bought illegally by a senior with a fake ID who was hoping to get into Chloe's pants. The world was ours, even if I just hitched the ride.

I was thrilled at that time, right before summer break, because the farm owner I was working for had decided to give me his son's old Honda Accord in exchange for a week's worth of work. I finally had my own car. Meanwhile, Chloe had fallen in love—or lust—with a senior named Bruce. All she did was talk about him. What he said, what he wore, what shampoo he used. How he touched her hand. How he kissed her. How they made love under the stars on the back seat of her convertible. And I listened. Her stories were the entire extent of my love life in high school.

Summer break saw Bruce disappearing, and a new guy, a dark and rather lanky waiter who worked at a local bar and grill, took his place. By the time the farm had started seeing long lines for the pony rides on Saturday mornings, the waiter was history, and Chloe was dating Dillon, a tall and brawny lifeguard who worked at The Ritz-Carlton. I knew all about it, of course. Every single detail. When I met Dillon, I shifted my eyes away from him, embarrassed I knew so much about how he liked to make love. The things he said during and after sex. I remember blushing and making up some excuse, and leaving the confused Dillon to savor sensual, daring, and unsatiable Chloe.

Then things changed forever, on the first day of my senior

year, when a new student transferred from somewhere on the East Coast. North Carolina, I believe. I was seventeen years old.

With piercing blue eyes that promised trouble, and a chiseled jawline that highlighted his sun-kissed skin, the six-foot-three newcomer strode into our classroom and stopped squarely in front of me. His toned body made me think *athlete*: baseball or perhaps football. His perfect smile radiated a level of magnetic charm that was impossible to ignore.

The chatter in the classroom dropped to almost zero, or so it seemed. Chloe drew close to me and grabbed my arm, squeezing it discreetly as if to say, "Look at *that*," and flashing her megawatt smile, paired with her signature hair toss.

His eyes never left mine. As if Chloe wasn't even there.

"Hi," I recall whispering, a little choked. Unlike Chloe, I was painfully new at the game. "Um, I'm Alana," I managed awkwardly. The hand I held out was slightly shaky.

He nodded, and his smile widened a bit, putting dimples in his cheeks. "Raymond Preston. Call me Ray."

FOUR

Chloe can't be that happy to see me. Not after everything that happened.

Not after the ten years since I last saw her, during which I tried my best to never cross her path.

I hold my breath while she hugs me, then gently pull away, my eyes shifting left and right while she holds on to my hands and sizes me up. As always, I'm a little uneasy under her scrutiny, in my worn capri pants and my simple V-necked T-shirt.

At first, I hesitate to look at her, but then I can't look away. She's stunning, even more so than I recall. A faint scent of top-shelf cosmetics fills my nostrils. Her clothes, even on her moving day, are pristine. The red, ruffled blouse is silk, an elegant match to beige tapered pants. Brown leather pumps complete the attire, the three-inch heels dangerously close to stepping into spilled apple pie.

Life has been good to Chloe.

"Look at you," she says, her voice raised with joy. "You haven't changed a bit. And I can't believe we're going to be neighbors!" To my surprise, she hugs me again and kisses the air near my cheek.

I smile shyly when she pulls away, feeling a bit odd about such a warm reception, secretly overwhelmed with her sudden appearance in my life. I realize I haven't been breathing for a while. I fill my deprived lungs with air and steel myself for what's coming. It can't be avoided any longer.

"Yes, it is a lovely surprise, isn't it? You look amazing as always," I say, still avoiding looking at the man standing next to the open door. But I have to. "Good to see you, Ray."

He's smiling, his blue eyes glinting with something I don't dare recognize. Nameless as it might be, that something stirs up feelings inside me I thought were long gone.

Damn. They should've stayed gone, just like Chloe should've stayed a part of my history.

Uncomfortable, I shift my weight from one foot to the other, my lowered glance fixed on the damage I've done. Pieces of pie have landed on Ray's slacks, on his shoes, on the floor, then splashed against the wall, staining the freshly painted stucco.

"I'm so sorry about this," I mumble. "Let me see if there's any toilet paper I can use." I slip in between them, careful not to brush against either, and disappear into the bathroom. Thankfully, Mrs. Moore has left some toilet paper behind. I grab a handful and rush back to the porch.

Chloe puts her hands up, her smile perfectly charming. "Oh, no, Alana, don't worry about it!"

I pick up the plate I dropped and start loading pie onto it, feeling awkward squatting at Ray's feet. He doesn't let me finish. He crouches by my side and gently grabs my arm. My hands start to shake, the danger of dropping the pie dish creeping up on me again.

"Don't worry, okay? I'll take care of it." He speaks to me in a low whisper, his voice kind, yet firm, commanding, just as I recall.

Defeated, I abandon everything on the floor and stand, wishing I could just run home.

He leads me to the kitchen, where the movers have lined six dining room chairs against the cabinets. He pulls one close to the island and invites me to take a seat. Without a word, I obey.

Chloe watches our interaction, her smile showing signs of waning.

Ray rinses his hands at the kitchen sink, then shakes off the water droplets in the absence of a towel. "So, tell me, is there a special someone in your life?" he asks.

From across the island, Chloe watches me with interest while Ray disappears into the bathroom and returns with the entire roll of toilet paper.

For a moment, I'm not sure what he means. A surge of anxiety rushes through my blood senselessly. "Yes," I reply eventually. "Daniel, my husband."

Chloe's smile widens just a little bit.

Ray stops in place and looks at me with the excitement of a little boy who's just discovered something new and shiny to play with. "So, get him over here! We'd love to meet him."

I frown a little. "What, now?" I look at the unopened boxes and furniture that needs arranging.

"There's no time like the present," he replies, then starts cleaning pie off his pant leg with a piece of moist paper, while I count my blessings. It would be so good to have Daniel by my side.

Quickly, I text him, knowing he will roll his eyes in frustration that he has to abandon his work to hang out with complete strangers. I try to make my text compelling.

> Come on over. New neighbors are old friends of mine. Bring another pie, a roll of paper towels, and some surface cleaner. I'll explain.

His reply comes quickly in the form of a question mark, an exclamation point, and the acronym OMW. I can easily translate his shorthand. He's frustrated, wondering if I'm okay, and he's on his way. It's Daniel's way of saying what the hell.

I stand awkwardly by the island, too nervous to sit any longer, while Ray continues cleaning the pie off his slacks with toilet paper that keeps disintegrating, too flimsy for the cleanup job. Unable to keep looking at him, I glance around the room, where the movers have stacked pieces of furniture one on top of another. Layers of boxes line the far wall and most of the dining room.

They have beautiful things. I'm not surprised. The silence too heavy to bear, I turn to Chloe and ask, "So, how have you been?" My voice is not nearly as shaky as I feel.

Her heels clack on the barren floor as she comes near, seemingly excited to start chatting like in the old days. She pulls up a chair, but the doorbell rings before she can take a seat.

I breathe. Daniel is here.

Ray is closer to the door, and he opens it widely. "You must be Daniel," he says, shifting the toilet paper roll to his left hand and extending his right hand.

"Yeah, nice to meet you."

They shake hands vigorously. For the first time since I've met Daniel, I realize how much the two men look alike. It's a disconcerting, unnerving feeling, although Ray's an inch taller than Daniel, and his hair is darker. Daniel's eyes are brown, not blue, and his cheeks don't have dimples like Ray's, so it's hard to figure out where the resemblance is coming from, but it's there, staring me in the face.

Chloe approaches with her power smile, her hair toss, and unshielded curiosity in her eyes. She shakes Daniel's hand while saying her name, then shoots me an approving glance. I'm too stunned to react.

My husband stares at the mess I've made and looks at me with unspoken criticism for my clumsiness, no doubt in his mind as to who was to blame. Then he sets down a shopping bag he's loaded with the things I asked for, and some others I didn't. A roll of paper towels gets Ray cheering loudly, and the cleaner spray is just as popular. Then Daniel pulls out a bottle of wine and offers to open it.

"Oh, God, yes," Chloe says almost sensually, "but we don't have any—"

"Got you covered," Daniel replies. "A gift for your new home." The last item in his bag is a four-glass wine set we received last Christmas and didn't quite like. It was taking up room in the pantry with a Post-it on it with the name of the giver, so that we wouldn't end up gifting it to the same person by mistake.

Chloe is opening the box with fluttering eyelids and a conspiratorial smile, as if it's the best present she's ever received. Whispering "Thank you!" to just him, not me, she tilts her head and tucks a strand of her silky blonde hair behind her ear.

She's shamelessly flirting with my husband, while I stand there speechless, feeling blood draining from my face.

The awkward moment is short-lived, or maybe it's only in my imagination. Daniel expertly pours the wine, then hands everyone a glass and joins me, putting his arm around my waist. I lean into him, grateful, then smile at him. He places a quick kiss on my lips, while Ray watches the interaction with a hint of amusement in his blue eyes.

"Cheers," Ray says loudly, and glasses clink in the air above the kitchen island. "Couldn't've hoped for better neighbors." His eyes linger on my mouth, and I'm unsettled. I decide to not look at him anymore.

Daniel senses I'm stiff as a board and shoots me an inquisitive glance. I shrug ever so lightly, and he shifts his attention to Ray. "You're into surfing?" He must've noticed the two humongous surfboards leaning against the back door.

"Yeah." Ray grins after emptying his glass. "You?"

"I don't have much time, but I've been looking for someone to go out on the water with."

"So cool!" They shake hands again. "We're so doing this."

Daniel, smiling like I haven't seen him smile in a long time, runs his hand through his hair and walks over to a mountain of furniture set in the middle of the living room. "What's going on here? You have movers coming tomorrow morning?"

Ray crinkles his nose briefly. "I have to find somebody. Those guys just walked out on us. Dumped everything and left."

My husband gives the heap of furniture a thoughtful look. "We got this, you and me," he offers. I repress a sigh. That's my Daniel, always willing to help. Even when I'm secretly hoping he wouldn't. "We'll have this licked in no time."

Chloe watches the interaction, shifting her eyes from one man to the other, like watching a game of tennis. I can tell she's pleased but can't say about what exactly.

"Sweet," Ray says, kicking off his shoes and rolling up his sleeves.

I still can't believe they're dressed like that for their moving day. *What happened to jeans and a T-shirt? Are those going out of style?*

"Sorry, we just got back from a fundraiser cocktail at my work," Ray says, as if reading my mind. "You look like a busy man," he continues, grunting a little as he lifts the dining room table in tandem with Daniel. "What do you do?"

Chloe still watches them, ignoring me although I'm right there, seated next to her.

"I—we have a restaurant," Daniel says, sweet to correct himself for my sake although the diner has always been his. I didn't bring much into our marriage.

"Here, in Half Moon Bay?" Chloe asks, springing off her chair and walking toward the two men. "Which one?"

"Dan's Diner," my husband replies, with a slightly proud smile. "You might've heard of it."

"Are you kidding? We love that place," Ray replies, and Chloe nods enthusiastically.

"Your oysters are to die for," she adds. "And the Caesar is delish. I always have that."

I stare at the exchange, cupping my chin in my hand. This is going to suck. Unless I do something about it. Like reminding Chloe I exist.

"What do you do for a living?" I ask Chloe, walking over there myself and touching the fine fabric of her blouse. I used to do that back in the day; the gesture creeps up on me with the unstoppable force of habit.

"Oh"—she turns to face me—"I'm a reporter for *Style Vignette*. I cover the latest fashions."

Of course she does. I manage a smile and instill a bit of excitement into it. "It's a great fit for you." I'm not lying. She always loved fashion. "Do you like it?"

She nods energetically, her full lips stretched in a slightly open, meaningful smile, her loose curls bouncing around her shoulders, as if to say, "duh."

"I get to travel, work with supermodels, try on loads of haute couture... just like you envisioned for me, remember?" She takes a couple of steps toward me and hugs me sideways. "Alana always said I should work in the fashion business," she tells the men. "And she was right." She plants a kiss on my cheek. "I never got to thank you for that. How about you? What do you do?"

For a split second, I lower my eyes, feeling a bit intimidated, as if my life is not good enough to stand comparison with hers. But I don't care, I tell myself, thrusting my chin forward and meeting her hazel eyes. I love my life and everything about it, regardless of how it measures up to hers. So screw her and her opinions.

"I teach fourth grade," I say simply. "At the K through twelve here in Half Moon Bay."

She claps her hands excitedly. Not the reaction I was anticipating. "Did you hear, Ray? Alana works with kids." She's beaming. Can't figure out why.

Ray looks at me briefly and smiles, his neck stretched awkwardly, because Daniel is having him flip the dining room table back on its legs.

Daniel grunts and sighs as he puts the table in position after moving it to where Chloe pointed her manicured finger. "I think we're done."

Finally.

Ray squeezes his hand vigorously. "Thanks, man. I appreciate it. Beers on me at the earliest, all right?"

"You bet." Daniel pats him on the back as he heads toward me, wiping a few beads of sweat off his forehead with the back of his hand. I'm itching to get home, and my pleading stare tells Daniel as much.

He makes our apologies, invoking a busy day tomorrow. It's actually true.

The two men pat each other's backs, and the women hug. I wish I could skip that part. Chloe's touch freezes me to the bone: feeling her breath on my cheek, her arms wrapped around my shoulders, her scent in my nostrils, triggers a whirlwind of chills, like a bad feeling lingering after a nightmare: one that won't dissipate when the light is turned on.

I let Ray hug me and that unsettles me even more. He's aware of it; I can see it in his loaded glance, in his slightly parted lips, in the way he whispers, "Good night." I pull away quickly, in time to see Chloe lingering in her hug with Daniel, her chest thrust forward against his, her eyelids lowered as if they're sharing some secret.

Then we leave, at long last.

For about twenty minutes after we get home, Daniel goes on

and on about the new neighbors, asking questions, wondering why I never told him about them, and telling me again and again how great it is to have such nice people move in next door. He likes Ray a lot; he has lots of plans for the two of them together. Fishing. Watching sports on TV with Ray and my brother-in-law, Jason.

I'm too exhausted to care about my husband's newly found bromance.

Later, by myself in the shower, I let it all out in bitter, stifled sobs. Neither the tears nor the strong jets of hot water manage to rinse away the bad feeling unfurling in my gut.

It's here to stay.

FIVE

The night that follows is restless, with so many questions keeping me awake. I feel as if fate is playing a cruel joke on me, slamming my painful, unsettling past against the peaceful present I worked so hard to build. Listening to Daniel's breathing, I want to scream. Not because he's sleeping so peacefully, but because I can't. And again, in a sickening déjà vu, it's because of *her*.

The day she came into my life twelve years ago I should've called in sick. Walked away. Or done something—anything—to avoid this never-ending train wreck.

When the alarm goes off, it finds me just having dozed off. I startle out of my sleep and silence the musical ruckus coming from my phone before it can wake Daniel. He works later hours; the diner doesn't open until eleven.

But my mornings start at six. This time, it's a particularly challenging one, as I'm preparing, more mentally than physically, for a visit to Dr. Ellefson's office in the early afternoon.

For a treatment I don't want.

No, that's not an accurate description of how I feel. Not even close.

I'm terrified of it. Some nights I wake up covered in cold sweat at the thought of it.

But I made Daniel a promise. He deserves a full life, a family, not just me faking smiles under the burden of all the emotional baggage he doesn't even know about.

Why did *she* have to move next door?

With that unanswered question, I enter the shower and spend less than five minutes under water I set colder than usual, to wake me up. To remind me that life is sometimes tough, and I have to figure it out like I always do. The past few years, in their peaceful, enjoyable routine, have done nothing but weaken me. I can feel my own weakness as I fail to repel the panic raising bile in my throat. At the thought of getting fertility shots.

Of getting pregnant.

And now of living next door to Chloe. And Ray.

Most of all, Ray. Her *husband,* Ray.

Getting dressed, my rambling thoughts go to the movie *Casablanca,* and I chuckle bitterly. Out of all people and all houses, they had to move next to mine.

I've always relied on humor when times were tough. I need to remind myself how to do that.

Still, the question lingers menacingly in my mind, despite the attempt to fight it lightheartedly. How is she here? How does something like that happen, if not intentionally? And if it was intentional, then why? What is she after?

Has she been stalking me?

I don't want Chloe here, in my life. I don't want her putting eyes on my husband, not even in passing. I have to find a way.

"Good morning, Ms. Blake." The cheerful, high-pitched voice belongs to a student of mine. Without realizing, I made it out the door and drove myself to school. A moment of irrational panic makes me check my attire, to make sure my shoes match and I'm not still wearing a wet towel wrapped around my body. I have no recollection of getting dressed, leaving the house, or parking the car in my usual spot. All I have on my mind is Chloe.

And Ray.

I force my lungs to take in some air and manage a smile. "Good morning, Paul," I reply, but the little boy is already out of earshot.

First period goes by uneventfully. Half my ten-year-old students are barely awake. All the nagging I do with the parents about ensuring their children get enough sleep at night goes to hell in the uphill battle against phones and texting and social media.

By second period, my students are getting a little rowdy for my frayed nerves and blooming headache, but I endure, willing myself cheerful and engaging. They take turns reading from the fifth chapter of *The One and Only Ivan*. Paul is one of the good readers, and Taylor, of course. That little girl makes me so proud. The moment I ask a question, her hand shoots up in the air and starts wiggling. Paul is the same, but he's a bit more reserved, as if concerned with appearing like a nerd or the teacher's pet, as I heard someone call him one time. After that happened, he didn't raise his hand in class for a week.

My students finish reading fifteen minutes before the bell, which gives me time for a quick set of comprehension questions. Paul talks for a few seconds about the captive gorilla's living conditions, describing them accurately, using some of the same adjectives the author used in the book, and managing to keep a straight face while a couple of kids in the back do their best to make ape sounds. Taylor's hand is the only one up when I ask about Ivan's emotions, and if any of the animals felt displaced or not belonging. Even she hesitates for a moment, but then her ambition prevails. She doesn't let anything stop her.

Hearing the bell, her words falter. The period is over. I raise my voice over the increasing commotion to give them their homework assignment. "Write a short dialogue between you and Ivan, exploring his past and his dreams of the future. Make it personal," I shout, to reach the kids who already left the classroom. Those are the ones who'll have to make phone calls later tonight to get the assignment or copy it from someone tomorrow over lunch.

I collect my things, including my own copy of the book, and leave the classroom, heading for the teachers' lounge. My head is pounding, and I need a cup of coffee more than I need air. Students are lingering in the corridor, ambling, unconvinced, toward the cafeteria. One of the boys in my class, a troublemaker by the name of Douglas Durazo, bolts past me. In passing, he shoves Taylor against the wall, intentionally, with both hands. Startled more than injured, she yelps as her books scatter on the floor.

I rush over to her side. "Are you okay, sweetie?" I help her pick up her books. She's a brave little girl, a little pale, but managing to breathe away the tears I notice pooling in her eyes.

"I'm okay, Ms. Blake," she replies in a small voice, as if afraid to be overheard by her classmates. "It's not the first time it's happened."

Her words break my heart and, at the same time, ignite today's very short fuse. I squeeze her shoulder gently, then walk away with a determined stride, looking for the offender. I find him in line at the cafeteria, laughing with the two ape wannabes from earlier.

I stop squarely in front of him. "Mr. Durazo, you will eat in detention today. Your tray will be filled last with whatever is left, after all the other students are done with their lunches. Meanwhile, I will call your parents."

"You can't do this," he shouts, leaning forward to get in my face, physically and metaphorically. He's too short to achieve the physical part, but he's on his toes trying.

"Watch me," I say coldly. "I have zero tolerance for bullies, and so does this school. Your detention will continue until you finish reading *You, Me and Empathy*, and write an essay detailing all your major takeaways from the book. Understood?"

"I want to see the principal," he says, throwing his empty tray on the floor and putting his hands on his hips. The tray clatters as it slides on the floor, its metallic sound reverberating loudly, until it stops against a table. "I want to see her now."

"What a coincidence, so do I. Let's go." With a hand gesture, I invite him to leave the line and follow me to the principal's office.

On the way over, I grind my teeth. I can't even look at him. Can't believe his attitude.

I find my boss, Destiny Jackson, seated behind her desk, her round face a bit sweaty and her brow furrowed, while talking on the phone excitedly and apologetically at the same time, seemingly with an angry parent. She gestures to me to wait, and I'm happy to oblige, considering the sour mood she's in.

She beckons me in as soon as she ends the call. I leave the bully in her waiting room, under the glaring supervision of her assistant, and enter her office. I barely notice the stale air and the slight smell of ranch dressing.

In a few words, I explain the situation, but she's not so quick to support me and send me on my way. Instead, she sits me down.

Oh, hell.

"Don't you feel you're being a little harsh?" she asks, steepling her hands together. Her long acrylic nails click almost imperceptibly when their ends touch.

I shrug, a little surprised. "I thought our zero-tolerance policy was clear. I followed it to the letter."

"The food tray part, which you left out, is not really in our policy." I swallow hard. "That was Mrs. Durazo on the phone, by the way. I promised her I'd look into her accusation that this school is feeding her son cafeteria leftovers."

The little shit. On the short walk between the cafeteria and the principal's office, he texted his mom, a pushy, overbearing, and entitled day-trader's housewife I was dreading to call. Now I've lost the upper hand.

"I'll call and explain," I reply. "She needs to know—"

Destiny puts her hand in the air. "*I* will call her," she says, placing a warning accent on the I. "I'll tell her it was all a big misunderstanding."

"It wasn't a misunderstanding, Destiny. I was there. I saw the kid, what he did. He's going to escalate if we don't nip this behavior in the bud. You know that." She shakes her head, giving me a clearly disapproving stare. "He needs to do the detention and the assignment. The food, I couldn't care less. But detention, that's per policy. What am I supposed to tell Taylor's parents?"

"Do they really need to know?" she asks, and I gasp. "That's the question you should ask yourself."

"Well, it's the policy—" I start saying, my tone raised, but then I stop, realizing I'm just wasting my time and making enemies.

"Be smart about this," Destiny says, laying it thick with a benevolent smile and a lowered voice. "We might be a public school, but some parents donate funds that make a difference. Some parents do, not all. We don't want to antagonize—"

"Ah," I say, cutting her off as the picture becomes crystal clear in my mind.

The interruption makes her angry. Her voice is cold when she speaks. "Listen, you're asking for a lot of things that aren't per policy. Your TV interview, which is going to happen here, on school grounds... that's an exception I made for you. I'm not even sure associating this school's name with the subject of kidnapping and building those binders is the best idea, but I've been willing to push it this far. For you."

She had to bring it up. She knows how important this project is to me, and she's using it shamelessly as leverage.

I stand, unable to keep on sitting when my entire being wants to run out of there screaming. The moment I do, I realize it's a mistake. Now I'm towering over her, and she hates that. I sit back down. "It won't hurt the school, Destiny. We talked about this. It only shows how much we care. And those binders are critical in the event a child goes missing. Do you think, in the heat of the moment, parents will remember everything they should share with the cops? It saves lives."

She nods as I talk, visibly losing her patience. "I get that, but people might think the school has a higher risk of kidnapping *because* you're doing this. They'll be afraid you know something they don't, and they'll line up in front of my office, demanding answers." She breathes a little heavily.

I don't interrupt anymore. The binder project is important to me. She knows exactly what buttons to push. I nod and smile, defeated. "I understand. And I appreciate it."

"Not to mention, next year you want to move to teaching fifth grade, instead of taking on new first graders for a new loop. Your decision created staffing issues, but you believe in it, and I supported you all the way. Wholeheartedly."

Oh, yes, she does know how to push, and she keeps on pushing. I'm out of cards to play.

"So, then, how would you like to handle the Douglas Durazo issue?" I ask.

She breathes, her large chest heaving as if there isn't enough air. "First of all, let's not call it an issue, all right?" She makes a brush-off gesture with her manicured hand. "It wasn't, really, an issue, was it?"

I sit still, willing myself to agree, but can't. I can't forget Taylor's tearful eyes saying it wasn't the first time it happened. All I can do is tentatively smile and wait.

Silence fills the stuffy room for a tense moment. "Let him do the detention," she eventually says. "But no more cafeteria punishments. And don't call the girl's parents, all right?"

I frown. Calling both children's parents is procedure for all bullying cases. "What if she tells her parents and they call us?"

"Then you're going to explain it was nothing, really, just someone who bumped into her by accident and was given detention for not apologizing."

"Ah," I say again, then cannot keep my mouth shut. "Is *that* what it was?"

Her smile vanishes and a glint of rage lights her eyes for a fleeting second. "Exactly." A pause, while she raps her finger-nails against her desk impatiently. "Alana, I hope we manage to find a way to be in agreement about these things. We're a team. If we're not, who knows where we'll end up." She waves me off, and I stand and leave without another word.

As I take a grinning and triumphant Douglas Durazo back to the cafeteria, I realize I'm going to be late for the stupid doctor's appointment.

I check the time on my phone. I have exactly seven minutes to get there, and it's a twenty-five-minute drive across the moun-tain. And there are two messages from Daniel I haven't noticed.

I just wish the day was over already.

SIX

"Alana..."

Daniel says my name in a disappointed tone. Hearing that brings the sting of tears to the corners of my eyes. "I'm so sorry, Daniel. We had an incident, a bullying issue I had to deal with, and it went ugly with Destiny. Turns out, the bully's mother is one of the principal's secret donors, so there. I just couldn't get out of it."

As I make my excuses, only silence comes across on the call. I drive impatiently, unusually close to the slow-moving Prius in front of me: yet another Arizona tourist who can't drive narrow, winding mountain roads without dropping to twenty miles per hour. I find the right opening and I floor it, passing the Prius in my Subaru Outback, while Daniel is yet to say anything.

After reentering my lane, narrowly avoiding a frontal collision with a truck I didn't see coming, I ask, "Are you there already?"

"Yes." Another long moment of disapproving silence.

"Let's—can you get started on my paperwork?" I hesitate to ask, because I can tell how he's going to feel about this. But it makes sense to save some of the time I've wasted.

"You want me to fill out your forms?" he asks, his voice lowered, probably out of embarrassment. "Seriously?"

"Please, Daniel. I'm driving as quickly as I can. I just don't want to miss the appointment if I have to do the papers when I get there."

He sighs, resigned. "All right. If they'll give them to me." He's about to end the call; I hear it in his voice.

"Call me if they don't, all right?" I ask, just as I take the southbound ramp toward San Jose. Eight minutes later, I barge into the small, quiet medical office, looking for Daniel.

He's seated in the corner, filling out forms with a quizzical expression on his face. Hearing the door whoosh open, he lifts his eyes and then springs to his feet. The frown on his face still lingers.

I kiss him quickly and rush toward the reception. "Alana Blake," I say, extending my hand with the driver's license and insurance card. "I'm so sorry I'm late." The receptionist takes my cards with an uninterested expression on her face. *She's way too young to be this spiritless*, I think, but then I put that thought aside and smile. "Can Dr. Ellefson still see us?"

She hands me the cards back after scanning them in the smallest scanner I've ever seen. "Take a seat," she says, not bothering to answer my question.

I'm too restless to sit. I walk over to the window and look outside, at the perfectly blue California sky. The deep azure mocks me, the anguish in my soul more suitable for a thunderstorm, a tornado even. *What am I doing here?*

Daniel clasps my hand and I have my answer. Still, the warmth of his reassuring touch doesn't soothe my fear. After a while, I breathe normally again, and my spinning thoughts settle.

I can't do this. I can't break Daniel's heart either. Feeling the urge to run out of there, I wring my frozen hands instead, as soon as I free them from Daniel's grip.

When the nurse calls my name, I almost don't react. Daniel tugs at my sleeve to get my attention, then we follow her into the exam room, where, again, I refuse to take a seat as instructed. After asking some routine questions, she finally leaves, closing the door behind her.

My eyes stay fixed on the stirrups while my stomach churns. The office is cold and dreary, impersonal, the AC setting a few degrees too low. Unlike the waiting room, there's no window to give me a glimpse of blue sky, of hope; only fluorescent lights above my head, casting a pale shade of bluish-purple over everything.

Dr. Ellefson knocks, then enters with a professional smile on her lips. She's in her late fifties with short, gray hair and kind eyes. She's perceptive: her smile wanes a little when she notices how I'm pacing the floor like a caged animal, avoiding her gaze.

"So, are you ready to become parents?" she asks, and Daniel's face lights up. I look at him, taking my fill of energy and courage from his joy. "Don't worry, there's nothing to it. Just an exam, to make sure everything is all right, then we give the future mommy a shot and send you home with a prescription for an ovulation-stimulating drug."

"Sounds good," I say, nodding as if to tell myself everything will be all right. I run my hand through my hair, then manage to look Dr. Ellefson in the eye. "Yeah, we're good."

"Excellent," she replies, clapping her hands. Her smile doesn't touch her eyes.

The door opens, and the nurse brings in a tray with a syringe, some disinfectant swabs sealed in tiny packets, and a vial. Then she leaves the room just as quietly as she entered.

Dr. Ellefson turns on the ultrasound machine and rolls the cart over next to the exam table. "Hop on," she says, patting the paper-covered vinyl with her hand. "Let's take another look at you."

I hesitate, painfully aware my eyes are darting all over the place as if looking for a way out. After a dreadful moment, I sit on the table between the stirrups and fold my arms over my chest, forcing myself to smile.

Probably feeling a little bit uncomfortable at the thought of witnessing a pelvic ultrasound, Daniel withdraws to the far corner of the small room, hands buried in his pants pockets.

Dr. Ellefson shoots him a quick glance. "Mr. Blake, why don't you wait outside for this part? I think everyone will be more comfortable that way."

"Sure," he replies, seeming relieved to leave the room.

The moment the door closes, I breathe.

Dr. Ellefson pulls over a lab stool and sits. "All right, Ms. Blake, it's just us girls now. What's going on?"

I look at her, no longer concerned about the tears rolling on my face. It's too late for appearances.

"I can't do this," I whimper, shaking my lowered head. Loose strands of hair slip over my shoulder and hide my face. "I really can't."

"I know, honey," she says, giving my forearm a quick, reassuring squeeze. "I'm not blind."

Holding my breath for a moment, I lift my eyes in an unspoken plea. "I'm on birth control," I whisper. "I-I can't..." I stammer, painfully aware of how little sense I make. "Something happened to me, years ago, and I—" Tears spring from my eyes as, choking, I struggle to breathe. It's as if pressure has built up inside my chest with no place else to go, threatening to release sobs I can't let Daniel overhear through the door.

Dr. Ellefson brings me some tissues and a paper cup filled with water from the faucet. A couple of sips helps me get a grip. I sniffle and look at her with gratitude, then pat my eyes dry and close my fist around the tissue, spasmodically crumpling it as if doing so can help me find a way out of this mess.

"I can't," I whisper, clearing my throat quietly. "Not after what happened." I stop talking, terrified she's going to ask questions I'm not ready to answer. "Daniel wants children," I add, as if she needed me to tell her that. I feel another sob swelling my chest. "What if I can't? What's going to happen to us? He's going to hate me for robbing him of a full life. He's such a wonderful man. He doesn't deserve this," I add bitterly.

Dr. Ellefson listens, not a trace of judgment in her eyes. "Why don't you ask him?" she says simply. She takes the tray with the syringe and serum and puts everything away in a cabinet, then returns to my side. "There are counselors I can recommend. A good therapist could help you navigate this dilemma. Past trauma can have a deep impact on your decisions. But you must have an open conversation with your husband, Ms. Blake. It's your body and your decision, but both partners have to be on the same page to have any chance at a happy life together."

The thought of having that conversation with Daniel fills my mind with raging panic. "Could we just pretend I had the shot, and—and just go on like this for a little while longer? Buy me some time?"

I'm being a coward. I press my lips together, disappointed with myself, feeling ashamed.

She sits on the stool and looks at me. Somehow, I find courage in her eyes, as if I can borrow her strength through a simple glance. "It's only going to make things worse," she says calmly, and I know she's right. "Your husband seems to love you very much. Don't sell him short. He might understand. And there are options. You can always adopt or have a surrogate IVF if you're not ready to get pregnant. Work together, find a way."

I nod, afraid she's wasting her time with me. I can't see myself explaining to Daniel what happened. Why I can't have his child and don't think I'll ever be able to. But he's just outside that door, waiting for me to tell him the first fertility treatment is done.

For now, the lie is the easiest way out.

"Will you at least not tell him? Today?"

She looks at me for a long, silent moment, a hint of disappointment coloring the kindness in her eyes. "Okay. Just this once."

Without thinking, I hop off the table and hug her. "Thank you."

"Tell him the truth," she urges me quietly, her hand reaching for the doorknob. "Promise me you will."

I nod and wipe away a rebel tear. She's right. I just have to figure out a way to tell Daniel. To make him understand.

Dr. Ellefson opens the door, and Daniel steps in, beaming. "How did it go?"

"We're done here," Dr. Ellefson says, plunging her hands into her lab coat pockets. "Call me with any questions," she tells me, then turns to leave. "If you'll both excuse me, I'm running a little late for my next appointment."

The air outside greets me with fresh warm sunshine. Relief swells my chest and I savor the feeling, deciding to worry about telling Daniel some other time. Maybe tomorrow.

A dozen red roses are waiting for me on the driver's seat of my Subaru. Daniel holds the door while I struggle to hold back tears. I love him so much. He deserves every bit of happiness.

"Let's go home," I whisper, roses in my arms, basking in the loving look he gives me.

It might be the last time he gives me flowers.

The last time he looks at me like that.

SEVEN

I drive home behind Daniel's Ford, letting my mind wander as the mountain road curves ahead of me, climbing and climbing through the redwood and cypress forest until the reservoir vista opens up in a breathtaking view. In the distance, the blue waters of the Pacific glimmer in the sun for a fleeting moment before the road turns again, and all I see is rolling hills. I lower the windows and enjoy the brisk wind that whips my hair, almost blinding me at times. I enjoy the sense of freedom it gives me. For a few minutes, my heart-wrenching troubles are forgotten.

Pulling into our driveway in parallel with Daniel's Ford SUV, my eyes veer sideways to the neighboring house. There's a black Mercedes GLE parked in front; I don't know whose. One of them is home. It's probably Ray. I don't see Chloe driving that huge vehicle. It's not her style. She's more convertible sports car than the bulky, heavy-duty SUV. At least, she used to be.

Our houses are almost identical. Single story, two-car garage homes built in the late nineties, when backyards were little larger than a handkerchief. Still, land is expensive in Northern California, and the two houses are built close together, merely twenty feet between them. I never cared much about the close proximity when Mrs. Moore used to live there. Now I have to keep in mind those walls are thin and the neighbors not the sort I want to eavesdrop on our lives.

On the other side of the house, a fence separates our street from the back of a convenience store and its loading ramps. It's not the most scenic of landscapes, but the former owner of our house did his best to keep the old, gray building out of sight by planting tall cypress bushes that obscure the view. In our peaceful cul-de-sac, it's just us. And our new neighbors.

I hate to admit it, but I just can't bring myself to believe their move is a coincidence. I keep waiting for something to happen, something that would explain why Chloe chose to live here, out of all places. She could've had a waterfront property, like her parents, or lived in San Jose, with all the glitzy Silicon Valley folks. And yet, she's here.

My car door swings open, and Daniel offers me his hand with a charming smile I can't refuse. I grab the roses from the passenger seat and follow him inside. Then I busy myself with finding a vase and arranging the red roses, one by one, until I'm pleased with the result. Rewarding myself with the velvet feel of rose petals against my face, I place the vase at the center of the dining room table as Daniel starts clattering dishes in the kitchen.

"What are you doing?"

"Making us an omelet." He takes a large frying pan from the cabinet, spinning it in the air expertly before he puts it on the stove. "You go take a shower," he adds, opening the fridge and retrieving a carton of eggs.

Grateful, I hurry into the bathroom, eager to get out of these clothes and rinse off the tension accumulating in my shoulders. A few minutes later, when I emerge with my hair still clumped in moist strands, wearing a comfy V-neck and sweatpants, the kitchen smells deliciously of fresh, cheesy omelet with herbs and hash browns.

While he sets the table, I linger aimlessly for a moment. "What if we sold this place and moved?" I ask, voicing a half-baked thought that doesn't make much sense other than putting some distance between me and our new neighbors.

Stunned, Daniel freezes in place, holding two square plates in his hand. "Move where? You want to leave Half Moon Bay?"

"N-no. The restaurant is here, and my school. No, just a different house. Bigger, maybe."

"I see." He frowns a little, but then gets wrapped up in finishing the meal. "I don't know how that would make sense. The cost of moving is horrendous. And I thought you were happy here."

"I am." There's no point insisting. He's right. It makes no sense at all.

The table is set, and a bottle of champagne awaits, covered in a chill mist. My own personal chef uncorks it with a loud pop, then pours the wine into tall flutes quickly, before it can spill too much.

"To our future family," he says, raising one glass and handing me the other.

My hand trembles a little when I take the glass, but I meet his midair and then drink a little wine. It's refreshingly cold and sweet, prickling my tongue with happy little bubbles. Yet it has a foreboding effect on me, as I remember the reason for his celebration is nothing but a lie. How will he think back on this moment, when he learns the truth? How will he ever trust me again? Will he remember how I smiled and clinked glasses with him, lying to his face?

After barely moistening my lips, I place the glass on the table and sit. My appetite is gone too, my stomach twisting in a knot of worry and dread.

"Enjoy," he says, pushing the plate toward me. Unable to do

anything but continue weaving my endless web of lies, I take the fork and load it with mouthwatering omelet.

It's perfect. As I chew one mouthful after another, my body remembers its needs, and hunger takes over, silencing the worries, even if only for a few minutes.

"I might be inclined to break our rule more often," I say, licking my lips when the plate is finally empty. "Seems to me you have all the talent in the kitchen. That's why there's none left for me." I smile, and a hint of sadness touches my voice. "Thank you for this."

He stands and comes next to my chair, leaning forward and kissing me softly. His tousled hair falls unruly on his forehead, smelling of shower gel and a hint of aftershave, a heady mix. "I could be persuaded to cook for you every day, milady," he whispers, his breath tickling the skin on my neck. Heat spreads throughout my body, ignited by his touch.

He scoops me up in his arms and carries me into the bedroom, then lays me down on top of the covers. I look into his eyes and smile when I see the passion smoldering there. Lifting my arms above my head, I wait, wanting, restless. Slowly, as if savoring every move, he draws close to me, his hands warm against my chilled skin, touching, exploring, releasing my body from the clothes that keep it captive.

I close my eyes and abandon myself to his embrace. My body starts responding to his, raising itself, lowering, thrusting. My hands explore him while I surrender, yearning for more.

In the dark space behind my closed eyelids, insidious memories swirl and collide, drawing Ray's face. The dimples he makes when he smiles, and how I used to trace them with my finger until he'd snatch the tip of it with his lips and hold it captive. His voice, sultry and low, whispering words I thought I'd long since forgotten. Asking me if I'd be willing to bleach my hair, as he played with the long, silky brown strands, fanning them with his fingers. Telling me I'd look so much better as a blonde, and how that felt: a little disappointing and crazy hot at the same time, unbearably sexy to hear he was fantasizing about me. His smile and the intensity in his deep blue eyes when I said no to his makeover idea. "Dare you to say no to me," he whispered, then made love to me like never before, passionately, all-consuming, as if we were the only two people left on earth.

The sound of my own moaning awakens me from the memories, rendering me brutally in the moment. Daniel is gasping for air, lying by my side.

"Whoa, baby, what was in those shots?" he quips as I frown, almost slipping to ask what shots he was talking about, the entire fertility issue completely gone from my wandering mind. "That was surreal, as if you were a different person. Wow." He places a kiss on my blushing cheek.

His words drop on me like stones covered in deceit.

Oh, God, what am I going to do?

Daniel wraps me in an embrace and closes his eyes. Within moments, his steady, shallow breathing tells me he's asleep. Yet I lie there, eyes wide open, afraid to let them close again. Afraid of my ghosts.

I thought I was over Ray.

I was wrong.

And he had to move in next door, to taint my life with the dark shadow of *what if*s and *maybe*s and everything I lost. There's no room in my life for the way he makes me feel. I won't give into that heady, intoxicating infatuation I remember so well. Daniel is my life now, and I love him too much to let Ray ruin what we have.

My breath shatters and I slide out of bed slowly, unwilling to wake Daniel and face questions I don't have answers for. Tiptoeing around the room, I gather my clothes and sneak out, closing the bedroom door gently, then walk into the living room naked, eyeing the window that faces our new neighbors' house. Thankfully, the curtains are drawn, and no one can see me.

I get dressed quickly, struggling more and more to fight my tears. There will be a time for crying, for coming to terms with everything that's happening, but that time isn't now, with Daniel sleeping in the other room. Maybe later, when he goes back to the restaurant for the dinner rush hour.

Looking for something to keep my mind off things, I walk over to the console table by the door. In an old, hammered-copper fruit bowl we keep there, Daniel has left the day's mail alongside his car keys. I grab the thin stack of envelopes and sift through them. The water bill is there and a notice of an upcoming sale event at the local furniture store. The last envelope in the stack catches my eye.

It's thin and doesn't have a sender's name. My name and address are handwritten hastily in green ink, the lettering heavily slanted. There's no postage; it must've been hand-delivered to our mailbox. Abandoning everything else in the fruit bowl, I open it quickly, sliding my finger under the flap and tearing it along its entire length.

When I pull out the letter, a picture falls to the floor, landing face up on the rug.

My heart skips a beat when I recognize it.

Unfolding the letter with trembling hands, I read the hand-written message as blood drains from my face.

It's time to pay for what you've done. I haven't forgotten.

My shaky knees give, and I land on the floor, crouching next to the photo I'm afraid to touch. Memories come crashing down, bringing the threat of revealing buried secrets that could destroy me.

I crumple the letter as I stifle the scream that threatens to rip through my chest. Heaving, I stare at the picture, desperate to understand how it landed on my floor. Who sent it? Who could've known what happened that day, when only Chloe was there with me? She was the one who took the photo. Chloe was the one who swore that day she would never share that image with anyone. That she would delete it from the phone's memory, as we both wanted to delete that day from our own memories. Forever. Completely.

And yet, the haunting image is there, staring at me from my living room floor in a four-by-six glossy print.

The picture—a glimpse into a carefree moment when three friends shared ice cream on the waterfront terrace of Miramar Beach before everything went wrong—has the power to destroy me.

And so does Chloe.

The name I haven't spoken in almost eleven years leaves my lips in a shattered whisper, chilling me to the bone.

"Nikki."

EIGHT

It was a couple of weeks after they found the body of Flavia Guzman, the girl who'd vanished without a trace from the parking lot of her church, eleven years ago. I remember that day clearly. Everything changed that afternoon, in one of those whiplash moments when life takes a sudden turn that forever alters one's existence.

We were in our senior year, just about a month before graduation, and riding the high of impending freedom from the rigors of school.

That was how everyone felt, and how I pretended to feel, while my heart was secretly breaking. Ray was no longer mine. He was with Chloe, and seemingly head over heels in love with her.

In retrospect, I should've done something, said something, not just given up when Chloe made her move. But that wasn't me; I wasn't that much of a fighter back then. I watched what was happening with eyes wide in shock, unable to say anything. While I pretended everything was okay, for everyone else's sake, not caring about mine for one moment. Maybe I should've—

Never mind. It's too late now. What's done is done. Was done a long time ago.

Back then, I had immersed myself in reading and listening to podcasts like *True Murder*. I became increasingly obsessed with a missing person case. A girl about our age, Flavia Guzman, had disappeared after attending a church service, and no one could figure out what happened to her. I was a recent subscriber to a true-crime podcast that was making waves, happy to keep my aching mind busy with anything else other than Chloe and her newly found romance.

Two weeks earlier, the cops had found Flavia Guzman's body in a dumpster behind a fast-food restaurant. Twelve days after that, an article in the local newspaper shared details of the girl's autopsy. She'd been kept alive for five days after she'd been taken. Five days when they could've saved her but didn't.

During my long shifts at the hardware store, I kept one ear bud in, wire snaking discreetly down my top, and listened to podcasts, perking up whenever I heard Flavia's name mentioned. Then someone—a guest speaker whose name I can't recall—went through a painful list of hurdles cops had had to go through to try to locate Flavia. It had taken them eight days to gain access to her phone. By then she was dead. Four more days to access her social media and messaging, to try to find people who might've lured her online. Too damn late. Her killer was long gone, never to be found. I suspected who he was—my personal knowledge of the community helping me get a grasp on what had happened—but no one cared what a schoolgirl working evening shifts packing screws and twine had to say. The cops wouldn't listen. The moment they figured out I wasn't actually an eyewitness, only someone who'd arrived at her own conclusions, they couldn't send me packing fast enough.

That was the day I learned about the If I Go Missing binders. They weren't called that back then: that came way later. The original idea was just a piece of paper with key information on it, not a real binder like it is today. We also had much less information back then; our lives used to be so much simpler. Nevertheless, the idea grabbed me, fascinating me with its simplicity and usefulness to the point I became—and remain—a dedicated champion of the concept. It's simple, really: collecting everything the police need to know to start looking for someone, in case they go missing, without any red tape delays that could mean the difference between life and death. Bringing insider knowledge of family, friends, relationships right in front of the detectives working the case.

My fascination with true crime made Chloe frown for a while. After all, it was something that belonged only to me, something she didn't share. Until she did. Later, she joined me in my passion for it, and being the friend I still was, I welcomed her, thinking two voices would speak more loudly than one. Advocating for such a simple means to save lives was well worth sharing my newly found passion with her.

But I digress.

The day after I first heard about what was to evolve into If I Go Missing binders, Chloe invited me and another girl to go for ice cream at the Miramar Beach restaurant, then maybe for a walk by the cliffs. I knew this other girl, Nikki. She'd recently transferred from Nevada. I remember that because I wondered why someone coming from a place with permanent scorching sun wasn't more tan. I would've expected her complexion to resemble that of a pirate, sun- and wind-burned. But no. Her skin was delicate, almost pale, her shapely legs just starting to show a little color from the strong California sun.

Chloe's invite came as a surprise. Usually, it was just the two of us, so she could share endless snippets of her love life with more detail than I cared to learn. I should've stayed away. I didn't. Maybe out of curiosity, force of habit, or just loneliness, I followed Chloe wherever Chloe wanted to go. Or perhaps it was my twisted, sickening way of stalking Ray, of keeping tabs on his latest activities. Of not letting him go.

At six, Chloe picked me up at the hardware store in her red convertible. The passenger seat was already taken by Nikki, her waist-long, naturally blonde hair waving in the ocean breeze. A delicate nose, a prominent jaw line, and eyes she kept squinting ever so slightly completed the striking appearance of someone who could've easily passed for Chloe's sister.

Maybe I was being replaced as Chloe's best friend. The thought didn't upset me much. Maybe some distance wasn't going to do me any harm. Distance would soon happen anyway, as we were mere months away from going our separate ways to different colleges.

But I remember wondering about Chloe's decision to invite Nikki. I didn't get a chance to ask her about it. Just climbed in the back seat of the Benz and let the cold wind whirl my hair around as Chloe drove a little too fast on the coastal highway.

A few minutes later, a blatantly flirty smile made a young, eager-to-please waiter at the restaurant give Chloe one of the coveted fireplace tables, the one closest to the edge of the patio, ahead of other patrons who were waiting their turns. Flustered and talking way too much, he then brought us cold drinks and dessert menus, while we watched the setting sun over the Pacific in silence.

The wind gusted at times, and the Pacific waves crashed against the shore in a melody that synced with my restless heart-beats. It was a chilly evening, the temperature dropping with the sun, soon to go below seventy as the winds picked up. Chloe had chosen the wrong day for ice cream, but she didn't seem to care.

The same waiter busied himself with firing up the patio heaters closest to our table, although a nice fire was burning happily in the pit between us.

Then, as we savored the chocolate-covered vanilla ice cream

and hot cocoa, I realized why Chloe had invited Nikki. As if it were just the two of us, she shared uncensored stories about Ray and her, dating, talking, making love, to the point where I couldn't breathe anymore. But Chloe wasn't noticing me at all. With the focus of a panther, she was getting her do-not-touch message across to Nikki. Marking territory. Nikki was pale and silent by the time she stopped pretending to finish her ice cream.

And I felt like I was about to faint.

Whenever I blinked, I saw images of Chloe moaning in Ray's arms, her lean body arching to meet his, her blonde curls fanned on the pillow, her red lips slightly parted, whispering sweet nothings in his ear. It was killing me. Yet there I was, unable to run from it, a deer in the headlights of the formidable Chloe Avery.

Oblivious to my agony, Chloe patted the loveseat pillows at her left and right with both her hands, inviting the two of us to join her for a selfie. I sat at her right, and Nikki at her left, the wicker loveseat wide enough for the three of us. Then all of us smiled widely, squinting against the sun.

One photo. That's all she took.

I was there, and I remember it clearly.

The angle was crooked, because Chloe overextended her hand to capture all three of us in the shot. The setting sun's glare, reflected in the Pacific waves, left streaks of sunshine over our smiling faces.

No one was supposed to have that photo but her.

As far as I knew up until a few minutes ago, Chloe never shared that photo with anyone and never spoke of it. She swore not to.

Had she? Apparently not.

And if she kept it, why?

That picture, together with everything else that had happened that day, was supposed to stay forever locked inside the vaults of our minds, never to see the light of day again. Never to be spoken of again.

For eleven years, I believed the past was just that, the past.

Not anymore.

The past came home to roost the day Chloe moved next door.

NINE

"You should get more sleep."

The makeup artist's verdict, as she dabs concealer under my eyes, brings a bitter chuckle to my lips. I wish I could sleep like I used to, before Chloe moved next door. She has no idea how much I wish I could just get a few hours of healing, of forgetting the tentacles of the past closing around my neck, leaving me breathless and already defeated.

But today is not about me. As she finishes her work, I dare to look in the mirror and almost don't recognize myself. The young woman has worked wonders. Now I regret not paying more attention to what she did, instead of spacing out and obsessing over the lack of sleep problem.

"Give us a smile, will you?" she prompts, and I comply, fascinated to see how I look. The tiredness and sickly pallor are gone, my skin now glowing, all the right shades of foundation and blush and eyeshadow working together to show the confident face of a beautiful woman.

Strange how I never thought of myself as beautiful until now, but it's there, in the mirror. I like what I see. My smile evolves naturally, instinctively, enchanted.

"Uh-huh," she mutters in a satisfied voice, collecting the Kleenex she planted on my shoulders and lapels to keep them free of makeup. "We're done here. I need a few more minutes for the principal, then a final touch-up on Jane, and you guys are good to go."

I stand and smile awkwardly, then shake her hand warmly. "Thank you. You're amazing."

"Don't I know it?" She turns toward Destiny, inviting her to take a seat, then starts working on her.

I'm a little surprised, but then again, not really, that Destiny chose to stay for my interview. She was never a big fan of the If I Go Missing binder. I'm actually a little anxious that she's inserted herself into my interview; something I've been trying to arrange for at least two years. Will she say anything incorrect? Yesterday, when we talked about it, she didn't tell me she was going to be here. I wish she had, so we could have coordinated our answers. But she probably just craves the attention, or perhaps she's still concerned with the potential negative impact this interview could have on the school.

I've been gracious about her presence and promise myself I'll continue to be just as gracious during the actual interview. It gives me the opportunity to repair some of the damage our relationship has suffered because of that cheeky little bully, Douglas Durazo.

At the same time, I'm worried. What if something goes wrong?

I breathe and tell myself everything will be okay.

The school is deserted at this late afternoon hour, a choice made by the reporter, *Top of the Morning TV Show*'s own anchor, Jane Fouch. She carries a lot of weight in the industry, and her show is syndicated for national coverage. This is a big deal for me. As I remind myself of that, my palms are slick with sweat. Discreetly, or so I believe, I wipe them against the butt of my black slacks, then button my jacket and arrange the collar of my white silk shirt, making sure the tiny clip mic the tech attached to my lapel is not rubbing against the rustling fabric.

"Are we ready, ladies?" Jane's voice reverberates in the school's reading room. The location wasn't my first choice, but Destiny decided against the teachers' lounge because of the messy layout, and Jane's cameraman shot down the assembly room because of its echo. But we're laid out neatly in here, on three armchairs set in a semicircle, with me at the center. Behind us, tall bookcases line the walls. In front of the armchairs, on a small coffee table borrowed from the teachers' lounge, I laid out a binder, open at the cover letter. It has colored dividers for each section, neatly indexed with printed self-adhesive labels.

"Yes, we're ready," I lie.

This is it. I breathe again, steeling my frayed nerves. *I'll be damned if I'll let Chloe ruin this for me.* I push the thought of her aside and focus.

We take our seats. Projected light lands on our faces in a blinding flood of white. I can feel the heat emanating from the lamps but try my best to ignore it, hoping it won't make me sweat. The makeup artist dashes through, arranging a strand of my hair over my right shoulder, then dabbing Jane's high forehead with a large blender brush.

"You're all set," she announces, then leaves hastily.

"We're rolling," Jane says, pairing her words with an illustrative hand gesture. The red LED on the camera is barely visible against the powerful light. "Look at the camera, ladies, and don't forget to breathe. This is a recorded interview. You can afford to relax."

Easy for her to say. Slowly, I let the air out of my chest and smile. "Thank you." My voice sounds surprisingly strong, positive, self-confident.

Jane clears her throat quietly and flashes her usual smile. "Top of the morning, everyone, it's Jane Fouch. Today I'm interviewing two amazing women who will share with you a little something that could someday save your life. Alana Blake is a fourth-grade teacher at the public school in Half Moon Bay." I nod a silent greeting when I hear my name. "Destiny Jackson is the school's principal. Thank you for hosting us, Destiny."

Destiny smiles, seeming a bit nervous. Her face is shiny under the strong lights. "It's my pleasure."

Jane turns to me, pointing at the open binder with a perfectly manicured finger. "Tell us, Alana, what is this binder and why do you so strongly believe we all need one?"

My throat is parchment dry, but I don't falter. "Eleven years ago, a young girl by the name of Flavia Guzman disappeared without a trace after attending church. Although she was immediately reported missing, the police had difficulties tracking her phone and accessing her social media because of the time it takes for warrants to be issued and executed. Telecom companies are famously sluggish when it comes to allowing access to people's devices—"

"And that's a bad thing?" Jane asks.

"In a few critical cases, like Flavia's, for example, it's a deadly thing. Of course, there are privacy concerns at play, perfectly justifiable ones. Law enforcement should never access personal information without due process." I swallow hard, suddenly concerned I'm not making much sense. But Jane nods almost imperceptibly, and I continue. "This solution prevents any delay for law enforcement, without compromising individual privacy."

"Very interesting," Jane says, leaning forward without lowering her head. "What's in the binder?"

"It's everything the police should know or have access to in the case of my disappearance. A letter detailing the contents and any concerns for my safety I might have." I turn the page to the next section. "My fingerprints, taken the best way I was able to, on my own. My DNA, in a few strands of hair with the root follicle still attached." I turn another page. "My phone passcode, in case it doesn't disappear with me. Computer passwords, email accounts, social media logins, bank accounts, credit card accounts—"

Jane holds her hand in the air, and I stop. "This is highly sensitive information. It's a deadly weapon in the hands of the wrong person. Identity theft made easy, to say the least."

"I agree. That's why it should never be left handy for just anyone to find. It should be kept safely, in a place only a trusted person would know of. A spouse or parent, maybe, or perhaps locking it in a safe or entrusting the family attorney with it," I add hesitantly, painfully aware she interrupted me halfway through the content review.

Jane notices my side glance. "What else is in there?"

"Anything I deem important in case I disappear. Am I scared of anything? Have I been stalked recently? Any bad breakups or threats I might've received? Is there something going on in my life, serious enough to worry me, but not serious enough to take to the cops?"

Jane nods and her smile widens, a glimmer shining in her eyes. "To be honest, at first I thought this was just some smart marketing gimmick to sell overpriced stationery."

I laugh quietly. "I'm not selling anything. Anyone who wants to build a binder can do so with whatever resources they have on hand."

"Exactly," Jane replies. "I think I understand where your passion is coming from."

I wait for a split second for her to continue, but she doesn't. "Flavia Guzman was alive for five days after she was taken. Yet the police were unable to gain access to her phone for eight days. It's possible the location of that phone could've saved her life." I shake my head, still reeling from it as if it were yesterday. "It's unbelievable. They tried their best, I have no doubt, but the thought that more could've been done sooner has kept me up nights. I decided to raise awareness of the one simple thing we could do to potentially avoid Flavia's fate."

"So, you don't believe family and loved ones could provide all this information to law enforcement in a timely manner?"

Out of habit I count on my fingers, as if I were teaching my ten-year-old students. "One, there's an immense emotional burden on loved ones if someone's disappeared. Critical thinking and memory are impaired, especially in older adults who might know essential information but can't recall it under duress. Then, number two is secrecy. Children or young adults don't want their parents to know their phone's passcode or social media passwords. Even happily married couples draw the line at sharing all their devices."

"You mentioned children," Jane says. "You work with them every day. You're an integral part of their lives, of their development. Do you believe children as young as fourth grade should have their own In Case I Go Missing binder? Isn't that a bit of a stretch?"

"Children more than anyone," I reply quickly. "Not only are they the most secretive members of the family, but their age makes them likely targets. It's an unfortunate truth of our society." I breathe and steady myself, hearing my voice tremble just a little bit. "Adopted children even more than that."

"Why do you say that?"

"First off," I count again, "the adopted child's DNA is not correlated with either parent. Parental samples cannot be used. Then, the child comes from a background parents know nothing about. Has a history they usually know nothing about. That history sometimes resurfaces, potentially with the kidnapping of the adopted child by their biological parent, for example."

"Fascinating," Jane says, then turns toward Destiny. "Is this something your school endorses?"

Destiny holds a slightly trembling hand in the air. "Not

officially," she replies quickly. "However, we care deeply about the safety of our students. Alana's passion for this simple yet powerful tool has raised awareness among the faculty." She looks at Jane as if seeking help, her eyes widening despite the strong light, but Jane doesn't intervene. "This doesn't mean our school is a dangerous place, or that our students must do this."

There. She couldn't help herself. Now Jane is gaping at her in disbelief, and I cringe. Then I try to fix it.

"I believe Destiny is saying that while our school is in no way more dangerous than others, my project can help parents be better prepared for this highly unlikely event."

Jane nods, a slight frown lingering on her brow. "One more question, Alana."

"Please," I say, with a welcoming hand gesture.

"Do you think it's healthy for people to spend time thinking about this kind of impending doom? Could it become obsessive for some? Drive anxieties in otherwise healthy, happy adults?"

Those were three questions, but I don't see fit to mention it. "Definitely, the binder shouldn't become an obsession. I've been asked how often you should update its contents, especially since some accounts require periodic password changes."

"Yes, exactly," Jane says, gesturing enthusiastically.

"The binder shouldn't be updated more often or thought of more often than a will, for example. To me, it's quite simple. You decide if you want it, then you build it, you place it in a very safe location, and share the details of its existence only with someone you trust wholeheartedly. Then you update it only if your circumstances change. No reason for any obsessions or anxieties."

"And still, the risk of going missing in the United States is infinitesimal," Jane says, and Destiny nods her agreement, seemingly relieved. Jane lowers her eyes to check the small note-book she keeps in her lap. "Less than point zero three percent of adults go missing in a year. Do we need to worry about such a small risk?"

"The risk is far greater for children," I reply calmly. "Over two hundred thousand cases of missing children are recorded each year. So that risk is ten times higher, at about point three percent."

"Still, it's very low. How is this binder warranted?" Jane's eyes become sharp, drilling into mine.

"The question we need to ask ourselves is whether Flavia Guzman would've benefited from having a binder like this. Could she have been saved if the police had access to her phone immediately? Could she still be alive today?" I pause for a moment. "If one life can be saved, then yes, it's warranted."

A lopsided smile emerges on Jane's lips as she tilts her head slightly. "And that's why I'll do mine. My son's too. Thank you, Alana, for caring about our community and our children enough to drive action."

"Thank you for your interest in it," I whisper, breathing fully for the first time since it all started.

A few more pleasantries are exchanged between Jane and Destiny, then Jane says, "Cut. We're done. Get me some B-roll." She turns to me and says, "Can we have you walk into the reading room, flip through the binder, maybe show it to Destiny?"

I do as instructed, while the cameraman takes different shots of us. After a few minutes, he's done and starts packing his gear.

I find Jane by the door, talking with Destiny. The principal doesn't look so happy.

Jane shoots me a quick look. "We're probably going to cut the piece about the school not being at risk and so on. It sounded weird to me. I'll watch it at the studio, but it might come out if it sounds defensive. We don't want viewers to freak out, thinking you're hiding something."

Destiny gives me a loaded side glance as if to say, "I told you so." I shift my attention back to Jane and shake her hand, thanking her again. This interview will bring great exposure to the concept. I finally believe I've made a difference.

I stay behind with Destiny to close up the school after the TV crew leaves. For a while, she doesn't say anything to me, other than telling me to return the coffee table to the teachers' lounge and to lock the door to the reading room.

Then, when we're outside, by the gate she's locking clumsily, I touch her arm to get her attention. "Hey, I wanted to thank you once more for doing this. It's very important to me, and I'm very grateful. I couldn't've done it without—"

"You sure hogged all the limelight in there, didn't you?" She glares at me with cold, squinting eyes. "You're not a team player, Alana. I'm really sorry to learn that about you."

My jaw drops. Speechless, I watch her climb into her car and drive off.

TEN

The show aired the following week, on Friday morning.

The entire time I waited for it I had a knot in my throat, avoiding Destiny as much as I could without making it obvious. She didn't comment on the interview or even hint at it, but there was static between us, a tension that hadn't used to exist.

Then, on Friday morning at seven, it finally airs. Halfway through getting dressed for work, I watch it in my underwear, seated on the edge of the sofa, cup of coffee in my hand, while Daniel is still asleep. Tempted to wake him, I click the remote and record it instead.

The woman speaking on television—me—seems like she does this kind of stuff on a daily basis. She's a natural. I feel proud of myself. I don't stutter, I talk clearly and assertively, my posture is perfect, my arguments logical and simple. Jane Fouch removed part of what Destiny said, but not all of it, and the editor was a pro. Everything flowed perfectly. The interview ends with Destiny speaking, so she should be happy.

But then, Jane adds something that wasn't included in the original material.

"We contacted Flavia Guzman's family and asked for

comment," Jane says, as I gasp in front of the TV. "This is what they had to say. 'We thank Alana Blake and the school for not forgetting our beloved daughter, Flavia. For not letting the world forget about her. We just wish we'd known about this when there was still time. Maybe things would've been different today.'"

The interview ends with Flavia's photo on the screen, displayed in a tasteful in memoriam frame. I watch with tears streaming down my face. I'm deeply moved; I struggle to get a grip.

A glance at the digital clock on the kitchen wall has me hustling to leave the house. I make it to school in the nick of time, barging through the doors together with the last busload of children, wondering if Destiny saw the interview. Should I ask her? Should I open the can of worms? I feel like such a coward for not daring to talk openly with her about it.

It doesn't matter, though. The interview is the hot topic in the teachers' lounge. Destiny is surrounded by teachers who are way smarter and more diplomatic than me. She's basking in their numerous compliments about how good she looked on TV, how great she did, how fantastic it was for the school. Better late than never, I join in with the crowd and lay it on too, at least in part fueled by my gratitude for her willingness to host the interview. When the bell rings and we have to go to class, she even smiles at me, a little unconvincingly, but still.

The day goes by incredibly slow. Now that the interview has aired, I feel drained. All that adrenaline has left my body a depleted husk that struggles to remember what's on my to-do list.

Friday is one of the busiest days at the diner, so Daniel will be gone till late. I have a dentist appointment and some errands to run in the afternoon; nothing I couldn't reschedule, but I don't. I like discipline, being on time, doing the things I have to do *when* I must do them. Over lunch, I speak with Daniel on the phone. He hasn't seen the interview, but he'll watch it tonight, when he gets home.

Then, an express oil change for my Subaru, and I can finally head home, dreaming of a long bubble bath with a book in my hand and a glass of wine on the side. Maybe after I soak for a while, I can figure out how to speak to Daniel about the fertility shots, getting pregnant, the other lies I've told.

Like Ray, for example.

Should I tell him Ray and I have a history? I'm dreading the thought, afraid it would ruin what we have. What if he somehow finds out on his own? Damn it to bloody hell, the day they moved next door. Why did it have to happen?

I almost miss my turn onto our small cul-de-sac, engulfed in my thoughts, but I make it, barely, with tires screeching on the asphalt.

The first thing I notice as I approach the house is Daniel's Ford, parked in the driveway next to his brother Jason's blue Mazda Miata. Frowning a little, I cut the engine and rush inside, curious to learn what made both of them leave the diner on a busy Friday afternoon.

I open the door to a hearty roar of laughter coming from the backyard. Dropping my purse on the sofa, I throw the car keys into the copper bowl and head outside.

The first person I see is Chloe, absolutely beautiful in a white, off-one-shoulder blouse and spandex jeans taut on her perfect body. I stop, frozen in place, stunned by her presence. And she's not alone.

"She's here," Chloe announces in a loud, cheerful voice, then rushes toward me. "Oh, my goodness, you were amazing! Congratulations!" She places a hearty kiss on my cheek before I can pull back. My nostrils fill with her scent, familiar and yet new, a mix of Acqua di Parma and high-end makeup. "I know what I'm talking about," she adds, her arm snaking around my waist in a side hug. "I do television for a living, and it's not easy. But you? You didn't skip a beat!"

"Thanks," I whisper, feeling drained, barely able to stand. Engulfed in smoke, Daniel smiles at me from near the barbecue, waving a greasy spatula in the air as if swatting flies. I smile back, feeling my heart tighten as I remember all the things I should've told him but haven't. With each passing day, the lies grow thicker, uglier, fed by my unwillingness to face the consequences of my actions.

"I couldn't believe you're still doing this," Chloe says, downing what was left in her wineglass and abandoning it on the table. "Remember, when Flavia was killed, and we were listening to those podcasts? For me, it was just a phase, I guess, but for you? Unbelievable. And you're right. These binders save lives. It's a worthy cause. Did I ever tell you I almost made one for myself?" Her voice drops to almost a whisper, tinged with undertones of fear that weren't there before.

I don't want to ask why.

Eager to put some distance between us, I nod and walk over to the table, where everyone is gathered, chatting enthusiastically. Ray is speaking with someone who looks vaguely familiar: a woman with an elegant hairdo who joined our impromptu barbecue in four-inch-heel pumps and a silver, shimmering cocktail dress.

As I approach, Ray turns and sees me. His eyes lock on mine, sweltering, and I'm suddenly breathless.

"Congratulations, Alana," he says, smiling widely. "Do you remember my mother?" The woman smiles at me and pats my cheek with warm, dry fingers, the way one does with a child. The way she used to.

"Ah, Mrs. Preston," I say, finally recognizing her. Must be her fancy 'do and dress that tricked me into not knowing who she was at first.

When we were in school, she wasn't that fancy. She used to

wear jeans and T-shirts like most moms her age, her hair tied up in an unpretentious ponytail. She's come a long way in eleven years. A big diamond ring sparkles on her hand. Her hair, almost entirely gray, is not dyed. She wears it natural in a long, stylish bob that gives her an eccentric look without making her appear old. Maybe her fashion-expert daughter-in-law had a say in her new look. Or she might've remarried. If memory doesn't fail me, back when I knew her, she was divorced, a single mom who struggled just like mine.

"It's Stella, darling girl. We're all adults now, and you're more beautiful than I remember." Her smile is charming. She's every bit as pleasant as she used to be when she was wearing jeans and worn-out tees, picking up Ray from school in an old Hyundai Accent.

Her attention and compliments make me smile. There's no reason for her to be so kind to me, and yet she is.

We chat for a little while, then I finally make my way over to Daniel, seeking refuge by his side. From Ray and his glances. From everyone else. When I reach him, I find myself afraid to look him in the eye, as if he will read the lies hidden behind my dilated pupils. My worries are unfounded. He welcomes me with a kiss and offers me a glass of wine.

"What's going on?" I ask in a whisper, tasting the chilled wine. Suddenly thirsty, I take a sip or two, and feel it rush straight to my head, courtesy of an empty stomach. My nostrils flare when a wind gust brings over smoke from the grill, where several hamburgers are sizzling. Buns are warming on the upper shelf.

Daniel laughs. "You're starving, aren't you?" I nod, my guilty eyes shifting. "You skip lunch again?"

"I'll take the Fifth. It's been a complicated day."

"Ah, the lives of celebrities," he quips, and I mock punch him in the side while he puts together a burger for me, just as I like it.

"You're the first one in our family to appear on TV, sis," Jason says, raising a misty bottle of beer. I smile and raise my glass, although there are several feet between us. He's dressed his usual way, in a dark-red hoodie and black jeans, sporting the bad-boy look that has girls wait for him in the diner's parking lot more often than not. He's a handsome man, my brother-in-law, although an entirely different kind of handsome than Daniel. Several tattoos cover parts of his neck, his hands, and his fore-arms, and probably other parts of his body I've never seen. There's no T-shirt underneath that hoodie, and the zipper, lowered halfway, reveals his naked, muscular torso. That's where Chloe's eyes are glued, when she's not listening to what he has to say. Probably some nonsense about sports or who knows what.

"Here you go, babe," Daniel says, handing me a plate with a loaded burger on it. I take a bite and close my eyes as the juices fill my mouth with artery-popping deliciousness. Why doesn't salad taste like this? People would have zero problems dieting if that were the case. But one burger, once in a blue moon, won't kill me. After all, we're celebrating my achievement. Which reminds me.

"Why are these people here, Daniel?" I ask quietly, stretching on my toes to be closer to his ear.

For a moment, he looks both surprised and guilty. "Well, it was Jason's idea to throw you a small party to celebrate your interview. We both know how important this is for you, even if" —he shoots Jason a quick glance—"I'm not sure he really under-stands the binder thing."

I nod, encouraging him to continue while I take bite after bite from my burger.

"Then we ran into Ray and his mother, just as we were pulling into the driveway. I introduced them, then Chloe showed up, and she'd seen your show, so—" He finishes the explanation, gesturing with his hands. "We thought you'd enjoy celebrating with your friends."

"I do," I lie effortlessly, then smile. "You're wonderful." I pat my lips with a napkin, then reach up for a kiss. He wraps me in his arms and kisses me, taking a little longer than I would've liked with so many people watching.

When I pull away from Daniel, I notice Ray's smoldering gaze fixed on me, on my body, on my lips. I look away, searching for Chloe. Ray's married, I'm married, what does he want? He should be staring at his wife instead, who's all over Jason, practically drooling over him. Or maybe that's just in my mind, because she's not really doing anything but chatting with him, at a party, behaving like people are supposed to in social situations. It's not her fault that her voice is so crystalline when she laughs, that her hair flows in golden waves so perfectly, or that men are drawn to her like moths to the proverbial flame. Jason included.

Selfishly, I'm grateful she has Jason in her sights now instead of Daniel. It's funny how the moment this woman appears, my entire life is thrown off-balance.

Stella speaks with Ray for a while, and I'm happy he doesn't stare at me the way he did earlier, because Daniel would soon notice. Relieved, I hold my glass out and my husband dutifully fills it. Chloe leaves Jason's side and walks over to me, her almost empty glass in her hand. Daniel fills hers too, and she thanks him with a smile and a hair toss, then she turns her attention to me.

We clink our glasses and drink, while she congratulates me again.

"Was that your real binder, on the show?" she asks, looking at me with genuine interest. Eleven years ago, she seemed to care about what happened to Flavia. Maybe she still does.

"It was a mock-up," I reply, wondering why it has kindled her interest so much. Doesn't she have enough excitement in the glittering world of fashion? Still, an endorsement or just mere advice from a journalist like her would help me advance this project. "I didn't want my personal information to be exposed to so many strangers. You can never be too careful."

Her arm wraps around my waist again. In just a few days, she's gone back to acting toward me just the way she used to, when we were both in school. Before Ray... before everything else that happened. I haven't. I still stiffen up when she draws near.

"Hey, I need to talk to you about something," she says in a low voice, pulling me to the side. All her self-confidence is gone, and her voice is now fraught. I look into her fearful eyes and wonder why I haven't noticed her apprehension before. "I'm worried... I might have—"

"So, I guess you're not pregnant yet," Stella says, cutting her off in midsentence, her voice unexpectedly contemptuous. I wonder if she heard what Chloe just told me, but it doesn't seem like she did. Ray's mom is standing about three feet away, pointing at Chloe's empty wineglass with an open-mouthed smile.

I gasp and do a poor job at hiding my gaping mouth with my hand. Chloe freezes by my side. Her eyes cloud with pain and regret and shame, all in one anguished glance she throws her mother-in-law.

Ray touches Stella's arm. "Mother, this isn't—"

"You're among friends, aren't you?" She laughs, wine prevalent in the slightly falsetto tones of her voice.

Chloe's face flushes with embarrassment. "We're working on it," she says, attempting to instill a bit of humor in her words, but I can tell she's thrown. I feel I should say something, compelled to stand up for Chloe, but I can't think of anything that wouldn't make things worse.

Stella draws closer to Chloe and touches her face just like she did mine earlier. "Well, work harder, sweetie. We don't live forever." Then she walks over to Daniel and starts chatting with him about living in Half Moon Bay's fog and humidity, while Chloe gapes after her, breathing heavily, fighting off tears.

"Let's get you freshened up," I suggest, and lead the way inside the house. She gives me a grateful and still embarrassed look, then disappears into the bathroom. Tired of everything and just yearning for some peace, I let myself slide onto the sofa and close my eyes for a brief moment. In the bathroom, the water is running, but I believe I can hear Chloe sobbing.

"Alana... you look more beautiful than I remember." Ray's voice, low and loaded, startles me. I open my eyes and find him seated on the armrest, too close to me for comfort, his hand inches away from my face. I pull away and then stand, putting much needed distance between us. "Don't worry," he whispers. "I won't bite." A lopsided smile stretches his lips. Dimples appear on his cheeks as he stands too and takes a couple of steps toward me. "Not unless you want me to."

"Ray," I whisper, at a loss for the words I need to make him leave me alone without sounding ridiculous. "This is wrong," I eventually manage, raising my hands in the air in a defensive posture that freezes him in his tracks. "We're both married."

He tilts his head and sizes me up shamelessly. "Is that the only problem?"

Tears burn the corners of my eyes as emotions swell and swirl inside me, threatening to break the floodgates open. "No." He takes one more step. "No. Stop." I raise my hand again to keep him at bay, but he grabs it and takes it to his lips.

"Oh, my God." I hear Chloe's tear-filled voice behind me.

I pull my hand out of Ray's grasp and turn to her. "Chloe, this is nothing," I say, but she's not looking at me. Her eyes shift around as if she's trying to find a way out of there.

When I look behind me, Ray is gone. Moments later, I hear him chatting outside in the backyard, his voice and Jason's louder than everyone else's.

"You didn't take long to go back to the way things were in school, did you?" Chloe asks. Her face is pale and scrunched in anger, her voice cutting and cold. I reach for her, but she pulls away, glaring at me. "Don't."

"I swear, there's nothing to worry about. I'm married, I love my husband, end of story. I was waiting for you, for crying out loud." I pause for a moment, watching the tension in her face slowly dissipate. "We're not in high school anymore, Chloe." I reach for her hand again and, this time, she lets me squeeze her frozen fingers.

A tear rolls down her cheek, and she wipes it quickly with the back of her hand. "I'm sorry, I've been struggling lately. I've been... there's something I need to talk to you about." She throws a tense look at the people gathered outside. "Not now."

"Whenever you need me, I'll be here," I offer reluctantly. I don't want to be swept into another Chloe drama, but I've never seen her so vulnerable.

She nods, her golden wavy strands floating on her shoulders as she moves. Then she hugs me, burying her face in my shoulder with a long, shattered breath. "Thank you. You're the best."

A couple of hours after they leave, Daniel goes back to the diner for the evening rush. I still can't take my mind off what happened. Why is she back in my life? To destroy me? Did she send me that letter, with the picture only she was supposed to have? What kind of sick, twisted game is she playing? How do I save myself from this slow-motion train wreck?

As I finally let myself sink into a warm, scented bath, the sense of uneasiness I've been having since Chloe moved next door increases tenfold, an ominous warning of things to come, while frightening questions swirl in my weary mind. I don't want to admit it, not even to myself, but I'm afraid. As simple and as nonsensical as it might seem, it's no less true. Dread has been churning my gut incessantly. In all that whirlwind of

worry and fear, the insidious memory of Ray is the most bother-
some of all. How his lips felt against my fingers. How his voice
sounded when he spoke my name. How his deep blue eyes saw
right through me.

Damn.

ELEVEN

My Subaru is stopped on the side of the small street, at a distance from a large, two-story house. The sight of it unnerves me, bringing a knot to my stomach. I shouldn't be here, and yet I can't keep away. It's one of the few distractions from the sense of danger that grows stronger with each passing day, while Chloe acts nice and Ray and Daniel forge a friendship I can't stop.

I've never been inside this house, but I'm sure it has floor-to-ceiling windows overlooking the ocean, and a stone-covered patio with a pergola and a firepit and comfy chairs to watch sunsets from. A lush lawn extends to the side of the house, where I can see it through the fence.

It's Saturday morning and the sun is shining brightly over Half Moon Bay. It's rare to see the perfectly blue sky so early, the night's dense fog burned and gone already. I relish the soft heat that comes in through the rolled-down window of my car. The peace of the small, deserted neighborhood. The sound of the little girl's voice calling the dog each time she throws a small red ball. The fluffy white dog chases it, then doesn't give it back to her. Playful barks and laughter fill the street. And my heart.

I can see them clearly between the boards of a shadowbox fence. I'm parked at just the right angle for that across the street. The little girl is wearing jeans and a bright orange shirt, already soiled with grass and sand. The dog, a Havanese most likely, is panting, out of breath after she chased him around the yard, squealing and laughing to get the red ball back, only to throw it again. The simplicity of their Saturday morning is profound, enviable, something I've always sought but never found.

In the distance, the Pacific glimmers with sunshine, completely ignorant of the restless, churning waves of emotion and angst swelling inside me.

Ray.

My thoughts speak his name, and it makes me heave a tear-filled sigh. I feel like I'm drowning, pulled down by a merciless undertow, deadly and yet hypnotizing, unescapable.

I close my eyes, and I see us walking on the beach, holding hands, skipping the last period in our senior year, eager to be alone together. It was the last time we made love, on the sun-kissed sand by Eel Rock, sheltered against the cliffs, the crashing waves a constant melody that lent us its rhythm. That was the last time I was happy with him, the memory of my blissful romance still so acutely real it feels like yesterday. My body shivered in his arms, grazed by the cold breeze and burning with passion at the same time, restlessly hanging on every word he whispered in my ear. He said he loved me, and I believed him. He said I was the one, and we were destined to be together forever. In my heart, it felt true.

It wasn't.

It was all lies. And it nearly killed me to find out.

I've never been the kind of girl who talks incessantly about her love life. In my friendship with Chloe, she was always the talker, and I was the listener. That's the excuse I found for Chloe's kiss-and-tell about Ray the following evening: that she didn't know I was in love with him. That somehow, being so self-absorbed, she had no idea. Otherwise, she would have said no to him. She would not have let him fold her into his arms, kiss her, then make passionate love to her in the back seat of her Benz.

Had she known I was in love with Ray, she would've said no.

That's the excuse I managed to find for Chloe.

I came up empty with finding excuses for Ray. There were none.

His betrayal hurt so badly I couldn't breathe for a while. I couldn't get myself out of bed for a couple of days, feigning illness for the benefit of my concerned mother and getting ready to lie to Chloe too, if she had bothered to ask or miss me that weekend. But she was too busy with him. With the man I loved.

School turned into a slow-moving journey through excruciating pain. Having to pretend everything was fine, for everyone's sake, took every ounce of self-control I could muster. I counted the minutes of every hour and every day, then rushed to my old, beat-up car and drove off. The standing lie was I had extra work at the farm. No one cared about me enough to ask other questions, like until when, what time I got off, or if I was okay. Still, over lunch and during breaks, Chloe found the time to whisper excited, endless details of her latest adventures with Ray. While I slowly died inside.

I didn't go out the following weekend. I was still reeling from the betrayal, and learning Ray was taking Chloe out on dates made me realize I couldn't take the risk of accidentally running into them. I would only make a fool of myself, letting him see how badly he'd hurt me. In school, at least during class, I didn't have to face them.

That weekend I decided, then and there, curled up in a ball under the covers and crushing a tissue soaked with tears in my trembling hand, that he must never know how much I loved him.

The week after his affair with Chloe started, he kept on calling, and I didn't pick up. At school, whenever he tried talking
with me, I claimed to be busy or sought other people's company
as a shield. Then, when I felt ready, steeled enough to face him,
I agreed to meet with him after school.

It was our senior year, and February was almost over. All
the joy of the upcoming graduation had been sucked out of my
life. I arrived first at the café and took a seat at an umbrella patio
table, facing the street so I could see him coming. The wrought
iron chair felt frozen under me, and the light jacket I was
wearing did nothing to keep the biting cold at bay. I thought I
was ready to face him, able to survive ten minutes without
falling apart, but when he pulled into the parking lot I was
shaking badly, feeling nauseous.

He approached smiling, heartbreakingly handsome in the
late afternoon sun, leaning in for a kiss as if nothing was wrong.
I turned my head and his lips landed on my cheek.

He sat slowly and reached for my hand. I didn't pull back
fast enough.

"You're frozen," he said, rubbing my fingers between his
warm palms, then blowing on them gently, his lips grazing
against my skin. "Let me get you a jacket from the—"

"No," I said, pulling my hand from his. "I won't be here long
enough to need it."

"What are you saying?" he asked, his eyes landing on my
mouth and staying there, intense and wanting.

"I had no idea you were seeing Chloe," I said, twisting the
story around like the master manipulator I was not. "She's my
best friend. You and I are over."

"You can't be serious, Alana." He leaned forward over the
table, pushing my coffee cup out of the way. I pulled it back,
cupping my hands around it to borrow the remnants of its heat.

How could he be so surprised and act as if I was dumping
him? I remember shaking my head in disbelief and forging

ahead with the script I had carefully constructed. "I'm sorry, Ray, but I can't do that to my best friend. You and I were never serious anyway. And now it's over." I tried to act carefree and indifferent and chose that particular time to try one of Chloe's signature hair flip moves and look away. A few strands got entangled in the umbrella crank handle, and I yelped. Tears burned my eyes, threatening to break the floodgates open.

Ray leaned over to help me get disentangled. His breath touched my face, the heady scent of his bodywash filled my nose. I closed my eyes and inhaled, knowing it probably was the last time I'd be that close to him.

When he was done freeing my hair, he remained standing and looked at me with regret. "I thought we had something special, Alana. I can't believe you're giving up so easily. I thought you'd fight for me."

I stared at him with my mouth agape and eyes wide open, discovering something about him I never saw coming. Or maybe I was misunderstanding something. I didn't even want to know anymore; it would've made no difference. "I'd never fight for you, Ray. That's not who I am. And you didn't have to fight for me either. You just had to choose. And you did." I forced a deep breath of air into my lungs. "I won't make things difficult for you, don't worry. You can enjoy your relationship with Chloe without concern for me. She doesn't need to get hurt. Goodbye, Ray."

He gave me a long gaze I probably misread. I saw desire in those blue eyes, unquenched desire and passion and a touch of sadness. Then he walked away.

I watched him leave, childishly hoping he'd turn his head and look at me one more time. But he didn't. Moments later, the tires of his car crunched pebbles and threw dirt up in the air as he sped out of the gravel parking lot.

It was over.

I don't recall how I got home that day, or how many days I

stayed in bed whenever I wasn't in school or working. Seeing them every day at school didn't help. Chloe, being who she was and always would be, remained oblivious to my sadness, and I was endlessly regaled with her stories. A few times, she invited me to hang out with her and Ray, but I gently refused, saying I would be a third wheel. She pushed back only once, saying it hadn't used to bother me before, but then started leaving me behind more often than not. No more weekends at the cabin in the woods. No more Sunday trips to San Jose for brunch and a movie. She still went, just not with me.

With him.

I open my eyes and let my pupils adjust. I recall thinking back then it would all be so much better after graduation, when the two of them would go to Stanford and I would start a science program at Berkeley. I'd just received the letter of acceptance, and I had breathed a sigh of gratitude that it would soon be over.

Little did I know.

A tear rolls down my face, but I don't let myself get drawn into agonizing memories anymore. Instead, I look at the fluffy white dog and see him stretch his front paws in a play bow, inviting the little girl to chase him. She doesn't let him wait too long. She pretends she doesn't want to, turns her back and tricks him into drawing closer, then squeals and gives chase in a flurry of white fur and grass-stained orange cotton.

Then the side door opens, and a woman appears, holding her hand above her eyes to shield them from the sun. She's wearing a colorful apron over jeans and a casual V-neck.

"Taylor," she calls. "Get Bear and come inside. Lunch is ready."

"Yes, Mommy," I hear her answer, while another tear finds its way down my cheek.

I'm glad she's okay after the run-in with that little asshole, Douglas Durazo. It's been a while since that incident, but victims of bullying sometimes take time to show signs of altered behavior.

I start the car, pausing to see if the black Beemer parked two cars behind me with its engine running is going to pull out before me. When it doesn't, I slowly drive off, then take a left turn, merging into traffic. My mind is on the brunch tomorrow with Ray and Chloe that I'd do anything to skip. Daniel said it was his idea, but the planned outing looks too much like Chloe's favorite Sunday pastime and too little like Daniel's to not suspect some influence from our new neighbors. Either way, I don't have much of a choice in the matter if I don't want to answer any difficult questions. Then, after said brunch, we're going to catch a movie in San Jose.

Just like bloody old times.

TWELVE

The following Monday morning finds me eager to get out of bed, after yet another restless night. It's the last week of school, and I'm looking forward to a break, to spend time by myself and think.

I survived yesterday's brunch and movie with the help of caffeine; it gave me the strength to display the right nonchalance. I try to keep my coffee intake limited to a morning cup, but yesterday I needed every drop I could get. First off, Daniel was late because of an unannounced health inspection at the diner. I had to drive into town with Chloe and Ray, in what must've been the most uncomfortable thirty minutes of silence of my entire life. When he finally showed up, I almost burst into tears.

By the time the stupid movie was over, I was a ball of frayed nerves, aching to go home. I held Daniel's hand during the entire feature and refused the popcorn offered by Chloe. She sat next to me, probably just as happy as I was to have herself inserted between me and Ray. Every now and then she made quick, funny comments on the movie's plot holes or acting blunders, just as she used to do when we were kids. After a while, I relaxed a little and laughed with her, until an older lady shushed us, and we clammed up.

There's a part of me that still likes hanging out with Chloe, as if somehow her youthful joie de vivre rubs off on me. It's contagious and enthralling. Those are the moments I forget I was just another girl for Ray, while she was the one he chose to marry. I tried hating her back then, and for a while I succeeded, but the jealousy-fueled hatred didn't last. Even if I was only eighteen years old at the time, I knew well that anyone could've been in her place, and Ray would've still done what he did. Cheating is not something that happens to people. Cheating is something that people make happen.

Ray was the one who cheated. Chloe was the ignorant party in the entire triangle, or so I chose to believe. Truth is, I never knew for sure if she was unaware that I was in love with Ray, or if she just steamrollered me when she felt like taking Ray for herself. I don't put it past her; she could do stuff like that with a candid smile on her face and not even blink. Probably I'll never find out.

One twisted thought has been bothering me. I remembered she did the same kiss-and-tell strategy with Nikki, her romantic confessions a bona fide girl repellent, for lack of a better way to put it. Had she done the same with me and I didn't see it? It's possible. I broke up with Ray almost two months before Chloe took Nikki and me out for ice cream, and that day ended in such disaster, I didn't even notice the pattern until recently.

But now it's too late for any of this speculation about the past. The real danger lies in the letter I received. Who sent it? Was it Chloe? Until I know for sure, I am playing with fire. Part of me doesn't want to see her ever again. The other part, fueled by a state of spiraling anxiety, wants to look her in the eye and see what that cunning, sharp mind is up to. Meanwhile, no part of me wants to see Ray again. Nothing good can come out of us crossing paths, not if he can't keep his distance. I don't trust him, and, more than anything, I don't trust myself around him. It's as if the wound I believed to be healed has cracked open, throbbing with pain.

I looked at Chloe yesterday, across the brunch table at the Whispers Café, and couldn't blame Ray for falling for her. She looked stunning, her face lit up with laughter over a joke Daniel just told, a touch of powdered sugar clinging to her upper lip from the crepes she's devouring like a teenager, although her waist has stayed just as youthful. Not a worry clouded her mood all day. Whatever's eating at her—that she hinted about at the barbecue—she knows how to hide it. Who knows what else she's not saying?

Anxiety washes over me in waves, ebbing and flowing almost all the time, urging me to do the impossible and put some distance between Chloe and me. The dread coiled in my gut reminds me of the sensation I had when I was hiking the woods at Presidio one time, when I came across a rattlesnake. I froze, staring at it, unable to move, as a pit of numbing fear opened in my stomach. It feels like that with her sometimes. I'm paralyzed, unable to save myself. Back then, the snake got tired of hissing and rattling at me and eventually slithered off. That's how I survived, through no merit of mine, but because I was too stunned to save myself.

Will Chloe one day tire of toying with me and just vanish? I should be so lucky.

Because if she sent that letter, she wants to destroy me. And she can.

First period bell finds me rushing through the corridors to get to class after missing the morning staff meeting, coming straight from the parking lot. I left the house late, finding it difficult to leave on time with so many things on my mind. I cringe at the thought of Destiny scolding me over this.

The first thing I notice when I enter the classroom, at three minutes past, is Taylor's empty seat. I frown, and worry rises through me like the tide. That sweet little girl hasn't missed a day of school in the four years I've been her teacher.

Throughout the math period, I challenge the students to perform basic operations in their minds, without pen and paper or calculators, slowly dictating long strings of additions, multiplications, subtractions, and divisions, then waiting to see who wants to give me the answer. Paul's hand goes up almost every time, and so do others, but fewer than I'd like. And all the time, I keep looking at Taylor's empty desk, as if expecting her to appear out of the blue, already seated and raising her hand.

The last thirty minutes I do a recap of fractions and give them simple exercises to practice the fear of them away, while tiny beads of sweat start to appear on my forehead. It seems awfully hot today. Maybe the air conditioning isn't working.

When the bell finally rings, I'm the first one out of the classroom, heading straight for Destiny's office. Her assistant, Eileen, takes phone messages from parents whose kids are sick and logs them into the school's attendance system.

I find her and Destiny chatting in her office, and two other teachers are with them, all standing and gesticulating and talking at the same time. Something's wrong.

"Good morning," I say, and notice how the chatter dies in an instant. "Eileen, is there a message from Taylor's family? She didn't show up today."

"Where have you been?" Destiny says, putting her chubby arm around my shoulders. "Didn't you hear? She's missing. We talked about it this morning in the staff meeting."

Blood drops from my face so quickly I'm about to faint. "What do you mean, she's missing?"

"It was all over the news last night. She vanished from her backyard yesterday." Her voice echoes strangely, fading as if she's walking away, but she's right there, squeezing my shoulder, bringing her face closer to mine with a concerned frown. "Are you okay?" she asks, but I hear her as if in a dream. I'm unable to articulate an answer. "Here, sit down."

She guides me to a chair someone rolled close to me, and I sit. Panting breaths enter my chest and leave it in rapid sequence, resisting my efforts to get a grip.

"Oh, my God," I whisper, my trembling hand covering my mouth. "W-what are the police saying?" I stutter pitifully, my voice weak and high-pitched, fraught with tears.

"They don't know yet, but they assume she was taken. They said they'll come by later, to speak with us. With you mostly, I guess."

Oh, no... of all the things I've been fearing, this has never crossed my mind. *Not Taylor.* I nod, forcing air to leave my lungs slowly, through my mouth, in an effort to steady myself. I don't have the time to fall apart. There must be something I can do. I can't sit still and wait and do nothing, yet I have to. At least for a while.

I somehow work through my classes for the day, moving and speaking in a nightmarish trance. I'm hopeful the children don't know anything about Taylor's kidnapping, but one of them does, a little girl with a long, strawberry-blonde ponytail. She raises her hand when I ask about their homework.

"Ms. Blake, my mom said Taylor's gone. Is that true?"

My breath falters. "She's not gone, sweetie. She's missing for a day or two, but she'll be back."

"Before summer break?"

That's in four days. "I hope so, yes."

Her questions light a fire in my chest. I give them their homework assignments and leave. The bell finds me starting my engine, then peeling off without thinking much about what I'm doing.

The entire way to Taylor's house I drive white-knuckled and out of breath, fighting back tears. I can't think of her in the hands of strangers. She must be scared out of her mind. In my frantic mind, I hear her crying, calling for help.

When I pull over in front of the house, I notice the news crews camped there a few moments too late, when I'm already out of my car and walking toward the front door with big strides. I have no plan and honestly, no business being there. Yet I can't stop myself.

Fighting off a pushy reporter who shoves a foam-covered microphone in my face, I ring the bell, while cameras flash behind me.

Maybe her parents know something.

THIRTEEN

My heart is thumping in my chest as I wait for the door to open. What am I doing here? It will be difficult to explain. I ring the bell again, pressed by the clamor building up behind me. Instinct tells me to turn and look, but I don't want to give the reporters a chance to snap pictures of my face on the Winthrops' doorstep, out of breath and frantic and about to fall apart.

The door opens a little, and I recognize Mrs. Winthrop. Her eyes are swollen and red, the sheen of tears she blinks away clinging to her long eyelashes.

"Oh, Ms. Blake, come on in," she says, opening the door barely wide enough for me to sneak inside, then quickly closing it behind me. "These reporters are driving us insane."

I find myself in a large foyer, almost devoid of furniture with the exception of a white credenza. A vase centered on its gleaming surface holds white lilies, the tips of their fragrant petals starting to wither. The floor is glossy white marble, lit by fractured sunlight coming through the frosted stained glass framing the massive door.

Tiny claws click quietly on the marble as Taylor's white dog appears, eager to see who's at the door. He approaches slowly, nose in the air, curious, and also fearful. Then, about a foot away from touching my leg with his wet nose, he turns and leaves, his tail lowered, his head too. He was expecting someone else. I'm not Taylor.

"Do you have any news?" I ask Monica Winthrop. We know each other from parent-teacher conferences. I've always admired her composure and her elegance. I can tell she's trying her best to hold it together, but she's probably exhausted and emotionally drained.

"No, they haven't told us anything." She sniffles and covers her trembling mouth with her hand.

I squeeze her shoulder gently, unable to think of anything to say that would bring comfort. I only have questions. "Has there been a ransom call yet?"

She shakes her head. A strand of her auburn hair breaks loose from her clip and falls over her face. With a quick gesture, she tucks it behind her ear. "We didn't hear anything yet. The police are here. They set up surveillance. David got them to send someone who stays here around the clock. In case they call." A sob rattles her chest. "Oh, my poor baby."

"How did it happen?" I ask, fighting off tears of my own. Something merciless twists and tears in my gut. I put my hand over my abdomen without realizing, while I wish I could shout, "How the hell did it happen? You have surveillance and video cameras and everything. Where were you?" But that won't help a tiny bit, not with finding Taylor, nor the heartbroken woman barely able to stand on her feet.

"I don't know, Ms. Blake," she replies, her voice colored with desperation and guilt. "I was here in the living room. The sliding door was open. I should've heard something, but—" She chokes and takes a moment to breathe, while I gently rub her arm to give her comfort. "She just vanished. No one saw anything, and our cameras don't cover that corner of the yard."

"Did she jump the fence?"

"We don't think so. She's too small to climb over a five-foot fence, and it's not something she would do." She looks away, devastated. "The police are assuming someone took her through the back gate. The padlock was cut."

"I'm so sorry, Mrs. Winthrop," I say, fighting back tears. I can't think of Taylor right now, of how she must be feeling, what she must be going through. I simply can't. "I wish there was something I could do."

"There is." David Winthrop's voice rings forcefully in the empty foyer. He's leaning by the archway leading to the brightly lit living room. His jaw is clenched in anger. He's pale as a sheet, and his shirt looks slept in. "You could leave us the hell alone. Why are you here?"

"David, please," his wife says, holding her hand in the air to stop him. He shrugs and walks away, mumbling something I can't hear.

Mrs. Winthrop turns to me and says, "Please forgive my husband. I know why you're here. It's because you love Taylor. I know that." She gives my hand a squeeze while my eyes burn with tears.

I nod, unable to speak for a few moments. "If you hear anything, please call me. Day or night. You have my cell."

"Of course," she replies, then takes one step toward the door. I get the unspoken message. The visit is over.

I grab the door handle but hesitate before I squeeze it. "One more thing, when did she disappear?"

Breath shudders on her lips. "Between one and one-thirty yesterday. I was just about to call her inside for lunch. I remember hearing the dog barking, but he barks all the time when they play together. I didn't realize—" She chokes and stops talking, squeezing her eyes shut. Tears streak down her face, and she turns her head away as if trying to hide them.

Between one and one-thirty, yesterday.

As if it carries any meaning, I remember what I was doing then. Standing in line for tickets at the movie theater with Daniel, Chloe, and Ray, my biggest concern being everything that was going on in my life, the present and past entanglements and relationships that could completely ruin me, like that letter and the picture that came with it.

In retrospect, that seems trivial, now that Taylor's missing.

I want to ask if they'd made her a binder but decide not to. They'll think I'm peddling something, and that's not why I'm there.

"I'm really sorry," I say again as I take a step sideways, making room to open the door. "Please call me if you need anything or you have any news."

"I will," she repeats her earlier commitment. But then she surprises me by giving me a hug.

When I step outside, the reporters rush to stop me before I can reach my car. I elbow my way between them mercilessly.

"May I know your name?" one of the more brazen ones asks, chasing me with his phone held out to record the interaction.

"No comment," I reply, then climb behind the wheel of my Subaru as quickly as I can.

Before I drive off, I hear one of them shouting, "It's Taylor's teacher, Alana Blake."

Just what I need. Now they'll come after me too.

FOURTEEN

I'm not crying.

Leaning against the tile wall in my shower, I stand under the jets with my eyes closed in a trance-like state, desperately fighting off the imagery my overactive mind is weaving inside my brain. I can't think of what Taylor must be going through right now. I can't control what's going on with her. I can't help her any more than I can help myself. All I can do is breathe. And wait.

Later, when I manage to leave the shower in my white terry robe and a blue towel wrapped around my head, questions I can't answer gnaw at my mind until it's raw. Who could've taken her? Did I bring this upon her with my binder interview?

No... it can't be about that. It's not about me. Most likely it's because of the Winthrop money. The family is wealthy enough to pay a nice ransom. Both David and Monica Winthrop are well-known in the community, a power couple. It makes sense they were targeted, and that sweet little girl is nothing but a victim of lawless greed.

Hope blooms in my heart, frail at first, then grows stronger.

If they took her for ransom, they'll keep her alive. "Be brave, baby, hang in there," I whisper, as if Taylor could hear me.

The doorbell chimes, startling me out of my thoughts. I look at myself, barefoot and clad in a fuzzy bathrobe, and decide to not answer the door. It's probably a delivery. They'll go away.

But the doorbell chimes again. Whoever it is, they're not going anywhere. Frustrated, I open the door just a little, hiding behind it until I recognize the unwanted guest.

It's Chloe.

She's smiling widely, gesturing to me to let her in. Resigned, I do, stepping out of her way as she enters the house with a spring in her step. I close the door and lock it out of habit, then turn to find myself wrapped in an enthusiastic hug.

"Did I pull you out of the shower?" she asks, dropping her Chanel purse on the sofa and landing in the armchair with her slender legs crossed. She's dressed for work and probably stopped here on her way home. An Evan Picone white suit with black trim that I remember seeing in this year's Macy's catalog and strappy black sandals with four-inch heels. She's always been frustrated with her petite stature and fought it the best she could by wearing impossibly high heels. Truth is, she looks good in them.

"No, don't worry," I reply, unsure what to do next. I unwrap the towel and start patting my hair to dry it out, head tilted to the side. I don't know why she's here, and I wish she'd leave me alone with my thoughts. "What can I do for you?"

She lowers her eyelashes for a brief moment. "I wanted to know if you're okay. I heard on the news that a girl from your school is missing. Is she your student?"

My hands stop the work they're doing for a brief moment. I look at her concerned face, wondering if this is how it's going to be from now on: Chloe, storming through my life whenever she feels like it, pretending we're best friends again. I don't know if I can do this. I don't know that I want to.

"I'm okay," I lie casually. Funny thing about lies. The more I tell, the better I get at telling them. At weaving them into complex alternate realities that make sense on the surface.

"You don't look okay," she insists, leaning forward to clasp my hand. "Tell me what to do."

Ah, hell. There's no escape. I could say I have a headache, but I'm not sure that would do me any good. Might as well find out what she really wants. Her concern for me isn't the reason she's in my house. Not if I know Chloe at all. "Let's make some hot chocolate," I say, and she smiles, quick to spring from the comfy armchair and head into the kitchen, her heels clacking on the tiles.

"I'll make it," she offers. "You dry your hair."

I take her up on it, even if I'm cringing at the thought of her rummaging through my cabinets and pantry, only because I'm too drained to push back. Minutes later, we're sipping hot chocolate on the living room sofa. My hair is dry for the most part, and the robe has been replaced with jeans and an Imagine Dragons T-shirt.

"It's awful when it happens so close to home," she says, talking about Taylor's abduction most likely. Her words echo my thoughts. All that crime we hear about on television or read in the news doesn't really resonate until it's someone we know personally. "It reminds me of Flavia Guzman."

My hands shake badly as I set the cup back on the table. I can't think of Taylor like that. Flavia was killed. The cops didn't find her in time. I draw air into my lungs and steady myself. Taylor isn't Flavia. She'll be all right. Her kidnappers probably want a Winthrop-size ransom. I must believe that.

When I look up from the table, I find Chloe's eyes riveted on me, curious, worried, a bit wary. "What about Flavia?"

"Remember how you knew who took her, before the cops did?" She chuckles lightly. "You were amazing. That's so you, always trying to get to the bottom of things, obsessed even."

She's right. I had forgotten that. "I tried to tell the cops, but they didn't listen."

"But how did you know?" She leans forward, seemingly as interested in what I'm about to say as if it's the biggest secret ever shared.

"It was right there, staring us in the face. No one saw Flavia getting into any vehicle after church. No one saw her leaving on foot either; that's what the cops said. The only scenario left was that she climbed into, or was loaded into, the delivery van that brought supplies every Saturday before the service. And Flavia would have known the driver, because she volunteered to set up the after-service brunch every Sunday morning. That was the pattern, her routine."

"You solved this!"

"I solved it all right, but much too late." I shake my head, still bitterly disappointed as if it happened yesterday. "Too late doesn't count." That's why I'd forgotten all about it.

For a moment, silence takes over the cozy living room. I stare into thin air, wondering yet again if Chloe sent that letter. I consider showing it to her, just to gauge her reaction, but decide against it. She examines her manicure closely, while a wave of sadness crosses her face.

When she looks at me, I barely recognize her, her expression completely changed. "Hey, could you do me a favor?"

"Shoot." A slight frown scrunches my forehead as I wait anxiously to hear why she's here, drinking hot chocolate in my living room.

"Can I see your binder?" A timid smile stretches her lips.

I gape at her, surprised. I didn't see that coming. "Um, sure," I say, wondering why she'd want to see it, and doubting it's a good idea to have her look at what I put in there.

"It's just that... I might be in some trouble," she whispers, shooting side glances as if someone else is there, lurking in the shadows, ready to pounce if she tells me what's on her mind.

Her words seed deep, dark apprehension in my gut.

"What's going on?" I ask, feeling cold sweat drench the back of my shirt.

She buries her face in her hands and shakes her head slightly. "I'm afraid," she says after a moment, lowering her hands and clasping them nervously in her lap. "I think I'm losing my mind." She shoots me a glance of unfiltered despair. "I want to make a binder, in case, you know, something happens to me. Not just disappearing... but anything."

I swallow hard. "You're scaring me, Chloe."

"I'm so sorry, I didn't mean to. Please don't tell anyone anything about this, all right? Promise me you won't." Her hands are pressed together in the universal gesture of prayer.

I squeeze her forearm in a gesture meant to comfort her. "Don't worry, mum's the word." I stand, ready to go into the bedroom and fetch my binder. It will do her some good to get busy with something. But I can't help wondering what could've scared her so badly. She doesn't seem willing to tell me, at least not for now. And it seems less and less likely it was Chloe who sent that letter. "I'll get it now."

Moments later, I emerge from the bedroom with my binder, then lay it on the coffee table, pushing the hot chocolate cups aside. "What do you want to see?"

She flips through the pages, seeming absent-minded. "I started one for myself, you know, years ago. These things save lives. I wish that little girl they took, the one from your school, had one."

I swallow hard, my throat dry. I can't think of Taylor. Not with Chloe there, watching my every move. "Too late for her, but there's still time for you," I manage to say, reciting the words almost automatically. I've said the same phrase so many times while promoting the concept at women's self-defense classes and advocacy groups. But just saying anything is too late for Taylor grips my heart in a frozen claw.

She flips through the pages slowly, then closes the binder. "I think I know what to do." Her head hangs low for a moment, then she looks straight at me, tears shimmering in her eyes. There's unspeakable fear in them, as if something terrifying is breathing down her neck. "Do you ever think about it?" she asks eventually, her voice a barely discernible whisper, her eyes veering toward the barely visible scar on the back of my right hand.

Her words freeze the blood in my veins. Speechless, I stare at her, while silence falls heavy on us like evening fog, all engulfing.

"I think about it every day," she eventually whispers. "About Nikki."

FIFTEEN

My heart thumps in my chest when I think of Nikki. As I recall the three of us huddled together on that loveseat by the fire, with Chloe's arm extended to take that selfie, a sense of dread sends shivers down my spine.

Right after Chloe took the picture, we all looked at it for a moment, poking fun at one another. I noticed a smudge of chocolate staining Chloe's upper lip. She laughed at Nikki's face and how the sun's glare seemed to run across her forehead like the tip of a light saber. Then Chloe put her phone away and that was the last I saw of the photo until it fell out of that green-inked envelope.

Chloe gracefully picked up the tab and spent two or three endless minutes flirting with the waiter who'd seated us. Then, right before leaving, Chloe gave the guy a kiss on his stubbly cheek, leaving him grinning like an idiot, stuck in place as if her kiss had turned him to stone.

"And that's how I'll get us the same table next time, ladies," she commented, undoubtedly proud of herself as she climbed behind the wheel of her red convertible. She touched up her lip gloss in the rearview mirror, and Nikki followed suit, smiling far less than Chloe or even me. "Let's walk by the cliffs, huh? What do you say?"

I shrugged, knowing she couldn't see me anyway. It wasn't like I had anything better to do that day. Nikki whispered, "Sure," sounding anything but.

Chloe drove off heading south, passing slightly over the speed limit through Half Moon Bay, heading toward the cliffs. She hadn't meant a specific area; just any stretch of the miles-long, rugged, and breathtakingly beautiful coastline.

As always, the scenery takes my breath away. The cliffs towering over the Pacific are mostly sheer, with striped façades that reveal layers of rock and sediment, constantly sculpted by wind and water erosion. Strong waves crash at the bottom of the cliffs at high tide, leaving a few feet of smooth sand or tide pools when the water ebbs. The land atop the cliffs is perfectly flat, level with the highway. The expanse is covered by lush grasses, ground-cover succulents, and hardy coastal shrubs, the greenery often hanging to the sides of the cliffs, tormented by strong winds.

Chloe had her favorite place along the coastline, where a bench had been erected in memory of someone whose name I could never recall, right by the edge.

That terrible day, she pulled over her convertible by the side of the road, then we all walked over to the bench, just in time for the final stage of the daily sunset show.

"Let's see if anyone escapes Davy Jones's locker tonight," she called, excitedly sprinting over to the edge of the cliffs as the sun started dipping into the sea.

The *Pirates of the Caribbean* reference made me smile then. But I have to admit I still look at every sunset hoping to catch a glimpse of the rarely seen, distinctive green flash.

"Come on!" Chloe beckoned with both hands, and we followed.

She stopped at the very edge of the cliff, restless waves

crashing noisily right beneath her, a good forty or fifty feet below. A fine mist blew high in the air, borne by mighty wind gusts, landing salty on my lips. A chill clasped my neck in its grasp, and I raised my collar and plunged my hands into my jacket pockets, not taking my eyes off the descending sun, eager to catch the green flash at the end of its fall into the ocean.

They say if you see the green flash, your heart can do no wrong. I don't know about that, but I do remember we saw a strong one that night and cheered at the top of our lungs.

"Yeah, break free, baby," Chloe shouted, stretching her hands out as if about to take flight into the chasm at her feet. "Come, join me! Let's take another pic."

I approached hesitantly, not a huge fan of heights and painfully aware, as a Half Moon Bay native, of how treacherous those edges were. But Nikki didn't hesitate much. She stepped right by Chloe's side and stretched her arms out too, imitating her, hooting loudly, with her long, blonde hair whipping in the wind.

"Come on, we're waiting on you," Chloe shouted, without turning her head to look at me. I took a few more steps, but stopped a foot from the edge, not daring to go any farther.

My phone chose that moment to chime, and I took it out of my pocket, frowning. It was a text message from my mom; she'd just picked up another shift and wasn't going to be back home until midnight. I started texting her back, reassuring her that I wouldn't stay out late, and I wouldn't starve either, when a shriek came out of my lungs as something cut the skin on the back of my hand.

My phone flew out of my grasp, and I looked up just in time to see, with horror, Nikki's body disappearing over the cliff, her high-pitched scream enveloped in the sound of crashing waves.

I stared at where her feet had been. A chunk of the cliff had broken off, taking her down with it. She must've flailed, desperate to grab on to something, because the bleeding gash that had opened in the back of my hand had one of her bright red acrylic fingernails still stuck in it.

Shocked, Chloe took a step away from the edge, her hands covering her mouth. "Oh, my God," she said frantically. "What are we going to do?"

I stared at the blood dripping from my hand, not daring to approach the edge to look at Nikki. "I'm going down there," I said, sounding much braver than I felt. "There's a place where I can climb down, a few yards that way." I pointed with my bleeding hand, the fingernail still there. I didn't dare remove it, for some unknown reason.

Chloe clasped my forearm with both her hands. "N-no, please, just... let's get out of here," she said, sobbing, pale, terrified. "It was an accident. No one knew this would happen."

"We can't just leave her there, Chloe." But she just shook her head and tugged at my arm, pulling me toward the car. "Hold it together, Chloe. She needs our help," I urged in a stronger tone than I'd ever used with her. She gaped at me, her mouth open, her eyes wide in fear. "She might still be alive, Chloe, and we're wasting precious time."

"N-no, no," she whimpered, not letting go of my arm. "She's dead. I saw her. Let's go. Let's just—"

"We don't know that!" I grabbed her shoulders and squeezed tightly. Her eyes were glassy with shock; she wasn't able to hear me. But I still tried to reason with her. "Even if she is dead, we can't just leave her there. An entire restaurant saw us with her. My DNA is under her fingernails, and"—I quickly scanned the short grass around us—"my phone's down there. What do you think is going to happen when they find her?"

"All right," she said, letting go of my arm. "You go, and I'll wait here."

"Don't just wait," I said, shaking her a little, to help her regain her senses. "Call for help, okay? Call now."

I rushed to the bottom of the cliff, descending the treacherous slope by sliding on my butt, too afraid to stand. Sandy sediment crumbled under my feet, and I had to slow my slide with my bare hands and my heels. I reached the bottom in a small avalanche of pebbles and dirt.

Nikki's eyes were open, the blue color of the dusky sky reflected in her frozen irises. Her neck was twisted at an unusual angle, and a thin rivulet of blood colored the sand near her head.

She was gone.

My stomach heaved, but I managed to hold it together, splashing some frigid seawater on my face.

A few feet away from Nikki's body, I found my phone on a higher stretch of soft sand. It was still working. I called Chloe, but she didn't answer. I texted her, asking if she'd called the cops. She replied,

On the phone with Dad. He'll handle it.

I looked at the sky and breathed out all the frustration and despair I was feeling in one long sigh. Of course she'd called her dad. He was an attorney, a powerful one, even if he practiced real estate law. And I was stuck there, unable to climb the cliff face without help, unwilling to leave Nikki and look for a way up, with only a short time left before the tide would carry away her body.

I did the only thing I could do. I called 911 myself, gave them the location, and explained what had happened as concisely as possible. I told them to bring a fire truck to lift her body and help me climb up. They didn't need me to tell them what needed to be done. Every year people fell to their deaths from the edges of the Half Moon Bay cliffs. It was usually tourists or people from out of state. Like Nikki.

It was almost dark when they got there, and I was relieved to see the flashlights flickering like fireflies at the edge of the cliffs above my head. Then a powerful projector was lit, its brightness thrown back at me by foaming white waves crashing closer and closer.

About twenty minutes later, I was wrapped in a blanket and seated on the rear bumper of a county ambulance, not even realizing my teeth were chattering. My clothes were wet from the surf and freezing on my body. An EMS technician had wrapped my hand after a crime scene tech, dressed in white coveralls, had swabbed the laceration left by Nikki's fingernail. The fingernail was gone, lost somewhere during my descent, or later in the surf.

But my mind was spinning and had been for a while, as I started remembering things. How Nikki had flirted with Ray a couple of times, and Chloe had seen it. How she'd watched their interaction from a distance, her face carved in white marble, her teeth clenched. Then, out of the blue, the invitation for ice cream and a walk by the cliffs.

A horrific thought bloomed inside my weary mind. Did Chloe push Nikki?

I wasn't looking when she fell. I was texting my mom. And the edge of the cliff, where Nikki had stood, had been showing signs of recent collapse.

It must've been an accident. Chloe wasn't a killer. She had means, motive, and opportunity, but she wasn't a cold-blooded murderer. I was sure of that, while at the same time wondering where she was while I was left there to deal with everything on my own.

"Alana?" A man flashed a badge in the dim light coming from the ambulance's rear lights. "Detective Fernandez, HMBPD." He seemed young for a detective, in his mid-thirties. His eyes were kind, or so they seemed to me at the time, and a bit tired looking. "I have a few questions, if you don't mind." He slipped his badge in his pocket and extracted a small notepad.

I nodded, swallowing hard, suddenly afraid, although I'd done nothing wrong. "Okay," I replied, choked.

What if they learned what I'd been hiding for months?

"Hold on a second," a voice intervened. It was Mr. Avery, approaching quickly with Chloe in tow. She averted her eyes when I looked at her, and that simple gesture sent new shivers down my spine. "You wouldn't speak with minors without representation and legal guardians present, would you?"

The detective groaned. He probably hadn't realized I wasn't eighteen. "No, I wouldn't." He flipped the notebook closed and put it in his pocket. "Should we do this tomorrow morning then?"

That's all I remember from that terrible day. Somehow, I got home. Chloe must've driven me like she always did. The next morning, an attorney Mr. Avery had arranged for me was present during the statement I gave. My mother was there too, shaking like a leaf, although I'd sworn to her time and again I'd done nothing wrong. My statement was simple and truthful, the attorney advising me to keep phrases short, stick to the facts. But I was more afraid than I'd ever been. My DNA was under Nikki's fingernails. Just as if I'd pushed her.

As a crime podcast fan, I deeply understood the weight of physical evidence, and I was terrified of it.

Then they put Chloe and me in the same room to interview us together. I was taken aback that Chloe had a different attorney, but immensely grateful that Mr. Avery had arranged one just as good for me.

Later, when we reconvened in the parking lot, I asked Chloe about the selfie she'd taken of the three of us at the restaurant. She swore to me no one had seen it, and that she'd delete it from her phone. That's what her lawyer had told her to do, and to not say a word to anyone about what had happened.

Until that letter landed in my hammered-copper bowl, I had no reason to believe she hadn't kept her word.

By the end of a very long day, we were both released with the reassurance that Nikki's death would be ruled an accident. It made sense to me. After all, that's what it was.

Or was it? I wonder now, looking at Chloe's pale face and trembling hands. Is there a guilty conscience fueling her turmoil? Or is she playing me with the letter she might've sent and the picture she was supposed to have deleted, reminding me she holds my fate in her hands?

All I know for sure is that I'd give anything to turn back time and never go out with her and Nikki. Better still, to have never let Chloe be a part of my life at all.

SIXTEEN

There's a lightness to the last few days of school before summer break, shared by students and teachers alike, one I usually enjoy. But I don't feel it today, when Taylor's empty desk reminds me of a stark reality. She's still missing. No one knows anything. There was no ransom call as far as I know. I still can't think of what she must be going through without feeling a sob swelling in my chest, threatening to choke me.

I've been going through the motions, following the syllabus and just doing my job, grateful it doesn't allow me much time to think, to slowly go insane with worry. My mind wanders at times, while my students take turns reading their assignments.

When Destiny opens the classroom door and beckons me outside, I hope for good news about Taylor.

Instead, she introduces me to Detective Fernandez, the same Detective Fernandez who's been haunting my nightmares since the day Nikki fell to her death. He's gray around his temples now, his forehead ridged by permanent lines. Since I last saw him, he's gained about ten pounds around his midsection, maybe more. And he doesn't recognize me.

I hold my breath. It won't take him long to remember. Cops are notoriously good with faces and names.

"Ms. Blake is Taylor's teacher," Destiny completes the introduction. "She'll answer any questions you might have." She touches my elbow in passing. "I'll take care of the little ones until you're done." Smiling and swaying her hips for the detective's benefit, she enters the classroom and closes the door.

"Ms. Blake, where could we talk privately?" he asks, his direct glance an overt scrutiny. There's a slight, curious tilt in the way he carries his head, a hint of a raised eyebrow. I probably seem familiar to him.

I invite him to follow me into one of the empty classrooms. He closes the door and remains standing, while I sit behind the teacher's desk, not trusting my knees to hold me much longer. "Do you have any news?" I ask, painfully impatient. I wring my hands in my lap, hoping against all logic that he won't notice.

"No, we're still investigating." He takes out a small notepad, just like he did eleven years ago, the first time we met. "The Winthrops said you stopped by their house the day before yesterday. I find that a little unusual." He stops talking, looking straight at me, waiting, but I don't say anything. "I can't remember a time when a child's teacher showed up on the family's doorstep like that."

I shrug, but still don't say anything. He hasn't asked me a question yet.

"Don't you find that unusual?"

"I wouldn't know." My voice is a little shaky. "I don't see that many kidnappings in my line of work. Actually, this is my first one."

"Why did you go there, Ms. Blake?"

"To show support." I breathe to steady myself, my voice, my shaky hands I'm clasping together in my lap to keep them still. "To see if they had any news of Taylor." He nods, encouraging me to continue. "I'm fond of all my children, Detective. You have to understand, having one taken is deeply disturbing to me, as well as to the students."

He looks at me for a long moment, as if seeing if I want to add anything, then looks at his notepad with a bit of a frown. "Alana Blake," he says softly, speaking my name slowly. "Your first name sounds familiar. You *look* familiar. Have we met before?"

Ah, hell. I might as well tell him. He'll find out soon enough. Or worse, he might know already, and he's setting me up, trying to see if I'm afraid of him connecting the dots.

"We did meet, yes, on one of the most terrible days of my life." His eyebrows shoot up. "The day Nikki Malkin fell to her death off the cliffs by Seal Rock, eleven years ago."

"Ah, yes, I remember." He scratches his forehead with the tip of his index finger. "Wasn't there another girl with you that day? The one whose father was a lawyer or something?"

I swallow with difficulty, realizing he remembered me just fine, and was playing games with me. "Yes. Chloe Avery." I will myself quiet, repressing the need to talk incessantly, to change the subject. He'd see right through me. And I have nothing to hide. Nothing, except the threatening letter I received.

"Interesting," he mumbles, flipping through his notepad. "You know what else is interesting? Your binders, Ms. Blake. You appeared on television talking about them. And now, one of your students has gone missing." I gawk at him in disbelief. "I can't help but think there might be a connection between those binders you're advertising and the little girl who was taken. Is this some twisted marketing gimmick?"

I gasp and spring from my chair, anger driving me to pace the classroom restlessly. "This is preposterous! How could you possibly think that?" I stop in front of him with my hands on my hips, breathing heavily as if I've been running. He just looks at me, visibly unimpressed with my outburst. "Well, let me tell you, Detective, first of all, I'm not making any money off those binders, just trying to save lives. Second, you're wasting precious time when you should be out there looking for Taylor. That girl's been gone for days already, and you know what that means, right?"

"No, Ms. Blake, why don't you educate me?"

I scoff and walk away from him, pacing again. "Are you kidding me? The likelihood of her being found alive drops like a river boulder after the first twenty-four hours, yet here you are, wasting your time on me. Please tell me the feds have been called and you're just doing busywork no one else would touch." I stop in front of him again and drill into him with resentful eyes. "Because it's a waste of time."

"All right," he says, closing his notepad and taking two steps toward the door. "Were there any incidents involving Taylor I should know about?"

For a moment, I can't recall anything, but then that little jerk comes to mind, Douglas Durazo. "Um, there was one minor bullying incident, but I don't think—"

"What happened?" The notepad is flipped open, and the detective's pen is hovering an inch above the paper.

"Douglas Durazo, another one of my fourth graders, slammed Taylor into the wall as he ran past her. She was a little rattled, but unhurt. However, she did mention it had happened before." I don't tell him I can still hear her tear-filled voice saying those words and that it still breaks my heart.

"Did you call her parents?"

Shit. I knew this was going to come back to haunt me. "The principal and I discussed the case. She talked with Mrs. Durazo, the boy's mother, and it was determined that the incident could've been accidental, not intentional. Nevertheless, Douglas was placed in detention for failing to apologize." I stop talking, giving him time to finish scribbling. "I don't think there's a connection. Douglas has the makings of a bully and a troublemaker, but he didn't orchestrate Taylor's kidnapping.

He's ten years old, for crying out loud, not some criminal mastermind."

"Well, I don't think so either, but that's why we investigate. To be sure." He walks over to the door and opens it, before turning to me. "Thank you, Ms. Blake."

The door closes slowly behind him, powered by a squeaky spring. I sit behind the desk again, feeling weak and drained, fighting the urge to hide in the broom closet for a while. *Nothing is wrong,* I tell myself for a while, but it's a big, fat lie. *Everything* is wrong. Taylor's gone. The letter. The lies I keep telling Daniel about getting pregnant, about everything, really. Chloe and whatever she's up to. And Ray.

And now this. A detective interviewing me, inches away from feeling curious enough to dig up old records. To remember that my DNA is on file since the day Nikki scratched my hand on her way down.

My head is spinning. Unsteady on my feet, I walk out of there and stop for a drink of water at the fountain, then head back toward my classroom.

My phone buzzes loudly in my pocket, set on vibrate as it always is during school hours. Chloe's name is showing on the screen. I stare at it for a second, while the same sense of dread that I've been fighting lately returns for another visit. What does she want now?

I take the call.

"Alana?" I recognize Ray's voice, colored with undertones of panic.

"Ray, what's going on?"

"Please come home as soon as you can. Chloe's gone missing."

SEVENTEEN

My mind is numb all the way home. I just drive, as fast as I can, simply unable to wrap my thoughts around what's going on. Chloe, missing? We were just talking about her concerns, about her intentions to make herself a binder like mine. A thought washes over me, in waves of anxiety, when I recall the only thing she'd mentioned about her fears was Nikki. Indirectly, just asking me if I ever thought of that day. She didn't say anything else, and I didn't think of asking, because the simple mention of the poor girl's name threw me into a whirlpool of dread.

And now, Chloe's gone. I feel as if I'm about to step into a trap, her disappearance menacing, terrifying, a bad omen I cannot yet comprehend.

As I turn the corner onto our street, I think again about how she wanted to make herself a binder in case something happened to her. Something worse than going missing. "Not just disappearing... but anything," she'd said, and she looked scared for her life as she uttered those words.

Three police cars with red and blue flashers on are stopped in front of Chloe's house, spilling over toward ours. A crime scene van is parked with the rear wheels on their lawn. A fourth vehicle, a dark gray, unmarked Dodge Charger, is blocking the access to my driveway, left sideways behind Daniel's Ford. I pull over on the side of the road and briskly walk the distance to Chloe's house.

The front door is wide open. I don't bother to knock, just head into the living room, guided by Daniel's voice. Cops and forensic technicians are swarming the place, collecting evidence, taking photos where they've placed yellow, numbered crime scene markers, dusting for prints.

The living room tells the story of a bitter struggle: toppled furniture, two broken wineglasses on the floor, a purplish-red stain on the cream-colored area rug, the glass top coffee table cracked, the TV remote on the floor by the window. Knowing Chloe, she would not have gone down without a fight.

Ray is seated on one of the wide armchairs, his head hung low, his hands resting on his knees. He seems to be in shock.

Daniel is standing by his side, squeezing his shoulder. "—anything you need, all right? And I'll bring food from the diner, so you don't have to worry—"

"I'm not hungry," Ray says, his voice brittle. A tear drops from his eye, staining his shirt cuff. "But thanks."

"Ray," I say gently, stopping by Daniel's side. "It will be all right," I manage to say.

Daniel gives me a quick, worried glance. There's something he's not telling me, something I don't know. I squeeze Daniel's hand and crouch in front of Ray to look at his lowered face. "What happened?"

He looks at me through a sheen of tears and shakes his head. "I don't know. Her car's in the garage. Her keys, phone, wallet, everything is here. I found the front door ajar, and this." He gestures with his hand at the destroyed living room.

One technician is swabbing the focal point of the crack in the glass coffee table, shaped like a spider web. He sprays something on the Q-tip he used to swab the cracks, and the cotton turns purple.

"We have blood," he announces, and his words make Ray's jaws clench. The technician's colleagues wrap the table in a large plastic bag and haul it out of there. Then he continues swabbing sections of the floor, the area rug, the furniture. "Take the rug too," he directs.

The rug is being rolled and slipped into another large evidence bag. Clipboards with forms are being passed around and signed, bags are sealed and initialed with silent efficiency, every move choreographed and executed smoothly.

While I hold my breath.

"Do you know anything?" Ray clasps my hand and I let him. "Did she call you?"

"No, I'm sorry," I whisper, taking my hand out of Ray's when I notice Daniel's gaze fixed on it. I slip it inside my pocket where I can clench a fist unseen. "They'll find her," I say reassuringly. "I'm sure of it."

Just another lie I tell as easily as I breathe.

I'm not sure of it, not in the least, considering what she told me that evening; that haunted look in her eyes, the mentioning of Nikki's name so soon after I received that letter.

A disturbing thought snakes its way into my brain, setting it on fire. What if it wasn't Chloe who sent that letter, but someone else? What if someone out there is seeking revenge for Nikki's death? I shudder as unspeakable fear turns the blood in my veins to ice.

"What's wrong?" Daniel asks, putting his arm around my shoulders. I can't bring myself to tell another lie, and the truth is impossible. I hide my face on his shoulder for a moment, and let his familiar scent instill some strength into my weary heart. Then I'm ready to face life again.

A crime scene tech comes by, holding an evidence bag,

already open. "We need her phone, sir," he says, and Ray hands it over without hesitation. "Do you have the code?"

"Yes." He smiles with sadness. "It's my birthday. Eleven, twenty-nine."

The tech seals the bag and scribbles the numbers on the back, right under his initials. "Thank you," he murmurs and disappears.

"Did she say anything to you? Was she worried about anything? A stalker, crank calls, stuff like that?" I ask.

"N-no," Ray replies, sinking back into the armchair. "I don't know where this came from," he says looking at me intently, desperately. "All I know is that I'm losing my mind."

But I'm not paying attention anymore. Instead, my eyes are riveted to the evidence pouch holding Chloe's phone, now being carried away to the crime scene van parked outside. What if she still has the selfie in that phone? She'll have changed phones many times since that day at Miramar, but maybe that photo survived the years, carried over from one phone to the next. Inherently, there's nothing wrong with it. Just three girls laughing and having fun together. But to the right detective, it could serve as a reminder of a troubled past.

"You, again?"

The familiar voice makes me flinch. I turn in its direction and manage a polite nod. "Detective Fernandez. Good to see you too." I feel the blood draining from my face as he studies me inquisitively. Then his focus shifts over to Daniel, whose surprised gaze is shifting from me to the detective and back. I make the introductions quickly, eager to be gone.

I expect Fernandez to shift his attention to Ray, who's now standing by Daniel, silent and grim, but the detective is still focused on me.

Irritated with everything about him, I can't help but ask, "Are you going to question me about this now? Waste some more time?"

A lopsided smile tugs at the corner of his mouth. "Unfortunately, Mrs. Preston vanished about the time you and I were talking things over at school. You have the perfect alibi, Ms. Blake. Me." He stares at me for another moment longer, his cold eyes giving me a chill. "One thing I'd like to know, though. How are you mixed up in all this?"

"We're the next-door neighbors," Daniel replies before I can. "And very good friends with Chloe and Ray. My wife went to school with both of them."

Ray nods to second that statement. He's pale and seems angry about something, but he's not saying anything.

Meanwhile, the detective is looking only at me, as if no one else is in the room. "Oh, it's *that* Chloe, huh?"

I nod almost imperceptibly, feeling my throat closing tightly, taking the breath out of me.

He runs his hand through his hair a couple of times, as if trying to sort his thoughts. "Somehow, you're in the middle of this," he adds eventually. "You and your binders."

I gasp and start to say something in my defense, but he shuts me up with a hand gesture.

"I'm willing to bet a month's pay this is no coincidence."

"What, exactly, are you talking about?" Ray asks, his voice cutting, his demeanor shifting from despair to assertiveness. The detective doesn't reply. "Tell me, damn it! I have a right to know."

"If you're such good friends with Ms. Blake, you must know about her binders, right?" Fernandez asks Ray.

"Yeah, I know about that, but what—"

"Did you know there was a kid taken from Ms. Blake's school? And all this happened since her TV show about the binders?"

"I heard about the kid, yes," Ray replies coldly, folding his arms.

"And you don't think that's strange? Two people gone

missing within two days of each other. You don't suspect there's a connection to Ms. Blake here?"

Ray shrugs, and a deep frown scrunches his forehead. "How could there be?" He gestures widely, seemingly frustrated just as much as I am. "This is nuts."

Fernandez doesn't say anything else, just stares at Ray for a long, loaded moment. Then he turns to us and says, "Well, I think you two are done here. We're keeping it close family only."

I look at Ray and he mouths "thank you" to me, then nods at Daniel as we leave. The detective has already turned his back, sifting through his notes quickly as if looking for something.

Back in our own living room, we watch the bustle next door through the sheers, keeping the lights turned off although it's almost dark outside. After a while, the marked cars and the forensic van leave. Only the detective is left. Apparently, the gray, unmarked Charger in our driveway belongs to him.

Daniel brews some herbal tea for the both of us, then places a cup on the table next to me on a cork coaster. "So, now, you two are holding hands?" he asks, pretending to be casual, but I can tell there's tension in his voice.

"It's nothing," I say, underlining my words with a dismissive gesture. "He's distraught, and we all go back many years, Daniel. There's nothing to be concerned about." I wrap my arms around his neck and smile, a bit too tired for a decent performance. "I love you. You're the best thing that ever happened to me." I mean it, which makes all the lies I keep telling him that much worse.

Noise gets my attention next door, and I peek out. The garage door is going up, and Fernandez is looking at something inside, probably at Chloe's car. Then he jots something in his notepad.

Before walking over to our driveway to climb behind the wheel of his car, he looks straight at me. I know he can't see me through the sheers, I'm sure of that, and still, his fixed stare makes me take a step back.

"Is there anything to his accusations?" Daniel asks calmly, taking another sip of herbal tea. "About the binders?"

I shrug and shake my head, then rub my aching nape for a moment. It's been one hell of a day. "I honestly don't know. I don't see why someone would kidnap people because of my binders. It must be just a coincidence." I look outside for a while, thinking I should move my car to our driveway, but then I realize something I should've mentioned to Fernandez. "I wonder why Chloe was home so early." I look at Daniel but can't read what he's thinking. A couple of lines run across his forehead, and his eyes have shifted away from mine. I don't like it.

When my phone rings in the deep silence of the room, we both flinch. I recognize Ray's number, although he's never called me from his own phone before. I take the call on speaker, thinking it will help me appease whatever suspicions are brewing in Daniel's mind.

"Chloe made one of those binders, like the one in your TV interview," Ray says, sounding a little out of breath. "Would you help me find it?"

EIGHTEEN

"I'll be right there," I say quickly, then end the call before I can change my mind. Before Daniel can change it for me. Without a word, I head into the bathroom and close the door. For a long moment, I look at my reflection in the mirror and don't recognize myself. What am I doing?

I don't dare answer my own question. I'm so good at telling lies I even tell them to myself and then believe them. The only thing I know for sure is I must go to Chloe's. I have to find her binder before anyone else lays eyes on it.

My nerves are frayed, sending fine tremors into my extremities. First Taylor's gone missing, now Chloe. I'd never admit it to anyone, but I see why the detective was probing to find the connection. It's too much of a coincidence to not make me wonder. And I'm scared, also something I wouldn't admit to anyone. So many things could go wrong, be revealed.

I splash cold water on my face, then brush my hair. It's instinctive, habitual, and still, it makes me feel guilty somehow, knowing I will be alone with Ray in the house next door. That's why I stop short of touching up my lip gloss, to better lie to myself that Ray's presence will have no meaning whatsoever. I'm just there for Chloe, not him.

When I leave the bathroom, I find Daniel dressed for work, jangling his car keys in his hand. He averts his eyes when I call his name, keeping his head lowered. His face is tense, his forehead ridged.

"Where are you going?"

"The diner. It gets busy about seven." A beat of loaded silence. "I'm going to take a leap and assume you don't need me over there."

"Daniel, I—"

He waves me off. "Yeah, I know. You have to go, you owe it to her, her life depends on it, and so on. You don't have to explain."

I recoil from the undertones of sarcasm in his voice, but I still have to do this. I don't have a choice. And I can't explain it to him.

"If she has a binder, I need to find it and give it to the cops before it's too late."

He scoffs and looks at me for a brief moment, a puzzled expression in his eyes. "To the same detective who's trying to pin this bloody mess on you somehow? *Because* of these binders?"

Speechless, I stare at him for a moment, slack-jawed. He has a point. Or maybe not. I haven't done anything wrong. Nikki's death wasn't my fault. I have to believe that the truth will prevail.

Only I desperately hope it won't prevail too much when it comes to the lies I've been telling Daniel.

And everyone else.

He throws me another glance and then opens the door. "Be careful, okay?" he says. I nod and smile awkwardly. "Don't do anything I wouldn't do."

The door closes, and silence regains ownership of the living room. After a brief moment, I hear the Ford's engine start, then fade into the distance. I hate to admit how relieved I feel he didn't want to come with me. Shivering, I drink a sip of tea and put on Daniel's rain jacket that's hanging on the coat rack by the door. Then I grab my keys from the copper bowl, but I stop short of opening the door, hesitating, wondering if I can really trust myself to be alone with Ray. Doubting I can trust him.

I cast off my doubts, remembering Chloe's fearful eyes and low whispering voice, her paranoid behavior, her unspoken cry for help. I have to do my best to find that binder. For us both, I remind myself with a shudder. I'm insanely afraid of what Chloe might've put in it.

It's amazing to realize the responsibility that comes with promoting these binders, and I didn't see it until now. I thought of them merely as a way to save lives, to shorten the time that law enforcement needs to access critical personal data in an emergency, like a kidnapping or disappearance. I never thought I'd find myself entangled so deeply in the mire of the consequences such treasure troves of evidence could have. In the wrong hands and used with ill intentions, they could do irreparable harm.

I walk over to Chloe's and ring the bell. When the door opens, Ray steps aside and I enter, painfully aware we haven't been alone together in eleven years. I will myself to stay focused on the task at hand, embarrassed with myself and my inappropriate thoughts at a time like this. The poor man is beside himself with anguish over his missing wife, and I'm reliving moments of our passionate past I'd be smart to forget entirely.

"Thanks for coming," he says, sounding tense. "If you have any idea where she might've stashed the binder, I'd appreciate it. Every second counts." He looks pale and tired and doesn't look me in the eye.

"She didn't tell you?"

He presses his lips together and shoves his hands in his

pants pockets. "I didn't know she had one. Her mother just called and told me." He throws a quick glance to the window. "They should be here any minute."

I breathe, slowly, hiding the relief I'm feeling at the thought of Ray and me no longer being alone in the eerily empty house. "I'd like to start in the bedroom." I feel my cheeks catching fire, but I look at Ray casually. He veers his gaze away, perhaps distracted by the sound of an approaching vehicle.

Moments later, Mr. and Dr. Avery enter the living room. Chloe's mom gives Ray a warm, tearful hug, a little rushed. Her dad shakes Ray's hand, the handshake turning into one of those brief half-hugs men do.

"We came as soon as we could," he says, pulling away. "We were in Monterey when you called."

As expected, they're worried, restless, and Dr. Avery's eyes are red and swollen. I don't expect them to remember me, but they do.

"Alana, so good to see you," Dr. Avery says, giving me a quick hug. She doesn't smell of dental office staples like disinfectants and rinses and eugenol. Chloe told me she retired a while ago. She's wearing a sharp black suit with a pencil skirt and heels and a silver chain with a starfish-shaped pendant. "Chloe's been talking about you and your husband." Then she covers her mouth with trembling fine, long fingers. "I-I can't believe she's been taken." She looks around her, visibly distraught, as Mr. Avery paces the living room, studying every corner, every surface.

"I asked Alana to help me find Chloe's binder," Ray says. His voice is different from what it was moments ago, when we were alone. There's no warmth in it. "I looked everywhere I could think of and couldn't find it."

"Great idea," Dr. Avery replies, heading into the kitchen. "Please, go ahead. Don't worry about us. I'll start on some dinner, coffee, whatever else you need."

"What do you think happened to my daughter?" Mr. Avery asks, looking straight at me from the other side of the living room, where he's been studying the traces of powder left behind by the crime scene technicians. "Do you have any idea who might've taken her?"

I shake my head. "No. I've been racking my brain to think of anyone who might've had a problem with Chloe. She's very well liked, as you know. I don't know much about her work, but she didn't tell me anything that could help us now."

"Do you have video surveillance?" Mr. Avery asks Ray. "An alarm system?"

"Chloe set something up for the front door. I gave the detective access to it, but he wasn't optimistic after reviewing it. He took the device to the police lab." Mr. Avery glares at Ray for a moment. "It's a safe neighborhood," Ray adds, sounding a bit defensive. "We didn't think we needed it."

Mr. Avery's displeased, but presses his lips together for a moment, keeping his thoughts to himself. "When did they release the scene?" The unexpectedly cold question makes me look at him again. His sharp, penetrating eyes drill into Ray mercilessly. Lines on his forehead, around his eyes and flanking his mouth, speak of late nights spent preparing for legal battles. Even if he's in real estate law—or he used to be, last time I heard—he's still an attorney and a highly successful one. He *thinks* like one.

"The scene?" Ray asks, taken aback by his father-in-law's choice of words. "You mean, our home?" Mr. Avery swats his concern away with a dismissive, impatient gesture. "I'd say within a couple of hours after they got here," Ray answers, frowning.

"So, they don't suspect she was killed here," Mr. Avery mutters. "Good. There's hope."

"Harold, how could you say that about my baby?" Dr. Avery starts sobbing, pressing her hand over her chest. She's bent over, gasping for air, and heaving with sobs, as if she's about to faint. I know her pain... I'm living through it. Rushing over, I help her into the living room, to the white leather sofa by the wall. She holds on to my arm like it's a lifeline, as Harold Avery stares at her from across the room, his gaze weary and apologetic.

"Denise... I—we need to know. *I* need to know. I'm sorry."

Dr. Avery nods, keeping her head lowered as if embarrassed by her tears. "I understand... it's just I can't bring myself to think of that possibility. I'm not used to you being so clinical." She wipes her tears quickly with the back of her hand and looks at me. "Don't waste time on me, Alana. Please, find my daughter's binder. Every minute counts."

With a nod and a hint of a hesitant, reassuring smile, I stand and walk over to Ray, who leads the way to the back of the house.

To their bedroom.

I hold my breath as he opens the door and invites me in. Being there feels awkward, the ultimate invasion of Chloe's privacy. My eyes land on the king-size bed with coral satin sheets, shimmering in the subdued light coming from the nightstand lamps. I know for a fact sleeping in satin is not necessarily Ray's idea; Chloe had satin sheets on her bed growing up. I remember staring at them as a teenager visiting her house—my first time seeing satin sheets—touching them shyly with the tips of my fingers, just another reminder that Chloe and I came from very different worlds.

The bed looks slept in, the covers thrown to the side where Chloe got out of bed, the sheets wrinkled, the pillows crooked, the white down duvet touching the floor. Standing there, trying not to breathe in the scent of their bodies, I can see them lying in that bed, making love, their naked bodies slick with sweat, their eyes lost in each other's afterglow.

In my wide-eyed daydream, Chloe's voluptuous body starts morphing into another's.

Mine.

"Are you all right?" Ray asks, touching my elbow.

"Ray," I whisper, startled back into reality. I nod, then I lie some more. "Yeah. I just... can't believe she's been taken."

NINETEEN

Get a grip, I tell myself, pushing away the stirring and at the same time disconcerting daydream. I remind myself of Ray's cheating, of the heart-wrenching day I learned he'd been dating Chloe, when I thought he and I were forever. When I still believed he was the one.

Reliving that anguish has the sobering effect of a cold shower, dampening the emerging, unwelcome fire, and leaving me a little rattled. But I have a job to do.

I must find Chloe's binder. Before anyone else does. I try to stay cool about it, to think rationally, but I can't help thinking maybe both Chloe and I are targets. And perhaps this has to do with the letter I received, and with Nikki.

I look around me in a different way than before, coldly, factually, wondering where to start my search. Ray is standing in the doorway, leaning against the frame, hands plunged deep inside his pockets, watching me with dark, nervous eyes. What is he afraid of?

"What does it look like?" I ask, then I realize it's a stupid question.

He shrugs, his hands still in his pockets. "I have no idea."

If he's afraid of what's in it, he's not the only one. Although, as little as I know about their life together since we graduated from high school, he doesn't have much to be afraid of. Not like me.

What if, in those pages, Chloe blames me for Nikki's death? That thought has been hanging over me like a dark cloud twisting faster and faster, threatening to become an all-destructive tornado that will rip my life to shreds.

She implied it one time when she was a little drunk. One week before graduation, she'd flipped out over Ray and me talking in the schoolyard, and threatened me later that night, indirectly. She referred to me as a problem that was so easy to eliminate it wasn't worth the effort, and ended her cautionary speech by saying Ray was her soulmate.

And so, I was warned off. Permanently. Whatever hope was left in my heart was destroyed. Later, feeling as intensely wretched as I'd ever known, I curled up on the sofa, in the dark, and listened to the sound of my own sobs until dawn.

I wished I'd never been born.

Now, looking at Chloe's bedroom, about to rummage through her things looking for the evidence she might've left behind to incriminate me, I feel nauseated again.

"Have you searched the closet?" I ask, opening the door and stepping inside between tightly packed rows of clothing on hangers, floor-to-ceiling shelves, and dressers with drawers. The scent of Acqua di Parma is stronger in here, and so is Chloe's spirit, present as if she were there in person, watching me. A bowl of her brown velvet hair scrunchies almost falls off the dresser when I clumsily turn on the light, a yellowish, anemic ceiling fixture. It doesn't do much to chase away the shadows.

"No." He's unusually quiet, disengaged. "Go right ahead," he adds, shifting his attention to his phone.

For a moment, I stare at him, wondering why he's not willing to search with me. He's probably offended by Chloe having kept secrets from him, or perhaps he doesn't want to be too close to me while his in-laws are in the other room. I start searching, feeling between stacks of clothing, touching underneath folded sweaters to probe for anything hidden, looking inside every drawer. As I search, my anxiety is raging. I'm afraid I'm not going to find the binder; while at the same time I'm terrified of what might be in it.

After a while, breathing heavily and covered in sweat, I have to admit defeat. Yet, I hesitate to leave the closet, as if something unseen holds me back. I linger, and in my wandering mind a new memory surfaces, covered in another heartache I had almost forgotten.

It was mere days after Chloe had warned me off about Ray. Pretending like none of that ever happened, she'd called me over for a special treat at her house. Her mother had made sundaes for the family, in celebration of our upcoming graduation. And for some logic-defying, incomprehensible reason that only a teenager's mind can conceive, I went. Thinking back on it now, I believe I wanted to still be close to Ray as much as I could. By proxy.

After we emptied the bowls, Chloe took me to her bedroom to share a secret with me, something she'd been whispering about since I got there. Then, after carefully closing the door and putting on some music to drown the sound of her whispers, she showed me a few naked selfies she'd taken for Ray's upcoming birthday. She had printed them on her father's laser color printer and kept them hidden in a safe place.

I recall looking at them while she shamelessly exulted. I was embarrassed by her nudity and, at the same time, felt sadness and despair overwhelming my broken heart at the sight of her stunning perfection. I realized then I'd never be like her, so flawlessly beautiful, so utterly sensual and yet vulnerable, a heady, irresistible mix no man could resist. Against her, I never stood a chance.

But I remember now what she did with those photos after showing them to me: she slipped them into an envelope and taped it to the bottom of a drawer, toward the back, where no one would ever think of looking.

Pulling the drawers open again, one by one, this time I reach far back instead of feeling through lingerie and socks and neckties, touching the bottom of the drawer above. I'm three drawers down when I feel something. With trembling fingers, I follow the contour of what seems to be a letter-size file, barely a quarter-inch thick.

This could be it.

Breath caught in my lungs, I keep searching, my slow, methodical movements now frenetic, feverish. Another object is taped to the bottom of the fourth drawer; this one is a thicker, smaller object, like a book. Or a diary. It might hold the answers I'm looking for.

After going through all the drawers, I stop for a moment and think. Ray is only a few feet away, but he can't see what's in that binder, not until I've seen it first. I need time.

I step outside of the closet and find him in exactly the same spot, looking at his phone, much too close for comfort once I start making noise retrieving that binder and flipping through its pages.

"Found it?" he asks, looking at me with hope in his eyes, while at the same time seeming a bit fearful.

I might be wrong; it happens a lot to me lately. His fear could be in my imagination.

"Not yet," I reply, letting out a long sigh and wiping my sweaty forehead with the back of my hand. It's a bit stuffy in the closet, but that's not why I'm sweating now. "Would you mind getting me a bottle of water or something?"

The phone finds its way into his pocket. "Sure."

I listen for a moment and hear him talking with his in-laws.

Rushing back into the closet, I open the third drawer and remove the object taped to the bottom of it.

It's Chloe's If I Go Missing binder. It says so on the cover in block letters written in black Sharpie. Pieces of blue masking tape still cling to its covers where it was taped to the drawer.

Holding my breath, I open it and find the first page is a typed letter. It starts with, IF YOU'RE READING THIS, I'VE GONE MISSING.

AND I HAVE JUST THESE PAGES TO GET YOU TO KNOW ME.

It goes on forever. I don't have time to read it now, but I rush to take a picture of it with my phone.

Then I turn the page and find Chloe's DNA in the form of a few long, blonde hair fibers extracted with their roots intact, sealed in a small plastic pouch taped to the page.

Then, an improvised ten card with her fingerprints. She followed my instructions to the letter, it seems.

The following page leaves me breathless. It's my own DNA, also in the form of a few hair fibers, light-brown and not as long as hers, taped to the page in a similar fashion. She must've swiped those from my bathroom, where I keep my hairbrush. Several of my fingerprints are pasted on the same page under clear tape, probably lifted off the glass I used when I drank wine at her house. All that is labeled clearly: "Alana's DNA" and "Alana's fingerprints." Why did she put my DNA there? Or my prints? When did she have time to do it? How is any of this relevant? Without hesitation, I rip out the page and crumple it in my hand angrily, then shove it inside the chest pocket of my jacket.

The next page has me shaking. It's the selfie she took with Nikki and me that day at Miramar. But that's not all. She received a letter just like I did, written in the same sickening, slanted cursive handwriting in green ink, with the exact same threatening message as mine. I tear off that page too and fold it quickly before I slip it into my pocket.

Tearing that page exposes the next one, and it's much worse. A newspaper clipping has been taped to a sheet of printer paper. The title of the article references Nikki's death and a witness coming forward after eleven years. Under the article, Chloe has written the words, "It wasn't me," in her highly recognizable cursive.

I'm going to be sick.

"You want flat or sparkling water?" I hear Ray calling from the kitchen. The sound of his voice jolts me, helps me get a grip.

Frantic, I tear off this page too, rushing to fold it and slip it into my pocket with the other two. "Still, please," I shout, knowing I only have a few seconds left. "Some ice too if you could."

The next page shows a photo of a girl I never met, small and rather blurry. It was taken at some athletic award ceremony, because she's wearing a gold medal, and it is printed on plain printer paper. I take a shot of it with my phone, then leave it be and turn quickly to the next one. The following pages are social media logins, bank and credit card accounts and passwords, and device logins and access codes, all perfectly organized and referenced clearly. Every page gets a picture, some blurry, some moving, but it's the best I can do right now, in the dim light of the closet.

Finally, the last page is a photo of some cars on a street, also printed on ordinary paper. I really don't have time to figure it out, because I can hear Ray's footfalls approaching. I just snap a picture of it and close the binder.

I barely have time to slip it inside a drawer when his head pops into the doorway, finding me with my arms up to my elbows inside Chloe's lingerie drawer.

"Got your water," he says, his words distant, neutral, cold as ice.

I pretend to reach deeper, then I say, "I think I found it." Fumbling some more, I extract it, blue tape still clinging to its edges. A pair of red lace panties falls out of the drawer, but I quickly put them back. "Whew," I say, breathing heavily, my hands still shaking. I trade the binder for the water Ray brought me and gulp down half the bottle breathlessly.

He's frozen there, holding the binder in his hands, looking at it as if it were a ghost. In a way, it is. "Don't worry," I say, feeling the need to comfort him. "All we have to do now is give it to the detective. Do you want to call him?"

He looks at me as if he doesn't know who I am. "Um, yeah," he says, walking toward the living room with the binder under his arm, dialing his phone.

I only have a split second, but it's all I need. I open the fifth drawer and reach deep inside, feeling the bottom of the drawer above where Chloe has taped that book or perhaps her diary. I'm hoping that's what it is. I can't have anyone else find that, not after what she's put in her binder. With a quick, determined yank, I pull that out of there and shove it inside the sleeve of my oversize jacket, where I can keep it out of sight as long as I keep my left arm lowered and tucked next to my body. Then I close the drawer and turn off the light before I leave the closet.

On the way to the living room, another flood of anxiety hits me as I realize my fingerprints are all over that binder.

On every damn page.

TWENTY

"Fernandez is on his way. He should be here in ten minutes." Ray ends the call and places the binder on the coffee table, then drops into an armchair with a heavy sigh. I remain standing, torn between the urge to run home and hide the diary and the three pages I took from the binder, and the instinctive need to be there when the detective shows up.

Chloe's parents approach the coffee table with curiosity, then take a seat on the sofa. Mr. Avery is the first to open the binder and flip through its few remaining pages, while his wife watches over his shoulder. Then he closes it and pushes it across the table in a gesture of frustration.

"Why would anyone waste their time obsessing over being kidnapped or disappearing or being killed? I don't get it." Mr. Avery resumes pacing the room, throwing me a cold glance in passing. He stops in front of the window overlooking the street, now shrouded in darkness. A lonely, yellow lamppost sheds some light over the cul-de-sac, its bulb wearing a halo of thin fog.

Dr. Avery takes the binder and opens it, then wipes a tear

from the corner of her eye. She's absorbed in reading the letter. I haven't had a chance to read it yet, but I'm anxious to, desperately so.

"May I join you?" I ask, and she pats the sofa next to her without taking her eyes off the page. I sit as close to her as I dare and try to read Chloe's letter from a distance, but it's too far. I watch the expression on her face closely, and there's nothing to tell me the letter mentions me in any way. There's no disappointed glare, no tearful accusations. Nothing, just a mother worried sick over the disappearance of her child. Her pain echoes in my weary heart, dangerously close to filling my eyes with tears.

She flips through the pages slowly, reading and studying everything Chloe put in there that I didn't take. "Do you know who this is?" she asks, pointing at the athlete with the gold medal hanging from her neck.

I look, but don't see the picture she's pointing at. My eyes are glued to a bit of paper still clinging to one of the binder's rings: physical evidence that at least one page has been torn out.

I struggle to control the panic that rages through me. After throwing the picture a quick look, I shake my head. "No, I don't." Sweat bursts into small beads at the roots of my hair. Who is that girl, and how is she connected with me? I'm not usually that self-centered, to assume that everything is about me, but the first three pages were. What am I missing? Is she someone else Chloe's trying to destroy with her baseless finger pointing, like she's doing with me?

Dr. Avery turns the binder toward Ray. "Do you know who she is?"

Ray looks at the photo from a distance, squinting in the dim light, then grabs the binder and sets it in his lap to study it closely. Without taking his eyes off the page, he finds the scrap of paper and tears it off discreetly with the tips of two fingers, then rolls it into a small ball and drops it on the floor, unnoticed by Dr. Avery or her husband.

I breathe again, wondering what I just witnessed. Did he already know about the binder, and having me search for it was just a strategy to help me save myself? Or am I imagining things?

Is he involved in her disappearance?

I look at him, and for a brief moment, our eyes meet. What I see in them rattles me.

"I don't know her," Ray says, handing Dr. Avery the binder. He seems a bit pale, his jaw clenched tightly, his shoulders stiff. "Seems my wife has secrets. I'm a little surprised."

"You and me both," Dr. Avery replies, turning another page. She scans quickly over the list of account names, logins, and passwords. "When she told me about this, I couldn't believe it. Why would she do this?"

"Because of me, I guess," I venture, my voice a little hesitant. "She knew I had one and knew why. We were high school seniors when Flavia Guzman was taken, and later found dead, before the police were able to gain access to her phone." I hear Dr. Avery's breath catch in a quiet whimper as I speak of the girl's death. "This is an excellent way to prevent that from happening," I say, with a slightly trembling voice.

I still believe the binder can save lives, although my confidence is shaken after seeing my project weaponized to blame innocents, to use as a revenge tool. I'm deeply upset to see the turmoil it has inflicted on Chloe's loved ones. And on me. For the first time in ages, I wonder if it does more harm than good.

"Yeah, I understand," Chloe's mom whispers, shaking her head as if to disprove her own words. She turns the page and looks at the three-by-four picture of the street with cars parked along the curb. From a distance, it looks eerily familiar, but I have to see it up close again to figure out what it is.

She closes the binder but continues to hold it.

"May I?"

"Of course," she replies, offering it to me. Casually, I start flipping the pages one by one, planning to go back and read Chloe's letter after I've left new fingerprints on all the pages, and after I've checked that last picture. Something about it is gnawing at me.

I'm just about to flip through the second page when the doorbell rings.

It's too late. Detective Fernandez is here.

I close the binder and stand, nervously waiting for Mr. Avery to open the door and invite him in.

The first thing he does is gawk at me, thankfully without any verbal sarcasm to go with it. I hand over the binder and look him straight in the eye. "Please read the letter carefully. Chloe intended for you to understand her, to know a bit more about who she is. She believed it would help you find her."

He keeps staring at me, and I can see the cogs turning behind his dark eyes. He can't figure out how I'm connected to all this, and, honestly, neither can I. I believed with all my heart that Taylor's disappearance was about money. Now, after Chloe has been taken, I don't know. It could be about money too, but it would be one hell of a coincidence.

"Any news about Taylor?" I ask, cringing as I realize my question is in very bad taste. Asking about one missing child in the presence of another's parents, that's a faux pas if there was ever one. But I can't help myself; it's my only chance of finding out.

His scrutinizing gaze becomes colder, steelier. "No. Nothing yet." His voice is just as cold. He opens the binder and reads a few lines from Chloe's letter, then starts flipping through the pages.

Mr. Avery is looking at him, concern digging trenches on his forehead. "And you're going to hand out all your family's financial information to the cops?" he asks Ray, his voice riddled with disbelief and disappointment.

Crossing his arms, Ray draws a little closer to his father-in-law. "It's what Chloe wanted."

Fernandez doesn't seem to care about the exchange. After turning a couple more pages, he sets the binder on the dining room table, slides it closer to where the ceiling lamp draws a bright white circle on the lacquered surface, then squints at that last photo I never got a chance to see properly.

Then he looks straight at me. My blood freezes in my veins.

"Was anyone alone with this for any length of time?" His question is punctuated by two fingers tapping against the open binder.

"No." Ray's voice is determined.

"And you're sure about that?"

My heart is thumping in my chest. I can barely breathe. What's he getting at?

"Yes, I am." Ray takes a step forward, but Mr. Avery touches his elbow as if to curb his rising ire.

"What is this about?" Mr. Avery asks. "If you have any concerns, now is the time to voice them. But I can assure you, my son-in-law had nothing to do with this."

"No concerns. Just doing my job." Fernandez is a worse liar than I expected. I see on Ray's face he doesn't believe him either. "Where were you today when your wife was taken?"

Ray scoffs and presses his lips together for a moment, probably appalled at being considered a suspect. "In a departmental meeting, with about eight witnesses. It started at eight in the morning and didn't end until one." He's glaring at the detective, fuming. "You have the damn binder. Do you need anything else before you start looking for my wife?"

Fernandez doesn't reply; he just turns and makes for the door. Before heading out, he looks at me one more time, a long, heavy look that gives me the chills. As if to tell me he's on to me.

Only I've done nothing wrong. Except tampering with evidence and obstructing justice, but there's no way he knows about that. And what justice? All I obstructed was the perpetuation of the lies she put in her binder.

When the door closes behind him, I'm a nervous wreck. I whisper my goodbyes and words of encouragement and head home, looking down the entire time, as if there were people on the street who could see right through me. Fog is rolling in, and I feel its silent, ghostly chill in my bones as I unlock the door.

Daniel's not home. His keys are not in the copper bowl, and the house is shrouded in dark stillness. I lock the door and rush to close all the curtains before I head into the bedroom and take off my jacket.

As I extract the diary from the sleeve and the three torn pages from the inside pocket, heavy sobs erupt from my chest. Crouching on the floor, I nestle my head on my folded arms. Leaning against the bed, I let it all out: all the tears I managed to keep locked in for so long.

Why? Why is this happening to me? Where is Taylor, and how is Chloe connected? Why was she taken? And why was she pointing at me in that binder?

Heaving spasmodically, unable to breathe, I wish I'd never heard that true-crime podcast, never spoken about the binder on television. It's brought me nothing but sorrow.

After a while, my tears run dry, pushed away by the urge to look at the photos I took of all the pages I didn't steal. I have to rush; soon Daniel will be home, and by then, I have to look and behave as if everything is all right.

Checking the time has the effect of a kick in the rear: it's almost ten, closing time at the diner.

I squint a little while reading Chloe's letter on my phone. It's not the best of images. Dark, a bit blurry and grayish, which makes reading a difficult task. She goes on and on about how she's asking the detective to find her and apologizes to Ray for hiding the binder. Promises everyone she'll fight back and survive. As with everything Chloe says and does, it's wordy and overly dramatic.

I don't need to study the Miramar selfie, or the threatening letter Chloe received. I have one just like it. But I take my time reading the newspaper article clipping. That's scary as hell. Seems a witness has surfaced, some tourist who visited Half Moon Bay eleven years ago and saw Nikki's fall from a distance. She went back home to Wisconsin without telling anyone what she saw, not wanting to talk to the cops for some reason. But when she returned for another visit this year, she asked about Nikki's murder, as she calls it in the article. She says she saw what happened, and that Nikki was killed. Her fall was not an accident. And the police now have her testimony on record.

Bile rises in my throat as I read Chloe's scribble across the page with the article pasted on it. "It wasn't me," she wrote. Well, I was the only other person there. I didn't push Nikki to her death, but the evidence against me is starting to stack up.

I realize that finding the binder and tearing off these three pages has done very little, just bought me some time. Nothing will keep Chloe from running her mouth off to the cops when they find her.

Not unless I find her first.

I slide through the pictures on my phone until I reach the one with the street and parked cars, the last page of Chloe's binder. I enlarge it as much as I can, before it turns too blurry to see anything, and stare at the familiar scenery. It takes me a long moment to figure it out, my heart beating faster and faster as I start recognizing details, pieces of a puzzle that catch the breath in my chest. One of the cars parked along the curb, second farthest in the frame, is my Subaru, part of its tag obscured by a white VW Beetle parked behind it. A strip of red-brick townhouses flanks the right side of the side-walk. At the very far end of the street, a familiar house sprawls on the corner, its yard enclosed with a shadowbox fence.

A guttural wail leaves my chest, echoing in the somber stillness of the house.

Chloe knows about Taylor.

TWENTY-ONE

I stare at the photo of my Subaru, parked on Taylor's street, my eyes brimming with tears. How could Chloe possibly know? And why did she point the police in my direction with that photo? How is this relevant to her disappearance?

A tear splashes on the screen of my phone, but I don't take notice. Memories rush into my mind, overwhelming me with the agony they kindle. Some things I've buried deep inside the most hidden crannies of my heart, too painful to think of. Others I've kept reliving, over and over, doubting myself, blaming myself.

That February, eleven years ago, when Ray and I parted ways at a small café on Main Street, I thought the worst of the pain would soon be over. When he drove off that parking lot, I believed only healing would come, even though it didn't always seem possible. Yet I survived, one day after the next, slowly emerging from the bottomless pit of despair his cheating had thrown me into. I couldn't afford to miss school, not when planning to go to Berkeley in the fall. I needed to graduate without issues and be gone, away from seeing Ray and Chloe every day, from hearing her telling stories I kept taking in, as if a glutton for torture.

As if to make sure I'd never forget Ray's betrayal.

Days melded together in a slew of sorrow and avoidance and lies, each lie a little bit easier to tell than the ones before, as I was weaving an alternate reality where I didn't have to explain anything to anyone or deal with my pain. Where I pushed everyone away.

That's why I didn't realize the worst of the heartache was yet to come. Ray and I were not over, not really. How could we be over, when a part of him was growing inside me?

I didn't believe it, at first; I couldn't. I spent weeks in denial, counting days, making excuses for being late. Blaming a resilient stomach bug for my morning sickness and lying to my mother, swearing I'd visited the local walk-in clinic to get looked at. I studied hard, keeping busy was a convenient escape from reality, and passed my finals with excellent grades, making Mom proud.

Only I knew there was little else for her to be proud of. If she had found out I was pregnant, she would've been so disappointed.

Everyone knew us in Half Moon Bay. I drove all the way to Milpitas, about an hour away, before I could summon the guts to enter a drug store and buy a pregnancy test. Then I couldn't wait to get home. I found a Starbucks and did the test in the restroom. Two clearly defined lines had me sobbing in there until the manager pounded on the door, threatening to call the police if I didn't leave.

I thought I was getting over Ray. I wasn't.

I never will.

Weeks passed by, bringing sunny, warmer days and the prospect of graduation closer. With the new life growing in my belly, surreal, illogical hope bloomed too. If Ray knew I was pregnant, he'd dump Chloe and... what, exactly? Marry me?

Embrace the future as a nineteen-year-old dad, forgoing Stanford and all his dreams?

I never once stopped to ask myself why I'd be willing to take Ray back after he cheated on me. I just knew I loved him. In retrospect, I can't blame anyone or anything else for wishing he'd come back to me, not even the hormones raging through my body.

So, I started hanging out with Chloe and him, accepting all the invitations with a smile, learning to hide my feelings just like I was hiding my expanding waistline under a newly acquired taste for wearing oversize sweatshirts and San Francisco Giants jerseys. Those days, as I watched Ray and Chloe hold hands on long walks by the cliffs, I remembered his words the day we broke up: "I can't believe you're giving up so easily. I thought you'd fight for me."

I should've fought for him. I should've told Chloe to go to hell and stay away from me and Ray.

But maybe it wasn't too late. I didn't have a plan; I only had faith.

The week before graduation, I ran into Ray in the schoolyard. I was coming from the cafeteria, and he from the tennis courts. His hair was falling over a soaked sweatband that ran across his forehead. He wore one of those mesh-like moisture-wicking T-shirts and carried a tennis racket in his hand, flipping it in the air every few steps.

He didn't see me coming: he nearly bumped into me. The racket clattered on the ground, but he didn't care. He looked at me with a yearning, unspoken, urgent desire glimmering in his blue eyes.

I got lost in them, a deep longing engulfing me and making me crave his touch. "Ray," I whispered, fighting the urge to draw closer to him, to become lost in his embrace.

He tucked a strand of my hair behind my ear with a soft gesture, then cupped my cheek in his hand. I leaned into it, aching for more. "Alana... I miss you," he said, drawing closer to me, frustratingly slowly.

"Ah, there you are," I heard Chloe say. He pulled his hand away and I took a step back from him, turning my head to see where Chloe was. She approached quickly, a wide smile on her lips and a spring in her step. "I was waiting for you two. Come on, let's go."

She dragged us shopping that afternoon, then Ray made some excuse and left. Chloe took me to dinner at one of the many seafood places that line the coast with oceanfront patios and space heaters and strings of lights. She downed a couple of glasses of wine without touching her clam chowder, avoiding my glance.

And then she flat-out threatened me. "Some problems are so easy to eliminate, they're not even worth the effort," she said, finishing her wine, then ordering another. "Just a change of perspective, a minor detail remembered, a new fact uncovered, and poof! The problem is gone forever, locked up somewhere far, far away." She stared at me for a while, and added, "I've fallen in love with Ray, Alana. It's serious this time. He's my soulmate."

It crushed me. Faced with the enormity of the threat, I realized I didn't have a choice but to let her be his soulmate instead of me.

I could never tell him about the life growing inside me. All I could do was walk away and never look back. Otherwise, Chloe would point her manicured finger at me, and I would go to jail for Nikki's murder.

She was too drunk to drive that night, so I drove her Benz and delivered her safely on her parents' doorstep. She sobbed in the passenger seat, apologizing to me and, at the same time, renewing her threats in inebriated gibberish. I pretended everything was fine, despite being heartbroken and secretly grateful we were two days away from graduating.

Then I went home and retched until I couldn't move, the cold tiles on the bathroom floor my only comfort. Mom was working late as she always did those days, killing herself slowly to make ends meet.

I wasn't going to disappoint her. That night, while lying there, sobbing unconsolably, I made my decision.

The following afternoon, after school, I drove over the mountain, heading to San Jose. I remembered seeing a highway billboard with a cheesy message, southbound on I-280. I didn't recall the words exactly, but it pertained to girls like me. Girls without options.

I was almost five months pregnant.

The billboard came into view after a wide, left turn of the interstate, right before the Santa Clara exit. It showed a mother holding her newborn baby, the picture so powerfully emotive it brought tears to my eyes. The text read, "Pregnant and alone? We can help." And a phone number I kept repeating until I was able to stop on the ramp and jot it down.

I called before I had a chance to change my mind. The receptionist was friendly and supportive and gave me an address in Santa Clara, saying I shouldn't wait before coming to see them. They always made time for young girls who needed help.

I was grateful for that. Ten minutes later, I entered a small, single-story building. A sign above the entrance read, "Westhaven Adoption Agency," the letters chipped and aged. The woman behind the small reception desk smiled encouragingly and asked for my name.

I shook my head and took a step back; I wasn't ready for that. She understood, and her kind smile reassured me. All she wanted to know was how far along I was, and I told her. Five months. I remember rubbing my belly with my hand, obsessively, soothing the kicks my baby decided to deliver at that exact moment. Then she said she was getting Mr. Patel, the agency's owner, to speak with me.

In retrospect, I should've wondered why, in the state that has you waiting for weeks for an appointment, any appointment, this man was available on a dime to someone who'd just walked in. But wisdom isn't something teenagers are blessed with. I didn't ask myself that question; I was just relieved it was happening quickly.

Nischal Patel was thirty-something years old and extended me a business card that identified him as an attorney. He was dressed in a dark suit and gray shirt, no tie. Polite and deferential, he invited me into his office.

I took a seat where he pointed and listened to what he had to say. He'd arrange for my baby to be adopted by a good family. The adoption would be sealed, and my healthcare costs would be covered during the pregnancy, delivery, and postnatal care. He'd ask his obstetrician to take a look at me and conduct some exams. An ultrasound, blood tests, nothing to be concerned about. If I couldn't stay home for the remainder of my pregnancy, he'd set me up in a nice apartment there in Santa Clara.

Then he stood and opened a safe tucked behind a picture on the wall and extracted a thick, white envelope filled with cash. Five thousand dollars to get me through until I was due.

And I took it.

After signing a heap of papers I didn't read, I left, arranging to return in a couple of days, grateful I had an option now, trying not to heed the desperate cry inside my heart.

Then I told more lies, big ones, without flinching. I told my mother I was going to Europe with Chloe for the summer. In fact, it was half a lie, the way I learned the best lies are; a core of rot wrapped in a shiny layer of truth. Chloe was going to Europe for the summer. That much was true. Only she was going with Ray, not me.

Then I asked Chloe to cover for me, to say I was with them.

She gave me a bit of a long stare, then winked and gave me a hug when I told her I wanted to spend the summer with a guy I'd just met. It was the perfect lie to tell her.

Saying goodbye to Ray was excruciating. He stared at me in disbelief when Chloe told him what I was planning to do, in unforgiving words that still reverberate in my mind. "Alana is going to get seriously laid this summer," she said. "She and her voracious new man will do a camping tour of the United States and explore every inch." She elbowed Ray, who kept on looking at me, the hurt in his eyes unbearable. "Of each other," Chloe added, bursting into sparkling laughter.

I didn't understand then, and I still don't now. Why did Ray cheat on me, if he looked at me like that? Why didn't he say something? Do something? Stop me, right there and then?

As Chloe and I had arranged, a few days later she picked me up to "leave for Europe together." I hugged my mom with tears in my eyes, at five in the morning, in front of our tiny place. Then we drove to the San Jose airport, where we parted ways. Chloe and Ray took a flight first to Los Angeles, then nonstop to Paris, while I took a cab to the adoption agency and waited on the doorstep for Mr. Patel to show up.

The attorney had a slimy feel about him, but I wasn't surprised. His line of work must've required it. As promised, he gave me the keys to a studio apartment and drove me there. It was a dreary building, smelling of food and stale smoke and weed. Loud arguments resounded from the floor above, in a language I didn't recognize, punctuated by slammed doors and stuff getting broken. In the studio apartment, roaches fled up the wall and hid behind the kitchen cabinets the moment I turned on the lights.

The bed had no sheets, and the mattress showed stains that looked as if someone's water had broken there. There was a small TV that worked, covered in a thick layer of dust. And there wasn't any toilet paper in the bathroom, I noted, making a mental shopping list.

The place was terrible. But it wasn't going to be forever.

I couldn't wait for Patel to be gone, so I said everything was fine. He gave me another one of his cards so I could call him the moment I went into labor and made me an appointment with his obstetrician for the following morning.

Dr. Das was an older woman who seemed patient and kind and understanding. She worked in a large hospital, her presence there relieving some of my anxieties about what was to come. I'd feared that if the healthcare matched the apartment, I wouldn't survive giving birth. She listened to the baby's heartbeat, then performed an ultrasound, turning the screen so I could see the baby in my womb in a black and white, grainy picture. Seeing that bit of life kicking and moving inside me sprung tears from my eyes. But then Mr. Patel shook his head at her, and she turned everything off with a sigh.

"It's a girl," Dr. Das said, "and she's perfectly healthy. She'll be due in mid-October. Blood tests will take a few more days, but I'll call you if anything needs attention. You need prenatal vitamins," she added.

But I'd stopped listening a while ago.

A girl.

Would she have blue eyes like Ray's?

And what would I name her?

Later, after making the bed with new sheets and finally lying down, I realized I wouldn't. She wouldn't be mine to hold and love.

She'd be gone.

It was a long summer, with hot days that heightened the smells in my building. I had arranged with a service to deliver food, and I never left the apartment. The risk of someone seeing me wasn't something I was willing to gamble on. I spent my time reading, watching TV, and wishing it was over already, so I wouldn't feel my little girl kicking vigorously, eager to be born and live and thrive.

I'd written a letter to Berkeley, asking them for an exception to my mandated semester start mid-August, spewing more lies: a sob story about my father dying of pancreatic cancer. Of course, they fell for it, and by mid-July they'd approved me to start in the winter semester, with the possibility to take the classes I had missed in other programs, until I was fully caught up. I wasn't due in school until January 9, when the winter semester started.

Every now and then I called my mom, instilling my voice with the enthusiasm and the joy of a carefree tourist wandering through Europe. Internet research gave me a vast collection of images to text her, none with me in the frame. She never asked... probably too weary from working two jobs for so many years.

Then one night in September, about five weeks early, my water broke, the contractions so painful they sucked the air out of my lungs and left me curled up in a ball, writhing. I called Mr. Patel, but the call went straight to voicemail. Unable to handle it much longer, I called a cab and gave the address of the hospital where Dr. Das worked.

My little girl was born at half past midnight. They wrapped her and put her in my arms, and my chest swelled. She grabbed my finger with her tiny hand and held on tightly, with unex-pected strength. About an hour later, she found my breast and started feeding.

Mr. Patel found me dozing off, my little girl in my arms. Daylight had filled the room with the promise of a gloomy, gray-skyed morning.

Without asking, he grabbed her and headed out the door.

"No, please, let me hold her a little longer," I cried, but he didn't stop. "No," I sobbed, getting out of bed with difficulty, my body sore and aching. But I didn't care. Touching the walls for balance, I followed him down the long corridor, then took a different elevator downstairs, just fast enough to see him loading my little girl into a child seat in his car.

Desperate I was going to lose her forever, I staggered outside and flailed my arms, not realizing I was a scary sight in the bloodstained hospital gown that was starting to come undone. But a cabbie stopped and picked me up, an expression of infinite pity on his face. He was grizzled and about fifty years old, with a kind smile that showed he understood more than I thought.

"Where to?" he asked.

"Follow that black sedan," I said, pointing at the attorney's car. "Don't let him see you."

"Uh-huh," he replied, then threw me a side glance. "You have money?"

I clasped my hands together. "I promise I'll make good. I have money at home. I will pay you, I swear."

Without another word, he started driving, following Patel's car from a distance across Santa Clara, then north on the interstate, and finally over the mountains into Half Moon Bay. I watched with my hand covering my mouth as his sedan came to a stop in front of a large, waterfront mansion. He took my little girl out of the car seat and rang the bell. The door swung open immediately, and a couple stepped outside to greet him. The woman, her features indistinguishable from a distance, welcomed my baby into her arms with a wide, loving smile.

For a moment, I thought of calling the cops. Something in what Patel had done had to be illegal, and they'd give me my baby girl back. But then I realized she'd be better off with them than me.

I had no means to raise her. They could give her a life worthy of a princess: safety, good schooling, a loving family. A mother *and* a father.

"Let's get out of here," I said, my chest heaving as I sobbed into my hands.

He nodded and drove off. "Where to?"

A simple question with a very complicated answer. "If you'll give me some more of your time, I would appreciate the help. The hospital first, then an apartment in Santa Clara, then back to Half Moon Bay."

He threw me a quick look in the rearview mirror. "Was that your baby?"

All I could do was nod, choked with tears.

He reached over to his meter and turned it off. "I'll take you where you need to go."

I found my purse in the hospital nightstand, just where I'd left it. At the apartment, though, whatever was left of the five thousand was gone, vanished from the bathroom cabinet where I'd stashed it. Perhaps the neighbors had seen pregnant women sheltering in that crummy apartment before and knew to go rummaging for cash right after the ambulance drove off. Or Patel might've taken a refund: I wouldn't have put that past him. Either way, there was nothing I could do.

When my mother came back from work that night, she found me lying down on the sofa, still wearing the bloodied hospital gown, crying.

I couldn't lie to her anymore. Wrapped in her soothing arms, I told her what happened, all of it.

Ray. Chloe. My little baby girl.

I was blinded by grief, thrown into an emotional turmoil that had me plead with my mom to help me get my little girl back, then voice strong arguments against it, because at least then she'd have a father. And money. A chance at a wonderful childhood.

Not like the one I had.

Slowly heeding the voice of reason coming from my mother's trembling lips, I agreed to go on with my life without her.

I let my baby go.

TWENTY-TWO

Daniel's key turning in the lock pulls me away from reliving the vale of tears that was my youth. Startled and anxious, I wipe my eyes quickly against my sleeve, stashing the binder pages in the diary and hiding it in my nightstand drawer, under some lingerie.

Then I meet Daniel in the living room with the best smile I can muster.

He looks tired. His face is drawn, and when I reach up for a kiss, I pick up the smell of fries and garlic butter, the two biggest mainstays at Dan's Diner. His lips are cold, and his eyes veer away from mine after merely a split second.

"Did you find it?" He takes off his jacket and hangs it on the hook next to the one I wore earlier, his back turned to me.

"The binder? Yes, I did. It's with the cops now."

He shoots me a quick glance. "Anything interesting in it?"

I shrug awkwardly. And I lie. "Nope, just the normal stuff. A letter to the cops, begging them to find her, samples of her DNA and fingerprints, that kind of stuff."

"Well, her husband should be happy then," he throws in passing, taking off his shoes.

"Relatively, yes, because she's still missing. Her parents were relieved too. They were both there," I add, and watch Daniel's reaction to my words. Less tension in his shoulders, a fleeting smile on his lips. He's relieved.

"Are you hungry?" I ask the pointless question I repeat every night.

"Nah... just tired. I'll take a shower and go straight to bed."

This time I don't plead with him to watch a movie with me or sip a glass of wine while we watch the evening fog rolling in.

While he's in the shower, I retrieve Chloe's diary and hide it in the bookcase. As soon as he climbs into bed, I close the door to the bedroom, grab the diary and the pages, and take my usual reading seat on the sofa, where the lamp is on.

For a while, I listen to the perfect silence that engulfs the house, disrupted at times by Daniel's distant, occasional snoring. With that silence comes anguish, rekindled by what I just learned from the last picture in Chloe's binder.

She knows about Taylor. I can't imagine how. No one knew, except for Mom, who's been gone for six years this November, after losing a battle with breast cancer. And that slimy lawyer knew about it, but he stood to lose a lot if he talked. It's safe to assume he didn't.

Then how does Chloe know? Anxiety grips my gut with iron fingers and twists mercilessly. If she knows Taylor is my daughter, she must know Ray is her father. I can only hope she won't fear that little girl as she feared me, because I know first-hand what monsters Chloe's fear can breed. Just thinking of it makes me shudder, then gasp at the possibility she kidnapped Taylor.

But why? It makes no sense at all.

I shake my head, unconvinced my theory has any merit. Scrolling through the pictures I took with my phone, I stop at the newspaper article clipping and read it again. What if someone from Nikki's family read that article too and spoke with the witness? And what if that witness pointed at Chloe as Nikki's killer? She could've been taken in an act of revenge, by someone close to Nikki, someone with nothing left to lose. Like a parent, for example, or a sibling.

She could be dead.

Whatever the reason Chloe is missing, if she's still alive, I have to find her before anyone else does. Otherwise, everything I've done, the stolen diary, the pages torn from the binder, won't mean a thing when she'll start spewing her lies to the cops. Her lies and some truths too: like telling them there was much more to the binder than they were given. Oh, she'd be so eager to throw me under the prison bus for that one.

Just like eleven years ago, the tendrils of Chloe's manipulations clutch me in their grip, suffocating me, sending me into a state of sheer panic. Where is she? Who took her? How is her disappearance connected with Taylor's? Is Ray involved in any of this? And how can I find her before Fernandez does?

The answer must be hidden somewhere in her diary. Knowing her, she must've said something in there about every single detail, no matter how minute, of her daily life. If her kidnapper crossed her path in the past, if it was someone she knew, they'll be in these pages.

I fold my legs under me and wrap a soft blanket around my shoulders, getting ready for a night of reading, and at the same time dreading it, as if I'm about to stare into an abyss filled with snarling monsters. I open the diary and turn the page to the first entry, dated at the beginning of our senior year in school. Bewildered, I start reading.

I hate her.

Whenever she's around, it's like I'm straight up invisible.

Why, though? She's so basic, just... totally meh. Her hair's that typical brown shade, straight-up flat with zero vibe, and she's out here like makeup is her enemy or something. Some-

times, no lie, she smells of stables. Those hands? So rough. And her nails? As basic as they come. I seriously doubt she'd ever had a mani before I treated her to one—consider it my good deed for the year.

Today was the most eye-opening, when the new guy showed up in class. From North Carolina or something like that. Okay, so he's kinda fire. Has that whole mysterious thing going on, bad-boy vibe and all. And those eyes? Hello, heart palpitations! Totally swoon-worthy. Every girl is gonna be all over that. They better step off, though.

Ugh... he literally breezed by me, without even a look, and was all about her. Like, hello? Am I a ghost? He was all chatty with Miss Plain Jane who's shoveling pony manure and shunning makeup.

I'm chillin' for now. Once Mr. North Carolina realizes he's been hanging with the farm girl for too long, I'll be right here, ready to show him what a real Cali girl is about. That switch-up is gonna be happening really fast.

At lunch, I totally "bumped" into him, and I swear, he was picking up what I was putting down. He even held my tray while I was "looking for something" in my bag, and our hands? Total spark when he passed it back—

I close the diary, unable to read more. Chloe's words are hurtful, stabbing me like daggers. And the paragraph about her and Ray in the cafeteria that day is a total fabrication. It didn't happen the way she described. I remember it clearly, because it was the first time someone made me feel special. I'd lived through high school entirely in Chloe's shadow, almost resigned to being her nonthreatening sidekick. But Ray didn't hold her tray that first lunch at school. He was with me the entire time, not even looking in her direction.

Why would she lie to her own diary?

Perhaps her mind contorted the truth until it became a

better version of the facts, some alternate reality she could actually live with. I shouldn't frown on it, though, since I've lied to myself on more than one occasion too. Although I like to think I never twisted the facts; just my emotional responses to them.

Whatever the case, I can't handle it anymore. The resentment seeping from those pages burns me, canceling the few good memories I had of my youth, spread sparsely among all that heartbreak. Now they're forever tainted, while I'm left here wondering why she pretended to be my friend. Was my Plain Jane presence reassuring to her? Did she need to shine even brighter, and I was there for contrast?

A sigh leaves my chest, making its way out between clenched teeth. How I wish they hadn't moved next door. I'd do anything if I could erase the past few months from existence.

Life doesn't work that way, unfortunately. We can't go back when present events leave us shattered and desolate. I will still have to read whatever's in that diary. Wherever she is, I must find her before anyone else.

I don't think past that point. I don't waste time wondering what I'd say to her, what I'd do. Instead, I pull up the photo album in my phone and scroll to the picture I took of her account details.

It's time for some cold, hard numbers, because the words deceive.

I tiptoe to the small desk in the corner of the living room, afraid the hardwood might squeak and wake Daniel. I fire up my laptop, impatiently waiting until it starts, then, in a new private browser window, load the details for Chloe's bank account. "Follow the money," they say on all good true-crime podcasts. I'm about to, the enormity of what I'm doing pushing my heart to beat faster and faster.

The online banking screen loads, displaying multiple accounts, just as I was expecting. She's doing more than okay financially. All her credit card balances are zero. She has investment portfolios and high-yield savings accounts.

And no mortgage payment.

I scroll back through her transactions, seeking the cash payment she must've made for the house next door, only it's not there. Probably Ray paid for it or perhaps her parents.

There are no cash withdrawals, no check payments to anyone, nothing that I could use as a lead to find who took her. There are no transactions on any of her accounts since yesterday morning, when she used her credit card at Starbucks for $12.63.

Frustrated, I log off, suddenly chilled by the thought the cops might be watching her accounts and notice the new login. They have the technology to track those things. In a state of panic, I erase the browser memory the best I know how, clearing the history, cookies, and all that, and stop short of taking the laptop to the backyard trash can and setting it on fire to hide what I've done.

What the hell was I thinking? This situation is driving me insane with worry, with fear, and with anger at the same time. Makes me do stupid things.

But the worst thing that's killing me is Taylor being gone. While she was safe with her posh adoptive parents, I could talk myself into believing it was best for her this way. But now, I don't even have the legal right to call Fernandez and ask him why the hell he's not finding my little girl.

I'm on the brink of madness.

TWENTY-THREE

Morning finds me dozing on the sofa, wearing pajamas and wrapped in a blanket, still freezing. It gets cold in the summer some nights, though not often enough to start the space heaters. The noise of the huffing and puffing coffee machine is responsible for awakening me, with Daniel at the controls. Daylight seeps in between partly open curtains and draws sharp lines of sunshine on the floor. It's obvious he didn't want to wake me; there's barely enough light in the kitchen to see what he's doing.

My first thought is one of sheer panic. The diary... where did I leave it? I pat the sofa around me and can't find it. Then, when I push myself up, I feel its hardcover corner poking me in the side.

I breathe. And smile. "Good morning, baby."

He throws me a quick, amused glance. "So you say. But I slept alone last night." He pours coffee into two mugs and brings one to me, then takes a seat by my side. "Did you sleep well by yourself?"

I stick my tongue out. "I'll never tell." It feels good to play our innocent games again, as if a heavy cloud has lifted. Only it hasn't.

As it starts coming back to me, it leaves me breathless. Taylor's missing. Chloe's gone too. Ray... and all those lies in Chloe's binder, and maybe more lies in the diary, lies I haven't discovered yet.

"What's wrong?" Daniel asks, noticing how I turned grim out of nowhere.

The doorbell rings, and I jolt to the side of the sofa. Daniel is at the window, looking out from behind the sheers. "It's that cop," he says, turning my blood to ice. Before I can tell him to give me a moment to get dressed, he opens the door. "Detective."

"Can I come in?" I hear Fernandez asking.

"Sure." Daniel steps aside, concern seeping into his expression. "What can we do for you?"

"I was wondering if you have any surveillance video here," he says, nodding in my direction. I wave at him, painfully aware I'm sitting on stolen evidence. I don't dare move.

"We only have Ring," Daniel says, firing up the laptop I used last night to log into Chloe's accounts. My hands are shaking, as if Fernandez could somehow see what I've done by looking at the device from a few feet away. "What time frame do you need?"

"Let's start with yesterday, about ten in the morning." Fernandez looks around the room, slowly, seemingly taking details in. People like him can tell a whole lot about people just by looking at their house, what furniture they have, what objects they have collected. I don't like his prying eyes. It's as if he's stripping me bare in his mind, but not my body, my entire life. "You have a unique setup here. Just two houses in this cul-de-sac. I bet you have zero traffic."

"Yeah. The mailman and the occasional delivery truck." Daniel is focused on the computer screen, where the warped image captured by the Ring camera shows a part of our driveway and a section of the street behind it. A piece of

Chloe's driveway is captured too, enough to see that none of their cars were there at ten yesterday morning. That doesn't mean anything; their cars could've been in the garage.

Unable to keep my distance, I wrap the blanket around my body, uncomfortable at being seen without a bra. Before I stand, I slip my hand behind me and shove the diary between the sofa cushions. As I get up, I make sure one of the smaller pillows covers that exact spot.

Then I approach the desk, my eyes fixed on the screen, where nothing happens for minutes in a row. "You can fast-forward," I say, curious to see what was captured on our camera, a little disappointed in myself that I didn't think of looking last night. It completely slipped my mind.

Daniel fumbles with the viewer controls, and I can feel he's becoming irritated. My husband isn't very technical.

"Here, let me," I say, reaching for the mouse. He steps aside and pulls up a chair for me, and I sit. I fast-forward, the image of the street changing ever so slightly, shadows shifting as the sun moves, birds flying in and out of view, and the mail truck making quick, cartoonish stops at both houses.

Then, at 11:07, we see Chloe's black Beemer pulling into the driveway.

"Can you freeze that for me, please?" Fernandez asks. I shoot him a side glance, wondering where yesterday's sarcasm and hostility went.

"Showing Chloe's car pulling in?"

"Yes, please." I stop the playback where he wanted, and he takes a picture of the screen with his cell. "Okay, good, let's proceed."

We watch several minutes more of the fast-forwarded video. Daniel paces behind me for a while. Then, probably having lost interest, he walks over to the kitchen. "Want some coffee, Detective?"

"No, thank you," Fernandez replies, not taking his eyes off the screen.

Behind me, Daniel is loading the dishwasher with whatever has collected in the sink, the chore I was supposed to do last night but didn't. I want to ask Daniel to leave it for me to do later. It's the first day of summer break; I have lots of time. But the last thing I want is for us to have housekeeping conversations in front of a stranger.

Instead, I use the opportunity to ask Fernandez the one question I'd ask every minute of every hour if I could. "Any news about Taylor?"

He shakes his head. "Nothing yet."

"How about ransom calls?"

He glares at me for a quick moment. "We can't discuss an active case with non-family members. You're not close family, are you, Ms. Blake?"

His question and the scrutinizing look in his eyes give me shivers down my spine. Could he know I'm Taylor's biological mother? My DNA is on file since Nikki's death, and he must have Taylor's. Yes, it's possible he knows, damn it to hell. But I won't confirm it. Even if he does know, he has no way to be sure I do. The adoption record was sealed. "N-no, I'm not," I stutter. "Just her teacher."

"Then I can tell you this much, and maybe this time you'll understand. I don't have any news about Taylor Winthrop."

The smug son of a bitch. Humiliated and defeated, I feel the burn of tears stinging my eyes.

"There," Fernandez says, touching the screen with the tip of his finger.

It's just a quick glimpse of a truck, the left back quarter flashing by.

I rewind a little, then play it back at normal speed. It's an older model, the faded green paint starting to peel off, as sometimes happens under the fierce California sun and corrosive salty air. The rear panel is dented above the wheel.

"It's an old Silverado," Fernandez says. I freeze the video without him asking. He just nods and takes a picture, showing the time code of the person's arrival: 12:14 p.m.

Then I hold my breath, fast-forwarding until the same truck leaves, seventeen minutes later. It has tinted windows, and I can't see inside. I play it back in slow motion and see that the truck is missing its rear tag.

My heart is thumping in my chest. I've seen this pickup truck before. It's unnervingly familiar. I'm racking my brain to remember where, but I can't.

Of course, I don't say a word about it to Fernandez, just wait for him to be gone.

He's already at the door when I ask, "What was on Chloe's security camera? Did you see who took her?"

Fernandez stares at me for a moment, not bothering to hide his annoyance. "Nothing. The camera was covered in bird poop. The video was unusable."

I frown, finding that a little unusual, but say nothing, and he thanks us and finally leaves.

Whatever I'm thinking, I can be sure he thought of first.

Through the sheers, I watch his gray Dodge Charger leave and turn the corner, then I breathe, relieved. For a moment, standing in front of the laptop, I consider asking Daniel about the truck, then I decide against it. If he knows who it belongs to, he'd immediately call Fernandez and tell him, and I can't risk that. I need to get to Chloe before he does.

Daniel finishes loading the dishwasher and pushes the button to start it, then washes his hands. "You owe me one," he says, walking over as I'm about to turn off the laptop. "Did you find anything?"

"Just a flash of a truck's rear end, no tags, nothing they can use."

"Huh. Interesting."

"Wanna see?" I ask, knowing just which buttons to push to deflate his interest.

"Nah, I got better things to do." He scoops me in his arms and takes me into the bedroom. Moments later, responding mechanically to Daniel's passionate embrace, I find myself trying desperately to forget about Chloe for just a few bloody minutes.

I can't.

There's nothing I can do to find Taylor, but I can still—maybe—save myself if I find Chloe.

The key to her disappearance is buried somewhere in the pages of the diary I tucked between the sofa cushions.

TWENTY-FOUR

Through the window, I watch Daniel's Ford stop at the corner of our cul-de-sac with the signal on, then turn right onto Miramontes Street, heading for the diner. I'm finally alone with my nightmares. Abandoning the nearly empty coffee mug on the kitchen counter, I head straight for the sofa and throw the pillows aside, digging underneath with both hands for Chloe's diary.

Then I curl up on the sofa, ready to start reading, anticipating more hurt while at the same time knowing it can't be avoided.

I flip through the pages and skip a few from the very beginning, where she does little but comment on what Ray looks like and how she can't stand me and I'm the worst. I feel sick.

But I trudge on, pushing myself to turn another page, looking for moments I remember from eleven years ago. I find one entry, dated February 12. That day resonates achingly in my heart. It was the last time Ray and I made love, on the deserted beach by Eel Rock.

I'm 99 percent sure my bucolic bestie got laid today. She was floating around all wrapped in this glow, eyes all dreamy and thoughts scattered, probably replaying what must've been an epic fuck. Ugh... no lie, I'm so over her little love drama. It's been lasting way too long. Gotta sprinkle some of my charm and make Ray see what he's been missing, or I'll seriously never forgive myself for letting such a hottie be wasted on a mediocre lay. He'll get it, I'm not stressing. Just gotta give him a VIP seat when I decide to flaunt my stuff. Blinding, irresistible, it'll have him begging for more.

Stunned, I have to stop reading. My heart is thumping in my chest, aching and aghast, my breath caught in my lungs as if about to turn into a desolate sob.

She knew! All that time, Chloe knew I was dating Ray, she knew I was in love with him, and she still decided to crush me. Oh, I must've been the dumbest little mouse in her game, the master feline barely entertained by how little effort it took to ruin my life.

In my infinite naïvety, I reread the paragraph looking for an inkling that she loved Ray. That she made her pass at him because of her feelings. But no... it was only out of spite. Or lust. Only because she could, and for a moment or three, it felt good to her.

Feeling dizzy, I force myself to breathe and count the seconds, inviting calm to bring relief to my racing thoughts.

She did me great harm eleven years ago and did it on purpose; there's no more doubt about that.

But she might not be done toying with me yet.

I can't explain why she filled both her binder and diary with so many lies. Nevertheless, I have to find her, as much to save her life as to save mine. For that, I must keep on reading, even if it kills me.

After the coffee machine spews out a second cup of coffee

and I take it over to the sofa, I feel the need to wrap the blanket around my shoulders again, even if the sun is high and it's a warm June day. It's as if a chill has taken permanent residence in my body and cannot be thawed.

After a sip of coffee burns my throat but fails to dissipate the shivers, I flip through the pages until I land on the Friday following the last entry I just read. I brace myself, knowing quite well it will get painful to read.

He likes me on top, and I'm game with that!

It took me like a hot sec to have Ray Preston wrapped around my finger. I was rocking a killer outfit today, a navy-blue pleated miniskirt over black lacy thongs and the white silk blouse with those sneaky little buttons. I invited him for a drive and let the top down to invite the breeze in. By the time I reached twenty miles an hour, my skirt's catching air, a button is free, and he's ogling like he's never seen a girl before. I get it... I was practically naked!

I was planning to take that eye candy home and nibble on it for a few hours, thanks to my parents vacationing in Baja, but we didn't last that long. The man's got mad skills. One hand on my thigh, slowly inching higher, and I'm pulling over by the cliffs, ready to kick it in the back seat. But nah, he's more of an outdoorsy type. We went for the bench. The biting cold almost blew it, but that crescent moon setting over the Pacific from my fave bench by the cliffs, and him getting hard under my touch, what a sight!

I could totally fall for him, no effort needed. Seriously. He might be the real deal.

Bitches, beware.

I'm losing my mind.

I can still recall Chloe's excited whispers, dripping poison into my soul with her breathless recounting of sex with Ray on the back seat of her convertible. I can still hear her words as if she's sitting right next to me, drinking hot chocolate and dishing it out, every moan and every sigh and every word spoken between them.

It was the back seat. That's where Chloe said they had sex for the first time. I'm sure of it.

Unlike the cafeteria on Ray's first day, I wasn't there when it happened. When did Chloe lie? When she told me about it, eleven years ago? Or when she wrote about it in her diary? Not that it makes a huge difference *where* they had sex, but, as I'm discovering a Chloe I never knew existed, I'd like to know if I can trust anything she says. Seems I can't.

Reeling, I let my thoughts wander for a moment, but don't like where they're going. Ray wasn't innocent in this whole thing; he still cheated on me. Yet knowing Chloe's role in Ray's betrayal makes me wonder. What my life would have been like with Taylor calling me Mom, instead of some stranger with a nice hairdo and an expensive home on the bluffs. How I would feel if Ray came home to me every night instead of her.

Out of all the irrational ruminations, thinking of Daniel fills me with guilt. All the lies I've been telling him haunt me, starting with the biggest one of all. I love Daniel very much, yet I deny him the child he wants because of Taylor. Because I can't bring myself to get pregnant again, to carry a growing life inside me, knowing I'd be desperately afraid I might somehow lose another baby. It would mean reliving every moment of that dreadful summer, all those years ago.

Without realizing, I put my hand on my abdomen to soothe the sense of wasteland emptiness that has resided within me ever since the adoption lawyer took my baby away. A sob swells my chest when I remember she's missing, held who knows where, scared and lonely and crying.

But she's still alive. She has to be. I would feel it in my heart if she'd left this earth.

It takes willpower to return to Chloe's diary, but I have no choice. Skimming over the lurid details of every romantic encounter she had with Ray that summer, searching for something I could use to find her.

Something I *don't* find gets my attention. There's no entry for April 19, the day Nikki fell to her death from the cliffs. The last entry before that date is five days earlier, something about Ray and Chloe making a beautiful couple. That's actually true, even now. People turn their heads and stare when they enter a room.

But I digress.

The next entry is almost two weeks after Nikki's death. Chloe's exuberance is gone, her snazzy writing style tame, almost somber. I read a few lines, then go back and start over.

I don't know who I am anymore.

A few nights ago, Ray told me he forgives me for what happened with Nikki. He was holding me in his arms, stroking my hair, and said the words that have kept me up at night ever since.

"It's okay, babe, I know it's been hard, but I understand," he murmured. "No matter what happened, I'm here and I love you. Never doubt that."

Those words... they shook me. Does Ray think... does he think I did something to Nikki? How could he even think that? It was just a terrible accident, right?

I never questioned him, but I keep questioning myself, obsessively. I replay the moments before her fall, as if I'm watching a movie from a distance, yet close enough to touch the screen.

Wondering if, maybe, without realizing it, I did do something.

This is my moment of complete and absolute honesty, reserved strictly for these pages.

I hate the hold Alana still has on Ray. Whenever she walks by, he's transformed somehow, and I resent that with every fiber in my being. And Nikki flirted with him shamelessly, knowing damn well he and I were a thing.

Maybe I wanted them both to stay away from Ray, but did I want something bad to happen to them right there, at the edge of the cliffs?

I remember being careful where I stood, making sure I was on solid ground. I love living on the edge, feeling alive, but was I hoping for them to join me and... and fall? How could I want that? I'm not a killer. I remember just enjoying the breeze, the view. And feeling the wind in my hair, there, at the edge of the cliff, what a heady high!

Then, I don't know. Alana said she didn't see Nikki falling, because she was looking at her phone. I didn't see it either, my eyes still riveted on the horizon after watching the green flash disappear.

I remember Nikki joining me by the edge, hooting and cheering, her straw-blonde hair whipping in the wind like she was some skinny, crazed Valkyrie about to take flight over the ocean.

Then her hoots turned into a bloodcurdling scream as she fell.

I didn't do anything. I didn't push her. I was just watching the Pacific waves crashing at our feet, painted in hues of purple and orange, garnished with pink foam.

Alana stood there, blood on her hand from where Nikki scratched her. She said she didn't see anything, but did she do something? That's my question.

Maybe I'm guilty of daring them to join me on the edge of the cliff. But I didn't do anything to Nikki. I know I didn't.

I just hope Ray believes it too.

I stare at the incriminating page, out of breath and shaking.

For an anxious moment, I see myself getting dragged away in handcuffs over Chloe's perjured testimony, screaming from the top of my lungs, "I'm innocent. I didn't do it."

Prisons are full of such stories.

Whatever it takes, I must find Chloe, and somehow make the inveterate liar speak the truth.

Before I turn the page, I realize Chloe took Nikki and me for a walk precisely where she and Ray had sex for the first time.

That's where Nikki died.

TWENTY-FIVE

This new side of Chloe, the symbolic meaning of her actions, is entirely new to me. I've never known her to care much about how she did things. She pretty much did whatever she pleased, when she pleased. Or at least that's what I thought, but it seems she chose a symbolic location, a place with meaning, at least once.

That's only if she was telling the truth about having sex with Ray on that memorial bench by the cliffs. If that's a lie, then the idea of her actions being symbolic is an even bigger lie.

For the heck of it, I assume it was true, and Chloe chose that location because of its meaning. Did she know ahead of time Nikki was going to die there? Hardly, if I'm to believe anything the woman wrote in her diary.

I read some more, faster and faster as I grow hardened enough to absorb lurid details about their love affair without falling apart. A few dozen more pages, and I can paint a clear picture of their relationship.

She might've started the fling with Ray out of spite or curiosity or just plain lust, but by the end of the school year she was in love with him. She changed her major to join him at

Stanford. She referred to him as her soulmate on a couple of occasions. And her jealousy had only grown of me and of any girl who crossed Ray's path.

She kept inviting me to join them, and I cluelessly went. I was heartbroken at the time, secretly pregnant, and still hoping against all reason that Ray would come back to me.

She hated having me around Ray, yet she kept inviting me.

I can't think why, but I have to conclude the behavioral paradox was fueled by a deep sense of inadequacy, the insecurity she felt in all matters Ray. She felt the need to show me he was into her, and to show him I didn't care about him anymore.

The master of the game was pulling the strings, and her puppets danced without even knowing about it.

I pause my reading for a brief moment, while a disconcerting thought blooms in my mind. What would Ray think if he read this? Does he know he's been played? Does he still—

I'm afraid to explore that thought any further, when I recall feeling his breath on my skin just a few weeks ago, and how it felt to hear him say my name. I can't... I won't think about it anymore.

No.

I've made the best out of what was left of me after high school. I went to college and got a degree. I met a nice, kind man who loves me and I married him. I managed to stay close to Taylor, to insert myself into her life discreetly, as her teacher, to watch over her from a distance and still make a difference. My life resembles a *kintsugi* bowl, built from the shards of a once perfectly fine existence, only the lacquer holding the pieces together is not powdered with gold dust, but with tears and resilience and courage. I have it together now, even if some of my cracks are showing, and I cannot let anything, or anyone, crush me again. There would be no coming back from it.

A long moment passes, while I listen to the birds chirping

outside my window, their happy voices endlessly and bound-lessly optimistic.

Then I read on, the next entry dated almost a year later, and find the only cloud looming over their relationship is Chloe's inability to have children. Just like Daniel, Ray seems to want kids very much, and Chloe is increasingly desperate about it. Unlike me, her fertility treatments are not lies she tells her husband. And still, she can't conceive. Reading this helps me understand her reaction when her mother-in-law asked her if she was pregnant yet, at the party in our backyard. She wasn't irritated by Stella's inappropriate comment; she was deeply hurt by it, shattered.

Throughout the years—I read about seven years' worth of sporadic diary entries—her obsession with Nikki's death resurfaces here and there, increasingly seldom, yet equally obsessive and slipping further from the truth with each iteration.

Her perception of what happened that day continued to evolve, gradually shifting toward believing I pushed Nikki off that cliff. I shudder when I read the latest such entry.

I think I know what happened.

How could Nikki have reached out and scratched Alana, if Alana was really standing that far off, glued to her phone like she claimed? It doesn't add up... I bet she pushed Nikki when I was lost in the view, and she wasn't paying attention. That's when Nikki scratched her, trying to clutch on to anything to keep from falling. Like the hand that pushed her.

Dad's money and his lawyers... it's probably what's kept a murderer walking free. How can I live knowing this?

But the why of it all, that's what's eating at me. If it was jealousy over Ray, Alana would've pushed me, right? Then, what's the real reason? It's driving me crazy. Nothing makes sense.

I look at the date, realizing the entry must've been written *before* Chloe found out about Taylor. I still don't know how she could've learned Taylor is my daughter, but, in her warped mind, that might've been one hell of a motive for me to push Nikki off the cliff. She could've thought that I'm out to get all women who were after Ray, perhaps including her. I stare at the diary as if a monster is about to leap off its pages and rip my throat open, knowing at some point I will find the entry that links the pregnancy and the reason why she thinks, in her deranged reality, that I killed Nikki.

But I still haven't found a lead, something I could use to find who took her. I know I should keep on reading, but I can't bear it anymore. Yielding to the sudden urge to find out if there's anything new with Taylor, I hide the diary in my nightstand and drive off to her house.

This time, I stop my car at a distance, looking with fear and frustration at the reporters camped outside the house. Everything I do or say will be reported and twisted and misquoted. Yet I can't let it stop me.

I walk the remaining distance briskly, not giving a crap I left the house in sweatpants and a worn-out shirt, and elbow my way through. Then I stop in front of the door, my hand hovering above the doorbell.

I don't ring it, though. The sheers behind the side window move gently, and Mrs. Winthrop's face appears veiled behind them, pale as a specter. She shakes her head slowly, then turns and walks away. She obviously doesn't want me there, or she would've opened the door.

I give her a minute to change her mind; she doesn't. Pushing back through the horde of reporters, I make my way to the Subaru at a light jog, then drive off fighting tears.

If Monica Winthrop had any news, she would've told me.

My sweet baby girl. Will I ever see her again?

I gasp as doubt slices through my gut, seeding fear and burning every bit of reason in its wake.

The rest of the drive home is merely a moment long, as I don't recall any of it, my weary mind absent from reality while it battles demons and despair.

But as I turn onto our street, I see Daniel's Ford in the driveway.

When I'm reasonably sure I can control the expression on my face, I unlock the door and walk in.

Daniel is seated on the sofa, still wearing his jacket and shoes. He's grim and looks at me with a hint of disappointment in his eyes.

"What's wrong?" I whisper, the silence unbearable.

He doesn't answer immediately but shifts his gaze away from me and toward the floor, his shoulders hunched, his hands clasped together, white-knuckled. "The cops were at the diner today, interviewing everyone."

"Oh." The syllable barely carries any sound as my gut churns, trapping my breath inside my lungs.

"They were asking questions about me and my whereabouts the day your friend Chloe was taken." He looks at me for a brief, intense moment, his eyes colder than usual, almost judgmental. "We're suspects, Alana. We are officially suspects in her kidnapping."

I quiver and have to find a chair to sit on, my knees suddenly weak. At a loss for words, I stare at Daniel as he runs his hand through his hair.

"This entire mess," he eventually says, "is coming from your past somehow. What is it about?" A beat of tense silence. "Or *who* is it about?"

I slowly shake my head, bitterly disappointed in myself as I get ready to spew another lie. "I have no idea."

The truth swirls in my head, a yarn of multicolored threads, each in itself a possibility. Taylor. Nikki's death and that threatening letter. Ray and his unsettling interest in me. Then Chloe's name comes to mind, the one truthful answer that rises above the rest, while the lie I told still echoes in the grim silence of Daniel's disbelief.

Where the hell are you, Chloe?

TWENTY-SIX

Chloe paces the dirty floor, not paying any attention to the squeaky floorboards or to the dust particles dancing in the narrow sunbeam cutting between the door and its frame. It's a rare sight, that sliver of sunshine, and soon to be gone. The cabin is deep in the woods somewhere, the redwoods and cedars so tall and majestic that sunlight rarely touches the ground. The air is charged with the mingling scents of earth and cedar needles, somewhat reminding her of petrichor, although it hasn't rained since she was brought there.

It's a dreary place, and Chloe wonders why anyone would keep it. It's small, barely a room and a carved-out section behind a plastic curtain for a toilet, a chipped grimy tub, and a sink. Only a tiny, barred window lets daylight in. She sometimes stops in front of that window and stares into the distance, where tall, dark tree trunks loom, a dense army of immovable soldiers with gnarly limbs and rugged bark.

If she screams, no one will hear her.

If she dies, no one will know. No one who matters.

The silence is heavy, engulfing like thick evening fog, and absolute. No birds are chirping. Yesterday, she saw a squirrel climbing a cedar tree quickly, as if something was chasing it. Later, she heard a warbler in the distance, and last night, an owl hooted nearby. She shudders when she realizes there might be mice to keep the owl interested.

Chloe wanders through the room again, pacing between the window she has tried opening many times and the door that is locked firmly, not even budging under her weight. Then she stands in the middle of the room, unwilling to sit on the tacky wooden chair or on the mildew-smelling bed she has to sleep on at night.

After a while, she pulls her hair over her right shoulder, running her fingers through its length in an improvised, ineffective comb, patiently disentangling it. The luscious blonde waves have dulled since she was brought here. Several strands give, hanging on her fingers, and she shakes them off and watches them fall onto the soiled floor. Then she quickly weaves her hair into a thick braid and ties it with the scrunchie she always carries in her jeans pocket. Absent-mindedly, she smooths the braid with her hands, her head slightly tilted as she listens intently.

The distant sound of a truck engine draws closer, louder, then dies with a sputter. A door is slammed shut, rattling. Chloe holds her breath and backs away from the door until she reaches the wall. Then, as the padlock outside is unlocked, she steels herself and takes one step forward, straightening her petite stature and thrusting her chin forward.

She's ready to face him.

The door creaks open, and the man comes in, bringing with him the heavy smell of stale fries and fast-food grease packaged in a brown paper bag he drops onto the wooden table.

"There," he says, "that's all you're getting today." She crinkles her nose, but she's hungry. Her body betrays her into craving the food she otherwise despises. When she grabs the paper bag, the man laughs, his voice raspy, his eyes sizing her up with easy-to-read intentions.

Chloe takes a bite of a flattened hamburger, chewing quickly.

"You're welcome." He laughs, reaching to touch her face. She pulls away and flashes an angry glare. His smile wanes. "Ah, so that's how it's going to be, huh?"

She finishes the hamburger and wipes her mouth quickly with the napkin she finds inside the bag, stained by grease already. "Thanks for the burger," she deflects quickly. "It was good."

He takes another step closer. "I can think of a few things that would be just as good," he whispers, the loaded undertones in his voice bringing a chill down her spine. "All of them illegal."

"Really?" She slips past him with a quick lurch and heads for the table. There are fries left in the paper bag, almost cold now, a faintly rancid smell lifting as she pulls them out. "Want one?" she offers, desperate to show she isn't afraid.

He takes a fry and eats it, then wipes his fingers against his jeans. "Not bad."

"Perhaps next time, you could get me something else?" She crumples the paper bag and throws it on the floor.

His hand finds her throat and squeezes it until she gasps for air. "What do you think this is, a fucking date?"

She whimpers and pulls at his hand, but it's like a vise. Slowly, just as she's starting to black out, he lets go and shoves her back against the wall. Air rushes into her lungs, dissipating the blackness in her brain. She breathes deeply a few times while she feels for damage on her throat with trembling fingers. It's sore, and she can't swallow without feeling pain.

Then she looks straight at him, her eyes filling with rage. "You son of a bitch," she says, her voice coarse, choked. "I swear, I'll—"

"You'll what? Make me regret this?" He scoffs. In two large steps, he's next to her, his breath scorching her skin, his hands forcing her shoulders against the wall. "Don't make me testify in front of a jury that you had it coming."

There's a lust for blood in his eyes she's never seen before. Defeated and scared out of her mind, she nods, holding her breath until he lets go. Moments later, she's alone again, the sound of the padlock clicking on the other side of the door reminding her of the choices she no longer has.

All she can do is wait.

And hope.

TWENTY-SEVEN

The afternoon has been tense and gloomy for Daniel and me. Few words were spoken after I told him I had no idea what Chloe's disappearance was about. I still don't; that part is true. But there are many things I should've shared with him, and I still can't, afraid of what it might do to our relationship. I put myself in his shoes and ask myself, what would I choose? To not know if Daniel's former girlfriend was living next door? Or to know, so I could spend my days obsessing over every interaction between them, no matter how innocent?

Ignorance is bliss for a reason.

At about six, I give up trying to lift Daniel's mood with low-key chitchat and a tour of the gossip-worthy celebrity headlines plucked from the day's news. A line was crossed when the cops showed up at the diner. That place is everything to him, all he's ever known since he was fourteen years old and helping his dad, bussing the tables and washing dishes after school with Jason. Daniel's more or less okay with everything happening here, I believe, even with Ray holding my hand out of the blue, or me searching through Chloe's things to find her binder. But having his staff interrogated by cops did a number on him, and it shows.

I wish there was something I could do to fix it, but there isn't. The truth will prevail at some point, as scary as it is for me to admit that, and they'll leave him and his diner alone. He didn't do anything wrong. None of this is about him.

I walk briskly into the kitchen, pretending that everything is fine, and ask, "What would you like for dinner?" I'm actually surprised he hasn't gone back to the diner. It's Friday, the second busiest day of the week. "I can grill us a steak," I say, when silence is the only answer I receive.

He's still seated on the sofa, staring into thin air, seemingly lost in thought, just the way I found him when I got back from Taylor's. He hasn't moved, still hasn't taken off his jacket or shoes. I stop in front of him and stroke his hair. "Hey, baby? Want a steak?"

He lifts his head, and I reel from the anguish I read in his eyes. There's no anger and no suspicion; just immense sadness. Somehow, he knows I lied to him, and this is the effect of it, my dishonesty gnawing at the fabric of our relationship like a cancer, leaving ugly holes that can never be fully mended, even if we both try.

"I have to go back," he eventually says, veering his gaze away.

"They'll do fine without you. It's okay to take the occasional day off, you know." I speak gently, in a soft, warm whisper. "Let's grab a bite, then go out for a walk on the beach to see the sunset." I pause for a moment, seeing his shoulders tense up. "Would you like that?"

He stands, still unwilling to look at me. "Not today." He shoves his hands into his pockets and paces slowly. "Not after the cops have been asking questions. I'd rather our employees don't decide I'm guilty before I'm even charged with a crime."

He's got a point. We live in a world where perceptions are everything. Where someone's off comment, innuendo, or just plain fabrication can render someone a suspect. Or even a convict.

"Then why don't I join you later tonight? We could eat at the diner and end the day with a glass of wine." I draw close and rest my cheek against his broad chest. His arm wraps around me after a moment or two of hesitation. Of him standing stiff and unwelcoming when I touch him, probably wishing I'd keep my distance.

I breathe, the sigh swelling my chest impossible to hold inside. I know I lied to Daniel about getting pregnant, and that's on me. But it wouldn't have happened if Chloe had never come into my life. I hate what Chloe's doing to my marriage, to my life. How her actions and her drama and her lies are threatening everything I am and everything I love. Like a ghastly, ominous reverse Midas, everything she touches turns to ashes.

Only this time, I'm going to fight back to my last breath.

"All right," Daniel eventually says, gently pulling away after placing a quick kiss on my forehead. "Gotta go."

The familiar sounds play in sequence, like a well-known refrain. The door closing behind him. The car engine starting, then waning in the distance as he drives off.

Then silence, with the faint sound of the television running in the background, its volume very close to mute.

I stand, frozen in place, exactly where he left me. Then I find the sofa and sit for a while, on its edge, unwilling to lie back and relax when I feel so deeply threatened, ready to flinch and run at the slightest noise.

A voice I recognize, although it's faint, announces the headlines of the local news. My mind wraps itself around that sound as if it's a vine clinging to a fence post, desperate to hang on to something and grow stronger. The volume is too low, yet I don't look for the remote, still too tired and dispirited to put in the effort to stand and walk over to the kitchen counter.

Then something the anchor says catches my attention. I hold my breath and listen intently.

"—Westhaven Adoption Agency was set ablaze last night, reportedly by this man."

Still holding my breath, I walk over to the kitchen counter and turn up the volume, then draw closer to the TV, squinting at the image to see it clearly. It's a blurry take from a distant surveillance video. The picture shows the silhouette of a man wearing black pants, a gray hoodie, and white sneakers, zoomed in on so closely it's broken into pixels. The hoodie covers his face entirely as he skulks close to the wall, keeping his face down. It's completely useless, but it shows the number for the Santa Clara Police Department, just in case someone recognizes him.

There's no way anyone could.

Meanwhile, the news anchor continues, "The agency owner, Mr. Nischal Patel, made a statement yesterday evening, after the police finished processing the scene."

The screen switches over to the Nischal Patel I remember, his raven-black hair turned silver at his temples, his face showing lines of worry and aging. His eye is swollen shut, and his lip is cracked and bleeding.

"He came in here and straight up punched me," Patel says, speaking with difficulty. Hearing his voice gives me the creeps. "He wanted me to show him where I keep all the adoption records. Then he proceeded to set everything on fire with the gasoline he brought in a gallon jug. You know, the kind you buy milk in, from Costco?" The interview has been edited, because the image flips and Patel is in a different position, holding a white napkin at his mouth as he speaks. "He didn't achieve anything. All our records were digitized a while ago, even the old ones. Everything we do here is documented with digital records, secured with state-of-the-art backup systems."

The image fades, and the familiar anchor reappears,

reporting from the studio. "The agency building was completely destroyed. Fortunately, no lives were lost. Police were not available for a formal statement."

The anchor changes topics and I mute the sound, while everything I just heard reverberates in my mind, seeding sheer panic in every fiber of my body. Feeling dizzy, I drop onto the sofa, pressing my hand on my chest in a pointless attempt to slow the beats of my terrified heart.

There's no doubt left. Everything that's been going on—Taylor's abduction, Chloe's disappearance, and now the adoption agency arson—it's all about me. It has to be. I'm the only common denominator. The cops will have already connected the dots between Taylor's kidnapping and the agency. It will only take them one look at the records to find out I'm Taylor's mother, if they don't already know from the DNA records they've had on file since the day Nikki fell to her death.

It's quite clear to me now, even if it's petrifying. Someone wants me destroyed: framed for murder, for Taylor's kidnapping, maybe even for this arson. That particular someone perhaps wanted to destroy the evidence linking Taylor to me or maybe is leading the cops to find out about it, drawing their attention with an arson that destroyed no evidence and claimed no victims. They even left a convenient witness to say that all records were still available.

If Chloe weren't missing, I'd say she must've been behind this somehow.

Someone out there wants me gone, locked up for crimes I haven't committed, and is willing to do anything, to risk anything, to make that happen.

And I'm nowhere closer to finding Chloe, whose role in all this I can't begin to comprehend. Until she moved next door, we'd lived separate lives for more than ten years. How is she connected to all this?

Is she?

Perhaps the binder and the diary are nothing but evidence of Chloe's obsession with me over Ray.

But she was there with me, having brunch at the Whispers Café when Taylor was taken. It wasn't her.

The doorbell rings and I jump out of my skin. A look through the living room window shows Ray at the door, his hands plunged deeply inside his pockets, the collar of his light jacket raised.

He looks so much like the day I said my goodbye on the patio of that windblown café. Maybe he was wearing the same jacket, or a similar one, but he was shivering just as he is now. I rush to open the door. For a moment, old, forgotten feelings are taking over my weary heart.

I swing the door open and step aside. "Ray," I whisper, my throat dry.

Our eyes lock and there's electricity in the air, an instant connection that can't be denied. That's scary and uplifting at the same time, swelling my chest with heartache yearning to be healed.

"Have you heard anything?" he eventually asks, remaining outside. "About Chloe?"

It's about Chloe. Of course it is.

I shift my gaze, grateful and disappointed at the same time, even a little ashamed. "No. You?"

He shakes his head, looking away in the distance. "I thought maybe she'd call you if she could. Instead of me or her parents."

"Me? Why?" I recall the hateful pages of her diary, but I stop short of mentioning that to Ray. There'd be no turning back until he learned everything, all of it, all Chloe did to me. To us. The finger she's pointing at me for Nikki's death. And Taylor. She knew about Taylor. That has to be in that diary somewhere. I can't fathom what Ray would do if he learned he and I have a child together. A baby girl I gave away.

"I don't know," he replies, looking at me ever so briefly. "I just... thought I'd ask." He stops talking for a while, seemingly undecided about something. "I'm sorry I disturbed you. Good night, Alana."

He looks at me and I lose myself in his eyes, the path to destruction I traveled before, oh-so-familiar, opening in front of me. Without thinking, but yearning for his touch, I offer a handshake. He takes my hand with both of his, holding on to it for a long moment, then taking it to his lips. His breath sears the skin on my fingers, making me restless, aching for more. Yet I find the will to resist, unwilling to take another step, aware how close I'm standing to the edge of the abyss.

He lets go of my hand with regret in his burning eyes. Moments later, the door is closed and locked after he leaves.

And I breathe.

Later, curled up on the sofa with Chloe's diary in my lap, I find it difficult to concentrate, a whirlwind of emotions taking its toll. It doesn't last long, the angst over Taylor's disappearance all-consuming and terrifying.

I can't lose my baby. It would kill me.

And the more I think about it, the more I realize Chloe could have the answer to Taylor's disappearance. Chloe and the person who took her. What if she found out Taylor is Ray's daughter? And mine? What if the two kidnappings are connected, just as Detective Fernandez suspects?

I must find her before it's too late.

TWENTY-EIGHT

Oh, how I hate that woman!

That's the opening phrase of what remains of Chloe's diary, dated only a few months before they moved next door. And the woman she hates is me, no doubt about it.

I'm nearing the end of the filled pages, maybe a couple of dozen or so left to read. I check the time and see I could finish before I have to head out to the diner, like I promised Daniel. Fighting off a shiver, I forge ahead, determined to finish everything she put in these pages.

I don't think Ray's ever truly gotten over her. The ghost of her just hangs around us, making me lose my mind. It's been almost ten years since Ray saw her last. Just yesterday, we were walking down our old chill spot, Miramar Beach, and he saw a girl who looked like her. Same plain clothes, jeans and a sweater and Converse shoes, her ordinary brown hair dancing in the wind. Her back was turned to us, but I could see Ray, his face lighting up, eyes stuck on her. "Could that be Alana?" he mumbled, and, ugh, the way her name rolled off his tongue almost brought me to tears. He rushed forward, pulling me with him, trying to reach her.

He called her name when he got close. She didn't turn. He gently touched her elbow, and she finally did, a look of surprise on her face.

It wasn't her.

Ray said sorry, and she left. It was nothing, but the glimpse of loss, of this deep, unspoken pain in Ray's eyes when he realized it wasn't her, when his hope of seeing her again was shattered... it's haunting me.

I can't shake off the image. I keep asking myself, has he ever looked at me like that? With such raw, unfiltered longing?

When he's with me, is his mind with her? Does he see her face when he touches mine? Does he still taste her lips after our kisses?

If I could give him a child, something she never gave him, perhaps I could still win this battle. Maybe he would finally forget her.

I stare at the half-written page in disbelief. A swell of emotions rushes over me, leaving me gasping for air. I can't believe it... Ray still loves me? Recent memories flood my mind with little moments I'd written off as a twisted game he wanted to play or wishful thinking on my part.

But what if it's true? What if he still cares, despite his cheating? Now that the dust of time has layered ten years over us, I can't help but think he was a nineteen-year-old boy, lured by a beautiful, sensuous, and ruthless predator, and he fell for it. He cheated. And I was quick to punish his betrayal with the ultimate judgment. I sentenced our love to death.

Only our love didn't die. It lived on inside me, where I've been trying my best to suffocate it for the past decade, to no avail. Now I learn it endured inside Ray's heart.

My chest swells with a bitter sob when I recall how he stood there, at the café, stunned and desolate, before he finally walked away.

A lone tear rolls down my face. For what I lost. For what it could've been.

What have I done?

More important, what am I going to do? Still sobbing quietly, I shake my head.

There's nothing I can do. I can't break Daniel's heart. I love him too much for that.

With a long, fractured sigh, I turn another page, sure I'm about to discover how Chloe felt after finding out about Taylor. Right after she wrote that a child was something I never gave Ray, while she still could.

The new page is stained with tears and dated about a month later. It seems to be the last entry, only a few pages long.

I'm... devastated. There's no other way to say it.

I thought I knew everything that went on between her and Ray, but was I in for a jolt... I'm still reeling, still in shock.

We're coming up on our wedding anniversary, and I wanted to surprise Ray with an unusual gift: DNA profiles for the both of us. I thought it would be fun to trace back our ancestries, to see if we came from the same places. I chose the couples package that came with a predictor of how our children would look, with the disclaimer that it was for entertainment purposes only, of course, and that our children could end up looking different. It sounded like innocent, lighthearted fun.

I didn't skimp. I chose the most expensive package, the one with portal access and the ability to view the profiles of people who are related to us genetically, long-lost family members we might know nothing about.

That was the plan, wrapped neatly in all the good intentions I had when I bought it. And it took me straight to hell.

I secretly swiped some of Ray's hair fibers from the bathroom counter and sent in a saliva swab for myself.

As I write this, I realize just how lucky I was that I decided to look at the results on my own, while he was away on a business trip.

I can't even put the words on paper, it hurts so badly.

He's got a daughter. My husband, Ray, has a child.

With her. With Alana, the bane of my existence, the ghost who keeps on haunting me and will haunt me until the day I die.

It's not difficult to figure out the girl is hers. The online portal shows the child's name, her age, and her family tree appears unlinked to Ray's. Her name is Taylor W something, her last name encrypted for privacy reasons. W or not, I still know she's Alana's daughter. She must be. Her age makes Alana the only possible mother, unless Ray was sleeping with someone else while Alana and then I were dating him. It's just not likely. I'd know. I would've known, back then, if Ray was seeing someone else. I would've smelled her on him.

The child's last name initial leads me to believe Alana gave Ray's daughter away for adoption. Must be the only intelligent thing that woman has ever done. She's not fit to be a mother. At least like this, I don't have to worry about her showing up on my doorstep with Ray's daughter in tow, expecting child support.

How many ten-year-old Taylor Ws could there be out there? I'll find her. I want to look at that girl and see Alana's features mixed with Ray's on her face. I want to see the person who could mean the end of me.

I cried all afternoon, mulling over what I should do. Ray can never find out about this. There's no telling what he'd do. Maybe he'd leave me in a heartbeat and beg Alana to take him back, to take both of them back somehow. I know it's not possible to undo an adoption, but I wouldn't put it past Ray to *try. I don't believe that, given a second chance, Alana would graciously bow out and leave Ray to me, like she did in high school.*

No... he absolutely cannot know he's got a daughter out there.

I lit the fire in the old fireplace, then I burned the test result, the folder it came in, the envelope, everything. Then I deleted the family DNA account and cleared the browser history.

When the fire died, the nightmare was gone, burned to ashes. All I can hope is that it stays gone.

And that I can have Ray's child myself, soon. As soon as possible. I've seen the way he looks at couples with children at the mall. At pregnant women. I can only imagine how he'd look at Alana if he learned she had his baby.

I still can't get over the fact she was probably pregnant when Ray and I started dating. She never said anything, never showed how much it must've hurt her to lose him. Or I just didn't care enough to notice.

I still don't. Screw her.

I thought I hated Alana before. Now... I have no words.

Maybe Ray needs to know Alana like I do, as the girl who coldheartedly pushed our friend off the cliff, because she was pregnant with Ray's child, and Nikki had flirted with him after class.

He needs to see her as the murderer that she is.

The last entry in Chloe's diary leaves me dumbfounded. Understanding washes over me, leaving few questions unanswered. I know how she found out about Taylor. I even understand why she felt motivated to incriminate me for Nikki's death. I still don't know where she is, or how I can find her before anyone else does. There are no leads in this diary, nothing I could use. And the shred of hope I had that I could somehow get her to stop telling lies about me has just vanished, realizing how jealous she is. How increasingly confused she grew over time, unable to deal with what had happened that night, with her guilt. Unable to accept that Nikki's death was an accident after all.

Or was it?

For a moment, I wonder if she kidnapped Taylor, now that she knows she's Ray's daughter. But it makes no sense. What would she do with my little girl? What could she hope to achieve, other than about ten years behind bars? It's not the first time the thought has come to my mind, but it just doesn't ring true. And although I'm still aghast after reading her diary, I don't believe Chloe could murder an innocent little girl. I can't accept it. I was wrong about everything to do with Chloe, but I can't be wrong about this. She was there with us, at the brunch, at the exact time Taylor was taken, and she was her normal self: chatty and flirty and a little bit over the top.

No... something else must've happened. Perhaps it is a coincidence, even if it seems so unlikely in the light of everything else. Or maybe the Winthrops have since received a ransom call, only I don't know about it, and I won't know anything until I hear about it on the news.

One thing I still don't understand. If she was so desperate to keep Ray away from me, if she hated me so much, why did she move next door? My life used to be peaceful before they moved in. Then all hell broke loose.

Suddenly.

Without normal transitions, without saying goodbye to Mrs. Moore over tea and chocolate chip cookies and more stories about Marcello the cat. Without the usual truck pulled up at the curb, loaders hauling furniture out of the house. Without a for sale sign or a forwarding address. Without a single hint, or explanation, or a wave goodbye as she drove off with Marcello in a carrier strapped to the passenger seat of her car.

I close the diary and stare out the window, where the light from Chloe's living room projects a yellowish shape on the asphalt.

Perhaps I've found a lead after all.

TWENTY-NINE

I still can't believe I don't have Mrs. Moore's phone number. I guess I just walked over to her house whenever I wanted to speak with her. I went through all my contacts twice, and she isn't among them. I tried calling 411, but they needed the city. I don't have it. She never said goodbye, and so I never got to ask.

But then I had a lot of time to think how I'd locate her, while spacing out during dinner with Daniel at his restaurant, late last night, after closing time. He was quiet and bleak, barely responding to his staff's parting wishes as one by one they left for the day, until it was just the two of us, engulfed in uncomfortable, heavy silence.

He didn't speak much and didn't look at me. He cut his steak into large pieces and stabbed his fries vengefully, as if they were life-long enemies about to jab him back somehow. And I'd almost forgotten why I'd offered to join him for dinner, my initial plan to lift his spirits long gone. Still suffering the emotional burden of what I'd learned from the last pages of Chloe's diary, my mind just wasn't on Daniel's sour mood.

I respected my husband's choice for silence, knowing he

needed time with his thoughts to figure out how he felt about everything, about me keeping things from him, about cops coming by the diner and interviewing his staff. I knew when he was ready, he'd speak with me, like he always did. Until then, I was alone with my thoughts while I sat across from him at a small table by the window, nursing remnants of chardonnay in a tall-stemmed glass.

The wine reminded me that about a year ago, Mrs. Moore had invited me over to her place for a game of bridge with two of her friends. One ended up being my partner for two rubbers. Her name was Mildred, and I remembered her well. I recalled the gold cross pendant she wore, and how she said, "Oh, my gosh," when a trick surprised her. Most likely, she was religious and probably went to church for every service.

I wake up this morning with that seed of a plan in mind and can hardly wait for Daniel to leave home. Nervous he might choose this particular day to go to work later than usual, I fidget in the kitchen, offering him coffee, breakfast, anything I can think of to get him off the sofa where he landed moments after he got out of bed. He's still gloomy, but at least he can look me in the eye now, an improvement that puts my mind at ease. I'm antsy because I'm hoping to find Mildred at church, and the service will end soon. The next one will be on Wednesday, and I can't see myself waiting three more days.

"What's your plan for today?" Daniel asks, starting to get dressed unnervingly slow.

His question startles me. "Nothing," I blurt out childishly, and he shoots me a quick glance, probably surprised at my reaction. I sounded defensive, my answer visibly a lie, as if I were about to cheat on him or something. "I mean, nothing important, just a bit of shopping, and then some cleaning. Maybe I'll read a bit in the afternoon." He looks at me without a word. "Do you need me?" I offer, desperate to fix everything that's broken between us, only I still can't tell him the truth. "I've got time, if you need help with anything."

I see him breathe out, some of the tension vanishing from his shoulders. "Not really." A pause. "Well, maybe you could pick up some air fresheners for the restrooms at the diner. I'm all out."

I stop in front of him and tilt my head playfully. "Should I deliver?" There was a time I used to love coming to the diner and hanging out on the patio, basking in the sun, looking at the ocean.

He finally cracks a smile, the first I've seen in the past day or so. "Sure, why not?"

A few endless minutes later, he's finally driving off, while I wave goodbye from the window, still sporting sweatpants and an old T-shirt.

A quick look at the microwave clock throws me into a frenzy. Church service usually ends at eleven-thirtyish. It's already fifteen past.

It takes me a few minutes to slip on a pair of jeans, a shirt I'm not embarrassed to wear in public, and to run a brush through my hair. Then, grabbing my phone and keys, I rush out the door. Moments later, I'm speeding on Cabrillo Highway, heading east. While there's more than one church in Half Moon Bay—more like five or six—I'm betting on the one Mrs. Moore used to attend.

When I get there, the service is just about to end. I sneak in and stand by the door, knowing everyone in the crowded building will have to pass by me on their way out.

A few minutes after the service is finished, the doors are opened wide, and people start leaving. I earn a few glares because I'm blocking the way and not budging, but I hold my ground, scanning for the familiar face I hope to find.

I see her among the last to leave, walking painstakingly slow and chatting with another woman. She's wearing a colorful floral blouse and a navy-blue skirt below the knee. She's put on a few pounds since our last game of bridge. I slip outside and wait for her to close the distance, while I pretend to check my phone. Then, when she's barely six feet away, I lift my eyes and smile.

"Mildred, right?"

For a moment, she looks at me a bit confused, shifting her hand to her forehead to block the sun. She wears gold bangles that jingle with every move. A look of recognition glimmers in her eyes, then she promptly hugs me. Her short hair smells of incense and candle wax and fresh-baked cookies.

"Sweetie, how have you been?" She places a hearty smooch on my cheek. "I saw you on television. Amazing thing you do with those, um, binders, right? Simply amazing." She backs off a little and looks at me head to toe. "You look fantastic. Ah, to be young," she says, and a bit of sadness clouds her eyes.

"I'm okay," I say when I get the chance to slip in a word. "You? Have you played any bridge lately?"

"Not since Easter, I'm afraid. I lost my partners. It's just me and Helen now," she says, pointing at the other woman who's been patiently waiting, giving us our space. I shake her hand and say my name.

"If you're up for a game, I can try to find us a fourth," Mildred continues.

"How about Mrs. Moore?"

She waves my suggestion away with a bangle-jingling gesture. "No, she's too far. It would take us ages to drive over there, and she's not much of a driver herself."

"Far? Where did she move to?" I hold my breath.

"Oh, she's in Los Gatos now. It's a nice townhouse, I've seen it."

"Do you happen to have her address, maybe her phone

number too? She left something in our backyard," I add unnec-
essarily, because she's already looking at her phone.

Moments later, armed with Mrs. Moore's number and
address, we say our goodbyes, share a hug and a promise to play
cards again soon. Then I climb behind the wheel of my Subaru
and enter the address into my GPS.

It's a one-hour drive, and I can't wait to get there.

When I arrive, I doublecheck the address. The townhouse
is about the same size as her old house, yet I can tell she traded
up. A small rose garden lines the wall under the window, and
the lawn is lush and perfectly trimmed. A wide driveway leads
to a two-car garage. White sheers block the view, fluttering
gently in the breeze. She always liked keeping her windows
open, although she feared for Marcello's life if he decided to run
away one day.

My heart is racing when I ring the bell. I haven't thought of
what I'd ask or how I'd explain why I'm there. I just know her
sudden move is what precipitated disaster, and I need to understand how it came to happen.

Mrs. Moore opens the door grinning widely, dressed in a
gray pullover and black slacks. She's wearing lipstick, and her
hair is neatly done. Los Gatos is definitely agreeing with her.
"Alana, come in, dearie!" I walk in and look around. Some of
her furniture is brand new, but it's still the same style as I
remember. "Mildred said you were coming, but she didn't know
when. I'm glad it's today. Let me get you something. Coffee,
right? You still like French vanilla?"

"Yes, please," I murmur, taking a seat on the edge of the
sofa, feeling shy, at a loss for words. While she makes the coffee,
we make small talk, about the new neighborhood, how's she's
really close to her children, who both work and live in San Jose.
How she misses her walks by the sea and the fog rolling in.
There's almost never any fog in Los Gatos, just sunshine.

She puts the coffee cup on the small glass table, and I thank her with a smile. I take it in my frozen hands and inhale the aroma, thinking how to broach the subject.

"I'm so sorry I left without saying anything," she says, and I'm grateful I don't have to bring it up. "You both work all day, and it happened so quickly, really. I felt bad. I've been meaning to call you, but life has been hectic over the past few months, with the move and everything, as you can imagine."

I take a sip of coffee and wince when it burns my throat. "Were you planning to move? I had no idea."

She shakes her head. "No. It just happened. One day, I got a call from a real estate agent who was representing—" She stops midsentence and frowns, looking sheepishly around for a moment before she looks at me again. "Well, to be entirely honest, I signed an NDA about the whole thing, but I don't think they meant I can't tell *you*, right?"

I smile, unable to bring myself to lie to her. Even after all the lies I've told, this one feels particularly bad and I just can't say the words. "Oh, I'm not going to say a word to anyone," I reassure her instead.

"I think a company wanted my house," she says, lowering her voice to barely a whisper. "The name on the sale agreement was a numbered LLC. I meant to look it up, but then I just forgot." She clasps her hands in her lap but doesn't seem afraid, only a little awkward. "They offered me twenty-five percent over market value," she eventually confesses, "but the move had to happen in three days, or the deal was off."

My forehead ridges with lines. I can't bring myself to understand the urgency. What was that all about? If Chloe wanted to move next door to me, why was she in such a hurry? I make a mental note to go over the dates once I'm back home. The date of the last entry in her diary, then the date they moved. Just to see if there's any correlation.

"I didn't want to move," Mrs. Moore continues, as Marcello appears from upstairs, quietly and elegantly coming down the carpeted steps. He weaves his body between my ankles but pulls away when I try to pet him. Tail straight up in the air, he jumps on Mrs. Moore's lap and starts purring, rubbing his head against her body. She smiles serenely, seemingly lost in thought. "The deal was sweet; you have to give it that. And I have grand-kids here. Now I get to see them every weekend. I couldn't say no."

I smile and nod understandingly, although I still don't understand the urgency behind Chloe's decision to move. That numbered LLC sounds just like what her father would've set up to buy a house under a trust or something, but I was never good at these things.

"But I could've at least said goodbye to my neighbors," Mrs. Moore adds, blushing a little. "I'm embarrassed."

"No, really, don't be. We reconnected now, and we'll stay in touch, right?"

"Sure, we will," she replies, as I finish my coffee and push the cup aside on the table.

"Excellent, I'd love that." I stand, ready to leave, but I can tell there's something else she wants to say.

"Um, Mildred said I forgot something in your yard?" she eventually asks, when I'm almost at the door.

"Yes, but I don't have it with me today." I lie without hesita-tion. "It doesn't fit in my Subaru." She's visibly confused. "Your rake? I'll ask Daniel to bring it in his truck."

Her eyebrows shoot up. "I don't have a rake," she says.

"Oh?" I zip up my jacket in the doorway. "So sorry... maybe it came with the house, and I forgot."

"I'm glad you came by," she says, giving me a hug, "because we're in touch now. Come back again sometime. I'm always home. Well, except for Saturdays, that is."

As I drive off, the smile I pasted on my lips drops off like a cheap, plastic mask. Whatever Chloe was up to, it had a strict and urgent time frame: so urgent it was worth paying a lot of money to make it happen. That incomprehensible sense of urgency fills me with dread and anxiety.

Only one person could answer my questions, although he might not be willing to.

Chloe's father.

THIRTY

I could waste a couple of hours digging up property deeds and sale agreements at the County of San Mateo Office of the County Clerk-Recorder to confirm that the LLC that made Mrs. Moore the generous offer for her house is, in fact, a front for Chloe's father. Or I can just drive over to the Avery residence and ask him. The overwhelming chances are I'm right about this, just as overwhelming as the chances he'll kick me out of the house and refuse to speak with me.

When I arrive back in Half Moon Bay, I stop by Dan's Diner with a plastic bag filled with air fresheners I picked up on the way, then spend some time enjoying a latte on the sunny patio overlooking the ocean. Daniel is busy and leaves me alone, after making excuses he didn't need to make. It's still lunch rush hour, and a perfectly beautiful summer day.

I take my time at a table for two, letting my mind wander while I watch the sun's reflection in the water, shards of sunshine restlessly undulating, hypnotizing.

What can I say to the Averys? How can I justify my questions, when they're going through hell over their missing daughter?

No matter how much I stare at the glimmering ocean, I have no answers. Still, I must go.

I find Daniel and tell him I'm leaving. He's filling in for one of his servers who called in sick and has about ten tables to wait on. If anything, he's relieved to see me leave.

I drive to the Avery residence on the coastal highway, too anxious and white-knuckled to savor its breathtaking beauty, hoping they haven't moved since I last visited them eleven years ago.

I hold my breath as I wait for someone to open the door after I ring the bell. The house is eerily silent, the only sound the constant crashing and retreating of the Pacific surf.

I'm about to ring the doorbell again when I notice a silhouette approaching through the frosted glass panels that flank the entrance. The massive door opens seemingly effortlessly, and Mr. Avery stares at me, speechless for a moment.

"Come on in," he eventually says, and I walk inside.

The house hasn't changed since I last visited. Mr. Avery, however, is visibly distraught, his face stubbly and drawn, his eyes marked by dark circles, his almost entirely white hair in disarray. His shirt and slacks look slept in, but he doesn't seem to have caught a wink of rest since Chloe vanished. "Have you heard anything?" he asks, leading the way into the living room.

"No, Mr. Avery, I'm sorry—"

"It's Harold," he says, inviting me to sit on the sofa. "That's how I remember it."

I feel my cheeks blushing. With a couple of words, he's made me feel like a high school girl again, and welcome, at the same time. "Thank you," I say.

The sofa is burgundy leather and deep, comfortable, the kind that entices you to fall asleep within seconds. "Do you have any news?" I ask, although I don't expect he does. As I realize that, I wonder why I find it so incomprehensible that there would be news about Chloe.

He shakes his head and paces with his hands deep inside his pockets. "No. Absolutely nothing." He stops in front of me, and I can see the despair written in his eyes. "I'm losing my mind, Alana. I can't lose her."

I can't think of anything to say. I just look at him, feeling sorry for his pain, for the anguish he and Dr. Avery must be going through. But I can't help them; there's nothing I could do that I'm not doing already to find Chloe.

The moment of weakness doesn't last long. Harold snaps out of it and asks, "What can I do for you, Alana?"

I swallow hard, my throat unexpectedly dry. "I was wondering if you knew how it happened that they moved next door to us, that's all." I wring my hands together, uncomfortable under his scrutiny. "I just thought it was a strange coincidence."

He sits heavily on an armchair and runs his fingers through his hair, looking into thin air as if trying to recollect what happened merely months ago. "It was a wedding anniversary gift. I didn't understand why, not until Chloe told me you were their new neighbor." He smiles with sadness. "Her and Ray's best friend, living next door. I'd say that qualifies for one hell of a ten-year anniversary gift."

So, she knew I lived there, and *wanted* to move next door to me. To be close to me and destroy my life, out of jealousy or revenge or who knows why.

"It was a surprise," he adds, staring at the gleaming hardwood floors, probably without noticing them. "I did the paperwork, had one of my people make the offer, arranged the move and everything. Even if it was a tight schedule, I pulled it off." That hint of a sad smile returns for a brief moment. "That's what I do, I make deals happen." His voice is bitter, as if he's embarrassed by his accomplishments.

"Ah, it was a gift from you," I say, remembering there was no history of mortgage payments in Chloe's account, nor of a house purchase in cash. "How wonderful."

He nods, still staring into the thin air at his feet. "From Denise and me, yes. You see, Ray isn't great with money. He doesn't know how to build wealth. But my daughter loves him, and he makes her happy. He treats her right, gives her what she needs, pays attention to her. Her face glows when he's around." A sigh quivers his breath, but he does his best to hide it. "So I was happy to foot the bill. She's my only child. What else would I do with my money?"

He doesn't expect an answer, and he wouldn't get one if he did. I'm overwhelmed by a cascade of conflicting emotions ripping through my chest. There's a paralyzing fear of losing Taylor, of never seeing my little girl again. There's anger and grief over losing Ray, now that I know I meant something to him and maybe I still do. There's confusion about the future, about my ability to put Ray out of my mind for good when, after all these years, all it takes is for him to look at me, to say my name or touch my hand, and I'm lost, falling again, unable to help myself. Then there's this swelling, emerging rush of betrayal, hurt, and disappointment, after reading Chloe's lies and seeing how badly she wants to destroy me. I wish I could scream at her, "Why? Why are you doing this to me? What have I ever done to you?" But it would be pointless. She would lie some more, while secretly plotting to end me once and for all.

Just because she can.

I stand and smooth my pants, resenting the wrinkle lines they get, a telling sign of cheap apparel from the local Walmart. Harold stands too, and we walk slowly toward the entrance. I stop midway, and turn to look at him as I ask, "When is their wedding anniversary, by the way? I forget."

"It's on—"

"I don't think you should tell her, Harold." Dr. Avery approaches quickly, her footsteps light and soundless on the hardwood, almost catlike.

I nod a greeting she ignores. "Hello, Dr. Avery." She ignores that too, staring intently at her husband with swollen, red eyes, still brimming with tears.

"Denise, Chloe said we should answer all her questions," he replies gently. I'm speechless. I wasn't expecting that. Chloe, who wrote endlessly about how much she hated me, instructed her parents to speak with me? To answer my questions? That can't be true.

"I know what she said," Dr. Avery replies in a cold voice.

"Dr. Avery, I didn't mean to—"

She finally turns her attention to me. "My daughter said we should answer your questions, but I don't intend to. My husband can do as he pleases," she adds, the threat in her voice clearly received by Harold, who slightly bows his head. "I believe you should go. The detective told us there's something strange about you and those binders. That Chloe is not the only missing person case you're involved in, and that we shouldn't speak to you anymore." She opens the door and holds it for me while I step out. "Goodbye, Alana."

The door closes slowly, leaving me astounded, frozen in place, my heart beating fast.

A moment later, when I'm able to move, I walk over to my car and climb behind the wheel. I'm about to start the engine when Harold raps his fingers against the passenger window. I lower it quickly.

He seems hesitant and ashamed, his eyes veering away after a split second of contact. "February twelve," he says. The blood drains from my face. The date resonates deeply in my heart, igniting an ache like I've never felt before. "That's their wedding anniversary." He leans against the door as if he's about to faint. "It's strange, I know, because ten years ago, February twelve was on a Wednesday. Valentine's Day was on a Friday, and I thought they'd want that, but Chloe was adamant. She wanted February twelve as their wedding day and didn't care that it fell midweek."

I thank him and watch him go back inside with the gait of an old man, not the powerful, successful attorney that he is. As the door closes, I can't bring myself to drive off. My head is spinning, and I can't breathe, even as I desperately gasp for air.

February twelve, eleven years ago, was the day Ray and I made love for the last time on the beach by Eel Rock.

Chloe had to have known somehow.

A year later, she took that day and made it hers.

THIRTY-ONE

Still reeling after speaking with Harold Avery, I turn the corner onto our cul-de-sac. It's not even six, and Daniel's Ford is in the driveway. My gut wrenches as I switch off the engine, afraid he's going to tell me the cops were at the diner again.

I find him seated at the dining room table, staring at a letter he's holding in his right hand. When I come in, he ignores my greeting and says somberly, "Please sit. We need to talk." The tone of his voice chills me to the bone.

I pull up a chair and sit, abandoning my keys and phone on the table with a loud clatter. I'm thirsty and wish I'd grabbed a glass of water first, but now it's too late. It will have to wait. "What's wrong?"

He pushes the letter toward me. It's a statement of some sort, some official invoice or something. I pick it up and see Dr. Ellefson's name. My heart sinks. It's a billing statement for medical services. It's for eighty-five dollars, the cost of a consult, not a fertility treatment. Those are significantly more expensive.

I look at him, petrified, at a loss for words. I don't blame Dr. Ellefson for sending the correct statement. She wasn't going to commit billing fraud just to cover my deception. She gave me everything she promised: time to come clean with Daniel. I didn't. All this is on me.

"Why, Alana?"

I stand and walk over to the kitchen, too nervous to sit still. My fight-or-flight response has been activated, and I consider grabbing my keys and running out of there, as if Daniel were chasing me with an axe. But I know how irrational that would be, how damaging. If I want any chance of saving my marriage, I have to fix things somehow.

I stop near the counter, leaning on it with one hand to hold my balance, and shake my hung head. "I-I just can't." I look at Daniel through a blur of tears. "I'm sorry I lied to you, Daniel. It's just... you weren't listening to me. I tried to tell you—"

"We talked about this," he replies. His voice is cold, his face pale, carved in stone. "You and I, countless times, we talked about it. You can't say we didn't."

I nod, swallowing a sob that threatens to choke me. "We talked, yes," I whisper. "I couldn't say no to you, even if I wanted to. You never really asked. You assumed having children was a given for us. Well, maybe it is for you. For me... it's terrifying."

"Why?" He stands and strides over to me, determined, menacing almost. I flinch and pull away. He stops in place, looking at me with an expression of hurt and dismay in his eyes. "Alana... what's wrong? I've never hurt you. Never raised a hand. How can you be afraid of me?"

"Sorry," I whisper. "It's just... I know you're upset. I know I lied to you, and I'm sorry."

His arms fall, inert, as he stares at me. "Yes, you did." He's back to being cold, distant, a stranger I've angered. "Are you on birth control?"

I turn my head away as if to escape the question, but there's no escape.

He walks toward me and stops mere inches away, staring at me intently. "I have a right to know, damn it."

I lift my eyes and meet his. "Yes, you do." Silence falls heavily as he waits for me to answer the question. My lips start forming words, but no sound comes out of my mouth. I know that the moment I speak the truth, he'll never look at me the same way, not ever, again.

The funniest thing about lies... they grow on you like a second skin, each new lie a patch stitched to other lies, while truth withers underneath, suffocated. And so, the truth dies smothered, making room for the new, shiny coat of lies to prevail, to grow stronger. But once someone or something rips off a piece, the entire web unravels, exposing the ugly, contorted nature of who we really are, who we were before we covered ourselves in pretense.

"So?" Daniel presses on. "Are you?"

I lower my head as a sob comes out of my chest. My shoulders are heaving, but I force myself to breathe, to control myself, and look at my husband's disheartened eyes. "Yes."

"Jeez, Alana," he snaps, slapping his hand against his thigh. He starts pacing the floor, angered, anguished, lost. "Why?" he asks, his voice filled with disbelief. "I thought you and I were together on this. I thought you loved me."

"I do love you," I say quickly, in a rush to keep him from drawing the wrong conclusions and letting them drive a wedge between us. "It's not about that."

"Then what is it?" He rubs his forehead with his fingers and turns in place, as if looking for a way out. "I can't believe you lied to me all this time. I just can't."

Speechless, I stare at him, feeling empty inside, barren, as I've been feeling since I gave away my little girl. I can't tell him the truth. Still can't. It would break him. It would drive him away. I'm sure of that just as much as I'm sure of his love, strong yet vulnerable, fragile, unable to survive the burden of the whole truth.

Daniel shakes his head slowly, then looks out the window at the setting sun layering the backyard with hues of orange and gold.

I pull a chair and sit, unsure my legs can still hold me. I can't think of anything to say. I rest my head on my elbow and cry silently, tears of despair for the peaceful life I used to have, for the love I'm about to lose. I wish I could tell him everything; I would feel so liberated. But how? I could lose him if he learned about Taylor, about what I've done. And with whom.

I flinch again when he strokes my hair, and his hand instantly withdraws. I look up and whisper, "I'm sorry I lied to you."

"Why, baby?" His voice is no longer cold. The Daniel I know and love is back, disappointed, heartbroken maybe, but still loving, still forgiving, still mine.

I shake my head, at a loss for words. How can I explain it to him? I just can't. "I'm afraid of what a child could do to our lives," I say, giving him the most truthful answer I can. "I love our life together. I love *us*. I don't want that to change."

He lets slip a long sigh, pulls a chair near mine, and wraps his arm around my shoulders. I lean against him, borrowing from his strength. "I don't know if I can take another lie, Alana." I hold my breath, fearing his words, knowing they come from the bottom of his heart. "If you can't be honest with me, we don't belong together. It's that simple." He searches my eyes, and I can't turn away, not now. "No more lies, baby. Promise me."

I cringe as I whisper, "I promise. No more lies."

There must be a special place in hell for people like me.

He kisses my forehead and wipes a tear off my cheek with his thumb. I lower my eyes, knowing the promise I just made is already broken. If the truth were to come out, my life would be destroyed.

With that scary thought I go to bed later that night, wondering how people know when it's the last time that they'll sleep next to someone they love.

But the truth is, they don't.

THIRTY-TWO

The chill from yesterday's revelation lingers in the house, in the air between Daniel and me, like a spider weaving gossamer in the corners where no one can see. It's in the words not spoken, the good morning kiss and smile not happening, in the questions not asked.

He didn't bring it up again, and neither did I. Still, I couldn't look in his eyes without shifting my gaze immediately, ashamed, afraid he'd see right through me and discover that so many other things I've said aren't true. I'm afraid. That's the word for it.

When he leaves for work, I look out the window and wait to wave as I always do, this time with a knot in my heart, hoping he'll turn around and smile at me. He doesn't. The fading sound of his car's engine leaves the house shrouded in silence, and me frozen, unsure of what to do or who I am.

After staring out the window at our deserted street for a while, as if hoping he'd come back, I move away and mechanically go through the motions of a typical morning when school is out. I load the dishwasher and clean the counter. I brew myself a second cup of coffee, but I'm unable to feel anything, or to enjoy the fresh aroma of my favorite blend. I just sit at the table, coffee cup in front of me, my stare vacant and my heart in turmoil.

When the doorbell rings, I jump out of my skin. I look out the window, hoping for something undefined. Maybe for Daniel's forgiveness. I recognize Detective Fernandez's gray Dodge Charger parked in front of the house. Heading for the door, I wring my hands in a lame attempt to keep them from shaking. What if they found Chloe? What if he's here to arrest me?

I unlock the door just as he's ringing the bell a second time, and I manage a polite smile I can only hope seems helpful and relaxed.

Fernandez nods slightly. "Ms. Blake, please come with me. We need to take your statement at the station."

I grab onto the door handle, afraid my knees will betray me. Is he arresting me? He's not saying the things cops usually say when they're arresting a suspect. But he's got lots of time to do that later, I suppose. "All right," I say weakly, frowning as I look at what I'm wearing. "I'll need a minute to change. Would you like to come in?" I'm hoping my hospitality will defuse his interest in me, but it seems he needs more than that.

He waits by the door, unwilling to sit or take a cup of coffee. He seems pressed for time, his face somber, almost hostile. I slip into a pair of jeans and a turtleneck, then grab Daniel's jacket from the coat rack and my keys and phone from the dining room table. With a deep breath to steel myself, I say, "I'm ready. I'll drive behind you." We step outside and I close the door, then lock it.

"No need," he replies, taking my elbow as I've seen so many times on TV. "Please, mind your head," he says, opening the back door of his Charger. I climb in, at a loss for words, sick to my stomach, his hand pressing down on my skull.

The drive takes under five minutes, all spent in the silence I know is my right.

I've never been to the police department before; I've seen the building many times, but I never thought I'd be escorted inside the yellowish building by a detective with a strong grip on my arm, as if I were a thug about to make a run for it.

Once inside, I notice the smells. Microwaved food, popcorn, pizza, something else with a Mexican flavor, and stale air. There's a low-key buzz of activity as several deputies hustle, make calls, talk to complainants, or just go about their business.

Detective Fernandez escorts me to a room labeled INTER-VIEW 1, and I'm left alone there. There's a faint smell of urine and something else just as disgusting, maybe old vomit. The walls are scratched and dirty around the doorframe and the light switch, and not exactly clean anywhere else. Obscenities have been written on the wall then painted over without being smoothed into oblivion by spackling paste first; someone did a very poor job at that.

Daniel was right. We're suspects. I wonder if they picked him up too; if he's sitting next door right now, inside the room labeled INTERVIEW 2. If his palms are sweating like mine are, or if he's cursing my name. I know he suspects I'm involved in this. He asked me that much, and I lied to him. He saw right through it.

Detective Fernandez finds me staring at the red LED on the video camera hanging in the corner. I've been doing that for a few minutes, hoping he'd notice and come back to get this over with. Waiting is killing me. Not knowing.

Fernandez brings Chloe's binder and drops it on the table with a groan. "Ms. Blake, how does this hell of a mess connect to you?" he asks, pulling out the chair across from me. The metallic legs scrape against the concrete, making me grind my teeth. I look at the binder and cringe when I see traces of finger-print powder staining its covers.

"I don't know," I reply, wondering if I should ask for an attorney. I don't have one. They'd need to assign me one, and

I'm not really sure whether it would do me more good than harm. It would definitely make me look guilty.

"Gotta do better than that, or we'll be here all day." He takes off his jacket, loosens his tie, and rolls up the sleeves of his light-blue shirt, as if preparing himself to be there for a while. It has the unnerving effect he was aiming for.

"Listen, you have to believe me, I have no idea."

His fingers rap against the cover of the binder. "You're quite the vocal advocate for these things, aren't you?"

"Yes. I thought, out of all people, the police would appreciate it."

He scoffs and shakes his head. "It has its value," he reluctantly admits. "But let's talk about you." He looks at me with a hint of curiosity written on his face. "Why were you stalking Taylor Winthrop, Ms. Blake?"

I knew this was coming, and I've rehearsed the answer in my mind, over and over. "Taylor was being bullied at school. I, um... the principal and I didn't call her parents after the last incident. I just wanted to make sure Taylor was all right."

He leans back against the chair and exhales loudly. "Do you stalk all your bullied students, Ms. Blake?"

My brow furrows for a moment. "No other student was bullied, so no, I don't. Or, rather, yes, I would, maybe—" I raise my hands and inhale, realizing I'd better stop before I dig myself deeper.

"So, you're not really sure, are you?"

"What I'm saying is, Taylor was the only student who was bullied since the school year started. I don't have another case of bullying to use as a baseline for your question." His eyes glaze over, making me realize I must use shorter, simpler phrases if I'm to get anywhere with him.

"Why the binder?" he asks, opening it at Chloe's letter.

"This one? Or in general?"

"Let's start with this one."

"That I can't answer. Only Chloe can."

"But she got the idea from you, didn't she?" I nod and clasp my hands in my lap, rubbing them gently to warm them up. "Did she speak to you about it?"

I hesitate for a moment, trying to recall if anyone overheard us talking at the party. "Only in general terms, nothing specific to her."

"When was that?"

"Right after the interview aired. We had a few people at our house: Chloe and Ray and his mother and my brother-in-law. It came up. That's what everyone was talking about that day."

He leans forward, his eyes drilling into mine. "I see. Why was Chloe stalking *you*, Ms. Blake?"

He must be talking about the photo in Chloe's binder, the one showing my car parked across from Taylor's house. I shrug. "You'd have to ask her about that. Do you have any news?"

He dismisses my question with a gesture. "Tell me about you two. What's your relationship with Chloe Avery Preston?"

Oh, boy... I'd need a year to explain that one, in the unlikely chance I'd be inclined to tell him the truth. "We're friends. We go back a long time."

"Would you say you're good friends?"

I nod without blinking. "We're close. We've been out of touch for a while, after going to separate colleges, but we were glad to reconnect."

"You're close, but you have no idea who might've taken her?"

"She didn't say anything that could be useful, no."

"But she built herself this binder." He pushes it slightly my way. I don't touch it; I pull away from it as it slides over the table, as if it might burn my skin. "I'd say she was afraid of something, wouldn't you agree, Ms. Blake?"

It drives me crazy how he keeps repeating my name. Must be some kind of tactic. "Again, I wouldn't know, because she didn't say. I thought she made the binder because of my TV interview. That makes sense."

"What was your relationship back then?"

"When, exactly?" I ask, bracing for the answer I know will come.

"When Nikki Malkin died. Were you friends then?"

A bitter smile flutters on my lips before I can catch and smother it. "Yes. We used to do lots of things together."

"Like what?"

I shrug again, shifting in my seat, increasingly uncomfortable. "The usual teenage stuff. Hanging out at the mall, at the movies, going for drives, that kind of thing."

"Was Nikki a close friend with you two?"

"She was new, but we liked her. Both of us did." I choose to bury both ends of the secret, not just mine.

"It was remarkable how Mr. Avery stepped in and helped you that day. The attorney he hired for you charges a thousand an hour." He whistles in admiration. "Wasn't that just a little unusual, Ms. Blake?"

I have to refrain from shrugging again. "No. Mr. Avery has always been nice to me. I was his daughter's best friend."

"And, because of that, he absolutely knew you didn't push Nikki Malkin to her death? Just because you were his daughter's BFF?" His voice modulates strangely as he says the letters, reeking of disbelief and a touch of sarcasm.

"It *was* an accident," I say, willing my voice to be calm, low-pitched, determined. "The edge of the cliff collapsed under her weight. The cops, um, police who responded that day took photos of the edge, showing how a piece of it came off. It should be in the case file somewhere."

He stares at me for a long, uncomfortable moment of silence. In the distance, a phone rings twice before someone picks it up. Fernandez leans back against his chair and slams his hands on the table. "I think you're lying to me, Ms. Blake. I'm positive you're involved in both kidnappings somehow; I just can't prove it yet." He reaches into his pocket and pulls out a wad of cash, then extracts a tenner and smooths it on the table before putting the rest back. "Ten bucks says you know who took them."

I stare at the tenner, then at him, unable to believe what I'm hearing. Am I supposed to place a bet to prove my innocence? Has he gone insane? I scoff quietly and shake my head. "I don't bet, Detective. Not even when I'm one hundred percent sure I'd win."

He takes the ten-dollar bill off the table and shoves it into his shirt pocket. "But you do lie, don't you, Ms. Blake?"

I don't respond, just sit there staring at him, too shaken to think straight.

After a couple of seconds of disquieting eye contact, he sighs and opens a notepad, then gets ready to take notes. "All right, Ms. Blake, let's do this a different way. Tell me, when did you first meet Taylor Winthrop?"

His eyes lock onto mine again and I can tell he knows about Taylor. It makes sense. Police had my DNA on record: they collected it after Nikki's death. And they must've obtained Taylor's as part of their investigation into her disappearance. As far as I know police procedure from true-crime shows on television, the moment they entered Taylor's DNA into their system, close matches were displayed, and I must've been one of those matches. With my entire history. With my name next to Nikki's.

Fernandez knows she's my daughter. But he can't be sure *I* know.

After listening to true-crime podcasts for more than ten years, after learning the only thing you should tell the police is that you want an attorney, I decide to take a leap and do the exact opposite, the only thing you should never do.

I decide to trust Fernandez.

My lips quiver for a moment, while I reconsider my decision, while I question it and my sanity.

"Taylor Winthrop is my biological daughter," I eventually say. There's only moderate surprise in his eyes: he already knew. He just didn't expect me to admit it. "I didn't have to tell you, but I hope it can help."

He nods. "Thank you for telling me the truth, Ms. Blake. I have to ask, because you admitted you're her mother: did you kidnap Taylor?"

With that simple question, I realize the enormity of the mistake I've made. "No, of course not." My voice sounds fraught with fear. "Look, I could've not told you. You probably already knew, because you already had my DNA, and you must've had Taylor's. But you had no idea if I knew, and no way to prove I did. And still, I decided to trust you, because the one thing I care about is finding Taylor and getting her home. To the Winthrops, not to me. Just knowing she's safe again is all I need."

"Sit down, Ms. Blake," he says, pointing at the chair I'd abandoned without realizing. "I had to ask."

"Oh." I take my seat, feeling like an idiot and, at the same time, afraid I've made a colossal mistake. But, as they say, in for a dime, in for a dollar. I fill my lungs with the stale air of the interview room, and add, "You might know the arson in Santa Clara, at the Westhaven Adoption Agency, could be related."

His eyes flicker with interest. "You're saying—"

"That's the agency where I gave my baby up for adoption. To your point, there are just too many coincidences to ignore. Mr. Patel was the lawyer who helped me ten years ago."

"I see." He sighs, closing the folder. He pulls the binder closer to him and flips through the pages until he finds the letter both Chloe and I received, the one handwritten in green ink.

"It's time to pay for what you've done. I haven't forgotten," he reads slowly, then looks at me. "Who wrote this, Ms. Blake?"

"I have no idea."

"You've never seen it before?"

I frown a little. "I did, when I found the binder."

"Ah, yes, how convenient. Mr. Preston couldn't find his wife's binder in his own house. He had to call you. Isn't that interesting?"

Now that he mentions it, yes, it is a bit interesting. I feel my cheeks catch fire, thinking Ray might've looked for a reason to be alone with me.

"And you've never seen it before, this letter? Other than when you found Chloe's binder?"

I hesitate for the tiniest of moments, and he catches it. "No, I haven't."

He nods, pressing his lips together. He doesn't believe me. Flipping back through the pages, he stops at the photo of the young athlete I didn't recognize. "Do you know who this is?" he asks, tapping the page with his fingertip.

"No." This time the answer comes out quickly and firmly, the way truth usually does.

He closes the binder and rubs his hands together as if to say he's done with me. "I'm charging you with Taylor's kidnapping. I don't care that you have an alibi. You could've paid someone to take her." I gasp and spring off my chair, but he glares at me. "Please, sit." I obey, slack-jawed, petrified. "I gave you plenty of opportunity to come clean with me. There's a lot you're not saying, about Taylor's and Chloe's disappearances, about Nikki Malkin's death all those years ago. Honestly, I'm tired of this binder mess and whatever the hell you're up to."

"B-but I didn't—"

He stops me with a raised hand. "I don't care. You had motive: you're Taylor's biological parent, and in eighty-seven percent of child abductions, a biological parent is involved. You were stalking the residence and the minor. You've encroached into her life; you managed to become her teacher and stay her teacher for four years. Taylor was taken from her backyard, the exact place you were casing the day before she disappeared. And then there's this." He taps on the binder's cover again. "If I Go Missing. What an interesting name, considering. Why not If I Get Killed or something?"

I stare at him in disbelief, my mind unable to process my new reality. I'm being arrested. I'll be thrown in jail for something I didn't do.

"Well?" He's actually expecting an answer.

I lick my dry lips and say, "Because it's when time is of the essence, and the information in the binder saves time. If you're dead... it doesn't matter that much anymore."

"Fabulous," he says, getting up and stretching his back with a groan, his hands propped on his hips. His back cracks as if he has arthritis, although he can't be more than forty-five or so. "I'll let twelve of your peers decide what to do with you. It's all the same to me."

He's almost out the door, Chloe's binder under his left arm, his right hand squeezing the handle, the door cracked open. "Wait," I plead, my voice riddled with tears. "You can't stop looking for Taylor. Please, don't stop looking for my daughter."

He turns in place and lets the door whoosh to a close. He looks at me as if he's never seen me before, with his head slightly tilted, his interest kindled by my words. "You're right, I shouldn't stop looking for your kid or for your best friend." He walks over to the table and drops the binder again, then takes his seat. "Where was Daniel the day Taylor was taken?"

Oh, no. A sob fills my chest with despair, then a chill spreads through my veins. Daniel? He can't be serious. "Um... we... the four of us had brunch in San Jose, then caught a movie."

"The four of you being...?"

"Daniel and I, and Chloe and her husband, Ray."

"I see. And was Daniel there all the time?"

"Yes, he was."

"That's not what I heard from other witnesses. People who saw you at the Whispers Café that day say Daniel arrived about half an hour later than the rest of you."

I stammer pitifully as I realize I forgot about that. "Y-yes, he... there was a health inspection at his restaurant, and he couldn't get away."

"Oh, so he was at the diner first? And then at brunch?"

"Uh-huh, yes."

"How about the morning Chloe disappeared? He was gone the entire morning, but the restaurant doesn't open until eleven."

"He usually does his shopping in the mornings, picks up supplies, or visits vendors."

"Do you *know* where he was that morning? Or are you just trying to cover for him?"

My shoulders heave and a sob climbs out of my chest. "I know he's not involved in this. He doesn't even know Taylor is my daughter. I swear to you, he's not the man you're looking for."

"One of us is terribly wrong about Daniel Blake." He stares at me, probably trying to see if his words throw me off, then slowly collects the binder from the table. He's made up his mind. "Do you know your rights, Ms. Blake?"

I swallow hard, my throat constricted and dry. "Yes."

"Then I suggest you remain silent and wait here until I verify the information you provided."

When the door closes behind him, I let the sobs come out. I don't care if they see me through that two-way mirror, or if the camera records every teardrop falling from my eyes.

My life is over.

THIRTY-THREE

I have no idea how much time has passed since Detective Fernandez left me in the interrogation room. He finds me resting my tear-soaked face on my folded arms, my mind wandering aimlessly, unable to deal with reality, senselessly looking for an escape. I can't bear to think of Daniel and how his life will be destroyed along with mine. I can't think of practical things I should do, like find an attorney, at least not now, when I'm about to be thrown in jail. I just can't function. Reality has proven to be worse than my darkest nightmares.

"All right, Ms. Blake," he says, and I lift my head and look at him, wiping my tears with the back of my hand. "We have a problem. There was no health inspection at your husband's diner the day of Taylor's disappearance. Whatever reason he had for being late for your brunch, he lied to you, or you lied to me. Which one is it?"

Desperation chokes me. This man will never believe a word I say. "I'm not lying. I swear I'm not. Maybe I remembered it wrong. I wasn't paying attention at the time. I had no reason to."

"So, when your husband is late for a date, you have no reason to worry or be curious as to why? Must be really nice and

sunny in the fantasyland you expect me to believe you live in." I
stare at him, at a loss for words. "But we'll get to the bottom of
his whereabouts, don't worry. We'll find out where he's been."

Fear ignites a searing knot in my stomach. "Please, don't tell
him about Taylor. He doesn't know she's my daughter. He'd
never forgive me. It happened before he and I met, but he
would never—"

"Ms. Blake, you have bigger problems than your husband
being upset with you over a kid you had in high school. You're
being charged with a serious crime. Do you understand?"

I look at him through a blur of fresh tears, clasping my
hands together in an unspoken plea. "All I know is I didn't do
anything wrong. This has to be about Chloe, or maybe even
about what happened to Nikki eleven years ago. You don't
believe me, but there might be a witness."

He slaps his forehead in disbelief. "What witness?"

I slow my breathing and try to keep my voice steady, calm.
"Chloe showed me a newspaper clipping of an article that said
there was a witness to Nikki's fall, someone who surfaced
recently. It seems that, back then, the witness didn't want to
speak to the police. She was a tourist from Wisconsin, I believe.
She came back this year, and learned that Nikki's death was
ruled an accident, but she claimed it was murder. She saw how
it happened."

"And this was a newspaper article you saw?"

I nod anxiously, my lips dry, my palms sweating. "A clipping. Chloe had cut it out from the paper."

"Which paper was it?"

He asks all the questions I should have asked myself before
mentioning it. "I don't know."

"Let me get this straight. Your friend shows you this
damning article incriminating one or both of you in a murder,
and you don't have the curiosity to ask her where she saw it?"

I take his tongue lashing with stoicism, because I can't tell him Chloe was gone when I saw it, or that it was pasted on a page I tore from her binder. I'd rather he thinks me foolish than add obstruction to the list of charges.

"Wait here," he says, then storms out the door, leaving me stunned, wondering why I brought it up. What possible good can that article do me, when mentioning it makes him even more suspicious of me? I'm such a cliché, the typical suspect, so afraid her crime will come out that she can't help but talk herself into the ground. Only I didn't commit that crime.

This time, he returns quickly, his face scrunched in anger. "There's no bloody article!" he shouts, slamming his palms against the table. It rattles loudly, and I jolt back, my heart thumping in my chest. "Nikki Malkin was my case, and any piece of evidence, any new witness, would've been brought to my attention immediately." He shakes his head, as if I've somehow invented it all. "No newspaper in California mentioned Nikki Malkin in the past year, not since the year she died."

I can't believe it. "I know what I saw," I say weakly. "I thought it might've been to blame for Chloe's disappearance, that's why I brought it up. If that witness said Chloe killed Nikki, maybe someone wanted revenge and took her." My voice trails off as I'm increasingly aware how all this must sound to him. How I'm digging myself deeper and deeper.

He scowls at me, his lips pressed in a tight line. "You people, and your twisted, mind-fucking games." He walks over to the door with an angry stride and opens it. "Get the hell out of here. Don't leave town; don't talk to anybody. Understood?"

I stumble out of the room, then he walks me to the door, holding my elbow just as firmly as earlier.

When I'm finally outside, inhaling the fresh air fills my lungs with a searing rush, as if I've been drowning.

I don't know why he let me go, but I sensed his attitude change when I mentioned the article. Perhaps he's starting to believe me, or maybe he wants to follow me and see where I go. I really hope that's not the reason he released me, because I can't afford to stop looking for answers.

It's dark already. I've been locked up in there all day. My fingers tremble badly as I call an Uber, tears falling on the screen of my phone. As I wait, I try to get a grip on myself, but one question keeps gnawing at me, throwing me into a spin.

If the article was fake, was the threatening letter real?

THIRTY-FOUR

I'm almost halfway home when I realize that's not where I want to go. With every weary fiber in my body, I need Daniel. His strong arms wrapped around me, his comforting whispers in my ear. Calling him won't do it; I need to see him.

I ask the driver to take me to the diner instead. He grumbles something about having to cancel his next fare, but I don't care. He turns around and heads toward the diner, while I look at my phone, determined to make it up to him with a nice tip.

Daniel called me four times while I was locked up. My phone just didn't ring. Probably there's no reception in those interview rooms. No, that's not it. As if through a daze, I recall switching the phone ringer off, terrified that Detective Fernandez might ask for it and find the pictures of the binder pages.

Daniel left two messages, and I listen to them both. One was routine, just a reminder I need to pick up his allergy prescription. The second, several hours later, was a worried "Where are you?"

I refrain from calling him, knowing I'm merely two minutes away from the diner. Instead, while absent-mindedly looking out the window at the town's myriad lights, I relive the lowlights of the day.

Yes, we're both suspects, and the detective's attitude toward us has evolved into open hostility, his suspicions fueled by my inability to keep my mouth shut. But that's not all. If that article was fake, why did Chloe add it to her binder? What was she hoping to achieve? She must've realized that, just like what happened with Fernandez barely an hour ago, the cops would immediately know it was fake.

Is it possible Chloe didn't know it was fake? Was that the reason she was so scared? In her diary, she gradually started to believe she was to blame for Nikki's death, until she sort of changed her mind and decided to blame me for it. And who was that other girl, the medal-winning athlete? How is she involved?

"We're here," the crabby driver announces impatiently. I thank him and get out of the car, filling my lungs with the chilly evening air one more time before I head into the diner.

I almost don't see it, my attention split between the Uber app blowing up my phone with prompts to leave reviews, the departing ride, a small group of patrons leaving the diner, and the thought of telling Daniel to brace for a long session with Fernandez.

But there it is, looking eerily familiar, one of the last vehicles parked on the side of the building. A green, beat-up Chevy Silverado truck, its weathered paint peeling off on the hood and the side panels, deep tinted windows, no rear tag, the left rear panel dented above the wheel.

Just like the one caught on video arriving at Chloe's the day she was taken, then leaving seventeen minutes later.

Heart caught in my throat, I stop and stare at the truck, ignoring the polite patron holding the door open for me. I can't take my eyes off it, feeling a chill traveling down my spine. Who does it belong to? One of the patrons? An employee? I'm tempted to walk by it, to study it in detail, but then dismiss the thought. I don't want to scare off the driver. This might be my best chance yet to find Chloe.

"Miss?" The young patron holding the door calls my attention as I'm stopped in the middle of the entryway. If he let the door go, it would probably hit me in the face.

"Oh, yes, thank you," I reply, heading inside in a hurry to reach our usual table by the window before the mystery truck drives away.

Once I'm in, surrounded by the lively chatter of the usual dinner crowd, the dim lights in the dining room, and the familiar smells of steak and clam chowder and garlic mashed potatoes, I feel better. Safe. At home. I look around for Daniel, and I find him chatting with a patron and his wife, seated at the bar. I wait for him to look in my direction, then I wave, smiling awkwardly. He makes a quick apology and comes to meet me by the door.

I rush into his arms, burying my face in his chest. The floodgates break open with the bitter tears I managed to keep in check until now.

He pushes me to the side, out of sight. "What happened?" He looks at my face, worried, a little pale in the dim, yellowish lights.

"You're right, we're suspects." I sob quietly, aware I'm making a spectacle of myself. "Fernandez had me locked up all day."

"What?" he says, his loud question drawing the attention of nearby customers.

I look at him pleadingly, holding a finger to my lips. "Let's go to our table. Can you get me a Coke or something? I've been in there all day," I add, my chin trembling as I try to stifle another sob.

"Tell me what he said," Daniel asks moments later, putting a misted glass of Coca-Cola in front of me. "Are they out of their minds?"

I gulp about a third of it, instantly feeling it bite my empty stomach, igniting hunger and nausea at the same time but perking me up enough to dry my tears.

"He asked me about you, why you were late for the brunch with Chloe, and where you were the morning Chloe was taken."

He runs his hand over his tense features as if to wipe the worry away. "Goodness... why does he care about the stupid brunch?"

"It's the day Taylor, my student, was taken. Why were you late for that brunch? He said there was no health inspection at the diner that morning. That's what you told me, didn't you?" I hate how suspicious I feel of him.

He frowns and clenches his teeth for a brief moment. "That's what I told everyone at the brunch. I had to go to bail the line cook out. He spent Saturday night in boozer lockup, with his second DUI."

I breathe, relieved. It's not the first time his line cook has got in trouble for his drinking. "They're suspicious of us for Taylor's kidnapping, although we weren't anywhere near where it happened."

"Ah. So now they want to pin that on us too?"

I don't answer his question. I just steal another quick look out the window. The green Silverado is still there, although late diners are thinning out. For a moment, I consider sharing what I learned about that truck with Daniel, but something holds me back. "He grilled me over Chloe's binder, where and how I found it, why her husband called me to find it, who the girl in the picture is, stuff like that."

"What girl? What picture?"

I remember he hasn't seen the binder, and I wave off his questions. "Doesn't matter. But we shouldn't talk to them without a lawyer present. Don't make the same mistake I made." Another furtive look outside. "I thought I could reason with the man, but that's not possible." I take another sip of Coke, preparing myself to deliver the really bad news. "He wanted to charge me with Taylor's kidnapping. Daniel, he wants to throw me in jail." My voice breaks. Tears are back with a vengeance, stoked by Daniel's reassuring squeeze of the hand.

"Why you, out of all people? Because you're that girl's teacher? That's insane. We'll get you a good lawyer. Don't worry. It's not going to fly."

He doesn't know what I've done, or who Taylor is, so he can say that, but I don't believe him. "Promise me you won't let him talk to you without an attorney. Please, promise me. He said you lied about where you were that morning, about the health inspection. He's coming after you for this. I don't know what I'd do—"

He squeezes my hand again, and searches my eyes with a strong, reassuring, honest look. "Don't worry, baby. It's not going to happen, all right? That's what the cops do: they lie to people and intimidate them. He's not going to charge you." He stands and strokes my head gently. I lean into his hand, my eyes out the window, riveted on the green truck. "Let me get you something to eat. Kitchen's always open for friends and family," he quips, but worry lines are still ridging his brow.

"Just some fries," I say, knowing by now he's probably put away most of his pots and pans. "Whatever's easiest."

Daniel disappears, leaving me alone to mull over my confusing thoughts. It feels as if my reality started spinning the day I dropped apple pie on my new neighbors' doorstep and, since then, it's been spinning faster and faster, at breakneck speed, and there's no escape.

But most of all, I'm disappointed in myself. How can it be that, after everything that's happened, I still believed what Chloe said or wrote in her diary or her binder? Haven't I caught her in enough lies? I should've known better than to speak of that article with the detective, without checking it myself first.

If anything had been published about a witness to Nikki's death, I could've found a note of it online and confirmed it before opening my big mouth. And still, something about that article, about what I said, made Fernandez change his mind about charging me. What was it? Am I on to something with that article? He wouldn't lie about the witness, would he?

For a really stupid moment, I consider calling Fernandez to show him the truck. His team has resources and can match the truck in my home security video to the one here, make sure it's the exact same one. Thankfully, I see the flaw in my thinking and give it up before I dial his number. If I call him, I'll never find Chloe before he does. Lately, I'm all over the place. It feels like I stopped making sense a while ago, when my entire world went insane.

I eat a heap of homemade fries with my fingers, my depleted body grateful for every last one of them. Something in the salty goodness of a plate of fries makes everything seem possible again and scatters the looming clouds of fear, replacing them with confidence in tomorrow's possibilities.

But even with their assistance, I still can't think of what I'd say to Chloe if I found her.

Feeling horribly powerless when my entire life is unraveling is frightening, paralyzing even.

Then, as tired voices say good night and mark their exit with chimes of the vintage bell above the door, and the dining room falls silent, I think of Ray. All this time, I buried my longing for him under the shock of his betrayal and the justifiable resentment that followed. But the love was still there, surviving like a tiny spring flower buried underneath a layer of ice that can endure the fiercest winter, just waiting for the right moment to thrive.

Only I can't let it. Regardless of what happens to Chloe, or what Ray wants, he and I are over. We've been over for eleven years, since the day he chose to make love to Chloe instead of me. Everything that's recently happened between us to spark the old feelings is just a memory, mere echoes of who we used to be.

His life is with her; it's what he chose. Mine is with Daniel, the man I love. It's confusing and disheartening that I can love Daniel the way that I do, and still have such strong feelings for Ray. They're not the same... I believe my longing for Ray comes from the same place as when an adult buys the toy they couldn't afford as a child, in an attempt to soothe the old self. That's what I'm doing with my fantasies... soothing the eighteen-year-old girl who was betrayed and abandoned, her young love crushed, her grief never resolved. I'd really like to think that's it, that I can blame it on some buzzy psychospeak, and that I'm not falling back in love with Ray against all reason.

Because having him next door makes it incredibly difficult to think of anything else. I walk over to the window every time I hear a noise, hoping to catch a glimpse of his face. I find myself wanting to go over there and ask how he is, how he's coping. After all, his wife is missing. But I'm not lying to myself anymore... such daydreaming fantasies end with me in his arms, breathless, my lips crushed under his, my hands fumbling with his belt, my back arched under his passionate embrace.

Instead, I've been planning my exits so I don't run into him. My willpower has been proven paper-thin, and I know, deep inside my heart, that if he says the right thing or does the right thing, my resolve will vanish, and I will fall again, hard, beyond repair. And I'd break the heart of a kind and loving man who's done nothing wrong other than marry a woman who never got over another man.

"Ready to go?" Daniel asks, and I startle. Thankfully, the truck is still there, but seeing it brings a chill back to my body.

"Let's stay a little bit longer, please." I hold up my empty glass with a timid smile. "Can I have a refill?"

"Sure."

"We're not holding anyone overtime, are we?"

"Nah, it's just me and Jason. Everyone else is gone. He's almost done with the patio, then he's going too. I'll tell him I'll close, so he won't have to wait."

I force my smile to bloom, my heart tightened with fear. Only Daniel and Jason? Whose truck is it, then? Jason drives a brand-new blue Mazda. It was in my driveway the day we had the backyard party after the interview aired. Daniel drives the Ford SUV parked by the entrance.

All the earlier excitement at the thought that I might be close to finding Chloe wanes, and the possibility that someone just abandoned the truck in the diner's parking lot emerges, withering everything it touches.

Daniel drops off my refilled glass, then disappears to finish his work in the kitchen. As I watch him walking away, the insidious suspicions seeded by Detective Fernandez take root in my mind. What if Daniel drove that truck? What if he's somehow involved in all this madness? My hands are white-knuckled around the glass and just as cold as its contents, as I picture Daniel snatching Taylor because he somehow found out she's mine. And that was why he was late for the brunch.

I push the nonsensical thought out of my mind. That's how people go insane, I tell myself. Too many questions, not enough answers. And an overactive imagination.

"Good night, sis," I hear Jason say. As I wave at him, the door opens and the bell chimes loudly in the deserted room. Holding my breath, I turn my gaze out the window and wait. After a moment, I see Jason walking toward the truck with his determined, youthful gait, unaltered by the long hours spent toiling at the diner. He unlocks the truck, then hops behind the wheel and drives off.

I'm speechless.

Jason? Why?

"Come on, baby, let's go," Daniel says, standing next to me. "I need a shower like you wouldn't believe."

I believe it. I think I need one even more than he does, after spending an entire day in that filthy interview room. But I don't say anything, and once we're home, I'll let him call dibs on the shower, because I'm too shocked by what I just saw, and I need time to process it.

"I thought Jason had that blue Mazda, the cute little sports car." I look back at Daniel as I'm walking out of the diner, while he stops to set the alarm and lock the door. "Saw him drive off in a piece-of-crap truck. Is he gambling again?"

"I don't know," Daniel says with a shrug, catching up to me. "He didn't say a thing."

I bet he didn't.

Or maybe Daniel doesn't want to tell me about it.

THIRTY-FIVE

I spent all last night awake, staring at the ceiling, connecting the dots. Why would Jason take Chloe? Does Daniel know more than he's saying? But I can't believe it. Not my husband. I've kept him out of all of this... there's no way he's involved.

His brother, however, is a different story.

Jason met Chloe at the impromptu party in our backyard. She flirted with him for about five minutes, but then again, Chloe flirts with any male who can fog a mirror. I recall she looked her usual fancy self, wearing her wealth on her sleeve.

Maybe Jason saw that as a quick way to make a buck. But that still doesn't make sense, although he's been in trouble over gambling debts before. No ransom call has been received, as far as I know. And I recall clearly that Chloe voiced some concerns for her safety that day. The day she met Jason in my backyard. Whatever those concerns were, they couldn't've been about a guy she'd just met.

If she's still alive, maybe she will be able to shed some light, or perhaps Jason will. In any case, for the first time since this nightmare started, I know exactly what to do. That certainty is energizing.

When Daniel wakes up, he finds me dressed, brewing his favorite blend of coffee. He looks absolutely lovable in his wrinkled pajamas, scratching his stubble as he rambles into the living room, squinting at the piercing morning sun.

Memories of my suspicions resurface for a while, putting a slight frown on my face.

"Good morning," I say, as cheerfully as I can muster with a tight knot in my stomach. "Want milk with your coffee?"

He yawns loudly, and it's contagious. "Yes, please." He lands on a chair at the breakfast table and settles his elbows on the glossy surface, then gives me a quizzical look. "Going somewhere?"

I cringe, remembering the solemn promise I made only two days ago, about not lying to him anymore. "Yes, I have a dentist appointment. Remember?" Lying has become so easy for me, it's uncanny.

"Ugh, sorry to hear that." He takes a sip of coffee, then sets the cup down and stares at it, probably still half asleep.

"Not a big deal, just a cleaning and a tiny filling." I finish brewing my coffee and take it to the table. I love our little morning routine. It only happens when I don't have to leave early for school. It's the cornerstone of my day, the moment I get my thoughts together. With him, today especially, I have to plan a web of lies, and it makes me sad. But I know for a fact that if he knew what I'm about to do, he'd never let me walk out that door.

A half-hour drive later, about nine, I park across from Jason's apartment building in Redwood City, hoping he's his usual self and won't notice the Subaru he knows so well. I keep my eyes on the beat-up Chevy truck, whose tagless rear end is visible in the building's lot, and I wait.

Just like Daniel, Jason's not an early riser, mostly because of the late hours they pull at the diner. But Jason's also the rebellious teenager who never grew up and never will, not even after serving time for his reckless impulsiveness. If it weren't for Daniel and his willingness to help his brother, Jason would probably be homeless right now, violating his parole to some degree.

Yes, my brother-in-law served time. For aggravated assault, no less. I guess escalating from that to kidnapping is not such an inconceivable leap, although the assault charge had more to do with his incredibly short fuse; while a kidnapping like Chloe's takes planning, focus, and a cool head. I never thought of Jason as a violent man, although he served time for it. To me, he's Daniel's little brother, *my* little brother, someone I love dearly. Someone who made a mistake once, when he was provoked, and ruined his life over it.

I remember the two of them chatting in our backyard: Jason and Chloe. He was ogling her, like he does with all the beautiful women who happen to cross his path, but not in an exaggerated way; more admiring and interested than lecherous. She was chatting him up in her excited, bubbly voice, leaning into him, lowering her voice at times as if she was telling him secrets, smiling, batting her eyelashes. A flip of her hair, the long, blonde waves of silk scented with Acqua di Parma; the clacking of four-inch heels; and the swaying of her hips as she walked away, only to come back moments later, in an ebb-and-flow game designed to arouse even the dead. All that while I was enthralled by Ray's burning gaze, wondering what it meant, afraid to find out.

About two hours into my stakeout, I'm tempted to go upstairs and bang on Jason's door, demanding answers. But there's no way he's holding a hostage in the cramped studio apartment, with paper-thin walls and a constant stream of people walking up and down the building's narrow corridors. It's best I wait.

A text from Daniel asks me if everything is all right. I almost forget my lie and ask why, but I catch myself in time and reply that all is good, that I'm almost done. His response is a thumbs-up emoji. When I raise my eyes from the phone's screen, the Chevy truck is pulling out of the building's parking lot.

For almost forty minutes, I follow Jason from a safe distance, anticipating his turns more than seeing them, and manage not to lose track of him. After he runs a couple of quick errands, including a trip to the bank's ATM for what appears from a distance to be a hefty wad of cash, he takes the interstate, then Highway 92, heading for Half Moon Bay.

Only he surprises me at the top of the mountain. Instead of keeping straight on 92 to start the descent toward the coast, he takes a left onto Skyline Boulevard. I fall farther back, as Skyline's traffic is sporadic at that time of day. Thankfully, the winding road is almost always shaded by large trees, making it difficult for him to spot me. He drives for a few miles, faster than I would normally dare, but I keep telling myself that if his weathered Chevy can make it, so will my Subaru.

He takes a right turn on an unpaved exit, more a trail than a road. His truck rattles and bounces, and I come dangerously close to being seen. I'm afraid to take the turn right after him, and I hesitate for precious moments, looking at the GPS map on my screen, wondering how far into the woods he'll go. Out of options, I eventually turn after him, driving slowly on the rugged trail, expecting to run into him after each turn.

I almost miss the Silverado as I pass by the long driveway to a small cabin tucked deep into the woods. The truck is stopped in front of the house, facing the road, and the front door is open. I continue driving until I find another path where I can hide my Subaru, behind a thicket dense enough to keep it completely out of sight. Then I climb over a small ridge and crouch down when the cabin comes into view.

Jason is loading several large black trash bags into the truck, sometimes grunting as he lifts and swings them before throwing them over the side. He makes quick work of the task. From this distance, I can't see the expression on his face, only his silhouette. However, what I *can't* see is what's most troubling. There's no Chloe anywhere, and there doesn't seem to be, considering the cabin door is wide open. There's no screaming coming from in there, no cries for help, nothing but the deep silence of the majestic redwood forest, occasionally punctuated by birds chirping and trash bags crashing in Jason's truck with the rattle of broken glass and empty tin cans.

After lifting and locking the truck bed, he hops behind the wheel and slams the driver's side door shut. I'm faltering back on my hands and knees, in a rush to get back to my car, but by the time I drive my Subaru back to the trail, he's gone. I drive as quickly as I dare, but once I reach Skyline, there's no telling where he went.

He's gone.

Desperate, I fight back tears. I must find Chloe before it's too late. Before I get thrown in jail and I can't even look for her anymore. What would I do then? Risk having her life on my conscience? Or dig myself even deeper, confessing that I withheld critical evidence from her binder? Would I tell the cops about Jason? How positive am I it's Jason's truck I saw in that surveillance video? But it is, I know it is. The same peeling green paint. The same dent on its side. It's the same damn truck. And it could be on its way to where Chloe's being held.

I need answers badly, and those answers just vanished, because Jason is gone.

For a moment, I consider calling him and telling him I know what he's done. It might work, or it might prove deadly. What do I really know about Jason? Until yesterday, I would've sworn he'd never hurt anyone, despite that one assault charge blemishing his record. I always thought that was just the hot-blooded, drunken mistake of a misguided youth. I thought I knew him. Turns out, I don't know him any better than I know Chloe.

Out of better choices, I return to the cabin. This time, I park right in front of it. I almost hope Jason will come back so I can confront him. Whose cabin is this? What's he doing here? Where's Chloe? And he better not say he doesn't know what I'm talking about.

I open the unlocked front door and enter, a late-emerging sense of anxiety making me breathe shallowly as I anticipate the worst, an undefined worst: someone else could still be in here, I realize as I open the door. Someone who could easily smack me in the head and lock me up somewhere, to keep Chloe company, to share her fate.

I can quickly see that the cabin's deserted, because it's only a room with a section curtained off to hide what has to be California's filthiest toilet and a sink to match. A small table, two wooden chairs, and a stained mattress on a wrought iron bed are the only pieces of furniture, alongside a small woodburning stove in the corner, by the window. The place smells of mildew something terrible, and of something else: a stench I always associated with rats, although I can't see any.

Jason must've loaded at least eight trash bags in his truck, and I can't begin to imagine what was in them. There's nothing left. No bedsheets or pillows, on the off chance those ever existed, no dishes or objects of any kind. The place has been sanitized, so to speak, although only fire could truly sanitize that hellhole.

If she was ever there, I'm too late.

As I'm about to leave, I recall something my mother used to tell me. "Don't be afraid to sweep under the bed, Alana," she used to say. "Who knows what lost treasures you might find there?"

I smile at the fond memory and go back inside, then kneel by the bed, trying my best not to touch it.

There's only one item, and I retrieve it with the tips of my fingers. It's a hair scrunchie, light-brown velvet, just like the ones Chloe always liked to carry with her, just in case. I recall how abundant they were: in her car, in the jeans she was wearing when we were caught in the rain one time, and she thought it best to tie her hair in a ponytail, a bowl full of them in her closet, when I went looking for her binder.

I take the scrunchie outside, where daylight helps me see better, and confirm my suspicion. A long strand of blonde, wavy hair is still clinging to it.

Chloe was here.

As heartbreaking as it is for me to admit it, Jason kidnapped her.

And now, she's gone.

THIRTY-SIX

It will crush Daniel's heart.

That's all I can think of on the drive back home. Regardless of what happens to Chloe, or if I manage to get to her before the police do, Jason is still screwed. What the hell was he thinking? If he's after her money, why didn't he ask for the ransom already? I guess I would've known by now if such a call were received. From Ray, if not from Chloe's parents. As I recall Dr. Avery's words when she threw me out of her house, I cringe with shame, regret, and a deep sense of loss. Even if I haven't seen them in years, I have fond memories of them both, memories I didn't realize I still cherished.

And then I think of Chloe, and a sense of dread unfurls in my gut, spreading bumps on my skin so intense I turn on the heat in my car. Who knows where she is and what she'll tell the cops when they find her? Now that Jason took her, I'm even more afraid of the damage she could do. It's not just me anymore... it's Daniel's little brother too.

Unlike me, Jason made his own bed. What the hell was he thinking? If he were here with me right now, I'd beat him senseless. That thought makes me wonder what I should do next.

Should I confront him or continue to follow him like I did today? Maybe he'll lead me to Chloe after all. All I know is I can't confront him without taking a huge risk. He might panic and run, or do something really stupid, as if his recent actions were not idiotic enough.

I drive by the diner but don't stop, just to check if Jason showed up for work in time for the lunch rush hour. The green Silverado is gone, but the blue Mazda is parked on the same spot the truck took yesterday. For a moment, I consider meeting Daniel for a meal, but the parking lot filled with chatty tourists tells me I'd probably be dining by myself, taking table space from a paying customer.

Knowing Jason's schedule, I plan to resume my stakeout at his place tomorrow morning. I can't do it tonight; it would be impossible to justify my absence to Daniel. I simply can't afford to get caught in another lie. But tomorrow, he might lead me to where she is.

I cling to this hope like a drowning person to a piece of driftwood, hoping to see the shore and not daring to look around much, afraid she'll spot the tip of a shark's fin drawing closer and closer.

After stopping to pick up Daniel's allergy meds from the drugstore, I head on home, eagerly anticipating the peacefulness of my living room.

As I turn onto the street, I notice a large, white Maybach blocking part of my driveway, the curb space between my house and Chloe's house too narrow to accommodate its length. A woman unlocks it with a simple touch on its door handle; a woman I recognize as I reach the driveway. It's Stella, Ray's mother.

I can barely squeeze my Subaru in its usual spot, passing the impressive car with two wheels on the lawn. Then I breathe deeply before getting out. She's waiting for me with a friendly smile on her lips, but I'm wary of her, as I am of all things Ray.

Regardless, I'm instantly wrapped in a hug I pretend to welcome, because life is so much easier when we pretend and lie and deceive.

"Darling girl, you're gorgeous," she says, pulling away and studying me head to toe. "You're gorgeous." She touches my face with gentle fingers, her diamond ring sparkling in the sun when she moves her hand. She must've done incredibly well for herself. I try not to stare, but there's no wedding band on her finger. Maybe she remarried, but that second marriage didn't last either. Or perhaps she found a way to provide for herself, and kudos to her. She looks fabulous: the body of a young woman, the looks of a comfortable and successful socialite. She's wearing jeans this time, high-heeled black ankle boots, and a white angora sweater so soft and lush I want to touch it again.

"Thank you," I reply, painfully aware I'm blushing like a schoolgirl. "You look amazing," I say, the compliment so easy to give.

She smiles and tilts her head ever so slightly, still looking at me, at my body, in a way that starts feeling a bit creepy. Her hand follows her gaze, and she touches my belly with a gentle caress. I have to summon all my willpower to stand still, although I don't know why I feel I must. "I bet you could bear my son children in a heartbeat."

My smile wanes, her words a veritable cold shower. I feel the urge to take a step back, and I do. "Mrs. Preston—"

"It's Stella, sweetie. There's no need for formality." She pretends not to notice she makes me uncomfortable, or maybe she genuinely doesn't know.

I nod, pushing myself to smile just a little. "Stella, thank you. It's good to see you," I say, getting ready to leave, but her hand lands on my forearm and I stop.

"Speak with Ray, will you?" she says, lowering her voice. "He's by himself, tortured and alone, and you're his best friend. Aren't you, my dear?"

A frown flickers across my brow. How did I end up being Ray's best friend in her mind after we haven't seen each other for almost eleven years? But I'm not going to tell her she's wrong; it wouldn't be the right thing to do. "I will. I can only imagine how hard it is to deal with Chloe's—"

"Promise me, all right? It would help me worry a little less about him. He's not like other men. He's so sensitive, so fragile even. And he loves you more than you think. He always has."

I almost blurt out that he didn't love me enough to be faithful, but instead I nod and whisper, "I promise."

She plants a kiss on my cheek and gives me another warm hug, then says, "I've always liked you more than Chloe, you know. But men are stupid, and my son is no exception. Maybe the wrong one won." She winks at me and adds, "You have my vote."

Then she climbs behind the wheel of her elegant vehicle and drives off. I stand there watching her leave, still shocked at her words. I have her *vote*? What the hell was that about? Probably just an eccentric woman's way to pay a compliment. I breathe away the feeling of uneasiness she left in her wake.

Warm hands land on my shoulders, squeezing gently in a tender gesture I relish deeply until I remember Daniel's Ford was in front of the diner only thirty minutes ago.

I turn around, startled.

"Ray," I whisper, unexpectedly out of breath. Our eyes meet and the silence crackles between us. His mouth is sketching a smile, but his eyes are burning with a longing I'm afraid to decipher.

"Alana," he says, my name on his lips throwing me into a spin. "I—"

He chokes and lowers his eyes for a moment, while I remember I must breathe. I start pulling away, but he clasps my hand, and our eyes meet again. I see he knows how I feel, and he wants it, he wants *me*. But he'd be cheating on his missing wife... how screwed up is that? Or is it? Is it so bad to feel lonely and lost and need someone during what must be the hardest time of his life?

"Have you heard anything?" I manage to ask, and the magic is gone in the blink of an eye. He lets go of my hand and I'm saddened by it.

He looks away, the longing still there on his handsome face, but his eyes avoid mine. "Nothing yet. No ransom call; no news from the cops either."

"I'm so sorry, Ray. Wish there was something I could do."

Without a word, he wraps me in his arms and searches for my lips with an intensity, a desire so overwhelming I forget myself. I respond to his kiss, my hands around his neck, wanting his touch like never before.

A honking truck in the distance breaks the spell between us and I pull away, breathless, ashamed. "Ray... I can't."

It's all I say before I rush inside my house and lock the door behind me. Then I drop to the floor, sobbing quietly as I will myself to be rational and faithful, while with every fiber of my being I yearn to rush back into Ray's arms.

But my sobs recede as I recall Stella's words. The strangeness of her behavior, the things she said, the hair-raising way she rubbed my abdomen, as if she knew I'd been pregnant with her son's child. A shiver crawls down my spine as I realize she might be the one who took Taylor. To her, it would seem almost like repossession, her fundamental right to be reunited with her own flesh and blood. But would she ever forgive me if she knew I'd given away her grandchild? Probably not in a million years. So what the hell was that all about?

Maybe she's seeking revenge against me, for abandoning the grandchild she so desperately wants. She knew about Nikki's death. Hell, everyone knew back then; everyone who had kids in school that year knew Nikki, or at least knew *of* her. Stella has the money to pull this entire scheme off. Taylor's kidnapping, and the adoption agency arson—probably to cover the tracks that could lead back to Taylor, to me. Then the punishment of the selfish mother who'd abandoned her baby. Ray's baby. That mother deserves to rot in jail. And who better to hire for the job than Jason, so she'd ruin his life too and Daniel's?

Holding my breath, I realize just how well this scenario fits. Except for one critical detail. Why on earth would she have kidnapped Chloe?

I can't think of a single reason why she would.

I'm not seeing the whole picture, and time is running out. I'm still free to dig into this, to follow Jason and try to find Chloe, but that could change in a heartbeat if the cops arrest me. Then I know there's no way a jury wouldn't convict me for Taylor's kidnapping. She's my biological daughter. I was stalking her. I inserted myself into her life and became her teacher. A good prosecutor could easily argue I was obsessed. And, years ago, a girl fell to her death with my DNA under her fingernails, which might sway a jury to believe I sometimes resort to violence to solve my problems.

They'd convict me and throw me in prison for years and years. What's worse, they'd probably give up looking for Taylor, and I'd never see her again.

Yet something Stella said is gnawing at me. Well, more like what she didn't say: that Chloe and I had fought over Ray. That's what she must've meant by "The wrong one won." It fits. At least, in her warped mind it does.

Then why did she say "You have my vote"? The answer that comes to mind makes my mind reel.

She meant Chloe and I are still fighting over Ray. Somehow, she believes the battle's still on.

Perhaps that's why she kidnapped Chloe. To tip the scales in my favor.

THIRTY-SEVEN

The following day, Jason doesn't leave his apartment until it's time to go to work. I follow his vehicle to the diner, occasionally wondering how come he doesn't get pulled over for driving without a tag. He always takes the small streets, and he has an interesting way to avoid cops. At one point, a police cruiser merges into traffic a couple of vehicles behind Jason. He must've seen it, because he immediately turns into a gas station and waits the cruiser out. His sudden maneuver causes some issues for me, because I can't follow him in time, but I find a way to wait for him a couple of blocks down without being seen.

He doesn't go anywhere but work; doesn't stop anywhere but the gas station. As I'm watching him pull into the diner's parking lot, I wonder if he still has Chloe. I don't know a whole lot about kidnappings, but from what I've seen in movies, holding someone hostage isn't easy. They want to escape. They shriek and make noise, hoping someone will hear them. They need to eat. If Jason has Chloe, he's bound to go there at some point, at least to check on her and bring her food.

Perhaps he goes after work, when I can't follow. I close my eyes, trying to recall if he was carrying food to go the other night when he left the diner, but all that comes to mind is the time I've been squandering. I can't afford to waste a moment longer. There was an awkward silence between Daniel and me this morning, when I invented another excuse for leaving the house early, this time something involving a school event. He's growing increasingly silent and withdrawn lately, as much as I try my best to cheer him up every night. A bit of suspicion still lingers, and I can't blame him. I think he's also hurt by my distrust in him and by my unwillingness to bear his children, whether he believes the reason I gave him or not.

I return home and text Daniel casually, asking if he wants anything special for dinner, saying I have time on my hands, just to deflate whatever suspicions he might still have. His reply is monosyllabic. Then, after retrieving Chloe's diary, I sit in front of my laptop and take out my phone, keen on reviewing every bit of information in her binder, including the pages I tore out.

I need to go back to square one, in case I missed something. There must be another way to find her, of understanding what's going on, and I'm just not seeing it.

As I scroll through the images saved on my phone, I stop on the photo of that girl I never met, the athlete wearing her medal. Who is she? After torturing myself with baseless speculations for a while, I remember there's an image search engine I heard about. After uploading the picture into the search engine, I click the button and wait for a few moments, staring at the girl's face in the faded photo.

Dressed in a white leotard with long sleeves and elegant vertical lines, the girl has her chin thrust out and her eyes filled with pride. She's not obnoxiously in-your-face conceited; rather, she's brimming with the delight of achievement, of winning. She's beautiful, about sixteen in the photo or even a bit younger. Her hair flows in loose, bountiful waves of blonde, silky strands, too long to fit entirely in the portrait cropping of the picture.

The image search is finished, and the list of results is extensive. All sorts of partial matches have me sifting through dozens of photos, almost all of them of blonde girls wearing white garments. I'm about to finish scrolling through the fourth page of results, when I see her.

I click the link where the image was originally posted. It's an article published by a local newspaper from Wilmington, North Carolina. As I read the headline, I gasp in disbelief.

LOCAL ATHLETICS STAR KILLED
AFTER SOCCER PRACTICE

I read the short article quickly, holding my breath, my hand absently covering my gaping mouth. The girl's name was Heather Davenport, and she was killed by another student, a girl who tripped her as she was running down the bleachers to meet a family member in the audience. If it weren't for someone's camera capturing the incident, Heather's death might've been ruled an unfortunate accident. But the amateur video, captured on a soccer mom's phone, showed another girl deliberately sticking her foot out when Heather was approaching. The girl fell down the stairs and broke her neck.

Why would the picture of a dead girl from North Carolina be in Chloe's binder? Ray moved to Half Moon Bay from North Carolina, that much I remember, but I don't see the connection. Another student killed Heather. As far as I know, Chloe never set foot in North Carolina, so it can't be that. The year Heather was killed, Chloe and I were attending school and hanging out together, here at home.

I check the date of the article, and see it was published about a month and a half before Ray started school in Half Moon Bay. That gives me pause, and enough reason to search for any correlations between Ray and Heather Davenport.

The web search doesn't return much information at all, but

social media is different. Heather's profile is still active, but memorialized: the word REMEMBERING appears above Heather's name. Her feed is an honor roll of photos from athletic events, both hers and her friends, where she just cheered along. There are finish shots, podium medal shots, and countless selfies with Ray.

They were dating, up until the day she died. I stare at the screen, at young Ray's face, and see the joy in his eyes, the undisguised enchantment when he held his arm around Heather's shoulders, when she looked into his eyes.

I'm jealous. Of a dead girl, no less.

I rid myself of the ridiculous feeling and start searching for Ray's social media accounts. I remember thinking, back when we were dating, how strange it was he didn't have any. He still doesn't, so that search is a dead end. But now that I have the girl's name, I can search some more. A few moments later, I know the school she went to, and I have the number.

Another quick search tells me the principal's assistant is Rose McCarthy, and she's been with the school for ages. My experience as a schoolteacher tells me she is the most likely person to spill secrets she shouldn't.

Nervous and a little apprehensive, I brew myself another cup of coffee and drink it slowly, savoring the sunshine in our backyard and planning my next steps carefully. I only have one shot at this.

I make the call from the privacy of my living room, hoping that Rose McCarthy will be there during summer break and has time for a bit of gossip.

After only two rings, a deep, husky voice fills the silence of my living room. "This is Rose." She sounds pleasant, good-natured.

"Hello, Rose, this is Alana Blake, a teacher in Half Moon Bay. How are—"

"California?"

I smile. "Yes, California. How are you today?"

"Oh, I'm fine, Ms. Blake." I can hear the excitement in her voice. "I always wanted to visit California, but never got the chance. So, how can I assist you today?"

"It's Alana. After all, we're practically colleagues, aren't we?"

She laughs. "Alana, yes, of course we are."

"I feel I already know you," I say, smiling widely so she can hear it in my voice.

"Really? How's that?"

"I'm doing a profile of one of our alumni. He's now quite the benefactor for our school. Said you were his guiding light during a challenging period in his youth." I pause for effect, and I could swear she's holding her breath. "Raymond Preston. Do you remember him?"

"Oh, Ray? My stars, what a gem of a boy. Always polite, charming, and a good student too. How could I forget him?"

"What can you tell me about his time as a student there? Any notable achievements? Was he featured in the school paper?"

"Um, I believe he was a football player. If I'm not mistaken, a quarterback. Quite popular with the girls." She laughs quietly, and her giggles turn into a bout of coughing, while I patiently wait. She must be covering the phone with her hand, because the sound is muffled until she's done. "My apologies. He was no ladies' man, though. He had his eyes set on one young lady. Tragically, she passed away during a school sporting event."

"He mentioned something, yes. How awful."

"Devastating, truly. We were all in shock."

"Did he see it happen?"

A pause. "No, he wasn't there. I believe the football team was playing that weekend, in Fayetteville, if I'm not mistaken. It's been years."

"Gosh, you have an amazing memory! To recall such details, wow. I envy you."

"Oh, well, it's because of the tragic loss of that dear girl. Otherwise, days meld together. You know how it is."

"What happened with the girl, if you don't mind me asking?"

"Not at all, it was in all the papers. Another girl was to blame, some say jealousy was the cause, but I don't know. Heather—that's the girl who died—she wasn't the kind to get sucked into any drama. She worked hard; she didn't have time for that kind of crap. She was an athlete, a gold medalist at state level. We were all so proud of her."

"And the girl responsible? Did she say anything?"

"She never really opened up about it, and her parents immediately hired a pricey lawyer and things were kept quiet, although she was charged and went to prison for it. No one could understand what made her do it. And Heather, that poor baby: one moment she's laughing, cheering, taking steps two at a time to be with her family; then next she's lifeless, her neck broken. A sight I'll never shake off." Her voice trails off in a shudder.

"Oh, wow. That's so tragic. Unbelievable. Must've been a tough time for Ray, being so young. How did he cope?"

"I think that's when the family moved to California." The state name rolls off her tongue in such a way I can tell she enjoys saying it. "The poor boy was devastated. And his mother was fierce about it. She wanted him away from there, so his academic and athletic development wouldn't suffer. I was taken aback a little by how determined she was about it. Just when Ray needed his friends the most, he lost them all. They moved the same month."

"And his father?"

"Mrs. Preston was a single mom," she says, a bit surprised.

"Yeah, sorry, Ray and I didn't speak much about Stella. I

met her, though, and she's amazing, a powerhouse woman. But I'm a little surprised she took him away from his hometown, from his community, especially at a moment like that."

"Oh, but Wilmington's not Ray's hometown. They're from Tennessee. They lived here for less than a year."

I bite my lip for a moment, frustrated. The call had been going wonderfully, until it wasn't. "You see, I completely missed that! In all honesty, Ray was more focused on Heather's death, on what was a very difficult time of his life. That's when he mentioned you, Rose. He said you were extremely helpful, understanding, and he expressed gratitude."

"He remembered... bless that little heart." I can hear the tears in Rose's voice. "I did help him. You see, his mother's a bit overbearing, if you ask me. Came on too strong and had this... ferocity about what Ray should or shouldn't do. His entire life, planned out move by move. Even Heather seemed to have Mrs. Preston's approval somehow. So, I stepped in whenever I could, bought the boy a bit of time to, well, be a boy, make friends, play football." A moment of silence. "I'm thrilled to hear he turned out all right. Big donor, huh? His mother was just as broke as the rest of us when they left."

How interesting. I wonder how she moved from broke to Maybach and diamonds in ten years or less. Sounds like the title of a cheesy clickbait article, but the story behind it might be worth uncovering.

"Thank you very much. I'll only put some of this in my article, but I'll make sure to name you as someone who made a difference in his life."

"Ah, thank you, Alana! Always heard folks in California have big hearts."

I chuckle quietly. If only she knew. "We do our best. One last thing—do you recall where they resided in Tennessee?"

"Huh?"

"Where in Tennessee were they living before they moved to North Carolina?"

"Oh, they were from Chattanooga, honey."

"Thanks again, you're absolutely amazing. If you're ever in California, lunch is on me."

She is still giggling, much like a schoolgirl, when she hangs up. Then I breathe, all the new information I've gathered swirling in my head, making absolutely no sense at all.

Why did Chloe include in her binder the picture of a girl who died when neither Ray nor his mother were present? What was she trying to say?

Maybe another call would bring some answers that I can understand. I don't know yet who I'm going to call, but I know exactly where I'll be calling.

Chattanooga, Tennessee.

THIRTY-EIGHT

It's easy to get embroiled in researching things that happened twelve or more years ago. What a kid's mom might've been doing while living in Chattanooga is not exactly newsworthy, unless, of course, it is. Stella had kept a reasonably low profile. Her name didn't exist in correlation with that place and that time, with one notable exception: she divorced Bradford Preston there, when Ray was fourteen. Aside from the divorce decree, which I was able to find relatively easily, there was only one other mention of Stella and Bradford Preston's names. A small, insignificant gossip column on a local blogger's site, titled WHEN CUSTODY BATTLES TAKE IT TOO FAR.

I read the poorly edited article quickly; it was only three paragraphs long. According to the blogger, the Prestons fought fiercely for custody of their only son, with threats and loud arguments and disturbances that eventually led to a police intervention, and without any regard for the teenager's well-being. She referenced it as an example of what not to do if you care about the mental health of your children during a nasty divorce. She also warned that getting the police involved could have unwanted consequences. In the Prestons' case, it seemed that

Stella used the police report to convince the judge that her husband was violent and careless of their son's welfare and then gained sole custody.

I go back and check the date on the divorce decree, then search for more information. After Stella was awarded sole custody, they remained in Chattanooga for almost three more years before moving to North Carolina, per the school's sporting events photo gallery.

Out of curiosity, I search for Bradford Preston. The search engine returns a cornucopia of information that isn't linked to the person I want. I decide to split the search results by year and location, and I find what I'm looking for with more ease.

After their divorce, Bradford Preston fell off the face of the internet for about a year and a half, then he was mentioned as one of the founders of a startup, something to do with music and digital streaming. Back then, streaming wasn't something most people knew about. My attention is piqued.

Another year later, Bradford Preston's startup was called "innovative, revolutionary, a game changer" for the music industry, and he moved to Nashville, sharing with an interviewer his intention to "stay close to the center of country music, for which I have a soft spot in my heart."

I change years again and, this time, a slew of articles fills the screen, along with several pictures. I recognize Ray's features in the handsome, elegant, and slightly grizzled businessman. His face shows self-confidence and strength, but it's not what makes me gasp. The third article on the page reads: SELF-MADE MUSIC MILLIONAIRE FROM CHATTANOOGA OPENS NEW HEADQUARTERS IN SILICON VALLEY.

He moved to California. Before Stella and Ray did.

Then, only a couple of months after Ray, Chloe, and I graduated from high school, Stella and Bradford remarried. I found a picture of them online, smiling, holding hands in front of a small group of people gathered inside a church. And about two years after that, Bradford's Porsche veered off the road and fell into the ravine, about a mile east of Albert Canyon. He died on the way to the hospital. Later, an extensive newspaper article noted he'd taken a few too many of his blood pressure meds that morning.

The sound of my own astonished whistle jolts me. That's how Stella went from broke to Maybach in ten years. But it doesn't help me in any way. I still don't know how to find Chloe.

As I'm about to close the browser window, another headline catches my eye. It predates Preston's death, and it's an opinion piece from a small tabloid that covers Silicon Valley celebrity gossip. Seems the second Preston marriage wasn't any more blissful than the first. According to the pretentious reporter, arguments were blowing up in the Prestons' posh Half Moon Bay residence just as they used to in Chattanooga, sure to shorten Bradford's life. Mr. Preston had recently complained of chest pain and shortness of breath, an unnamed source was quoted as saying.

That reporter must've been psychic. Her column was published mere weeks before Preston lost control of his car and crashed into the canyon.

Did he really overdo his blood pressure meds that morning? Or did Stella dose him? It's too late to ever find out.

Closing the browser window, I get ready to call Ray's school in Tennessee and play the same part I did with Rose. But the thought of Stella's creepiness doesn't let me. There were several mentions of her in Chloe's diary. For the most part, I didn't pay much attention to those sections when I was reading, but one entry keeps nagging at me. I flip through the pages of Chloe's diary quickly until I find it, then I read it again.

Last night, it happened again. I was tense, overwrought, help-lessly tearful. I received an invitation to attend a memorial service for Nikki Malkin, a year after her death. It upset me deeply; got me wondering if Alana received one too, if she's going to show. How about me? Should I send flowers? Should I simply not attend? Then what would people think? That I was feeling too guilty to show up and pay my respects? There have been whispers in the community... Ray overheard some people talk.

Ray came to my side and took me in his arms like he always does when I'm crying. Then he whispered words that brought a chill to my heart. "I'm right here, sweetheart. Doesn't matter what happened; I understand."

At first, I didn't realize what he was talking about. I looked at him inquisitively.

He continued to whisper ever so gently, stroking my hair, my face, wiping tears off my cheek with his thumb. "It happened, baby. It's just something that happened. Just forget everything about it. I know it's difficult when you have doubts, when you blame yourself. But I will never blame you. I promise you that."

"What are you talking about?" I finally asked, still sniffling.

"Nikki."

That name on his lips buried me under the weight of guilt, of doubt, of insanity. He still believes I killed her. How can he believe I killed that girl and still love me? And why does he think I killed her in the first place?

Did I? What if he knows what I'm not yet able to accept? I invited her to join Alana and me for ice cream, then a walk on the cliffs. No one else... I did that. I did it all. I knew the terrain, I knew where to stand, I knew what I was doing. And she fell to her death. How is that not my fault?

That's what's driving me insane: that I can't really be sure. Alana said she didn't see Nikki falling. What if she did, but she didn't want me to go to jail? I believe she genuinely cared *about me. What if she saw me do something, or noticed I chose the solid rock footing for myself, then invited Nikki next to me where it was sandy, unstable, about to give way?*

Is that what I did? It must be, but I don't remember. I feel like everything's mixed up in my head.

I sobbed last night, lying in Ray's arms, willing him gone and willing myself sane again. If I did all that on purpose, if I wanted Nikki dead, then... I don't know how I'll be able to live with myself.

I didn't fall asleep until four in the morning, and today I was a zombie, still obsessing over what happened that day, over Ray's kindness when I'm not sure I deserve it. Then, just an hour ago, Stella stopped by. She brought me a nice Hermès scarf that must've set her back quite a bit and some chocolate truffles I can't afford to touch. Then, as I was trying on the Hermès in front of the mirror, she hugged me and said, "Darling girl, I'm so proud of you."

What's she so damn proud of? What did Ray tell her about me? Was she talking about Nikki? If she also believes I killed Nikki, how can she be proud of me?

I'm going crazy. And it scares the shit out of me.

I close the diary, reflecting on what I just read, and on what I recall from reading the rest of the diary. Over the years, Chloe's guilt diminished as she convinced herself it was I who pushed Nikki to her death.

Unlike her, however, I'm not confused. I know for sure I didn't kill Nikki, nor did I dare her to stand close to the edge of the cliff.

But I still don't understand what Stella's game was, and why Heather's photo was pasted in Chloe's binder. What did that girl mean to Chloe? If she meant anything, why isn't there anything about her in the diary?

As for Stella, she was, and perhaps still is, an overbearing mother, a bit arrogant, and a bit of a jerk. Remembering the way she asked Chloe about being pregnant at my party makes my skin crawl. The thought of her having taken Taylor is numbing me with unspeakable fear.

Shaking my head, I realize I still have more questions than answers. And I have to admit I do know a little bit more now, after following the breadcrumbs left by Chloe in her binder.

It's time to follow the trail a little further. I pick up my phone and dial the number for the school where Ray attended high school, although now I have more questions about Stella than Ray.

THIRTY-NINE

Looking at the website for Ray's Chattanooga high school, I realize the principal's assistant is much too young to have been on the job when Ray was a student there. I'm afraid to ask for the principal, thinking they might see right through my lies. Out of any other options, I ask for the admissions director. They're usually the ones who talk with parents, who deal with transfers and enrollments. Her name is Michelle Coachman, and she seems, at least from the wide smile in her professional photo, friendly enough to answer some questions.

I give her the same bit as I gave Rose McCarthy earlier, about the article I'm writing. She's far less excited to speak with a teacher from California, but she reluctantly agrees to give me a few minutes.

Unfortunately, I can't skip straight to asking questions about Stella. I have to work my way to it, so I ask about Ray first.

"Do you recall why they moved to North Carolina?" I ask, after pleasantries are exchanged briefly.

"I don't recall exactly." I can tell from her voice she's a little annoyed that I expect her to remember things that happened so long ago. "I do remember it was after the young man's girlfriend had died. Maybe that's why."

"But—" I almost blurt out that she must be confused, because Heather didn't die for another year. I catch myself in time. "Um, what was her name?"

"Olivia Robinson," she replies, clearly inching a little more toward slamming the phone down on me. "It was in all the papers."

"I'm sorry, I had no idea. What happened to her?" A pause, while she's probably considering whether I'm worth her time. "I do appreciate your help with this. I know you're very busy; I promise I won't take much longer."

She sighs. "It was a hit-and-run, right after class. She was walking home with her two best friends, and she stepped in front of a speeding SUV. Such a terrible tragedy."

I barely hear her anymore, my mind spinning, wondering what the odds are. The same thing, more or less, happening twice in a row. "And Ray was her boyfriend at the time?"

"Yes. Now that I'm telling you what happened with Olivia, I remember a few more things. He was struggling with school already. His parents had gone through a nasty divorce. Everyone was talking about it here, in Chattanooga, their bitter fight over Ray's custody. Then this happened."

"And they moved?" I ask the obvious.

"His mother was adamant about it. But I think she was running away from her husband, and their move didn't have anything to do with Olivia's death, or how much it screwed Ray up."

"How so?"

She sighs impatiently, as if infuriated at how dense I am. "When cops have to be called to break up fights between warring spouses, you don't wonder how a boy will end up. You *know*. Then, after the divorce, he was just starting to get back on his feet, and his girlfriend died in a stupid accident. The day after it happened, his father took him back to Chattanooga. Probably the boy wanted to be there for Olivia's funeral. I remember it clearly, because the cops were checking the boy's alibi, and I had to testify. It was... scary."

"Where had he been?"

"Mr. Preston took him on a business trip, someplace exotic, I don't recall exactly where. He didn't miss more than two days of school." She sounds apologetic, as if the statement carries some deep meaning. "We have rules about missing school days here, and we're strict about it. I remember how he pleaded with me to let him go, saying he was probably going to lose custody of his son soon. He kept saying, 'I have to fight for my son, Mrs. Coachman, please.' I guess he lost the battle. A month or so after Olivia died, Ray and his mother were gone. We were given a North Carolina forwarding address."

"How about his mother, Stella? How was she during all these events?"

She scoffs quietly, and I sense hesitation in the dead air between us. "Well, I've always believed that it takes two to argue. I'm not judging what happened between her and her husband; people get divorced all the time. But it hurt me to see an intelligent, hard-working student fall apart because of his parents' marital problems. As a mother, she handled things very poorly. She tried to control everything, came to school much too often." She pauses for a moment, while I hold my breath, hoping she doesn't stop here. "I don't mind involved parents. They're much better than the ones who can't be bothered to give a crap about their kids. But that woman was something else. She had to approve everything her son did, his playmates, his curriculum. Even Olivia. I remember hearing a rumor Ray took her home to meet his mom when he was only a sophomore. She told her girlfriends about it, how formal the whole thing was, and how Stella Preston had touched her face and said, supposedly, 'I approve of you.' It stuck with me because of how weird it was. The entire school made jokes about it. Kids kept asking them if they were getting married. I thought it was creepy. Even Olivia's parents agreed. They liked Ray, but his mother? Not so much."

Creepy.

The word resonates in the silence.

"Thank you, Mrs. Coachman," I eventually say. "You've been most helpful."

"Well... I'm glad he managed to make something of himself, that young man. You know how we educators love hearing success stories."

I thank her and end the call, feeling the urge to run over next door and give Ray a hug. That poor boy, going through so much loss, and now his wife is missing too. I stop myself, knowing quite well how it would end, and how wrong it would be, despite my good intentions. The need to soothe Ray's pain would last about three seconds, then my yearning for his touch would take over and we'd careen down a dangerous slope, unable to stop.

What are the odds? I ask myself, running an internet search for the name Olivia Robinson, limiting the results to Chattanooga, and the time frame to the years Ray was attending high school.

There are many results, most of them to do with her death. The hit-and-run driver was eventually caught and charged: a fifty-two-year-old man who'd had three drinks for lunch and didn't see her step in front of the vehicle. Nothing to do with Stella or Ray. Still, I'm astounded, looking at Olivia's picture.

She could be Heather's sister. Or Chloe's. Same long, wavy, blonde hair and light complexion. Same charming smile and slim, athletic build. I'm at a loss for any logical explanations, other than the obvious: that Ray has a type. It's sad for me to accept it, but I'm not his type. I'm not a petite, slender girl with long, blonde hair, who looks as if she just stepped out of a salon.

I am Plain Jane, with my brown hair that runs boringly straight down to the middle of my back. My shoulders are broad, from sports but also from farmwork as a teenager. I'm more muscular than delicate, but I'm not bulky, just strong. I'm me... nothing like them.

That simple thought brings an icy claw around my heart. Seems that Ray is rather superficial, going after the physical appearance more than any other traits. And seems I'm weaker than I thought, obsessing over what Ray likes or doesn't like, when the main questions still remain.

Where is Chloe, and what does all this have to do with her disappearance?

I followed her breadcrumb trail until I reached the end, and I learned a few things. One, that Ray's mother was always a bit creepy, famously so, her weirdness leaving lasting memories in people's minds. Two, that there's an unusual coincidence involving Ray's girlfriends. They died in freak accidents, he was never involved and neither was Stella, end of story.

It happened twice, and that's incredibly unusual.

Actually—I realize as my throat tightens—it happened a third time.

With Nikki.

Three girls died in freak accidents, while there were other people present. Only it can't be.

This can't be happening.

"Oh, no, no, please, no," I whisper nonsensically, moving around the living room at a frantic pace as my vivid imagination runs away with me. With it come memories, snippets of life that fit the puzzle laid out in front of me.

They fit well, even if I don't like the resulting image.

Who likes blondes? Who makes that choice? Is it Ray? Or Stella?

I recall Ray asking me to bleach my hair, while he played with my long, brown strands, lying by my side after we'd made love. How conflicted his request made me feel back then: disappointed for not being liked the way I was, and at the same time hot and bothered, realizing he thought of me, he dreamed of me with different hair. I found my inner strength back then and resisted, although it took all the willpower I still had, lying naked in his arms, his fingers playing my body like an instrument until it sang symphonies. He'd pleaded with me, whispered that I'd look so much better as a blonde, but the fire in his eyes intensified. "Dare you to say no to me," he'd whispered, as if aroused by my defiance, and then he'd made love to me like never before.

Just thinking about it, reliving that moment, makes me emotional, tears about to fill my eyes. At the same time, I'm wondering, clear-headedly and almost clinically, if he was so aroused because I was rebelling against Stella's preferences, not his.

I like to think of myself as lucid right now, but who am I kidding? Even now, I'm looking for validation. Because very soon after that day, he went and replaced me with Chloe. Blonde, ethereal Chloe.

It must be I'm still searching for validation, after all these years. Or am I looking for the truth? For Chloe? I've followed her trail so far and fast it makes me dizzy, and I believe I'm lost. Where does Ray come into all this? Or Stella? How does it all tie back to Taylor? Is there a connection with the lies Chloe wrote in her diary? Most of all, one question keeps coming back at me: why does Chloe want to frame me for murder?

I believe I might know the answer to that.

I still don't know how to find Chloe, but I can find another answer. Abandoning the last bit of common sense I still possess when it comes to all things Ray, I grab my keys and storm out the door, heading for a place I haven't visited in years.

Chloe's favorite hair salon.

FORTY

I look at myself in the mirror and doubt stabs me with tiny needles of anxiety. What the hell was I thinking? Yet I'm fascinated by my new look. I run my hand through the length of my light-blonde hair, amazed at the soft, wavy texture. The strands are luminous and fall naturally around my face, complementing my features. I'm a different woman. I *feel* different, although I'm embarrassed to admit it, even to myself.

Yesterday afternoon, I rushed to Chloe's favorite hair salon, the one where she used to take me occasionally. Back then, I resisted getting the makeover she offered, her voice lowered to a whisper: "Come on, Alana, trust me on this. Blondes have all the fun." But Chloe is a natural blonde; she didn't have to endure the bleaching process or worry about roots showing the following week. She just added some lowlights to give her hair dimension—her words not mine—as if the lustrous waves cascading down her shoulders needed any help.

I found the stylist who used to do her hair back then. It seems she stayed loyal to him over the years, because he was willing to take me without an appointment when I mentioned her name. He was a little surprised at my request, and I believe

I saw a flicker of disbelief, maybe even contempt, when I asked him to make my hair look like Chloe's. He tried his best, though, for two endless hours. But when he was done, my hair looked just as if Chloe had been given a drastic haircut. He offered me extensions that matched the new color and texture of my hair. I'd never seen extensions before, but I accepted his offer gratefully.

On the way back to my Subaru, I noticed something unusual: attention. I turned a couple of heads. A handsome young man smiled at me. A woman glared at me. It was as if I had entered an alternate reality, a place where I was noticed, where I existed. It made me feel like crying. I wanted to shout out from the top of my lungs that I was the same person, and all of what they seemed to like so much was merely four hundred dollars' worth of fakery.

After stopping to pick up some makeup from a high-end cosmetics store, I went home and anxiously waited for Daniel to come back from work. For a while, I obsessed over hiding my new hair, tying it up in a ponytail, and stashing the extensions in a drawer, because my makeover wasn't meant for him. It was mere bait I was planning to dangle in front of Stella, hoping the surprise would make her tip her hand somehow.

Remembering the unexpected attention I received from that handsome young stranger, though, I decided to treat Daniel with my new looks, hoping it would smooth things over between us, even if just a little bit.

When I heard his truck pulling into the driveway, I posed on the sofa, my new hair waving over my left shoulder, the only light coming from the end table lamp. He unlocked the door, threw me a quick look, and said, "Hey," in a tired-sounding voice. Then he turned on the lights in the living room and whistled. "Whoa. Nice hair." I smiled widely, happy to see him smile too. "What happened?"

I frowned slightly. "Happened? What do you mean?"

"What caused this?" He gestured with his hand, probably unfamiliar with the word makeover.

"Nothing," I lied again. "Just something I've been meaning to do. Do you like it?"

"Ah, I see. Yeah, I do." The smile on his lips waned. He took off his jacket and shoes, then went straight for the shower.

Very few other words were spoken last night, and I can understand why. It must've been strange, to say the least, to see me borrow a missing woman's hairstyle, and then refuse to be honest about it.

I can't tell him the secrets I keep are meant to protect him.

This morning is no different. He's withdrawn and quiet, monosyllabic with me. He gives my blonde ponytail a cursory look and doesn't mention it. Then he tells me he's leaving for the diner earlier than usual, just when I'm about to invent a new excuse to resume my morning stakeouts in front of Jason's building. I don't hold much hope he'll take me to where he's keeping Chloe, but I can't ignore the only lead I really have. Then the plan is to pay Stella a visit, in the highly likely scenario Jason doesn't lead me to Chloe first.

As soon as Daniel drives off, I rush into the bathroom and apply makeup, getting ready to show off my new looks to Stella. But I'm missing one tiny detail: I don't know where she lives, and I don't have her phone number. I can't ask Ray for it without providing a good reason, and no reason comes to mind. In yesterday's excitable pursuit of this new look, I didn't think things through. As I apply a touch of eyeshadow, I'm hoping Stella is listed online and I can get her number and address from Whitepages.

Attaching the extensions doesn't come easily to me, but I pull it off, while tiny beads of sweat burst at the roots of my hair. If I find her address, then what? How could I possibly justify landing on her doorstep, me and my new look? I need a plan. Maybe I'll keep it simple and just ask her out for coffee.

If I really have her "vote" and she is who I think she is, she'll bite.

The sound of a car door slamming outside the living room window draws my attention. I head over to see what's going on. I recognize Detective Fernandez's Dodge Charger just as the doorbell rings.

For a moment, I freeze in place, staring at the car with eyes wide in fear. Is he here to arrest me? I feel an irrational urge to run, to flee through the back door and escape somehow.

The doorbell rings again, followed by loud knocks. The sudden noise startles me into action, and I open the door. No matter how hard I try, I can't force myself to smile. I'm too scared.

"Oh, wow, look at you," Fernandez comments, sizing me up shamelessly. His reaction makes me both happy and angry at the same time, just like yesterday. "Can I come in?"

I hesitate for a moment, then step out of the way, inviting him in. As soon as he comes in, I close the door and make for the dining room table, eager to take a seat before he can sense the weakness in my knees, the slight tremble in my hands. He sits too, seemingly unable to take his eyes off me. It's unnerving.

"What can I do for you, Detective?" I ask, eager to get to the reason for his visit. I'm still clinging to the hope he's not here to arrest me, or he would've done that already. On the doorstep, slapping cuffs on my wrists, like I've seen in countless crime shows on TV.

"I hope you have some idea how screwed up it is to adopt Chloe Preston's hairstyle when she's gone missing." He shakes his head. "You've been really busy lately," he says, his words driving a stab of fear through my gut. "Made some very interesting long-distance calls."

I stare at him in disbelief. "Is this how you're looking for my daughter? And for Chloe? By wasting time tracking my phone?" For a moment, I hide my face in my hands, a gesture of desperation as I feel like screaming, like smashing something. "You'll never find them if you keep focusing on me! How many times do I have to tell you, I don't know where they are! I don't know who took them, and I don't know why." My voice sounds honest and seems to resonate with him. It should, because I'm telling the truth.

Well, for the most part.

"Not so fast, Ms. Blake. Let me remind you what we know." He grins at me, self-assured and downright annoying. "You're Taylor's biological mother. You were stalking her and her residence, casing out the exact spot where she was taken. You had knowledge of the adoption agency arson, including the apparent motive behind it. You confessed you knew the victim, Nischal Patel, personally." A pause, probably for effect, to give his words the time to sink in and terrify me some more. "Where is Taylor, Ms. Blake?"

I look straight into his eyes and speak the truth. "I don't know." I grind my teeth, the way he says my name repeatedly drawing instant ire.

"Where is Chloe, Ms. Blake?"

"I don't know."

"Who were you calling in North Carolina yesterday?"

That does it. I decide to take my own advice, the one I gave Daniel so insistently. "I believe it's time I call an attorney before I answer any more of your questions."

He stares at me for a long moment, his jaw clenched, his eyes cold, menacing. "It's your right, Ms. Blake." He stands, and I follow suit, eager to see him gone already. "I won't ask you any further questions, but I will tell you this. I have more than enough to charge you with conspiracy, or at the very least with obstruction of justice. You're somehow involved in all this, and every moment you refuse to cooperate endangers the lives of your biological daughter and your best friend. You know this, and you don't seem to care, which strongly suggests to me that you're involved and willing to sacrifice anything to stay out of jail. It won't work. I'll do everything in my power to get to the bottom of this, and I don't care how deep they bury you or how far away they throw the key."

I shudder and hope he doesn't notice. "You do what you have to do, Detective."

He continues to stare at me, but I'm not budging, not lowering my eyes, not even asking him how come he wants to charge me with conspiracy and obstruction now, when he wanted to charge me with Taylor's kidnapping the last time we spoke. I just remain silent, knowing it's probably the best thing I can do for myself at the moment.

He breaks eye contact with a frustrated groan and takes two steps toward the door. Then he turns to me. "I think you know who that girl was, the one in Chloe's binder. That's who you called about in North Carolina, didn't you? At Raymond Preston's old school? Now, why the hell would you do that?" I look at him coldly. "Feel free to not answer that," he adds quickly. "But think whose sickening mind game you're playing. Sure as hell isn't yours." A lopsided, disappointed smile blooms on his lips. "Starting from Chloe's oddly contrived letter, and all the way to that girl in the photo you've been chasing, you're being set up, toyed with like a puppet on a string. I don't know why, but when you finally see it, it will be too late." Hand on the door handle, he adds, "They took your kid, for crying out loud. Who are you protecting?"

Without another word, he opens the door and leaves, pulling it shut after him, while I remain where he left me, stunned, my mouth agape. Something he said about Chloe's letter filled my heart with dread. I never read it carefully, because I didn't feel it was addressed to me, and because of everything else that was going on. I just saw it as some fluff meant to make the detective on the case care about her, and I was relieved I wasn't named as Nikki's killer in it.

But what I did read of it made me think, at the time, how unusually worded it was, how elaborate it sounded. Back then, I blamed the uncommon writing style on her job. After all, she's a fancy magazine journalist. They don't write like the rest of us common mortals.

Taking my phone out of my pocket with frozen, trembling fingers, I find the picture of the letter and squint to read it, word for word this time. By the time I finish, an unequivocal question arises from the torrent of memories and thoughts stirred by Chloe's writing.

What if the crime fighter she addressed the letter to was *me?*

She used to call me something like that, back when I got into true-crime podcasts, and I kept telling her what I would and wouldn't do in certain cases we talked about. And, again, after Flavia Guzman's disappearance, when I'd figured out who took her. She called me "obsessed with the truth" and something else I don't recall exactly, like I was on a mission to uncover the truth. I thought that was merely a figure of speech.

Yes, the letter could definitely be addressed to me; otherwise, she might've just addressed it: "Dear Detective."

Holding my breath, I read the specific section again, this time assuming it's meant for me.

Most people like crime in fiction, on television, or in books. Those people shy away from looking at crime's realities, repelled, shrouding themselves in disbelief, thinking that denial will be the protective shield that will keep their lives pristine and safe. Others are the exact opposite, eager to stare at blood puddles and flare their nostrils at the first whiff of death, unrelentingly looking for scapegoats and making up lies to support their fictitious scenarios as they go along. To them, the lure of someone else's misery is heady and unescapable.

Neither can be trusted to find the truth. Especially when

*that truth is wrapped in a lie, shielded from the light of day in
such ways that no one can see it. Serving the lie in perpetuity,
just as a host organism serves and feeds the parasite coiled
around its heart.*

*This is the kind of person you'll need to be to find me:
different; someone who chose to fight crime, not just be entertained by it in fiction and the news media. Someone with an
unrelenting passion for making people's lives a little better at
the worst moments of their existence. I'm hoping that's who
you are, hell-bent on a mission to find out what's real, and that
you won't stop until you get answers.*

You were meant for this.

Only you can find me.

Please do.

A truth wrapped in a lie? What is she talking about? But
yes, I can recognize myself in her description, although I've
never thought of myself as someone who makes people's lives "a
little better at the worst moments of their existence." The
notion flatters me but doesn't take from my focus.

If the letter was intended for me, what else did she say in it
that I might've missed?

For starters, she tells me every bit of information in the
binder is relevant. She also says she doesn't know what's going
on, which makes a lot of sense; we never know when fate will
strike us.

Then, things turn weird again. She talks about knowing
how to choose the right tidbit of information from all the facts,
memories, and snippets of life to form the right picture. And
then, under the guise of a cherished memory, she talks about a
cabin she and I used to spend weekends at, the one with the
nauseating smell of mothballs so thick it gave us headaches.

I know exactly what cabin she's talking about.

Most important, she mentions our childishly encrypted

letters using the da Vinci mirror technique, as if to say her letter to me is encrypted too. She tells me to find the right mirror, the one that will help me decipher all her secrets. Finally, she apologizes to Ray for not telling him about the binder and encourages her parents to stay strong until she's returned.

Her last two paragraphs give me pause.

> So please flip through the pages and find answers to your questions, some of which you haven't yet asked. It's in your power to save me. No one else can.
>
> Please find me.

I read it aloud, a couple of times, wondering if I'm grasping everything Chloe wanted me to. *Flip through the pages and find answers to your questions, some of which you haven't yet asked.* A list of questions starts forming in my mind, each belonging to a reality that's a slightly different mirror image of another.

Somewhere at the center of this dizzying mirror chamber, I stand unsure of myself, trying to catch my breath, to find answers.

Why didn't Chloe tell Ray about the binder? How did she know I was going to be the one who found it? If she needed me to find her and take her home, why did she accuse me of something I didn't do? Didn't she realize I'd also find her diary, where her contempt and hatred for me were so explicit? How did she think this was going to entice me to help her?

Is Fernandez right, and Chloe's disappearance is just a game to set me up? Is it because of the way Ray still feels about me?

Looking beyond these questions, I discover something I know for sure: the address of that mothball-smelling cottage from our youth. Grabbing my keys from the copper bowl by the door, I slam the door behind me, in a rush to leave.

Because I believe I know where Chloe is.

FORTY-ONE

"I'm tired of this kidnapping bullshit. I'm going home tonight. I need a bath and a mani-pedi." Chloe leans against the dusty windowsill and looks outside, yearning for the moment she can put everything behind her and be free again. Splotches of sunshine make it through the dense foliage, staining the ground with the promise of warmth. It's chilly inside the cottage, nights on the mountain seeing drops in temperature several degrees below the coast. She represses a shudder and turns to Jason, who's staring at her in disbelief. "You have to let her go." Her voice is steady, calm, commanding. She can't afford to let him know how scared she is.

"The hell I do," Jason replies, taking two menacing steps toward her. She doesn't flinch, but steels herself, getting ready for the blow that will eventually come.

In the corner of the room, the little girl starts whimpering. She sits on the floor, hugging her knees, shaking, and crying. In the last two days, she started refusing her food, and Chloe can barely get her to take a sip of water every now and then.

"All you need to do is drive her to San Francisco or San Jose and let her out of the car somewhere. She'll be fine. And she won't tell a soul."

Jason glares at her, his mouth slightly open. "Are you crazy? Half the county is looking for this kid. And you want me to just... let her go?" A quick, loud burst of sneering laughter makes Chloe flinch. "I don't care what you have to say, all right? I know who her parents are. Her daddy is forking out five hundred large ones for any information."

"You're already getting paid. That's the deal."

Jason puts his hands on his hips. "That deal was before you completely fucked up my life with your scheming. That money doesn't cover the arson, keeping this girl for days while the entire FBI is looking for me. It doesn't cover any of this! My life is over, don't you get it?"

Chloe sighs, tired of the argument, of dealing with Jason, of everything. "I needed a service, you offered to provide it. You got greedy, that's what happened. Well, too bad. You're letting the kid go." She smiles calmly, a touch of resentment lighting a fire in her eyes. She isn't used to men resisting her in any way.

This time, Jason doesn't react too well to her smile. He tilts his head and brings his face close to her, slamming his hand against the wall right next to her head. "Remember how you got more than you paid for by blackmailing me? How you got me to set that place on fire? What do you think the agency owner did the moment I walked away, huh?" Another slam of his hand against the wall has Chloe shaking. "He went straight to the cops and had a composite done. Of me. By now, it's in every precinct in the county. I got nowhere to go. So, nope, half a mil ain't cutting it no more, when I'm supposed to live the rest of my life holed up in places like this."

"What are you going to do?" Chloe asks, her voice still sounding calm, while she's panicking inside.

"Her daddy's going to pay for it. I bet I can squeeze two mil out of the man. Then yours. I heard you're pretty loaded too. Thanks for the crash course in blackmail. It will come in handy."

Chloe bites her lip. She promised Jason half a million dollars, but she was never going to pay a dollar more. She doesn't have it. All right, so perhaps she made a mistake and underestimated Daniel's little brother.

Daniel seemed so gentle and accommodating, she didn't expect his brother to have such grit.

"If you make the ransom call, they'll catch you." Chloe looks at Jason. "You'll never see a dime from me, because you'll go to jail for a long time. You're taking a hell of a risk making that call."

"I don't have a fucking choice," he bellowed. "Do you understand what I'm saying? This kid ain't going nowhere until I get my money."

The little girl starts crying again, her incessant whimpers driving Chloe nuts. Everything drives her mad. The small, dusty cottage by Coal Creek, a place she used to love now holding her hostage. The tiny bit of road she can see in the far distance, where occasional traffic passes at high speed, reminding her of the freedom she's lost. Most of all, the fear that she ruined her life for nothing.

What if she fails? What if everything she planned so carefully has somehow crumbled to bits, just like her deal with Jason?

"If I play my cards right, I'm going to get the money," Jason says, his voice sounding less convincing than his words. He starts pacing the room slowly, running his hand obsessively over his stubbly chin. His jaw is clenched. The tension in his shoulders stretches his shirt taut. Maybe that gumption of his is wearing thin.

"If you do that, I'll testify against you. They'll put you away for life."

In two long steps he walks over to her and slaps her face hard, making her see stars. Tears burst in her eyes, uncontrollably, and she hates every one of them. Nevertheless, she looks straight at him, defiantly. "Sure, go ahead, build some more evidence against yourself."

"Argh!" he shouts, driving his fist through the wall right next to Chloe's face. His knuckles bleed, but he doesn't seem to care. There's a flicker of rage in his eyes, of insanity, that puts a chill down Chloe's spine.

The man is mere seconds away from killing her.

She definitely made a mistake when she chose him for the job.

"Be smart about it, that's all I'm asking," she says, giving it all she has so her voice isn't shaky, while her heart thumps, panicked, in her chest. "If you want money from the kid's family, that's fine by me. Just as long as you let her go in the next six hours."

He frowned and stared at her with piercing eyes. "Why the hell is there a time frame on this?"

"Because the kid isn't eating, that's why. Kidnapping is one thing, but killing a kid? Just think about it. I'd just cut my losses and let her go. She won't know how to identify us to the cops. I'll pay you, and you can get the hell out of Dodge."

The girl stops whimpering and looks at them, her eyes brimming with tears. Jason looks at her for a moment, then grinds his teeth angrily. "She's not going anywhere."

"You're crazy, you know that?" Chloe shouts, feeling her anger rise. She's losing control, heading into dangerous territory. "We had a deal!"

"And now we don't," he replies in a singsong voice, mocking her. "What are you going to do about it?"

A faint noise coming from outside catches their attention. Jason rushes to the window, then pounds on the sill with his clenched fist. "Shit, they found us."

Chloe watches the approaching vehicle in the distance, barely visible through the thick woods, and smiles.

Then, she turns and looks at Jason's scrunched face. He's transfigured with fear and rage. "You should go."

FORTY-TWO

I cut the engine in front of the cottage, no longer doubting I remembered the address correctly. It looks familiar. I'm definitely in the right place. Yet I sit behind the wheel, my heart beating hard and fast, afraid of what I might find once I open that door.

If Chloe is there, exactly where I believe she said she'd be in the binder letter, that means she set this entire thing up. It means Detective Fernandez was right, and I was played like a puppet on a string, right into Chloe's hand.

It also means I might soon find out why Chloe set me up.

I draw a lungful of fresh air and get out of the car, then walk over to the door. As I approach the cottage, memories rush to my mind. The place has the same weathered shingle roof that was leaking in the corner of the kitchen when we were kids. It exudes the same rustic charm I remember well. Made of darkened logs in redwood hues, the walls blend smoothly into the deep woods. Large windows overlook the mountains behind me. Moss-covered boulders flank the path I walk slowly to the entrance, wondering who's watching me.

I knock, then I try the handle. The door opens with a low-pitched creak, and the smell of mothballs greets my nostrils, now faded and slightly musty. I walk inside warily, not knowing what to expect, when an ear-piercing squeal rips through the somber silence.

"Ms. Blake!" Taylor rushes to me and I kneel on the floor with my arms wide open. She crashes against my chest, crying tears of joy. "You came to take me home." I close my eyes and gently rock her back and forth, stroking her hair. She's alive. She's okay. Gratitude and love fill my chest.

I let myself savor the feeling of my little girl's body cradled in my arms. It's not likely to happen again soon.

"Yes, yes, I'm taking you home," I eventually whisper, feeling a sob choking me.

"I miss my mommy," Taylor cries, her face buried in my chest, her hands clinging to my neck.

Her words slice through my heart like a knife. "I know, sweetie," I reply, my voice cracking. I barely resist the urge to run out of there with Taylor in my arms, to take her away, to safety. But I desperately need answers. Reassuringly, I murmur, "We're going home soon, I promise."

Then I open my eyes and see her.

Chloe.

She stands by the window with her arms crossed, looking at me as I hug my little girl, her face devoid of the hatred I expected. A little pale and dressed plainly in a T-shirt and jeans, she's not wearing any makeup and looks rather tired. Her hair is braided simply and brought over her right shoulder. Her lip is swollen and split, her cheek and left eye bruised.

Reluctantly, I stand, not letting go of Taylor's hand, and I approach her, stopping a few feet away, a glass coffee table between us. "Well... hello, Chloe."

A timid smile flickers on her lips as she looks at me. "You figured it out, Alana. Thank you. I knew you would."

"Where you were? Sure, I did." I'm stiff with rage. "Whatever this sick game is, Chloe, you crossed a line. You took my kid," I say, realizing a bit too late that Taylor can hear me. She doesn't react, though.

"No, I mean, this." She gestures at my hair. "You finally saw it. Just like I wanted you to."

I frown, a little confused. What is she talking about? And why the hell can't she make sense like a normal person, say directly what's on her mind?

I let out a long, frustrated sigh. "What are you doing here, Chloe?"

"Running," she replies in a soft whisper. "Hiding. Trying to save my life."

As if through a haze, I recall the words I read in her diary. *I hate the hold Alana still has on Ray,* she wrote at some point. *Oh, how I hate that woman* was another entry. Whatever the flavor of her drama might be this week, I don't believe the woman standing in front of me deserves any more of my time. After rushing to find her and save myself from the lies she's been telling, I realize I have absolutely no means to get her to speak the truth. She's completely incapable of it, a bona fide pathological liar. I should take my baby and get the hell out of there.

"All right, whatever. I'll take Taylor home now. You... good luck with everything." The little girl's fingers clench tighter around mine, filling my heart with joy.

"I wasn't lying in that letter," she says, quickly taking a step forward, as if to stop me. "Only you can help me, Alana. Please."

I scoff angrily, propping my free hand on my hip. "Why the hell should I care? You have only contempt and hatred for me. You've always despised me. I'd be an idiot to care about you anymore. You've made your point."

She's smiling, a little crookedly. That broken lip must be smarting. "You found my diary. Just as I intended."

"You wanted me to read that?" I can't help myself from

being dragged into it, but I have to know. "Why? You accused me of killing Nikki, when you know damn well I didn't. What are you trying to do to me, Chloe?"

She unfolds her arms as she walks closer. When she reaches out to touch my shoulder, I take a step back. I don't want that woman touching me.

She lowers her hand. "Nothing. I just wanted you to see. I needed you motivated to come looking for me before anyone else did. And... you're here."

I shake my head as if a sticky clump of fog is clinging to my mind, swallowing it whole. She speaks words I understand, but the meaning of it all escapes me, like scattered pieces of a puzzle. "Why? What is this all about?"

She looks at me silently for a moment, her eyes grim, a glint of fear in her gaze. "I'm next in line to die, Alana. And I won't see it coming. I won't know when or how." She clasps and unclasps her hands together, tormented. "No one believes me. I tried, even spoke to the police, but they didn't believe me. Our family lawyer listened, then asked my father if I was losing my mind. But I know I'm right. And it's going to happen soon."

My brow furrows as I try to make sense of what she's saying. "What do you mean?"

"Heather Davenport in North Carolina, Olivia Robinson..." Her voice trails off, trembling. "Even Nikki," she whispers, lowering her head as if under a heavy burden. "They never saw it coming. Never knew who was going to give them the final—"

"Wait a second, what are you talking about? Olivia died in a hit-and-run."

She nods silently a couple of times. "Just like Nikki died in a completely random landslide. Two other girls were there with Olivia when she happened to step in front of oncoming traffic. Did you actually believe that?" She takes another step toward me. She reaches for my hair, and I let her, curious as to what she'll do. "Are you sure neither of those two girls pushed Olivia in front of that SUV?"

She slips her fine, long fingers through a few strands of my hair, lifts them slightly, then lets them go with a sad smile. "I thought you saw the pattern. When I noticed your new style, I was certain you did. I thought maybe you had a plan."

I bite my lower lip, wondering if I should share anything with her. She's the most duplicitous and deceitful person I ever met. Yet I'm willing to give her one last chance. "Maybe I did. I was about to test my theory when I realized I knew where you were."

"That's my brave crime fighter, hell-bent on a mission to see what's real." She smiles sadly. "Now you know why I needed you to find me before anyone else did. Only if you were furious at me, desperate to clear your name after I wrongfully accused you of murder, would you be able to look past your love for Ray to see—"

"I don't love Ray anymore, Chloe." The lie comes naturally to me. I really don't know why I bother, but I don't believe the truth would be helpful at this point. Or is it the truth? How can I love Daniel, yet have such strong feelings for Ray still?

She holds her palm up as if to stop me. "I know what I saw between you two, and it's all right. I should've never taken him from you. I always regretted that. But I fell so hard for him I couldn't help it."

Right. She never said no to anything she wanted in her entire life. Not for someone else's sake, anyway. Chloe is selfish to the extreme, and nothing will ever change that. And I doubt that regret she's mentioning is sincere.

I shrug, deciding to let it go. Let her believe whatever the hell she wants. I just want to take my sweet little girl home to the mother she knows and loves, and then go back home and cry myself to sleep after downing a glass or three.

But something Chloe said piques my curiosity.

"You're saying Olivia's death wasn't accidental?"

"I can't prove it, except with highly circumstantial evidence: one of the girls she was with when she died has been in and out of rehab ever since, as if her conscience bothered her, pushing her to drugs and alcohol. The other one is married, has kids, a normal life."

"That's not nearly enough. Not unless she confesses. How about Heather? Another girl tripped her."

"I spoke to that girl." I gawk at Chloe, surprised. She went further than me looking for the truth. "She's been out of prison for years now, and I traveled to North Carolina and talked to her." She scoffs bitterly. "Guess what? She's a blonde too. She told me she'd just started dating Ray two or three weeks before it happened. She didn't make much sense when I asked her why she tripped that other girl, but she did say she felt like she had to fight for his love."

I gasp as she says the words. "Stella," I say softly, and a flicker of agreement glimmers in Chloe's eyes.

"She really screwed him up with her custody battle. She kept telling him things like, 'Real love deserves a good fight' or 'Mommy will fight to the death for you' and 'Anyone who really loves you must be willing to fight for you.' That kind of thing. Can you imagine what that did to him? He didn't stand a chance."

The thought of a young boy's mind being twisted like that tugs at my heartstrings.

Chloe shoots me a glance. "I related with that girl on a different level, because of Nikki." A beat of tense silence. "Because of what I did."

My lungs deflate when I realize where she's going with this. "I read your diary, Chloe, and you didn't kill Nikki. I was there."

"You were on your *phone*," she shouts angrily, and Taylor whimpers, drawing closer to me. "I lured Nikki there. I wanted her to fall. And she did. I stood on the solid rock outcropping and dared her to join me on the sandy edge. She didn't have a chance."

"Chloe, I'm not going to say you're innocent here. Yes, you recklessly endangered Nikki's life, and now you have to live with that. But you didn't drag her to the edge. You didn't push—"

"You don't know what it's like. To have your mind twisted slowly until it turns on you."

I contain a bitter smile. After dealing with her, I'm an expert in having one's mind twisted. "I think I do—"

She holds her hand up again, and I fall silent. She has tears in her eyes that she's barely holding back. A heavy sob makes her chest heave. "It started slowly, so gradually I didn't sense it at first. A word here and there, misunderstood, taken out of context and twisted. Just what you read in my diary about Nikki, and how I was shown only support and love, deepened my guilt, my self-doubt, my shame, until I couldn't live with myself. Unlike the diary, where I shifted the blame to you, in reality I crumbled under the weight of it. From one day to the next, in slow-moving increments, the atmosphere shifted until I was the murderous wife everyone forgave because she did it out of love." She covers her mouth with her hand and inhales abruptly, a sharp gasp that's meant to hold back tears. "But I know what I did, and what I didn't do. I tried to explain, and it didn't matter. I know what my thoughts were that day, with Nikki. It's almost as if Stella knew what I was thinking, because she told me one time that Ray was worth everything I did and would ever do." She lets the air out of her lungs with a heavy sigh. "And so, to myself and to my family, insidiously, I was labeled a killer, and even I grew to accept it." She paces the room slowly, her eyes glued to the floor, her silent tears staining her shirt. "What's worse, and what I cannot begin to compre-hend, is that I felt that way about Nikki. Those thoughts... were not my thoughts. I'm not a killer, Alana. I need you to believe me. I didn't push Nikki; I swear I didn't."

I'm not sure I believe her. It's difficult, after peeling off so many layers of deception.

Silence fills the room for a brief moment that I don't dare interrupt. Taylor tugs at my hand gently, and I stroke her hair. "Then what happened?" I eventually ask.

"Then something changed again. Now it's my turn. I know it's coming, but I don't know when or how."

Ah, that thing again. And it means I can't just turn around and leave her there like that, even if Taylor keeps tugging at my hand.

Much to my misfortune, I have a conscience.

"What exactly are you afraid of?"

"You heard Stella at your party. I can't have kids, Alana. I tried, and I can't. She hates that... she wants another little Ray to fuck with. If I can't give one to her, I'm not good enough anymore. She called me out, almost like a warning, that day at the barbecue." She sniffles and wipes a tear off her face with the back of her hand. "I'm going to die. I won't even see it coming. Some woman, a blonde just like you are now, like me and Heather and Olivia, will come by and ease me into oblivion." She locks eyes with me, and I can see all her desperation and fear glinting in her wide, almost maniacal eyes. "But now you see it too, the pattern. And you'll save me, right?" She rushes forward and clasps my left hand, while Taylor tugs at my right, fearful, stepping back. "Please, Alana, help me. It's in your hands."

"What are you talking about?"

For a brief moment, she looks out the window, into the wooded distance. "I didn't know where we were going to move to. When I saw you through the window, I knew." She looks back at me. "You were the chosen one. And I was finished."

For a moment, I consider giving into my urge to run away,

carrying Taylor in my arms, screaming from the top of my lungs. Let everything Chloe become someone else's problem.

But there's something in those frantic eyes that just won't let me.

For a long moment, I consider the facts in perfect silence. Is there really a pattern of deaths in the wake of Stella Preston? How did Bradford Preston die? Way too many accidents happen around her, although she's never there, and neither is Ray.

But I have a million questions—holes in Chloe's story—that keep me from believing her.

"You're asking for a lot. You spent years writing about your hate for me in your diary, and now you tell me it doesn't really matter? That the blame you put on me for Nikki, it doesn't matter?"

Her lips flutter with the hint of a smile, and her eyelids drop. "I wrote that diary in three days, after your party. From scratch. Your binder interview gave me the idea."

I gawk at her in disbelief. "I don't buy it. The cover is worn, the fabric is pilling, the pages yellowed."

Her smile blooms a tiny bit more. "Four cycles in the dryer will do that for you. And a few drops of coffee."

A long, weary sigh leaves my parted lips. "Jeez, Chloe... is there anything real about you?"

Her smile dies and her eyes lock into mine. "Yes. I will die unless you help me. That's as real as it gets. You've seen it yourself. All those girls... looking just like me." A sad chuckle and a gesture punctuate her words. "And now, like you."

Her words send a chill down my spine. I don't know if I believe her, but I'm not done grilling her. I crouch down to hold Taylor in my arms, because she has started whimpering, eager to get the hell out of there, my poor baby. I can relate... this nightmare can't be over soon enough.

"You were at some cabin first, then you moved here. Why?"

"In case we were followed. I didn't want them to find Taylor."

"Wow," I whisper, stunned. "Whose cabin was it?"

She shakes her head. "I don't know. It seemed abandoned. We just used it for a day."

"That newspaper clipping, about a witness to Nikki's death. Which paper did it come from?"

"I don't know. Stella found it and gave it to Ray."

Of course she did. "It's not real, you know. The cops checked. It's fake."

"Oh." She gasps, her eyes instantly brimming with tears. "Oh, God. She must've wanted me going insane with fear over Nikki's death. You see? First, they made me believe I killed her. Then—"

"How about the letters?"

"Letters?" She frowns a little and paces slowly, wringing her hands. "What letters?"

"The ones handwritten in green ink, with the threatening message. I got one just like it."

She frowns and looks at me a little differently, wary of me, as if a chill has descended between us. "I just—it was in the mail one day, right after we moved. I don't know why you got one."

I don't know what to think anymore.

I've been on the Chloe carousel for way too many rides to not feel dizzy and disoriented. I could forgive and understand a whole lot, but one thing I will probably never be able to do is forget.

"You took my daughter," I say in a low, menacing voice, holding Taylor's head at my chest and covering her ears. "*Nothing* justifies that."

"I took *his* daughter!" Her voice is taut with anger and fear. The two emotions are basic: primal, raw, almost mirror images of each other. One can instantly transform into the other and then jolt right back, in endless interplay. "I was desperate to draw people's attention to their family history, to all the people who die around them. And it didn't work. I wrote about it in the diary in case you didn't know Taylor was your daughter. I wanted *you* to know."

I stare at her and see her chest heaving, her pale lips parted as she's breathing heavily. She's scared; there's no doubt about that. But is her fear legitimate? Or has she completely lost her mind? "Who took Taylor? Was it you?"

Her gaze shifts. "It was Jason." I glare at her. She destroyed my brother-in-law's future, just because it served her purpose. "I paid him to do it," she adds quickly, reading me correctly. "I'm so sorry. I didn't think—"

It's my turn to stop her. I've heard enough, and the more I hear, the sicker I feel. Many times before I've wished I'd never met her, but never like today. She's the ultimate spider, patiently readying her web of lies to catch the prey she sets her eyes on. My reality is unrecognizable, disfigured under a constant bombardment of lies and deceit. And still, if I walk away like I should, a question will always haunt me.

What if she's right?

What if tomorrow, or next month, or who knows when, I turn on the news and hear about some freak accident that claimed her life? How would I live with myself then?

As I stand and look at her, my resolve strengthens. I know exactly what I have to do. I will be the metaphorical broom, ripping cobwebs from the corners until the sun can shine through.

I look at my reflection in a faded wall mirror, then take out my phone and dial a number I find on the internet.

Detective Fernandez picks up immediately.

"Hello, Detective. I have a package for you. But it comes with strings attached."

FORTY-THREE

I'm almost out of the Coal Creek Preserve, heading toward Half Moon Bay, when I realize I forgot to ask Chloe an important question. She said the idea for this charade came to her when she saw the binder interview. But then, why did she move next door in the first place? That happened months before.

As I drive along the picturesque and winding Skyline Boulevard, I go over all the puzzle pieces in my mind, because I don't want to call her. I don't want to ask her. Honestly, I don't want to speak with her ever again. She was probably targeting me for my "crime-fighting abilities," and she used me like she always has.

Then I recall the price tag for her rushed move and frown. She paid a whole lot of money just to live next door to me. Am I really worth that much?

Perhaps I'm not, but she could have believed it, especially if she thought her life depended on it.

I stop and yield to traffic before I merge onto the highway, heading west into Half Moon Bay. As I wait, I check my reflection in the rearview mirror. My makeup is perfect, my hair shines with sun-kissed highlights. I look sophisticated and alluring, something I've always envied in Chloe.

I smile to myself, content. Excited with anticipation.

When my phone rings, it startles me back into reality. A look at the screen reveals Ray's name in bold letters. I let it ring for a moment, asking myself, once more, if I know what I'm doing.

Then I take the call.

"Alana... hey." His voice does things to me I can't begin to understand. All I know is that it's wrong. Everything is wrong. All that's happened. How I feel. What I'm about to do.

"Hey," I reply, keeping my voice casual.

"Can I see you?"

I hold my breath, unable to speak, knowing quite well I won't be able to say no.

"Please? I need you, Alana."

I breathe slowly, steadying myself for what's to come, and ask myself, once again, if I'm ready for it. If I know what I'm doing.

I'm not. And I don't.

Then I say, "I'll be there in ten minutes."

I can still turn away. I can go to the diner and seek refuge in Daniel's arms, in his kitchen, where my unwanted feelings should stay locked up in his freezer until they die. And yet, butterflies swarm in my belly as I forge ahead, impatiently weaving through traffic until I turn onto our little street, eager to get to Ray. To find out, once and for all, how he feels about me.

Our driveway is empty, and I'm guiltily grateful Daniel's not home yet. I park in my usual spot, grab my purse, and steady my panicked breathing before getting out of the car. As I do, I throw my front door a quick look. I still have options.

Then I walk over to the adjacent house.

I don't get to ring the bell. He must've seen me coming,

because he opens the door and I melt into his loaded gaze as he takes in my new look.

"Alana," he says softly, as I wonder again why my name on his lips has such a powerful effect. He folds me in his arms and his lips find mine, hungrily, his breath melding with mine as my body starts craving him like a drug, with an urgency I can't possibly resist. Still holding me, he leads me in a slow dance away from the doorway, then pushes the door closed with a kick.

"Oh, my sweet Alana, you're so beautiful," he whispers when I pull gently away. He strokes my face, his fingers leaving trails of fire in their wake. "I missed you so much," he whispers, his breath on my neck, his fingers in my hair, his body pressing against mine.

It takes everything I have to pull away a little more. "I missed you too," I say, the words resonating to my very core. I look into his deep-blue eyes and almost lose myself. "I'm so sorry. I didn't realize." He looks at me questioningly, visibly confused. "But I wanted to apologize now, even if it's too late."

He frowns briefly. "For what, sweetheart?"

I look away for a brief moment. "For not fighting for you. For giving up on you. On us." My eyes brim with tears. "I threw away our future, Ray. I never forgave myself."

"Oh, baby," he whispers, cupping my face in his hands and drawing me close in a breath-stealing, feverish kiss, filled with the longing I've been feeling since that day on the café patio.

I respond passionately, my body betraying me, luring me to give in, to forget where I am and why. "Please," I whisper, pushing him gently away. "I need you to hear me first. Then... the night can be ours." My words make his eyes shine, his desire so intense it electrifies the air between us.

Reluctantly, he walks into the living room and invites me to take a seat, but I can't. I remain standing, nervous and restless, while he plunges into a leather armchair.

"I'm listening," he says softly, a hint of a smile tugging at his full lips. "But don't be deceived, I might not be able to sit still for long. I'd miss you too much."

It doesn't help one bit that he's so damn sexy, or that I'm so hot and bothered I could cry.

"If you still want me to, I will fight for you now." My voice is choked, hesitant. I've never made myself so vulnerable before, but the look in his smoldering eyes is rewarding, enticing. I bite my lip and continue, even more hesitantly. "What happened with Nikki... do you remember her?"

"I do." He clasps his hands together in his lap.

"That's how badly I'm willing to fight for you now, if you want me to." His eyes glint intensely. "But I have to know... how did you feel about Chloe after that day? Did you hate her? Did you despise her for what she did, even a little bit?"

"No." The word rolls off his curved lips in a low, charged whisper. "She fought for me. You wouldn't. She took care of things, and I loved her for it."

I blink, surprised at how much it still hurts to hear him say how he felt about Chloe. I let that sadness show and he's visibly entranced. "Do you still love her?" I ask him.

"I love you more."

I clench my fists until my fingernails dig into my flesh to keep myself still.

"I always have."

"And Chloe?" I draw near, dropping my purse on the sofa. Then I sit on the armrest next to him and run my fingers through his hair, down his face. He closes his eyes, savoring my touch, then kisses my fingertips. "I need to know for sure if you want me. If you can forgive me."

He clasps my hand with his and takes it to his lips. "Why do you doubt me? You always doubted me."

I bite my lip and refrain from telling him the truth. But one thing I feel I must clarify, once and for all, my morbid curiosity too insatiable for my own good. Did Chloe lie when she wrote in her diary that they made love on that bench? Did she choose that place to take Nikki and me because it had some secret meaning, like a pilgrimage to the sacred, soon-to-be sacrificial place where their love was first consumed? "Tell me where you and Chloe first made love." His smile turns lopsided, almost mischievous. He thinks this is a game. I place a soft kiss on his lips to encourage him. "Maybe you and I could make love there. Erase her memory."

"Uh-uh, no, ma'am." He laughs and lowers his eyes for a moment. "Do you know that bench, over by the cliffs?" He tilts his head back and laughs. "It was hard and cold and very uncomfortable. There are way better places we could go instead." He kisses my fingers slowly, deliberately, as if savoring an exquisite feast. "A luxury hotel. A cabana in the Dominican Republic. The French Riviera... wherever you'd like."

I pull my hand away from his restless mouth. "This is serious, Ray. That day, you chose her instead of me. You—"

His look shifts, turning colder. "What are you talking about? It happened weeks after you left me in that café."

His words hit me hard, trapping the breath in my chest while pain sears through my body.

I look into his eyes and know he's telling the truth.

Oh, how blind I was, how easily deceived. How naïve... Chloe had my number all along.

I believed her when she said she'd made love to Ray on the back seat of her Benz. It hadn't happened. Ray had not cheated on me. Because of her lies, I broke up with him. I ripped my heart out of my chest for nothing. And thus, Chloe delivers one last blow, just when I thought she couldn't hurt me anymore.

Ray's still staring at me, his hand on my thigh, his thumb moving slowly, soothing, caring.

I smile with sadness, holding back bitter tears. "She fought well for you. She deserved you because she earned you, my love."

He frowns and looks at me with a hint of worry in his eyes. "What are you saying?"

I shake my head, and my hair flows around my shoulders in golden waves. "It doesn't matter. I'll fight for you now. I'll do anything you want me to." I hold my breath for a moment, watching his gaze soften and his lips stretch into a sweet smile that puts dimples in his cheeks. "Because we have a daughter, Ray. You and me."

"Oh!" he exclaims, and springs to his feet. For a moment, he's stunned. Then, he wraps me in his arms and gives me a deep, fiery kiss that leaves me breathless. "We have a daughter? How wonderful. Why didn't you tell me?"

"You were in love with someone else. Going with her to the same college. Starting a life with her. I thought I never meant anything to you. I was just a girl, while she was the one you married. She must've meant more."

"Only after you left me. And she doesn't anymore. Not for a while now. If I could be rid of her somehow, if she could just vanish, I'd be immensely grateful. I'd be free to be with you. Forever." He looks at me with an intense stare I'm afraid to decipher, his words sending shivers down my spine, frightening, shocking in the clarity with which they paint a picture I never wanted to see.

I manage to get a grip. "And us? What about us?" He looks at me with immense longing. "What are we going to do, after she's back?" A beat. "*If* she's back?" I begin to pace the floor, one hand at my forehead, another instinctively touching my abdomen, the sense of loss still curled up in there, as strong as it's always been since I brought my little girl into this world and gave her away. "I can't lose you again."

"And you don't have to," Ray says. "I promise you that, my sweet Alana."

Our lips are about to touch when I hear a commotion at the door and I stiffen and hold my breath, listening intently. Ray pulls away just a couple of inches, his arm still coiled around my waist.

The door swings open and Chloe walks in. As she takes in the scene, her jaw slackens and her pupils dilate. Ray springs away from me, bewildered. I take a step or two back, until I feel the sofa against my legs. I can't think of anything I could say.

She's wearing the same clothes as earlier and looks just as pale. Her eyes take in the scene, then she shrieks, her mouth wide open, her fists clenched and close to her chest as if getting ready to fight.

"I knew it!" she shouts, heading straight for me. "You lying, homewrecking slut! I can still smell the manure on you, you whore."

The insults rattle me, but not nearly as much as the maniacal rage in her eyes and the determination in her step as she pounces. Moving lightning fast, I grab my purse from the sofa and take out a gun. "Hold it right there," I say coldly, aiming it at Chloe's chest.

She freezes in place, her eyes wide with shock, her mouth slightly agape.

"Back the hell off," I say coldly, finding it difficult to hold the heavy weapon aimed at her chest. "I still remember how you stole Ray from me." Holding the gun aimed at her chest while I say those words feels intensely rewarding. Alluring. Dangerous.

She takes a step back, while I look at Ray, a sense of dread unfurling in my gut, paralyzing, suffocating.

He's staring at both of us, mesmerized. His eyes are glimmering with excitement, his parted lips can barely contain an aroused grin.

"Pull the trigger," he says, his voice hypnotizing. The control he exerts is irresistible. "No one would blame you."

A beat of heavy silence as I reel from his words. I heard him loud and clear, and still, I can't believe it.

Worse, I can't forgive myself for how tempted I am to obey him.

I swallow the knot in my throat. "You sent the letter, didn't you?" I ask Ray, my voice gentle, warm, as if Chloe isn't there anymore and it's just the two of us. "You wanted me to know she killed Nikki." It's a statement, not a question.

He nods and smiles. "I knew you'd get it."

"And the article?" I'm afraid of what he could say, but I press on. "The one about the witness?"

A flicker of uneasiness washes over his blue eyes. "You knew about that?" He looks at Chloe for a brief moment, his eyes cold, merciless. "Someone was bound to have witnessed what happened that day. I was just the messenger." He keeps staring at Chloe, whose eyes are glistening with tears. "I thought you'd do the right thing and turn yourself in."

Turning pale, Chloe stares at him without a word for a long moment.

"Tell me what to do, baby," I whisper. "Tell me you'll still love me if I do this."

From where he's standing, a few feet away, his eyes are electrifying, hypnotizing. "I swear." His whisper hits my heart like a knife. It all makes sense now. Calling me to find Chloe's binder. The bit of paper that had clung to the rings, that he disposed of so discreetly. The threatening letter he sent to us both, with solely one purpose.

For me to pull that trigger.

Slowly, I turn the gun toward him and see the blood draining from his face. The scene plays out as if in slow motion. Chloe drops on the sofa and starts sobbing, her face buried in her hands. Detective Fernandez barges through the door with a few uniformed deputies in tow. Several guns are aimed at Ray's chest now, and he's bellowing with rage, transfigured, his beautiful eyes bloodthirsty, the face I used to love contorted with hatred.

I lower the weapon, my hand shaking under its weight. Then I remove the mic taped to my chest and throw it on the floor, sick of everything I felt and said and did.

Handcuffs click around Ray's wrists, while he desperately calls to me. I can't bear to look at him. His voice, screaming my name, will repeat in my nightmares for a while.

I never really knew him.

It's damning and liberating at the same time. For the first time in forever, I'm free of him.

I hand over the weapon to Fernandez. My hands are trembling badly, my fingers frozen. "You could've trusted me with a loaded gun, Detective," I joke weakly, although I'm grateful he didn't. It would've weighed a ton.

"Yeah, right," he says, then pats me on the shoulder. "You did good today, Ms. Blake."

I roll my eyes and he laughs, then starts barking orders at the other cops.

It's over. I can finally breathe. I extend Chloe a hand and she takes it, then lands in my arms, sobbing hard. Despite everything that happened, I almost feel sorry for her.

"Thank you for believing in me," she says between sobs. "You saved my life."

A wave of exhaustion washes over me. It's the adrenaline leaving my body, turning me into a weary, fatigued mess.

I pat her on the back and pull away. "Honey, that's what friends are for."

FORTY-FOUR

I'm shaking badly as I watch them haul Ray away in handcuffs. A deputy offers me a soft throw blanket he peels off Chloe's sofa, and I wrap my shoulders in it, holding it tight with white-knuckled fists. The living room window gapes black with flashes of red and blue from the police vehicles parked outside. When I finally step outside, the evening chill cuts me to the bone.

In the distance, fog is rolling in from the sea in a dense, all-engulfing wall of silence and moisture. My house is still shrouded in darkness, but Daniel's Ford is in the driveway, and he's leaning against it, his arms crossed, his lips pressed tightly in a disapproving line. The moment our eyes meet, he turns and leaves, slamming the door behind him when he enters our house. Our living room window paints the sidewalk yellow for a moment as he turns on the lights inside, but then he pulls the curtains shut and darkness resumes its reign over that section of sidewalk, in between flashes of red and blue.

My heart tightened with fear, I turn around and stare at Chloe's living room window. It's curtainless and brightly lit. Everything Ray and I did in there, the passionate kisses, the smoldering embraces, Daniel could've seen all that. I falter forward, about to fall, and lean against a car I don't recognize, desperate for some support.

"Easy there," Mr. Avery says, offering me his arm. When did Chloe have the time to call her parents? But, as always, they're there when she's in a bind. "Detective Fernandez filled us in. Thank you for what you've done. We had no idea." He clears his voice, then continues, looking in the distance at his daughter. "She tried to tell us a couple of years ago. We just didn't listen. We couldn't believe it. We thought... well, she's always been a little too dramatic, sometimes living in a fantasy world at the cost of truth and reality."

What a fancy way to say Chloe can't really be trusted. The Averys have a way with words, that's for sure. I look at Harold Avery feeling infinitely tired and yet awake and scared at the thought of facing Daniel. But then I gather my last bit of strength to ask him the question that's been bugging me for a while. I have to know the truth. "Some anniversary surprise it was, moving next door to me," I say with a hint of a smile. I feel embarrassed, unsure of what he saw. "I guess Chloe wanted to surprise Ray, and she didn't realize."

"No, it was the other way around. Ray wanted to surprise Chloe. Talk about it backfiring," he quips, but there's no smile stretching his lips or touching his eyes.

I follow his gaze and see Fernandez holding Chloe by the elbow, while he talks to a man dressed in a suit worth more than I make in a month.

"What's going to happen to her?"

Mr. Avery lowers his head for a moment. "I have the best criminal attorney in the state on retainer. For the hours law enforcement spent looking for her, we'll gladly reimburse the police department, and we hope that will do away with any charges stemming from faking her disappearance. I'm assuming charges will still be brought, just so the authorities are not seen as condoning this behavior. As for the girl's kidnapping and the agency arson, it seems someone else perpetrated those, but she was nevertheless involved. My colleague suggested we postpone trial until Ray's criminal charges are brought. If he's given a guilty verdict, it will be easier for us to get Chloe an acquittal."

I nod, amazed she might get away with it all. "What are they charging him with?"

"Criminal solicitation for now. He'll serve time." A long sigh leaves his chest. His jaw clenches as he looks at Ray, who's being loaded into the back of Fernandez's car. "I was very wrong about that man. But now that they believe Chloe, they'll start digging into his past. They'll interview those girls in North Carolina and Tennessee and who knows where else." He rubs his forehead forcefully, as if looking to dislodge the bad thoughts there. "This entire Nikki Malkin business could crop up again if they start investigating."

Oh, no. Not Nikki. Not again. I feel an urge to throw up.

"Excuse me for a second," I say, and rush over to catch Fernandez before he drives off. I wave at him, and he gestures that he'll wait.

He's already behind the wheel, but lowers his window as I approach, the white throw fluttering around me in the wind like a fuzzy shroud. Ray's glaring at me from the back seat, and I look away. Then, unable to resist, I look at him, unspoken questions trembling on my lips. His rage fades slowly, turning into something I recognize, stirring and scary and haunting.

"Yes, Ms. Blake, what's on your mind?"

"Did you tell my husband what was going on here?" I ask, holding my breath.

"Yes, of course. However, I also told him we're looking for your brother-in-law. If you hear anything, please let us know."

I nod, unable to agree verbally to what he's asking, and he probably knows it. He drives off, and I walk over to where

Chloe and her attorney are talking to a deputy. She's not hand-cuffed, nor is she being loaded into a cruiser.

"We'll do the official surrender the day after tomorrow at nine," I hear the attorney say. "That works with my schedule."

"All right," the deputy agrees, then takes to chatting with Chloe's attorney about the latest Giants match.

I stop squarely in front of Chloe.

She smiles weakly and touches the throw I'm wearing around my shoulders. "Ray gave me that, a few years ago for Christmas." I consider throwing it away right that moment, but I'm too cold. "You can keep it."

I draw close to her and lower my voice. "Listen, you will make my family whole again, and I don't care how much it's going to cost you. You have to make it right for Jason. He was walking the straight and narrow, getting his life back together, and you screwed him up badly."

"I promise," she says softly, her eyes locked onto mine. For no logical reason whatsoever, I believe her. Hopefully, she's telling the truth this time.

"And I mean money, lawyers, everything he needs to walk away from this a free man. He's got a record, you know. He's not like you." She nods, still holding my gaze. "And I'll testify for you. I'll tell them how Ray wanted me to fight you back then, and I refused."

Her pupils dilate slightly. "Is that true? He asked you to fight me?"

"Yes, it's true." She squeezes my hand. I put my arm around her shoulders and bring my lips to her ear, our heads close together like in the old days, when she used to whisper about boys, and I mostly listened. "If you clear Jason's name, I'll never say a word about Nikki."

There's nothing to tell, really, but she shouldn't doubt for a moment I'd be willing to lie to protect my brother-in-law. Chloe Avery Preston has destroyed enough lives.

"I promise," she repeats, and I feel her shoulders trembling under my arm.

"One more thing, and it's not negotiable."

"Anything."

"Sell the damn house. Tomorrow."

She plants a quick kiss on my cheek before I can pull away. Her lips are cold and chapped.

"Consider it sold."

FORTY-FIVE

The red and blue flashes are gone. The last of the cruisers drove off a couple of minutes ago, leaving me standing in front of my house, wearing Chloe's fuzzy white throw like a cape I don't feel worthy of. It does little to keep the cold wind at bay, or maybe the chill nestled in the depths of my heart is to blame for my chattering teeth and trembling hands.

It wasn't Stella after all... it was Ray.

And I never saw it. It was right in front of me, since the day he said I had to fight for him, instead of telling me the truth when I accused him of seeing Chloe. His words are forever burned into my memory. "I thought you'd fight for me," he said. Just as his mommy dearest had taught him to expect of love, to demand of it. It only took me eleven years to make sense of it.

Even if he hadn't slept with Chloe yet, he led me on, fueled my sense of betrayal instead of straightening things out. He wanted me to fight for him, because that's what mattered in that twisted, deformed mind of his.

Part of me still can't accept it, but now I see him for what he is. A monster. A murderer. That day on the café patio, when I said goodbye, I saved myself, even if I thought it was going to kill me.

Stella's fingerprints are all over Ray's murderous psychology. She probably fueled his obsession with concepts of love earned and defended and protected, to secure his loyalty during the prolonged custody battle. Unforgivable. I remember her creepy comment about me being her favorite, and I find myself wondering if she was choosing me, as Chloe suspected, to be Ray's next wife. Or perhaps he did. The thought creeps up my nape with a chill.

I was the one who got away. He probably couldn't deal with it. Couldn't let me go.

I shake my head, deciding to lock all those memories in the deepest, darkest recess of my mind. A gust of wind blows my hair in a twirl of silky strands, while I look at the dark living room window of my own home. I fill my lungs with air and open the front door quietly, afraid of what all this has done to Daniel. To our marriage.

The living room is lit only by one of the lamps by the sofa. Daniel is sitting at the dining room table, his chair turned sideways, his right elbow resting on a placemat, so he can see me when I walk in. My heart sinks when I notice he's wearing his windbreaker, and his car keys are right by his hand. I close the door softly.

"Daniel, I'm so sorry—"

He raises his hand in the air and turns his head away, as if he's unable to look at me anymore. Tears spring to my eyes seeing him hurting so badly. I stand there, by the door, not sure if I should come closer, not knowing if he wants me near. I just continue shivering, as if the cold coastal wind is still blowing, here, inside our home.

"I can't unsee what I saw today, Alana." His voice is fraught with sorrow. "His hands on you, the way you kissed him, I-I just can't." He buries his face in his hands for a moment, then looks at me with a deathly cold stare. "Police custody is the safest place for that man right now. I swear to God, if I could wring his neck I would, with my own two hands. If the cops hadn't stopped me, I would've..." He looks at his hands as if there's already blood on his knuckles. "But it's you, not him, isn't it? With your lies, your cheating, your—"

"Daniel, I—"

"Shut up," he hisses, and I freeze. I've never seen him so mad. "There was no dental appointment the other day. No school assignment yesterday. Just lies. You've turned me into the laughingstock of the neighborhood, ever since your so-called friends moved next door. You played this sick game with Chloe at the price of our marriage. Jason's life too. Well, Alana, I hope it was worth it."

I rush to him. "Please, let me explain."

The look in his eyes stops me in my tracks before I can reach him. Disappointment, sadness, and grief, all too heavy for me to bear. Tears burn my eyes, while a sob climbs from my chest, suffocating me.

He points a condemning finger at me, stabbing the air angrily. "The cops told me *why* you did it. I know you were trying to bring down a killer. But you never trusted me. Never thought of coming to me with whatever the hell was going on, not even after they moved here and started dragging you into their fucked-up game." He frowns and looks at me with curiosity, like he's never seen me before. "What am I to you? A companion animal? Like a dog you keep around you but don't need to explain things to?"

I look at his face through a blur of tears. I can't stand seeing him so hurt. His pain sears me inside, the truth in his words making it ten times worse. He's right about everything. I feared a day might come when I'd have to pay for my many deceptions; I just didn't want to accept the risk, the damage it could do. And now the damage is done, irreparable.

"Her name is Taylor," I say, my voice shattered with tears.

"The girl who was taken?"

"She's my daughter," I manage to say before I break down. "Mine and Ray's."

"Bloody hell, Alana..." He stands and grabs his keys, frozen in place, looking at me with unspeakable sorrow in his eyes.

I grab my stomach and bend over, my wails threatening to rip me apart.

He takes a few steps toward the door and stops, looking at me with pity. It's worse than anything.

"My mother once said you must've had a child before you and I met." My blood turns to ice as he speaks. It's the first I heard of that; I'm appalled. His late mother was no fan of mine, but I never knew she'd said that about me. "She was an OB-GYN nurse," Daniel adds, as if I could ever forget. "She used to tell me how easy it is to know things about women just by looking at their bodies. The shape of their hips. Their breasts. Their waistline. I never listened to that stuff, never believed a word of it. But I never thought, in my wildest nightmares, Alana, that you would lie to me about having a child."

"Daniel, I—"

"You know, out of all the things my mother could've been right about, it had to be this." He scoffs bitterly and opens the door.

"Daniel, please, don't go." I rush after him and grab his sleeve with both hands. "I never cheated on you. Please, Daniel. I love you."

A long sigh leaves his face weary, drained. "I need some time." Gently, he frees himself of me and steps over the threshold.

"I'll be here, waiting for you," I whisper, watching him walk away, past his truck, and onto the path that cuts through the grass field behind our house straight toward the highway. Until I can't see him anymore.

I stand in the open doorway for a while, ignoring the biting cold, hoping against all logic that he'll come back. Fog rolls in dense, heavy clumps that meld with my tears and leave droplets of water in my hair, but I don't care.

Daniel's gone.

It breaks my heart, but deep down inside, I know he's right. I could've told him. I could've stopped at any given time and said, "Hey, there's something you need to know." Perhaps that wretched day when Chloe moved next door. It would've been difficult and unpleasant, but not nearly as heartbreaking as it is today.

Guilt claws its way inside my chest and another wail leaves my lips. Not long ago, I was losing my senses with desire for another man. And now here I am, finally seeing the love that was right in front of me, but only after I've lost everything.

FORTY-SIX

I don't know how much time has passed since Daniel left.

After a while, I close the door and falter over to the sofa, where I find nothing but loneliness and tears.

And regrets.

It's strange how the past few months are blurred together, a blob of falsity and fear and deceit. If I had to testify today about what happened, I'd doubt every single detail, unable to tell the truth from the lies anymore, barely able to say my own name without hesitation.

The enormity of what I've done crushes me, and knowing I was a pawn in a sociopath's mind game does little to bring comfort. I don't want excuses; I don't need them. I want penance, atonement for my lies, for the lives I've ruined.

Detective Fernandez's words resound in my weary mind. "You did good today, Ms. Blake," he said, right after Ray enticed me to kill Chloe. Little did he know.

He'd be shocked to learn that for a gut-wrenching moment, I wondered what my life would be like if I left everything behind and started a life with Ray, *after* I'd discovered the monster hiding behind those mesmerizing blue eyes. He'd probably be disgusted to know I wasn't acting when I kissed Ray so passionately, even if I landed in his arms as part of a plan to expose his lust for blood. He'd shake his head in disbelief if he knew all that transpired between Chloe and me over the years, and still, I decided to help her. I don't understand it myself.

Most of all, I'm shocked at how completely and utterly I destroyed my marriage. Even if Daniel comes back to me and forgives me, I'll never forgive myself. But I'd give anything for another chance.

The sound of the doorbell jolts me to my feet. It's almost nine, quite late for any visitors, but this has been as far from a normal day as I can imagine. I peek from behind the curtains and spot a black Mercedes SUV parked by the curb. I don't recognize it. Perhaps it's the lawyer Chloe promised she'd provide for Jason.

Wiping my tears with the back of my hand, I open the door.

"Ms. Blake!" Taylor squeals and rushes to hug me. I crouch down and open my arms, in a toned-down yet still heartwarming replay of this morning's emotional reunion. Yet, unlike this morning, the Winthrops are standing right behind her.

"We're sorry for the late hour, Ms. Blake," Monica Winthrop says, "but this young lady wouldn't go to bed unless we thanked you for getting her back."

I let Taylor go, after stealing a kiss on her cheek, and stand, holding on to the doorframe for balance. "Please, call me Alana."

"Monica," she says, extending her perfectly manicured hand for a shake as if it's the first time we meet.

Her husband follows suit, smiling with tense, thin lips. He isn't too happy about being here. "David Winthrop."

"Would you like to come in?" I ask, wondering if it's just gratitude bringing them to my door at this hour.

"Oh, no," Monica replies. "We don't want to impose. It's late." She shifts her weight from one foot to the other, a bit unsure of herself, then takes Taylor's hand in hers and crouches by her side. "Taylor, Ms. Blake is your other mommy," she says.

Tears spring from my eyes as I cover my mouth with a trembling hand.

"Really?" Taylor exclaims, her eyes wide as she momentarily frowns and looks at Monica. "So, do I call her Mom too, or something else?"

I crouch back down, and she approaches me cautiously, glancing over her shoulder at Monica Winthrop, who's just as tearful as I am. "No, sweetie," I manage to say. "Your mom is still your mom. I'm, uh, more like a really good friend." I hug her tightly and blink away tears when she returns the embrace. Then I look at Monica Winthrop and mouth silently, "Thank you."

"We heard what you did today," David Winthrop says. "Detective Fernandez told us. You're incredibly brave, Ms. Blake." He scratches his receding hairline with two thin, nervous fingers. "I don't know what we would've done if something happened to her." He looks around at the deserted cul-de-sac, then says, in a lowered voice, "That man is a serial killer or something. And his wife? Goodness gracious. She should be grateful Taylor wasn't harmed."

Taylor pulls away from my arms and rushes to the middle of the lawn, where she stoops to pick up our sprinkler, shaped like a fire hydrant with a rotating top. The street fills with her delighted laughter. "Check it out, Mom, it's like a dog toy!" She glances first at Monica, then at me. I wink at her and share a warm smile. We all follow her to the front lawn, her joy irresistible.

I wish Daniel was here, so my heart would be complete.

"Taylor, leave that be. It's not yours."

I smile reassuringly at Taylor's mom, and she smiles back. Monica Winthrop has a quiet elegance about her, kindness touching her features, and a glow that speaks of a gentle soul.

"All right, let's go," she says, waiting for Taylor to take her hand. David opens the back door of the black SUV. "If you like, you can invite Alana to all your parties from now on."

I turn my face away from Taylor to hide my tears.

"For my birthday and Christmas and all that?" my little girl asks.

"Sure." Monica extends her hand to me, and we share a warm handshake. "Thank you, Alana."

Out of the shadows, a figure appears, and my heart skips a beat as I recognize the silhouette, the unruly gray hair caught in the breeze. My body tenses, fear gripping me.

"Stella," I whisper, my voice barely audible.

Her eyes glint with rage as she approaches, staring at me mercilessly. They lock onto mine as she steps closer, the gun in her hand now evident. "Go on, say your thanks," she hisses at Monica, her aim shifting to Taylor. "Thank her for taking my son away."

Monica gasps, but I almost don't notice it. Eyes riveted on the barrel of the gun, I take a couple of rushed steps and shield Taylor's body with mine. "Please, Stella, don't do this." My voice is steady, but my heart is pounding in my ears, drowning out the rest of the world. "She's just a child. Your grandchild."

Her hand, holding the revolver, is now firmly aiming at my chest. "You took my son. I'll take your daughter. It's only fair." Her laughter sends shivers down my spine, a hint of madness in her tone. "Maybe I'll let you live. Live with the pain. But if you make me, I'll shoot you too."

"Ma'am," David Winthrop intervenes, holding his hands up in a pacifying gesture. "Whatever it is you're upset about, we can discuss it."

As if without thinking about it, Stella turns her aim at him and fires. David cries and falls to the ground. Taylor shrieks and rushes to his side.

"Dad!" she cries out, while I can't take my eyes off Stella's gun. In the corner of my eye, I see David's arm wrapping around Taylor's body, holding her down, shielding her. I hear him whispering something to her, the tone of his unintelligible words soothing, encouraging.

I take a few more steps sideways, trying to insert myself between Stella and Taylor again. I look at her in the faint, yellow light coming from the fog-enveloped lamppost and see the immense pain Ray's arrest has caused her. She's disheveled, her face drawn, her eyes bulging, swollen and red. "I misunderstood him, Stella," I say gently. "All those years ago, he needed me to fight for him, and I chose to walk away." The hand holding the gun wavers a little. "You can't begin to understand how sorry I am for what I've done. I still love him very much, you know."

"Shut up," she snaps. "I know exactly what you did. He's locked up like an animal, with drunks and addicts and thugs, all because he trusted you."

"They won't keep him," I blurt out, pouring lies on top of lies without a clear strategy. All I know is I have to buy us some time. Someone must've heard the gunshot and called 911. In our peaceful California town, that rarely ever happens. "They've got nothing on Ray. He'll be arraigned tomorrow morning and released. Then, when his trial is on, I'll testify. I'll say what a terrible mistake I made. How wrong I was." I look at her pleadingly. "You chose me for a reason, Stella." She lowers the gun a little more, her eyes riveted on mine. "He's done nothing wrong. No matter how hard they look, there's nothing they can find. He was never there!"

"You don't know what you've done," she whispers. "He was there with Bradford. He did what he had to do, for me. He fought for me, my darling boy. And you took him away." Rage comes back in full force in her baleful voice, her stiff, threatening posture, in the firm aim of her gun. I see my death sentence in her eyes, and I fall silent. There's nothing more I can say.

The gunshot is loud, echoing in the fog. The bullet rips through the air, missing me narrowly, Stella's aim deflected by Daniel wrestling the gun out of her hand. He came out of nowhere, materializing out of the thick mist, not a second too soon. She sees me still standing and shrieks, a desperate cry of hatred and sorrow and rage, as distant, flashing red and blue lights spark in the night.

FORTY-SEVEN

There's a sickening sense of déjà vu, albeit only partial: the flicker of flashing lights coming from the two police cruisers parked in front of our house; Detective Fernandez's Dodge Charger with its rear door open, while he holds a resisting Stella by the elbows, forcing her onto the back seat; an ambulance stopped at the side, David Winthrop seated on its rear bumper while an EMS technician tends to his superficial shoulder wound.

Monica and Taylor, huddled inside their vehicle, looking out the window at me, their faces still retaining a little of the horror we all endured.

All that, while I stand in the middle of my lawn, trembling, my teeth chattering, wrapped up in a blanket Daniel borrowed from the ambulance.

Daniel came back to me.

He's there, by my side, his hands on my shoulders, his body behind mine, lending me strength and warmth. I don't dare look in his eyes yet; it's too soon and I'm afraid the mirage will tear to shreds like gossamer in the cold, gusty breeze, and I'll end up alone, curled up in a ball on the sofa, crying myself to sleep.

"Any more surprises?" Detective Fernandez asks, after he slams the passenger door shut on his Charger. Stella glares at me through the window, and I don't look away. I stare at her curiously, trying to decipher where in that woman's mind the idea was born. The idea to torment her son into becoming a sociopath. How does someone do that? One day, do they just decide, I'm going to twist my kid's mind and screw it up beyond any recognition? Or did she repeat an earlier cycle of abuse that goes back for generations, something I have no knowledge of, and she had no control over?

I will probably never know. As I think of it, I see her, the younger Stella I remember well, holding her son's hand and teaching him all the wrong things about love. The damage it can do, leaving broken hearts in its wake. The powerful weapon that it is, making lovers into slaves with a few powerful words and the promise of addictive bliss.

I look at the departing cruisers and wonder about my life: how it was irreparably damaged the day Raymond Preston walked over and introduced himself to me. I still recall how powerful his charisma was, how special he made me feel, without words or actions, just with his presence. He was intoxicating, like a drug or a poison one can heal from but never forget.

Daniel's laughter awakens me from the reverie. Fernandez has come over, and Daniel's chatting with him, probably just as eager as I am to see everyone go away.

"This is an active investigation," Fernandez says, gesturing with his hand to the deputy who's rolling yellow crime scene tape around our lawn. "Until we finish measuring everything tomorrow, please don't move your cars."

I roll my eyes, then smile. In the grand scheme of things, calling an Uber for a ride isn't exactly a disaster.

"Thanks again, Ms. Blake," he says, shaking my hand. "We were actually conferring with the DA on what to charge Stella

Preston with. I was afraid she'd vanish, and I was sure she's not exactly innocent."

"Well, that problem's taken care of now, isn't it?" I ask weakly. I'm bone tired.

He laughs heartily. "For twenty-five-to-life, it is," he says, walking over to his car. Moments later, he's gone, and with him, the specter of the enraged woman cursing my name from the back seat of his Charger.

One by one, the players bow out and disappear, the second police cruiser the last one to go. Yet I hesitate to walk inside, to be alone with Daniel again, with the weight of everything that's happened between us lying open like a bleeding wound.

Daniel clasps my frozen hand. "Let's go." His voice isn't fraught with pain anymore. Hopeful, I look at him for a brief moment, then follow him into our home.

"Brrr," he says, turning on the lights and rushing toward the thermostat like a man on a mission. I hear the air starting to flow through the vents and rub my hands together. It will get warm soon.

"Thank you," I whisper, still a little afraid to look him in the eye.

He smiles at me quickly, a faint smile, more like the promise of one. Then he opens the fridge and takes out a bottle of white. With quick, expert moves, he uncorks it and pours the wine into two glasses.

"Drink this, it will help," he says, then clinks his glass against mine. "Cheers. We survived."

I take a reluctant sip, the idea of putting anything cold in my mouth not that appealing. But the wine works its magic and sends waves of heat through my body.

He takes a few thirsty gulps, then looks at me with a strange intensity. "I left earlier and went crazy, thinking I'd lost you. I couldn't bear it, couldn't take one more step. I came back and saw I was about to lose you for good." Another couple of gulps, and he sets the empty glass down. "It drove me insane. I'm still screwed up some."

"I'm so sorry, Daniel, for everything," I whisper.

He takes a step closer. "What now? How do we move past this?"

A flicker of a smile blooms on my lips. "Well, no more secrets, if you're up for it."

"Always," he replies, his brow lined with worry. He knows me so well.

"Thank you." I stop there, at a loss for words. Where do I start? How do I mend what's broken? "Taylor, she's, um, she's been adopted by a very nice family. And Ray didn't know she existed until today. It's a lot to take in, I know, but if you'd like, I can—"

He shakes his head slowly and smiles. "I'm ready to move on past all this. Are you with me?"

I take another sip of wine for courage, then abandon my glass on the counter. "I'm on birth control, but if you're still interested, I can stop taking it, and in about a month or two, things could start happening."

He looks at me, desire lighting up his gaze, then folds me in an embrace, crushing my lips with a deep, passionate kiss. I respond with increased yearning for his touch, my weary body slowly awakening in his arms.

"This'd better be the last of your secrets, woman," he whispers in my ear.

True to the promise I've made to myself, I pull away gently. "Nope. I have one more, and it's a doozy. I also committed a crime you need to know about."

"Oh, jeez," he whispers, stepping back from me, leaving me standing there, feeling deserted and desolate. "What did you do?"

I bite my lip, wondering how much I should tell him, then decide. Everything. "I believe the legal term for it is aiding and abetting," I say in a low voice. "Jason is in Mexico, in hiding, until Chloe puts together his defense. It was the best I could do." I look at him with an unspoken plea in my eyes. He's stunned and not in a good way. His mouth is slightly open, his eyes wide in disbelief. "He has a record. They would've thrown away the key."

He continues to stare at me for a long moment of silence. "Thank you." He pauses for a beat, then smiles and tilts his head appreciatively. "You're dangerous, you know that?"

I guess he could say that. I nearly destroyed our lives. "One more thing. You might see a for sale sign next door tomorrow."

He looks at me with an open grin that touches his eyes. "I don't dare ask how you got those people to do what you wanted. I'll only ask one thing."

"Shoot."

"Dinner?"

I nod happily and empty my wineglass.

Daniel reads my gesture correctly and asks, "Here? Or at the diner? It's kind of late."

I look at the time, but then decide not to care how late it is. San Francisco is just a short Uber ride away. "What do you say we check out the competition tonight? Let's eat out."

We get dressed quickly. I'm feeling energized by the wine, its effect likely to wear off and render me sleepy when I least expect it, but for now, I'm happy to go out with my husband for a peaceful, romantic dinner. We have lots to celebrate, including—no small feat—a future without Chloe or Ray.

I touch up my makeup and brush my hair. As I leave the house, Daniel strokes a long, shiny strand of hair extensions.

"I kind of like you better as a blonde," he says, his loaded smile ignoring the gawking Uber driver who's staring at the crime scene tape zigzagging over our property.

I throw a wicked grin over my shoulder. "Ah, shut up."

Later, after dinner, we find each other between sheets, and

make love slowly, endlessly. Our bodies recognize and welcome each other, lit by the same fire, driven by the same wants.

In my mind, Daniel's features shift ever so slightly, starting to morph into another's. I close my eyes and let the fantasy take over. It fills my body with a desire so intense I'm afraid it could end me. My hands touch his heated skin, caress his face, run through his hair, pulling gently. My body arches forward meeting his in perfect synchronicity, as his face continues to change, to evolve into someone I recognize. Someone I'm still aching for. His eyes become a deep shade of blue. His hair turns a little darker. And when he smiles, dimples appear in his cheeks. A silent whisper carries his name off my lips.

"Ray..."

In the darkness of our bedroom, my eyes snap open.

A LETTER FROM LESLIE

A big, heartfelt *thank you* for choosing to read *If I Go Missing*. If you did enjoy it and want to keep up to date with all my latest releases, just sign up at the following link. Your email address will never be shared, and you can unsubscribe at any time.

lesliewolfe.com

When I write a new book I think of you, the reader: what you'd like to read next, how you'd like to spend your leisure time, and what you most appreciate from the time spent in the company of the characters I create, vicariously experiencing the challenges I lay in front of them. That's why I'd love to hear from you! Did you enjoy *If I Go Missing*? Your feedback is incredibly valuable to me, and I appreciate hearing your thoughts. Please contact me directly through one of the channels listed below. Email works best: LW@WolfeNovels.com. I will never share your email with anyone, and I promise you'll receive an answer from me!

If you enjoyed my book and if it's not too much to ask, please take a moment and leave me a review and maybe recommend *If I Go Missing* to other readers. Reviews and personal recommendations help readers discover new titles or new authors for the first time; it makes a huge difference, and it means the world to me. Thank you for your support, and I hope to keep you entertained with my next story. See you soon!

KEEP IN TOUCH WITH LESLIE

www.LeslieWolfe.com

facebook.com/wolfenovels
Amazon.com/LeslieWolfe
bookbub.com/authors/leslie-wolfe

ACKNOWLEDGMENTS

A special, heartfelt thank you goes to the fantastic publishing team at Bookouture. They are a pleasure to work with, their enthusiasm contagious and their dedication inspiring.

Very special thanks to the wonderful Ruth Tross, who makes the editing process a pleasant experience and who is the best brainstorming partner an author could hope for. She is my guiding light in all things publishing and doubles as a muse when I need a nudge. I can't thank you enough.

A special thanks goes to Kim Nash and Noelle Holten for tirelessly promoting my books across all channels. Alba Proko is the wonderful audio manager who turns my written stories into audible recordings, nurturing the productions throughout the process and making me proud of each and every one of them. Your work with my stories is nothing short of inspiring.

A huge shoutout for the digital marketing team, who work seamlessly and tirelessly in ensuring that every book launch is better than the one before. You are simply amazing.

My warmest thanks go to Richard King and his enthusiastic efforts to take my work to other markets in translated versions and perhaps one day to the screen. A heartfelt thank you for everything you do and for your keen interest in my work. It's much appreciated.

Be thrilled by Leslie Wolfe's first
psychological thriller!

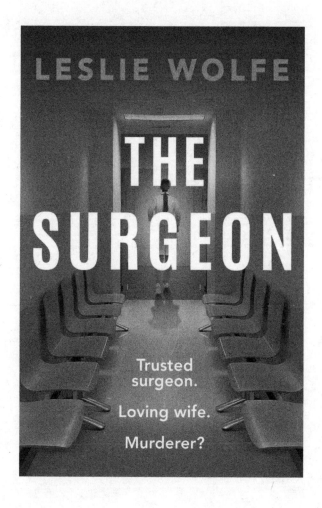

Please turn the page for a preview.

ONE

THE PATIENT

What have I done?

The thought races through my mind, searing and weakening my body. The rush of adrenaline fills my muscles with the urge to run, to escape, but there's nowhere to go. Shaky and weak, I let myself slide to the floor; the cold, tiled wall against my back the only support I have. For a moment, I stare at my hands, barely recognizing them, as if I'd never before seen them sheathed in surgical gloves covered with blood. They feel foreign to me: a stranger's hands attached to my body by some inexplicable mistake.

A faint, steady beep is sounding incessantly over the constant whoosh of air conditioning. I wish I could summon the strength to ask them to turn it off. The operating room is at a standstill, all eyes riveted on me, widened and tense above face masks.

Only one pair of eyes is glaring, drilling into mine whenever there's a chance, the steel-blue irises deathly cold behind thick lenses and a face shield. Dr. Robert Bolger, still seated by the anesthesia machine, doesn't need to say anything. We've said to each other everything that needed to be said. Too much, even.

"Turn that thing off," Madison whispers. Lee Chen presses a button, and the ghastly sound is muted. Then she approaches me and crouches by my side. Her hand reaches for my shoulder but stops short of touching me. "Dr. Wiley?" she whispers, her hand still hovering. "Anne? Come on, let's go."

I shake my head slowly, staring at the floor. I remember with perfect accuracy the properties of the polymer coating they apply on all the operating room floors. Useless information taking space in my brain for no reason, since I'm the surgeon, the end user of these blue mosaic floors, not someone who decides what coating should be used.

"Anne?" Madison says my name again, her voice reassuring, filled with warmth.

"No," I whisper back. "I can't."

A bloody lap sponge has fallen from the table, staining the pristine floor inches away from the tip of my right foot. I fold my leg underneath me, staring at the sponge as if the bloodstain on it could come after me.

Madison withdraws under the fuming glare of Dr. Bolger.

He sighs and turns off his equipment, deepening the silence of the tense room. "Well, I guess we're done here." He stands with a frustrated groan and throws the echocardiologist Dr. Dean a loaded look. "Let's grab a cup of coffee to rinse off the memory of this disaster."

Dr. Dean throws me a quick glance as if asking for my approval. He probably feels guilty for being singled out by Bolger. I barely notice.

I don't react. I can't.

My mind is elsewhere, reliving moment by moment what has happened since this morning.

The day started well for me, without a sign of what was to come. A capricious, windy spring morning that made my daily jog more of an exercise in willpower than in physical endurance. Chicago has a way of showing its residents some tough love, with chilly wind gusts that cut to the bone, so to speak—there's no surgery involved; just weather and people's perceptions of it.

Like the past couple of weeks, I ran the usual three-mile loop through Lincoln Park looking at elms and buckthorns with renewed hope that I'd find a budding leaf, no matter how small. I was ready for spring and flowering gardens and warmer sunshine. Nothing else was on my mind; at six thirty in the morning, it seemed to be just an ordinary Thursday. Deceptively so.

At about seven thirty, I drove into the hospital employee parking level, taking my reserved numbered spot. I had reviewed the details about the day's surgery a final time the night before from the comfort of my home office, another set routine I have.

The procedure on schedule was an ascending aortic aneurysm. The patient, a fifty-nine-year-old male by the name of Caleb Donaghy. We were scheduled to start at ten sharp.

I'd met Caleb Donaghy twice before. The first time was during a consult. His cardiologist had found a large aneurysm and referred him to us for surgical repair. I remembered that consult clearly. The patient was understandably scared by the findings, and became more so with every word I said. He kept his arms crossed firmly at his chest as if protecting his heart from my scalpel. His unkempt beard had streaks of yellowish gray, and the same gray adorned his temples, as much as I could see from under the ball cap he had refused to take off. I let him keep it.

He was morose and argumentative for a while, disputing everything I said. What had he done to deserve the aneurysm? His parents had only recently died, and not of any heart-related issues. Only after spending a good fifteen minutes managing his anxiety was I able to evaluate him.

That was the first time we met.

Then I saw him again last night, after completing the surgical planning session with my team. Caleb Donaghy had been admitted two days before and had all his blood tests redrawn. He was sitting upright in his bed, stained Cubs ball cap on his head, arms folded, leaning against the pillows doing absolutely nothing when I came in. The TV was off, there were no magazines on his bed, his phone was placed face-down on his night table. The room smelled faintly of stale tobacco and boozy sweat. He was brooding, miserable, and alone. And he was pissed. He'd just learned they were going to shave his beard and chest in pre-op. To add insult to injury, someone in hospital administration had swung by and asked him if he was a registered organ donor. For seven long minutes, he told me in various ways he wasn't going to let himself be sold for parts. He knew what we, doctors, did to people like him, who had no family left to sue us and no money to matter. We took their organs and transplanted them into the highest bidders. Why else would entire buildings in our hospital be named after Chicago's wealthiest?

I promised him that wasn't the case. He wouldn't listen. Then I told him that all he had to do was say no and organ transplant stopped being a possibility in case of a negative surgery outcome. Which is surgeon lingo for death on the table. That silenced him in an instant.

But that was yesterday.

This morning, Madison had my coffee ready for me when I got to the office. She's the best surgical nurse I've worked with, and my personal assistant when she's not scrubbed in.

Madison; Lee Chen, the talented second surgical nurse on my team; Tim Crosley, the cardiovascular perfusionist who operates the heart and lung machine we call the pump; and Dr. Francis Dean, the echocardiologist, are part of my permanent surgical team. Then it's the luck of the draw with anesthesiologists, and I drew the short and very annoying straw with Dr. Bolger.

There's something off-putting about him. Could be his undisguised misogyny. Rumors have it he's been written up twice by the hospital administration for sexist diatribes insisting women don't belong in a clinical setting anywhere above the nursing profession. Contempt for women seeps through his pores, although recently he's grown more careful about letting it show. He's also an arrogant son of a bitch, albeit an excellent anesthesiologist. His professional achievements fuel his hubris and dilute the resolve of the hospital administration when dealing with his behavioral issues. That's who Dr. Bolger is.

When we're in surgery together, I always try to make it work as well as possible, for the good of the patient and the surgical team.

It never works. It takes two to dance in harmony.

I remember swearing under my breath when I saw his name on the schedule, then pushed the issue out of my mind.

Dr. Bolger was already in the operating room when I came in. "Good morning," I said, not expecting an answer. None came, just a quick nod and a side glance from behind the surgical drape that separates his world from mine, before he turned his attention back to the equipment cart at his right. The anesthesia machine helps him deliver precise doses. He controls the patient's airway from behind that protective drape. During surgery, I rarely, if ever, get to see my patients' faces.

My focus is on their hearts.

I'm forty-one and I've been doing this for twelve years, since I finished my general surgery residency. I moved to cardiothoracic right after that, and I never looked back. It's what I've always wanted to do. And I've never lost a patient on the table.

Not until today.

The thought of that hits me in the stomach like a fist.

For an instant, pulled back into the grim present moment, I look around me and try to register what I'm seeing. The surgical lights are off. Madison is still there, looking at me with concern. Lee Chen is sitting on his stool, ready to spring to his feet when needed. Tim Crosley is seated by the pump, his back hunched, his head hung low. If he could, he'd probably rest his forehead against his hands, but he's still working, still keeping sterile. As long as that pump's whirring, he's on duty.

My thoughts race back to the surgery. The operating room was filled with excited chatter, like normal. Virginia Gonzales, the semi-scrubbed nurse who runs back and forth, keeping us all organized and bringing us what we need, was sharing her experience with online dating. She's just been through a terrible divorce. She'd recently decided she could still go out there and meet people. I admired that resilience in her, and secretly hoped it wasn't desperation at the thought of living an entirely lonely life. But her first Tinder match had proven to be a man who'd misrepresented himself dramatically, and everyone on the team was laughing as she shared the details. He'd said he was a transportation executive, when he was in fact a truck driver. Nothing wrong with that, Ginny was quick to say, but the man had never heard of flossing, and during the twenty-five-minute encounter he'd let it slip he used hookers while he was on the road. Cheap ones, he immediately reassured a stunned Ginny.

Hearing her speak, I couldn't help thinking how grateful I was for my husband and my marriage. I'd die a hermit if I had to date again.

A quick bout of laughter erupted in the operating room when Ginny added, "I just ran out of there."

Dr. Bolger glared at her. "Let's try to have some professionalism in here, if at all possible," he said, speaking slowly, pacing his words for impact. "If I'm not asking for too much."

I refrained from arguing with him. Everyone was working, doing their jobs. Surgical teams perform best when they have a way to let off some steam. If there's silence in an operating room, if no one's sharing a story, if the music isn't playing, then something's going terribly wrong.

I'd rather have them laughing all day long. That's how you keep death at bay. It's worked for me anyway. So far.

"What will you have?" Madison asked me, standing by the stereo.

"Um, let me think." The early morning jog had me thinking of The Beatles. "Do you have 'Here Comes the Sun'?"

Madison grinned from behind her mask; I could see it in her eyes. She loved them. "I've got the entire greatest hits collection right here."

"Punch it," I said, moving between equipment and the operating table until I reached my station, by the patient's chest. Music filled the room.

Humming along, I held out my hand and the scalpel landed firmly in it. No need for me to ask; Madison knows how I work. I'm sure she can read my mind, although that possibility isn't scientifically proven.

From the first incision—a vertical line at the center of his breastbone—every step of the procedure was routine.

The sternotomy to expose the heart.

Opening the pericardium, the thin wrapping around the heart, and exposing the aneurysm.

It was big, one of the biggest I'd seen. But I knew that already from prior imaging studies. We were prepared for it.

"On pump," I said, instructing Tim to start circulating the patient's blood through the heart and lung machine.

"Cross clamp in position," I announced. "Cold flush," I asked. A cold solution of potassium was administered into the chambers of the heart. I flushed the exterior of the heart generously with the solution, knowing the cold fluid preserved the heart tissue while we worked. Within seconds, the heart stopped, its death-like stillness announced by the droning sound we were waiting for. The sound of flatline, or the absence of a heartbeat.

With the heart perfectly still, I started working to replace the aortic aneurysm with a graft. It took me almost an entire Beatles album to finish sewing it in.

It feels strange how I remember the cold above all else. It's always cold in the operating room. The air conditioning system blows air at sixty-two degrees. The cold flush that lowers the heart temperature and renders it still is delivered at forty degrees, barely above freezing. My fingers become numb after a while, but I move as fast as I can. Yet today it seemed colder than usual, the only premonition I can say I had.

I don't believe in them. I have my reasons.

When I was done with the sewing of the graft, I examined my work closely, checking if the stitching was tight enough. The final test would be when the blood started rushing through that graft. Then I'd see if there were any leaks and fix them. Usually there weren't. For now, I was satisfied.

"Warm saline," I asked. Those two words marked the end of the cardioplegia stage of the surgery, when the heart is perfectly still. I flushed the organ generously with warm saline solution, relishing the feeling of warmth on my frozen fingers, then used suction to get rid of the excess solution. "Releasing clamp."

The clamp clattered when it landed on the pile of used instruments. I held my breath, knowing this was the moment of truth.

The heart remained perfectly still.

Not fibrillating, not barely beating. Nothing. Just perfectly still.

And that almost never happens.

"Starting resuscitation," I announced. Madison gestured toward the stereo and Ginny turned it off, then started a second timer with large, red digital numbers. Silence filled the room, an ominous, unwanted silence underlined by the flatline droning of the heart monitor. "Epinephrine, stat."

"Epi in," Dr. Bolger confirmed.

The shot of epi should've done something. It didn't. I massaged the heart quickly, feeling it completely unresponsive under the pressure.

"Paddles," I said, my voice tense, impatient. Madison put the paddles in my hands. Placing them carefully on opposing sides of the heart, I called, "Clear," and pushed the button. A brief interruption in the steady droning, then the sound of bad news was back.

I tried that a few more times, then returned to massaging the heart with my hands. "I need another shot of epi. Time?"

"Seventeen minutes," Madison announced, grimly.

"Damn it to hell," I mumbled under my breath. "Come on, Caleb, stay with me."

For a couple of minutes, I kept on with the massage, but nothing happened. The pump still kept his blood oxygenated and delivered to his organs, but the heart was another issue. Its tissue was no longer preserved by the cold potassium solution. With every passing minute, it was deteriorating, its chances of ever beating again waning fast.

"Come on, already! Live!" I snapped. "Come back."

I felt the urge to look at the patient's face as if it could hold some answers. I took a small step past the surgical drape—and froze, mouth agape under the mask, hand stuck in midair. I believe I gasped, but I don't think anyone noticed under the hum of air conditioning, the whirring of the pump, and the blaring of the monitor.

I recognized that man.

My blood turned to ice.

The face I'd seen yesterday and hadn't recognized was now clean-shaven. The ball cap was gone, his bald forehead marked by a port-wine stain on the right side. The birthmark was an irregular shape of red splashed across his forehead as if someone had spilled some wine there.

It took all my willpower to step back behind the drape. Breathing deeply, thankful for the cool air that kept my mind from going crazy, I abandoned the paddles on the table and stared at the heart that refused to beat.

"Time?" I asked again, this time my voice choked.

"Twenty-one minutes," Madison replied.

I slipped my hands into the chest and massaged the heart, knowing very well the heart compressions I was delivering wouldn't work.

I forced one more breath of air out of my chest, then said, "I'm calling it."

"What?" Dr. Bolger sprang to his feet. "Are you insane? Keep going."

I was expecting that. "I could do that, but he won't come back, Robert. We tried everything. The heart's not giving me even the tiniest flutter."

His steely eyes threw poisonous darts at me. "Giving up already? Why? Are your pretty little hands tired, sweetheart?"

I let that one go. It wouldn't help anyone if we argued over the open chest of Caleb Donaghy. "My case, my call." I held his seething gaze steadily for a moment. "Time of death, one forty-seven p.m."

Heavy silence took over the room. Then people started shifting around, collecting instruments, peeling off gloves, turning off equipment. Only Tim stayed in place, the pump still working, still preserving Caleb's organs and tissues.

"It's unbelievable what happened here today," Dr. Bolger said. "You're unbelievable. Pathetic even. You didn't just lose your cherry... you threw it away."

The sexualized reference to the fact that I'd never lost a patient before left me wondering how much of his disdain was in fact envy. But that thought went away quickly.

Then reality hit me like a freight train.

What have I done? Have I just killed a man?